Gill Paul is the bestselling author of twelve historical novels, many of them describing real women she thinks have been marginalized or misjudged by historians. *The Second Marriage* was longlisted for the Historical Writers' Association Gold Crown in 2021; *Women and Children First* was shortlisted for the 2013 RNA Epic Novel of the Year award, and *No Place for a Lady* was shortlisted for a Love Stories award in 2015. Her novels have reached the top of the *USA Today*, Toronto *Globe & Mail* and kindle charts, and been translated into twenty-two languages. Gill also writes historical non-fiction, including *A History of Medicine in 50 Objects*, and she speaks at libraries and literary festivals on subjects ranging from Tutankhamun to the Romanovs. Gill lives in London, where she swims daily in an outdoor pond.

## ALSO BY GILL PAUL:

# *The* MANHATTAN GIRLS

## GILL PAUL

avon.

Published by AVON
A division of HarperCollins*Publishers*
1 London Bridge Street
London SE1 9GF
www.harpercollins.co.uk

HarperCollins*Publishers*
1st Floor, Watermarque Building, Ringsend Road
Dublin 4, Ireland

First published in the United States by William Morrow,
HarperCollins*Publishers* 2022

1

This edition published in Great Britain by HarperCollins*Publishers* 2022

A catalogue copy of this book is available from the British Library.

ISBN: 978-0-00-853094-5

Typeset in Berling LT Std
Printed and bound in the UK using 100% renewable electricity
at CPI Group (UK) Ltd

For Vivien Green

# Cast List

*Professions and status given are as in 1921, when this novel begins.*

## THE BRIDGE CLUB

Jane Grant, reporter at the *New York Times*, married to Harold Ross (qv)

Dorothy "Dottie" Parker, writer of short stories and poems, famous wit

Winifred Lenihan, Broadway actress

Margaret "Peggy" Leech, advertising sales agent at Condé Nast

## OTHER ALGONQUIN HABITUÉS

Alec Woollcott, drama critic at the *New York Times*

Harold Ross, writer and editor, married to Jane Grant (qv)

Franklin Pierce Adams, known as FPA, newspaper columnist

Bob Benchley, freelance writer

Heywood Broun, writer for the *New York Tribune*, married to Ruth Hale (qv)

Ruth Hale, feminist and freelance feature writer, married to Heywood Broun (qv)

George Kaufman, drama editor at the *New York Times*

Marc Connelly, playwright and drama critic

Helen Hayes, actress

Edna Ferber, novelist

Charlie MacArthur, reporter for the *New York American*

Frank Case, manager of the Algonquin

## BOOTLEGGERS

Arnold Rothstein, gangster whose associates include Lucky
    Luciano, Legs Diamond, and Meyer Lansky

Larry Fay, gangster

## EXTRAS

Edwin "Eddie" Pond Parker, stockbroker and husband of Dottie
    Parker (qv)

Woodrow Wilson, terrier belonging to Dottie Parker (qv)

Max, agent of Winifred Lenihan (qv)

Tony Soma, speakeasy owner

Neysa McMein, magazine cover illustrator

Jack Baragwanath, miner

Peter Costello, motion picture distributor

Hawley Truax, businessman

Carr Van Anda, managing editor at the *New York Times*

Herbert Swope, editor at the *New York World*

Alvan Barach, doctor and psychoanalyst

Elinor Wylie, poet

Bill Benét, associate editor of the *Literary Review* of the *New York
    Evening Post*

Eva Le Gallienne, actress

Raoul Fleischmann, heir to a baking company

Tommy Smith, editor at Boni & Liveright publishers

Seward Collins, socialite

Ralph Pulitzer, publisher of the *New York World*

# Chapter 1
# JANE

Jane Grant squeezed into a wooden Bell Telephone cubicle in the lobby of the Algonquin Hotel, took her reporter's notebook from her worn leather satchel, and dialed the number of the *New York Times* copy desk. While she was waiting for the switchboard to put her through, she took off her hat and smoothed back some wayward strands of brown hair, then lit a Lucky Strike, screwing her eyes against the smoke.

"I've got a story for tomorrow, page two," she said when someone answered.

"Ready for you," a young man's voice replied.

Jane began: "Ruth Hale, founder of women's rights organization the Lucy Stone League—"

"Is that H-a-i-l?" the voice interrupted.

She tutted with exasperation. "Don't you read the news? She's a well-known journalist."

"Never heard of her," he said.

"H-a-l-e," she spelled out, then continued, "has won an important legal victory by getting a real estate deed issued in her maiden name rather than her married name."

"What's her married name? Should I put that in?"

"Lord, give me strength!" Jane exclaimed. "The whole point of

1

the Lucy Stone League is to campaign *against* women being forced to take their husbands' names."

"Why don't they want to?" He sounded puzzled.

"How long have you been on the job?" The standard of copy-takers at the paper was haphazard but she had never come across one quite as clueless.

"It's my first week. Second day, in fact." He sounded proud.

"Did no one test your general knowledge at the interview?"

"I didn't have an interview," he said. "My uncle got me the job. He's a chief sub."

"Figures." Jane tapped a column of ash into an amber glass ash-tray with the hotel's logo on the bottom. "Well, if you want to make it to your third day, you'd better sharpen up. Savvy?"

The blatant nepotism made her cross. She'd had little help as she clawed her way up to become the first female reporter in the paper's history. Nothing about it had been easy; she'd gotten there by bringing in more stories and working longer hours than any-one else. Her male colleagues were still disparaging, calling her "Fluff," but at least she got sent out on proper news now and wasn't just covering society balls and the new season's hemline.

She dictated the rest of her story to the youngster on the other end, telling him he was "dumb as they come" when he said he hadn't realized the Nineteenth Amendment gave women the vote. She stubbed out her cigarette with gusto at the end.

After hanging up, she walked through to the hotel's Rose Room. It was empty, apart from a group of her friends spilling messily out of a booth at one end, as if the room had been tipped on its side and they'd tumbled in a heap. Their chairs were encroaching into the passage to the kitchen so waiters had to squeeze past, balanc-ing trays on their shoulders, as they set tables for dinner.

At one end of the booth Harold Ross, her husband of not quite a year, was sitting with their friend Alec Woollcott, the *New York*

*Times* drama critic. She stopped to plant a kiss on Harold's gnarled forehead, and listened to a snatch of their conversation.

"You've got the wrong idea about thanatopsis," Harold said. "It's from the Greek 'thanatos,' meaning death, and 'opsis,' meaning view. It's not a *wish* for death but a *meditation* on it."

"Ah, but you're forgetting . . ." Alec began, and Jane stepped back. The pair of them loved their long-winded highbrow debates, in which neither would back down, and she preferred to steer clear.

At the other end of the table, Dorothy Parker beckoned and moved up to make space for her on a banquette, so she squeezed through the crowd and shuffled in.

Dottie was resplendent in a green spring hat and black feather boa, smothered in her customary cloud of chypre perfume, a mossy, woody scent that always reminded Jane of embalming fluid in an undertaker's parlor. Jane never wore scent and dressed in practical clothes without any fripperies, but that didn't stop her from admiring Dottie's style.

"They're starting a Saturday night poker club for men," Dottie told her, gesturing toward Harold and Alec. "I should get Eddie to join. Maybe they would teach him how to flush." She flicked her feather boa over her shoulder, hitting the face of a man Jane didn't recognize, who batted it away with a snicker. Dottie often made her husband, Eddie, the butt of jokes; it was no wonder he chose not to socialize with their crowd.

Jane felt a pang of worry about the poker club. Harold loved poker but he was terrible at it. She'd met him at a poker game in Paris in 1918, when she was a volunteer for the YMCA and he was managing editor of the US Armed Forces' newspaper, *Stars and Stripes*. He'd thrown that game because he lost concentration when he started flirting with her, and he'd had bad luck at cards ever since.

"Harold will lose his shirt again," she said out loud.

"And no one wants to see *that*," Dottie murmured.

She was forever sniping about Harold's lack of physical charms, but Jane ignored her. It was just Dottie being Dottie. Someone passed her a hip flask and she sniffed the contents before pouring an inch into a glass. She guessed from the amber color it was whiskey, although you'd never have known from the taste or smell. The Algonquin hadn't served alcohol since Prohibition became law the previous year, but the staff turned a blind eye if you brought your own.

There was a cheer from the other end of the table, and Alec stood and tapped the rim of his glass with a spoon to demand silence. He had taken his jacket off and Jane was reminded of Dottie's cruel but accurate description of his figure: "Like a beer barrel on stumps."

"A decision has been reached. Henceforth, the Saturday night poker club will be called the Thanatopsis Pleasure and Literary Club, and it will take place at an upstairs room of this establishment, courtesy of the long-suffering management."

Jane rolled her eyes at Dottie, mocking the pomposity of the announcement. Typical Alec!

"Can we girls come and watch?" called an ingénue she hadn't seen before, who was wearing something that looked more like a peach satin negligee than a day dress.

"Men only," Alec replied. "Women ruin poker. They can't control their emotions."

Winifred Lenihan, the Broadway actress, was sitting opposite Jane and Dottie. "Gee!" she commented. "I thought that's what I did every night when I walked out onstage."

Alec raised his glass to her. "You're the exception, my dear, but you still can't join our game."

"Why don't we start our own Saturday night club, just for girls?" Jane suggested. "I fancy learning bridge. How about you, Dottie?"

4

Dottie shrugged: "Why not? So long as you have low stakes for the unemployed." She had lost her job the previous year and was still sore about it.

"I was in the bridge club at Vassar," said Peggy Leech, a bookish friend of theirs who worked for Condé Nast. "I'd be happy to teach you."

"I play a little," Winifred chipped in quickly. "Can I join you?"

"That's a four then," Jane said. She hardly knew Winifred, but she would make up the numbers. "Shall we take turns to host? I don't want to be here at the Gonk, with the poker club upstairs. Speakeasies are too noisy and coffee shops are too dry."

"Fine by me. I'll host the first," Dottie offered. "Next Saturday?"

"Are you sure Eddie won't mind?" Jane asked. "He might not approve of his home being invaded."

"Mind? Are you kidding?" Dottie said. "With Winifred Lenihan in his parlor, he'll surely *lose* his mind . . . which would be no bad thing, come to think of it."

Winifred smiled politely. She *was* beautiful, Jane thought, with gray-green eyes and bone structure like a Classical sculpture. She never felt jealous of good-looking women; to be so perfect must be a burden.

A stout woman in a beige check suit edged toward the table clutching a notebook and pen, her gaze fixed on Dottie.

"Pah-don me for interrupting, Mrs. Pah-ker," she said, with the dropped *r*'s and long *ah*'s of a Boston accent. "I've been waiting all evening for a chance to ask for your autograph and now we have to leave to catch our train and . . ." She was flustered, her words speeding up as if she didn't want to waste their time. "I would just never forgive myself if I missed the chance. I'm such a big fan of all those witty, clever things you say. I always read them in the papers."

Before Dottie could reply, Alec Woollcott chipped in: "Are you sure you don't want my autograph too? Anything remotely funny I've ever said has been attributed to Mrs. Parker."

Dottie ignored him and took the book and pen, smiling sweetly. She scribbled her signature on a blank page and handed it back, saying, "Don't believe what you read in the papers. These scoundrels are the types who write them." She waved a hand vaguely in Alec's direction.

The woman muttered her thanks, almost knocking over a chair as she backed away, and for a moment Jane thought she was going to bow, as if to royalty.

Dottie turned to Alec: "Don't you know, dear, that attribution is the sincerest form of flattery?"

"Is Mrs. Parker being nice?" he replied. "I'd have thought you would disapprove of flattery."

"A little is fine," Dottie said. "So long as you don't swallow."

As JANE AND Harold took a trolley home that evening, she told him about the young *New York Times* copy-taker who hadn't realized women had been given the vote. "I could tell from his tone that he wasn't keen on the idea."

"Goddamn punk had no idea who he was talking to," Harold said. "I hope you showed no mercy."

"Not a lot." She chuckled. "When did I get to be so *fierce*?"

"It's your Kansas spirit. Cattle and women: they breed 'em tough." He slung an arm around her shoulder. "You don't mind about our poker game, do you, mushkins? I hear you girls are starting one of your own."

Jane sucked air through her teeth. "I worry whenever I hear you're playing poker, sweetest. We're supposed to be saving money, not doling it out to our friends."

Their first plan was to get a home of their own and move out of the cramped, down-at-heel apartment they were sharing. The next plan was to start a new magazine with Harold as editor. It was his long-cherished dream, and Jane was excited to be a partner in the venture. They had agreed they would live on her *New York Times* salary and save his entire pay as a writer at the humor magazine *Judge* until they achieved their goals.

"In the spirit of matrimonial compromise, I promise I'll walk away from the table if my losses ever reach five dollars. How about that?"

"Five dollars a week is two hundred and sixty dollars a year," she replied.

He laughed and punched her jokingly on the arm. "Oh ye of little faith!"

She persevered: "We could have used that money to eat out once in a while, instead of me rushing home every evening to cook dinner."

It was a chore having to shop for and prepare a meal every evening, especially since she often had to head back to the office afterward to tie up loose ends before the morning paper went to press. She could see why most women gave up work when they got married; she was worn out trying to combine the two.

Harold whirled her around and kissed her on the lips. "I'll buy you a steak dinner with my first winnings," he promised.

Jane bit back the retort on the tip of her tongue. She didn't want to be a nag. "Hey, why don't you invite Eddie Parker to your Thanatopsis poker club?" she asked instead. "Dottie's worried he doesn't feel part of the Algonquin scene."

"I don't think he'd feel part of any scene," Harold replied, "unless he managed to find a shoal of dead fish floating in the harbor."

Jane snorted with laughter. Eddie was certainly lacking in the

# Chapter 2
# DOTTIE

L et me get this straight," Eddie said. "You want to bring a bunch of broads around to guzzle my hooch? Why don't you get a job and buy your own?"

He was slumped in an armchair, his shirt unbuttoned and his face shiny with perspiration. Dottie thought he had never looked less attractive. She crouched to pet her terrier, Woodrow Wilson, and immediately he rolled onto his back begging for his tummy to be rubbed, legs spread like a two-dollar hooker.

"Look at Woodrow," she said. "Reckon we could get work for him at Polly Adler's house of ill repute?"

Eddie didn't glance over. He topped up his whiskey glass and took a slurp, without adding water, then launched into a diatribe that sounded as if he'd been rehearsing it all evening. "The thing I liked about you before we married was that you were a working girl with a good job and plenty of gumption. But then you got smug and arrogant and reckoned you could say what you liked because you were irreplaceable. And guess what? Turns out you weren't."

Dottie didn't argue because everything he said was true. She had gotten swept away with the power of being *Vanity Fair*'s theater critic, swanning off to premieres and theatrical soirees with a sense of entitlement, and scribbling off a review just moments before the copy deadline. At first she'd tried to give an honest opinion but often couldn't resist a little mischief for the sake of a sassy punch line. For one show, she'd recommended that audience members bring along knitting to occupy them; for another, instead of reviewing the play, she'd written a detailed description of the woman fidgeting in the next row.

When her boss invited her for lunch at the Plaza Hotel, she was planning to ask him for a raise—and then he dropped the bombshell that they were replacing her. He denied it was because she had trashed three big Broadway shows in a row—shows that spent a lot on advertising in Condé Nast publications. He denied it was because she'd likened the wife of one bigwig producer to an erotic revue dancer. But she was sacked all the same.

Her best buddy, Bob Benchley, walked out in support, and they rented a tiny office together, setting themselves up as "Freelance Writers." She planned to concentrate on verse and short stories, but when she stared at the blank page in her typewriter, the ideas wouldn't come—and if they did, the words sounded trite and pathetic on rereading. She'd had a few pieces published, but her main achievement since launching herself as freelance was the ability to toss scrunched-up paper into the bin from six feet away, with unerring accuracy.

Maybe she wasn't cut out to be a writer; maybe entertaining friends with one-liners was the most she was capable of. That woman who asked for her autograph in the Algonquin had only heard of her because Franklin Pierce Adams, known to all as FPA, often quoted her in his "Conning Tower" column at the *New York Tribune*, but sadly no one paid for her bon mots. She and Eddie were living off his salary, and it was clear he wasn't ecstatic about it from the lecture that was still droning on.

She went to bed before him that evening but was wide awake

when he turned in, his weight on the mattress tipping her sideways. He pulled at the quilt so she was partly uncovered and started snoring with a *squeee* sound almost as soon as his head hit the pillow.

This would have been the ideal time to start a family, she mused, if only they were getting along well enough for some marital whoopee. Eddie had an idea that he wanted to move back to his hometown of Hartford, Connecticut, to raise his children, but that sounded like hell on earth to Dottie, who considered herself a New Yorker to the marrow. It was a sore subject between them, one of many.

Truth was, as she confided to Jane, they'd only been married five minutes when he went to war in 1917 and then he arrived back two years later seeming a different person from the smooth-talking guy she'd met on vacation in Branford. *That* man had been handsome, well dressed, irreverent, and sexy. In his company she'd felt her brain turn to mush, her heart turn to liquid, and her insides catch fire—all the well-trod clichés come true. The wedding day was quiet—her parents were long dead, and his family didn't approve because she was part Jewish—but she was still fizzing with happiness and cheap champagne.

And then the United States entered the war and Eddie signed up for the ambulance service without so much as asking if she minded, and he was gone before she could blink. Two years later it was as if they'd sent back a different man; as if she'd put a suit in the French cleaners and when she picked it up they handed her one that looked similar but was older and saggier and had lost all the characteristics she once loved. Somehow she had to fix their marriage, to rediscover the man he used to be, but she was clueless where to start.

She had the idea that if she fell pregnant, they'd work things out . . . but if there was ever a stirring in his pants these days, it sure didn't happen when she was around. Was it the booze causing his lack of interest? Was it the war? Or was it just her?

EDDIE INSISTED ON heading out come Saturday rather than hang around for the first girls' bridge night. Dottie tried to persuade him to stay and say hello—"My friends think you're an imaginary husband," she joked—but he insisted her set didn't like him, and none of her protestations would persuade him otherwise.

"Where's Eddie?" Jane asked, glancing around the room.

"He's got a date with his dear friends Haig & Haig," Dottie told her. "They're so close they're inseparable."

Jane gave her a quick hug, then pulled back. "Dottie, there's poop on your carpet," she scolded.

"Don't blame me, it's not mine," Dottie said, remembering she'd forgotten to take Woodrow Wilson for his constitutional earlier.

Jane ripped off a sheet of newspaper and picked up the offending turd, taking it to the bathroom to flush away.

Dottie bent to pet Woodrow. "We think humans are more intelligent than dogs, but I'd say they've got the edge since they've got us cleaning up their shit."

Peggy arrived straight after, clutching a tray covered with a tea towel. "A few canapés," she said as she handed it over. "To save you the bother."

Frankly, Dottie hadn't considered providing food. She had set out a bottle of Eddie's bootleg gin and a jug of lemonade on her card table, along with four mismatching tumblers. Wasn't that enough for a hostessing gold star?

"Did anyone give Winifred the address?" Jane asked, glancing at her watch.

"I did," Peggy said. "Don't worry, she'll be here."

"I scarcely know her," Dottie said. "Is she more than just a pretty face? There are so many of them these days, you can't leave home without bumping into a few blocking the sidewalk as they toss their Shirley Temple curls."

Peggy smiled. "Trust me, you'll like her. She'll laugh at your jokes."

"The surefire way to my heart," Dottie agreed, pouring them each a drink.

"How do you know her?" Jane asked Peggy, taking a sip and wincing at the strength of the concoction.

"From the Gonk," Peggy said. "We were sitting next to each other one night and the men were being bores, so we swapped life stories. She's Brooklyn Irish, unpretentious, and sharp as a needle."

Dottie didn't often chat with women at the Gonk, apart from Jane and Peggy. She couldn't abide the novelist Edna Ferber, who had a grating manner and a grossly inflated self-opinion; she had no time for the posturing of the women who flocked around actress Tallulah Bankhead, declaring themselves bisexual as if it were a new religion and they were the only ones who would be saved on Judgment Day; then there were the feminists, such as Ruth Hale, who needed to be imbibed in small doses, like schoolmarms whose hearts were in the right place but whose hectoring manner left her mildly nauseated after a while.

There was a knock on the door and Dottie answered to find Winifred standing outside, breathless. "Speak of the devil," she said, noticing that although Winifred looked fashionable in a navy-blue jersey dress with a sailor-tie collar, her hair was mussed and her eyeliner was smudged beneath one eye.

"Sorry to be late," she said, sitting down to catch her breath. One of her stockings was ripped and the other was sagging around her ankle, having detached itself from the suspender.

"I hope the other guy looks worse," Dottie remarked.

Winifred glanced down. "Don't ask," she said, and bent to try

13

and pull up the stocking. It was clearly in tatters, so she slid off her shoe, removed it, and wriggled the shoe back on. Her feet were dainty and elegant, her legs smooth as eggshells. Dottie mused that it must take a lot of effort—and vanity—to look so burnished.

"We're asking," Jane said gently.

"Professional hazard," Winifred replied. "I had dinner with my agent. Classy place, divine food, but he wanted payback in the taxi."

"What a creep!" Jane exclaimed. "You should get yourself a new agent."

Winifred wrinkled her nose and shook her head briefly. "They're all the same. Besides, he's one of the best."

Dottie was watching, fascinated. "Best what? Best taxi pest? I hope he's very proud."

Winifred grinned. "That's the trouble: I suspect he probably is."

Dottie had been prepared to dislike Winifred on the basis of her impeccable grooming, but there was something intriguing beneath the shiny surface. She decided to give her a chance.

# Chapter 3
# WINIFRED

Winifred was more shaken by Max's lecherous lunge than she let on to the others. Lots of men thought actresses were fair game, but her agent was supposed to be her protector in the industry. He'd been amused when she fought him off, and the taxi driver stared straight ahead, careful not to notice.

She accepted a gin and lemonade from Dottie but winced and put it down after one sip. The booze was of shocking quality, with an aftertaste like carbolic soap. She noticed none of the others were drinking it either.

Despite the cheap gin, she was honored to be in the apartment of the inimitable Dorothy Parker. It wasn't as glamorous as she'd expected, but it was three times the size of her own place, with hardwood floors and wooden partitions separating the bedroom and kitchen. Trains rumbled along the Sixth Avenue elevated railway outside, their lights flickering through the drapes and vibrations humming through the floor.

Inside, no concern had been paid to the décor. Mismatching chairs and cluttered tables were arranged almost at random, as if there had been a party the night before and no one had cleared up. She could smell the perfume Dottie habitually wore, combined with the harsh aroma of the gin and a hint of urine she assumed was that of the dog sleeping in an armchair. A cage hanging in the corner contained a yellow canary that was watching them from its perch, head on one side as if sizing them up.

"We call him Onan," Dottie said, noticing the direction of her gaze. "Because he scatters his seed on the ground."

Winifred laughed. "Of course you do!"

She was flattered to be included in the bridge group. Max had taken her to the Algonquin one night and encouraged her to sweet-talk the bigwig theater reviewers, Alec Woollcott, Marc Connelly, and George Kaufman. It was the men you focused on first because they dominated the conversation, but soon she'd found herself fascinated by the sharp-witted women. She learned to sit close to Dottie and listen for the devastating one-liners delivered in her ladylike accent and peppered with swear words that would have made a bricklayer blush.

"Shall we start?" Peggy asked, shuffling the pack with smooth sleight of hand. She dealt them each thirteen cards and told them to arrange their hands into suits, then demonstrated how to win tricks. "Ace is high, but any trump card will beat another suit."

Winifred was surprised to see Dottie slip on a pair of black horn-rimmed glasses that took up half her face. She never wore those at the Gonk. Was it vanity that stopped her?

Peggy suggested they play a rubber with diamonds as trump, so Dottie and Jane could get the hang of it. That went smoothly, with Jane looking surprised to win five out of the thirteen tricks in her first game.

Peggy dealt again. "Now, I want you to look at your hand and try to estimate how many tricks you think you will win. That's what you need to get—no more, no less." She wrote down their estimates on a score pad, smiling when Dottie's was wildly over-optimistic. Jane chose spades as trump and they played again. This time Peggy got the six tricks she had bid and Dottie failed to win a single one.

"Next, let's try splitting into pairs," Peggy said, "and bidding with our partners . . ."

"I can't concentrate while I'm drinking this goddamn coffin juice Eddie brought home," Dottie interrupted, putting her drink down and making a sour face. "I'm going to Neysa's to borrow some Scotch." She stood up and removed her glasses, leaving them on the table.

"Borrow?" Jane queried with a raised eyebrow, but Dottie was already on her way out the door. She turned to Winifred. "Have you met Neysa McMein? The magazine illustrator?"

"I have." Winifred explained she had posed for her once, and knew her apartment was across the hall.

"Dottie treats Neysa's place as an extension of her own. Actually, lots of people do. Her salon is an institution because there's an open-door policy and she always has plenty of booze—which is a more or less guaranteed route to popularity these days. Neysa has a talent for cultivating those who can further her career or social standing: lion hunting, I call it."

Winifred didn't know how to respond. Weren't they all guilty of lion hunting to an extent? Wasn't that why Max had brought her to the Gonk?

Peggy had rinsed out their glasses and now brought them back to the card table, then laid out the food. There was cornbread, deviled eggs, and some celery sticks neatly stuffed with Roquefort. Jane grabbed a hunk of cornbread and attacked it hungrily.

"Tell us what's so great about your taxi-pest agent," she said to Winifred, spitting crumbs without a hint of embarrassment.

"He gets me work. I've just got the female lead in a new A.A. Milne play opening at the Bijou in December. I need to perfect my English upper-class accent," Winifred said, switching into it. "I play an ingénue who has eloped with the wrong man. It's fun, but hardly Ibsen." She pulled a comic face.

17

"A lead at the Bijou? You're doing well." Jane reached for an egg. "Most actresses I know are happy to squeeze into the back of the chorus line and do a few high kicks."

Winifred knew she was lucky. Max had spotted her in a show while she was still at drama school and signed her up on the spot, so her path had been smoother than most.

"I can't complain," she told Jane, "but it's not all flowers and curtain calls."

She explained that acting was a tough career choice when you didn't have family money to fall back on. She worked shifts in the millinery department at Lord & Taylor to cover the rent, but didn't want to be stuck squeezing hats onto rich women's coiffured heads for the rest of her life. Sometimes there were months between plays when she was scared she might never get acting work again, and she had to pretend to be pleased for them when she heard of other actresses getting roles she would have cut off her pinkie for. And auditions were the pits. She shivered, pushing a memory firmly to the back of her brain.

"It's hardly a secure career. Why not do something else instead?" Jane asked. She had almost finished the deviled eggs.

You could tell she was a reporter, Winifred thought—her staccato questions, delivered in a Midwest accent, were like an interrogation—but she didn't mind.

"Don't get me wrong—I adore acting. It's a thrill stepping into someone else's skin and inhabiting your character's life," she said. "I love the *smell* of the theater, and the camaraderie of being part of a team. I like the challenge of using your instincts onstage, because every show is different. There are frustrating aspects, sure, but I can't think of any other way I'd like to earn a crust. Certainly not fitting hats."

"What about marriage and kids?" Jane asked, lighting a cigarette.

18

"They're definitely not for me," she answered, so vehemently that the others laughed. "I grew up in a huge family, tripping over toddlers with snotty noses and drooping nappies, and it holds no appeal."

The faint scent of urine in Dottie's apartment was bringing back memories of home. All the men in her family were stocky, baggy Irishmen in construction, while the women were in the baby-making trade and aged beyond their years. As a third-generation immigrant, Winifred had been determined from childhood to forge a better life than that of her parents. She wanted to make something of herself, and acting seemed to offer a way.

"So what *do* you want?" Jane asked. "Fame and fortune?"

Winifred thought hard. "No, not that. Artistic fulfillment, I suppose. To be allowed to grow as an actress."

Jane turned to Peggy. "And what about you?" she asked. "Are you looking for a husband?"

"I am," Peggy said. Winifred already knew that, because they'd talked about it at the Gonk. "And kids. I'm also writing a novel that I would love to get published one day, but that's probably a pipe dream. What about you, Jane?"

"To get the magazine off the ground." She explained to Winifred that she and Harold were saving to start one, and Winifred was asking about it when Dottie returned with a bottle and a soda siphon.

"We're talking about ambitions," Jane addressed her. "We've all confessed ours, so it's your turn. What's yours?"

"To be a genius, of course," Dottie replied. She poured an inch of whiskey into each of their glasses, then topped them up with soda.

Winifred took a sip. It was marginally better than Eddie's gin but not much.

"Why does anyone drink?" Dottie asked, slurping her own

drink, then shuddering. "It tastes vile, turns you into a moron, and poisons you so you feel like death the next day."

"Ah, but it shows you're a free thinker," Peggy said. "A nonconformist. I'm all for that."

"Prohibition has certainly given booze more cachet than ever before," Jane said. "In direct contradiction of the predictions of the Temperance movement, arrests for drunkenness have *risen* sharply. I wrote about it for the *Times* last week. New Yorkers don't like being told what to do, and they're rebelling against the ludicrous aspects of the law. Did you know that sanctions for possession of a hip flask are now the same as for carrying an unlicensed handgun? It's absurd."

"I don't know, hip flasks can be lethal too." Dottie's voice wobbled and Winifred was amazed to notice she was crying. Proper crying, with real tears. What had brought that on?

Jane leapt up and put an arm round her.

"Everyone has to drink now, or they're accused of being saps," Dottie sobbed. "I sometimes wish they would repeal Prohibition so we can all go back to sobriety."

"Are you worried about Eddie's drinking?" Jane asked, pressing a handkerchief into her hand.

"Never mind *pro*-hibition," Dottie replied, mopping her eyes, "I wish he'd have more *in*-hibition."

If she had known her better, Winifred would have advised Dottie to run a mile. She had grown up surrounded by hard-drinking men and knew you could no more change a drinker than a zebra could change its stripes or a robin could change its red breast.

"Is there anyone who could have a word with him?" Peggy asked. "Someone he respects, whom he'd listen to?"

"Not really. It's fine," Dottie backtracked, wiping her eyes and smearing her black eyeliner in raccoon style. "He's just taking his time to find his feet after all he went through in the war. I'm sure he's not alone."

Winifred had heard her mother making excuses like that for her father—often lisping through a lip split by a backhander. She exchanged glances with Peggy.

"Shall we play another rubber?" Dottie asked, picking up the cards and putting on her glasses. "That's why we're here. I think I'm starting to get the hang of it."

Winifred looked at her watch and pulled a face. "I'm sorry, I've promised to meet someone at Tony Soma's speakeasy on West Forty-Ninth. I didn't realize we'd be playing so late."

"Who is he, have we met him, and what's your current status?" Jane asked, grinning at her own nosiness.

"Peter Costello. He's a motion picture distributor. We've been stepping out for a few weeks." Winifred spoke without enthusiasm.

"You don't sound giddy about him," Jane observed.

"It passes the time," Winifred replied with a cheeky smile and a half-wink. She wasn't in love, but he was better company than most men she met so she felt she should persevere. "He's bringing a friend. Do you want to join us, Peggy?" Peggy was shaking her head before she finished the sentence, so Winifred urged her: "Don't think of it as a date. Just come for one drink."

Peggy blushed crimson, making them all laugh. "I'm not wearing the right clothes," she said. "And I had a late night last night. Besides, I'm not much of a drinker."

Winifred decided to push her. "You'll never find a husband if you head home at midnight in Manhattan. All the best ones are only just coming out then—if they can slip away from their wives, that is." She raised an eyebrow. "Put on some lipstick and let's have some fun."

"Peggy's too much of a bluenose for fun," Dottie said. "She

21

doesn't indulge in any pursuit that doesn't have an '–ology' or an '–ism' at the end."

Winifred took Peggy's hand. "Come on—prove her wrong."

"Oh, alright," Peggy agreed. "But I warn you, I won't stay long."

As they said their goodbyes and headed down to the street, Winifred wondered why she had made such a big deal of it. She didn't think Peggy would like Peter one bit, so she was unlikely to fall for his friend. Maybe she was being selfish; she always felt safer with another woman around because they could watch each other's backs.

She found it hard to get her actress friends to come out on the town with her. They said she was "too beautiful" and they wouldn't stand a chance beside her. Peggy was different; she didn't rely on her looks to get by. She was a walking encyclopedia, the smartest person in any room, and nice as pie with it. Someday a man would fall in love with those qualities, hook, line, and sinker. Probably not at Tony's, though. That would be pushing it.

# Chapter 4

# PEGGY

I'm a friend of Tallulah's," Winifred told the chubby, bald, black-clad doorman behind the grille, who nodded and ushered them through a doorway and down a darkened flight of stone steps.

"Are you really?" Peggy asked. It had become a byword for bisexuality in their crowd, since Tallulah Bankhead was known for her steamy affairs with other women.

Winifred laughed. "No, but Peter told me that's this week's password. At least it's memorable!"

She opened a door and the noise and the reek of booze and cigarette smoke assaulted Peggy's senses. The room inside was heaving with customers: they were three-deep along the bar, clustered around tables, and standing in the middle too, all of them sipping from white coffee cups that she knew for certain didn't contain coffee. The décor was Italian in style, with rose-colored walls adorned by paintings of Venice, the Leaning Tower of Pisa, and the Trevi Fountain.

"This way!" Winifred called over the clamor, waving to a man at the far end of the bar. She pulled Peggy by the hand as she wove between customers.

Peter had mischievous eyes and black hair slicked to his head like shiny tar. He whispered something in Winifred's ear that made her laugh, then took Peggy's hand and kissed it, saying "*Enchanté*."

23

Peggy had a pet hate of people who dropped foreign words into conversation, but she smiled and said, "Pleased to meet you."

He introduced his friend Fred, a tall angular man who was pouring drinks for them from a bottle on the bar. He handed them a cup each, and raised his own, saying, "Bottoms up!" Peggy took a sip and grimaced. It tasted like pure ethanol.

Winifred started telling Peter about the bridge group so Peggy turned to Fred and asked what he did for a living.

"Stocks and shares," he said, with a self-important air. "Predicting trends, seeking the winning stocks of the future. Making money from money. Helping the rich to stay rich, and making me rich too."

"I suppose you must be a connoisseur of human behavior," Peggy said. "For example, I would guess that domestic appliances are bound to be a burgeoning area, with all these new labor-saving devices coming on the market and women seeking more time for leisure and self-improvement."

Fred looked at her with a puzzled expression. "Say, did you swallow a dictionary?" he asked. "You talk real fancy."

"Do I?" Peggy fluttered her fingers in a gesture meant to indicate she wasn't fancy at all. "Blame the Vassar education."

"I bet you read a lot of books," he said in a damning tone.

"Why? Don't you?" She glanced at Winifred, hoping to draw her into the conversation, but Peter was in the midst of a lengthy anecdote.

"You sound like a virgin. Are you a virgin?" Fred asked. "I bet you are." His expression was weaselly, with a glint of nastiness.

Peggy felt her cheeks burn as she sought a frivolous answer. What would Dottie say? "None of your business, mister" was the best she could come up with.

He nudged Peter. "Hey! What are you doing bringing me a virgin? Is this some kinda joke?"

Winifred looked from Peggy to Fred, and in an instant her expression transformed into fury. "Go boil your head, you moron!" She pointed toward the kitchen doorway. "Don't come back till you've learned how to talk to a lady."

"What's the problem? I'm just razzing ya," he said, but Winifred stepped between them, so Fred was forced to talk to Peter.

"I apologize," she said to Peggy. "I've got no idea what Peter's doing with a fella like that."

"Thanks for rescuing me," Peggy said with relief. "I was hoping to get a chance to ask about your new play. When do you start rehearsals?"

As Winifred answered, Peggy tried to swallow her mixture of irritation and humiliation at Fred's behavior. Her mother had drummed into her that "nice" young women kept themselves intact for their future husbands, and her contemporaries at Vassar had mostly been well-brought-up girls who felt the same way. But when she started work in the advertising department at Condé Nast just before the war, she realized times had changed and her virginity had become a disfiguring flaw. The office was full of hotshot types with lascivious expressions, who whispered things like "Anytime you want help with your little problem, dear. . . ." She'd begun to think she should choose one of the least offensive ones and get it over with.

In her spare time she was writing a novel that explored this societal change through the eyes of a character called Vergie, who was searching for a husband. She wasn't sure how it was going to end since, at the age of twenty-seven, Peggy had failed to find one herself.

It wasn't for lack of trying. There had been a nice but dull boy back home in Newburgh who took her out on old-fashioned dates for a while before announcing, unexpectedly, that he was marrying someone else. Then there was the son of a family friend, who bought her a few dinners before he stopped calling. In 1918 she had volunteered to work for the American Committee for Devastated France, thinking it would be an interesting experience as well as a potential way of meeting single men. But on arrival, when the organizers heard she could drive a car and speak fluent French, she was tasked with touring rural villages in a mobile library instead of hanging out in Paris with the soldiers on leave. Jane had been in Paris with the YMCA and that's where she met Harold; Peggy came home with a few pen pals but no proposals.

Now, she was beginning to panic. It was her dearest wish to have children, but none of the men she met were husband material. She'd hoped there would be someone in the crowd who hung out at the Gonk, but the men there were too busy laughing at their own witticisms and seldom paid her attention. Besides, few of them were single apart from Alec Woollcott, and everyone knew he was in love with Neysa McMein. She had confided in Winifred, hoping she might know a suitable candidate in the theater world, but instead here she was in Tony Soma's with a man who thought she talked "real fancy." She felt frumpy and unattractive. What hope was there?

Suddenly Fred leaned over, hands outstretched, and grabbed Peggy's breasts, squeezing hard as if on a pair of Klaxons and yelling, "Honk, honk!"

Before Peggy could react, Winifred drew back her hand and slapped him across the face with a sound like a whip crack. "How dare you!" she growled, her expression terrifying.

Fred clutched his face, momentarily stunned. When he took his hand away Peggy could see red fingermarks. It must have hurt.

He tried to recover his bluster. "She's got saggy tits," he said, "like an old maid. Few more years and she'll be grateful if any guy gives her the time of day."

Winifred raised her hand to slap him again and he dodged behind Peter, who murmured at him, "Lay off."

Peggy considered telling him he was no Michelangelo sculpture, but she doubted he'd have heard of Michelangelo. Besides, there was such meanness in his eyes she didn't want to encourage any further dialogue.

"I'm going home," she told Winifred. "Please stay. Don't let me ruin your evening."

"I wouldn't dream of staying in present company," she said, grabbing Peggy's arm.

Peter protested to no avail, while Fred smirked behind him. Peggy couldn't bear to look at him now. He made her skin crawl as if there were ants swarming over her.

In the taxi, she asked, "Where did you learn to slap a guy like that? I'm very impressed."

"I was a scrapper as a kid." Winifred chortled. "My Brooklyn neighborhood was rough and you had to stand up for yourself against older brothers and kids on the block."

"It was as if Fred hated me," Peggy said, "even though he doesn't know me."

Winifred agreed. "There's a subset of guys who feel inadequate in the company of clever women. Forget about him."

Peggy remembered Dottie calling her a bluenose earlier. Was that her problem? Maybe she needed to find a bluenose type of a guy.

"Is Eddie smart?" Winifred asked, and Peggy shook her head firmly.

"Not nearly as smart as Dottie. They're a mismatch if ever I saw one. It's such a shame. Of all the women I know, Dottie is the most in need of a stable marriage."

Winifred was curious about the tears earlier. She'd thought of

27

Dottie as a hard-edged sophisticate. "Are things that bad between them?"

"She's always been a weeper," Peggy said. "I remember bouts of unexplained tears when she worked at *Vanity Fair*." She paused, deciding whether to confide in Winifred. Now that they were all part of the bridge club, it felt as if there was a common bond. "Thing is, Dottie's had a lot of loss in her life. Her mother died when she was four, her stepmother when she was nine, then her father when she was nineteen. And she also lost an uncle on the *Titanic*. She once said to me that death follows her around, like a stray dog snapping at her heels."

"Doesn't she have siblings?" Winifred asked.

"Two brothers and a sister, but her brother Harry walked out on the family years ago and hasn't been heard of since. She's not close to Helen and Bert—they're much older. That makes Eddie feel like her only family—and he fell in love with the bottle when he got back from Europe. It's not been easy."

Winifred exhaled with a whistling sound. "Poor Dottie. It makes me want to look out for her. I'm glad we can keep an eye on her at the bridge club."

Peggy smiled. "I'm glad you're in the bridge club. Do I know you well enough now to ask a favor?"

"Of course you do!"

"Any chance you could tell me where you buy your clothes? I badly need a style update."

"Let's go shopping next week," Winifred suggested. "We can use my staff discount at Lord & Taylor. As long as I live, I will never tire of the glittering allure of Fifth Avenue."

She was a beguiling mixture of warmth and toughness, Peggy thought. Remembering that slap, she made a mental note to avoid getting on the wrong side of her.

# Chapter 5
# JANE

Jane popped her head around the door of the cubbyhole office Dottie and Bob Benchley rented above the Metropolitan Opera House, where there were two desks, two chairs, a single skylight window, and no standing room. Bob was hunched over his typewriter, stabbing the keys with two fingers, and he gave her a wave without stopping. Dottie flung a cover over her typewriter. She was always fiercely protective of any work in progress.

"I'm not here to steal your ideas," Jane told her. "I wondered if you can take time off to come and view a property Harold and I are thinking of buying. I could use a second opinion."

Dottie cocked an eyebrow: "I think you've got the wrong gal. I'm known for many things but homemaking's not one of them."

"But you're a New Yorker." Jane glanced at her watch; she only had an hour to spare before she had to interview a congressman in a Midtown hotel. "And this is slightly off the beaten track—in Hell's Kitchen, west of the Ninth Avenue El."

"I forgot to bring my Colt .45 and getaway horse," Dottie drawled. "You wanna come, Mr. Benchley?"

"Can't. Deadline. Head in noose if I miss it," Bob said, without skipping a keystroke.

Dottie rose and stepped around the desk, slipping her arms into

29

her coat sleeves and checking the angle of her hat in a compact mirror.

It was a new hat, Jane noted, black with bright pink and orange taffeta flowers pinned on one side. Dottie loved her hats. Jane hadn't bought a single item of clothing for over a year because she and Harold were saving for the magazine. It would be worth it one day, she told herself.

Jane had intended to walk there—she was a fast walker with a long stride and generally walked most places around Midtown—but Dottie was tottering along on heels and it would have taken too long at her pace. Reluctantly she hailed a yellow cab, and was annoyed when the driver quoted a fare of fifty cents.

"It's less than a mile," she complained. "It should be half that."

"Take it or leave it," he said, with a shrug, and Jane knew she had no choice. She'd never get Dottie in a subway and the trolleys didn't go that way.

They drew up outside number 412 West Forty-Seventh Street, two small brownstones that had been clumsily knocked together by a previous denizen.

"This is it!" Jane indicated, paying the driver the exact fare with no tip.

There was a man sleeping on the sidewalk outside, blocking their path to the front steps. He looked peaceful, wrapped in a worn brown coat and homburg, with an empty bottle clutched in his hand.

"The doorman, I presume?" Dottie commented. "Very chichi."

The property was in dire condition, with peeling paintwork, crumbling walls, and a stoop that looked set to collapse imminently. Jane pulled a key from her pocket and stepped around the sleeping man.

"The plan is that Harold's friends Hawley Truax and Bill Powell would be lodgers on the upper floors to help with costs. We'd have a communal room for entertaining but we'd each have separate apartments," she explained, opening the door into the hallway.

It was worse in broad daylight than it had seemed when she and Harold had viewed it the previous evening. A crop of mushrooms was growing from the ceiling and there were scary cracks in the walls, as if the whole structure could crumble at any moment.

"Is this a joke?" Dottie asked, eyes wide. "You're not seriously thinking of living here?"

Jane bit her lip. "Harold wants a house rather than an apartment and this is all we can afford. I'm not quite sure *why* it has to be a house. All he said was it's so we can get a cat."

"You're buying *this* for the sake of a cat?" Dottie looked aghast as she stepped carefully over holes in the floor, clutching her coat so it didn't brush against anything. "I'm sure, given the choice, it would rather have fillet of salmon and a bowl of cream."

Jane felt gloomy. She liked the idea of all the space but was daunted by the work that would have to be done to make it habitable, and she suspected she would be the one in charge of the building operations because Harold wasn't the practical type.

"You can see the potential, can't you?" She whirled around, looking up the dim stairwell.

"As an opium den?" Dottie answered. "Why, sure."

"It will give us a base for planning Harold's magazine." Jane tried to summon enthusiasm. "If we can't afford offices to start with, there's plenty of room here."

They stopped to light cigarettes in a sunny front room, which had floor-to-ceiling church-style windows with domed tops. Outside, a few scrappy lads were taking turns kicking the man sleeping on the sidewalk. He roused and shouted curses at them, punching the air with futility, whereupon they ran off hooting with laughter.

"I guess if you have kids, they can grow up playing with those charming boys, and become upstanding members of the community." Dottie's expression was deadpan.

"We're not having kids." Jane felt strongly on the matter. "I didn't fight to become a reporter only to throw it all away by getting pregnant." She'd once interviewed Margaret Sanger, the birth control advocate, and had obtained a wishbone diaphragm on her recommendation. "There are plenty of men at the office who think the *Times* shouldn't be employing married women. I'd never persuade them to keep me on if I had children."

"Do they still call you Fluff?" Dottie asked, grinning. "I love it—although you're the least fluffy woman I've ever met."

"'Course they do." Jane smiled. Even now, her male colleagues tested her, sending her out on spoof stories, hiding her reporter's notebook, rigging her chair so it collapsed when she sat down. It only made her more determined to write better stories and get more bylines than them. "What about you?" she asked. "Are you and Eddie planning to produce some little heirs?"

Dottie looked pensive. "Sure, I'd like to. But turns out Eddie fell in love with me because I was a career girl who earned her own dough, and he's not best pleased that's dried up lately." She sucked hard on her cigarette as if trying to inhale strength from it. "He wants me to keep the house spic and span, transform into a cordon bleu chef, raise a brood of little Parkers, earn lots of money, and what's more, he wants me to do it all in Connecticut, close to his beloved mama. . . ." Her voice trembled. "If I'd read the small print in the wedding vows, I'd have eaten my ovaries before letting him anywhere near me."

Jane was concerned. Dottie was the antithesis of a "little wife in the suburbs" type. "It seems he doesn't know the woman he married. What about you? What do *you* want from him?"

Dottie paused for a long time and blinked rapidly before she replied. "It would be nice if he could just pat me on the head from time to time and tell me I'm swell."

Jane squeezed her arm. "You two need a proper talk. Tell him how you're feeling."

Easier said than done, she knew. She had tried to talk to Harold about her misgivings over buying this dilapidated house, but he was swept along by enthusiasm for the project and couldn't see any view but his own. She loved his ambition but feared his lack of practicality.

"I'd have to kidnap him immediately when he stepped out of his Wall Street office, before he reached the nearest speakeasy." Dottie crushed her cigarette underfoot as if it were a cockroach. "That gives me about twenty yards."

"Was he always a drinker?" Jane asked. She was grateful Harold wasn't. He quaffed his fair share but knew when to stop.

"He drank before the war, but turns out that was a little light training before the main event." She shrugged. "I hope it's a phase he'll pull out of. Maybe living in the same town as his darling mama would help in that respect—but I'm not sure I could bear her scrutiny of my domestic arrangements and criticism of my child-rearing methods. Can you imagine?" She gave a mock shudder. "What's Harold's mother like?"

Jane laughed. "She's baffled by my lack of domesticity. She mails me recipes clipped from magazines, then wants to know how they turned out—but she's otherwise harmless."

"You're lucky if your worst problem is having to fib about an angel food cake. Come on then, show me the rest of this slum."

As Jane led her around, she wondered why she had brought Dottie, of all people. It was obvious she wouldn't like it. Had she wanted to be talked out of it? Was she looking for ammunition to persuade Harold it was a mistake?

She and Dottie had only met a year earlier, but right away Jane had felt a strong kinship. They both worked in journalism and battled to be taken seriously. They were allies in the competitive male-dominated atmosphere at the Gonk. And they were both young married women trying to forge a place in the world who didn't think looking after their husbands was their sole purpose in life. Jane had never been drawn to the kind of women friends who swapped fashion tips and went to beauty parlors together, and Dottie wasn't like that. She was funny and cerebral and refreshingly cynical.

Viewing the building in daylight, Jane felt a little more optimistic. The front rooms were sunnier than she'd thought, the kitchen yard was larger, and the area they planned to be a communal space would be perfect for parties. It would be tough going for a year or so but it could work.

"You think we're mad even considering it, don't you?" she asked.

"All madness is relative," Dottie said. She had a naughty look in her eyes and Jane could tell she was biting back a satirical comment. "But you and Harold are still just about young enough to make mistakes."

Jane laughed, and glanced at her watch. She had to go. "Are you young enough to try living in Connecticut? Or can you persuade Eddie to stick it out in Manhattan?"

"You gave me an idea earlier," Dottie said. "I'm going to write a story about a man who marries an independent, career-oriented woman, then tries to turn her into a younger version of his mother. It will be called 'Revenge of Oedipus' and the ending won't be pretty."

"Leave it on Eddie's nightstand," Jane suggested. "And send me a copy for Harold's mother too."

# Chapter 6
# DOTTIE

Dottie's legs felt leaden as she climbed the stairs to their third-floor apartment. It was all very well Jane advising her to talk to Eddie about the state of their marriage, but in truth she never saw him sober, except in the morning when he was hungover and foul. She only hoped it was a phase he would get over—and please let it be soon.

She unlocked their door and saw right away that he was slumped in the armchair, like a boxer out for the count. There was a half-full glass of amber liquid balanced on the armrest so she moved it to the table, then watched him for a while, trying to summon a vestige of affection. It was hard when she got nothing but criticism.

Sighing, she took off her coat, reapplied her wine-red lipstick, and headed across the hall to Neysa's studio. The door was ajar. Neysa was painting at her easel, dressed in baggy overalls, her unruly hair secured in a knot with a paintbrush stuck through, yet she still managed to look glamorous. A dozen people were dotted around the large room. One man was playing jazz tunes on the piano—rather well, Dottie thought—but no one seemed to be listening. He was sumptuously good-looking, with a high forehead, dark hair, and a hint of mustache.

She wandered over to Neysa. "Who's the pretty new boy?" she

asked, nodding in his direction. "And have you unwrapped him yet?" She glanced at the painting Neysa was working on, one of the lithe, languorous women she created for *McCall's* magazine covers.

Neysa blinked her tawny cat's eyes and grinned. "Jack something or other. Don't you think he looks like he stepped out of an Edward Hopper painting of a man nursing a drink in a late-night diner?"

Dottie sensed he was aware they were talking about him although he didn't look over. "Are you sure he's interested in the fairer sex? He might dance on the other side of the ballroom."

Neysa winked: "Let's just say there have been signs of his preference."

Neysa had dozens of male admirers and collected broken hearts like other women collected lipsticks, Dottie thought. Not callously, but carelessly. She bestowed her favors, the guy thought he'd struck gold, but by the time he tried to register his claim she'd be off dazzling some other gold miner. Dottie wandered over to introduce herself to Jack and couldn't stop cackling when he told her his profession was mining.

"What has made Mrs. Parker so merry?" Bob Benchley called from the couch, where he was sitting next to Alec. "Did it come in a bottle?"

"No, it's seeing you two," she said. "Move over, and tell me all the gossip, like the village fishwives you secretly are." She squeezed between them.

Bob didn't deny being a gossip. Scarcely lowering his voice, he told Dottie that Harpo Marx, of the famous Marx brothers stage show, had been there earlier. "He brought his harp and played for us—very painful it was too—then he got down on bended knee and invited Neysa to accompany him to Hollywood, where he is soon to shoot a motion picture."

Alec laughed, cruelly. "Of course, one doesn't know where to look when a man humiliates himself quite so publicly."

"What did Neysa say?" Dottie took Alec's glass from him and tried a sip, then screwed up her nose and handed it back.

"She ruffled his hair and whispered something I couldn't hear," Bob said. "His face fell and he left soon after, trailing his instrument behind him. Neysa, as you can see, carried on painting, as if she hadn't just destroyed a man's entire life."

Dottie knew that Alec was in love with Neysa too. Hell, every man in that room was. They hovered around her like blackfly on a June day. "That's one less rival for you to see off, I guess," she said with a conspiratorial smile. "And you can make notes for when you set out your own proposal. Number one: ditch the harp."

Alec swirled the drink in his glass, and didn't comment. Dottie caught eyes with Bob, who was struggling to keep a straight face.

She felt sorry for Alec. A rotund man with piggy eyes behind round wire spectacles, he hadn't a cat in hell's chance of snagging Neysa. She had never known Alec to have a lady friend. There was a rumor he was impotent after a bout of mumps in childhood but she hadn't presumed to ask if it were true. The Gonk crowd goaded one another mercilessly about trivia but never probed far beneath the surface.

IT WAS AFTER two a.m. when Dottie sloped back to her apartment. She hoped Eddie might have gotten himself to bed but he was still slumped in the armchair. The sound of the door woke him and he swore and clutched his head.

"Shall I get you an aspirin, honey?" she called, and went to the kitchen to dissolve a powder in some water without waiting for an answer.

His hand was shaking so badly when he took it from her that

some spilled down the front of his shirt. After he had drained the rest, Dottie held out an arm. "Let me help you to bed," she said.

As he rose, unsteadily, his arm swung out sideways and his fist connected squarely with her eye socket, sending her hurtling backward. Her head smacked the corner of the table before she landed on the floor, where she lay, shocked and winded. He hadn't meant to do it, she told herself. It was a clumsy accident. But there was no apology. Instead, he staggered to the bathroom and she heard the drumbeat of his urine hitting the pan.

She tried to raise herself on her elbows but her head was spinning. Eddie lurched to the bedroom and she heard the mattress springs creak as he toppled into bed. He was going to leave her on the floor. What if she'd been knocked unconscious? Wasn't he at all concerned?

Waves of pain radiated through her cheekbone and pulsed behind her eye. She leaned on the table to raise herself to her feet and walked slowly to the kitchen to dissolve an aspirin powder for herself. After she drank it, shivering at the bitter taste, she crept into the bedroom and lay on her side of the bed, too shaken to get undressed.

Eddie wasn't a violent man, she told herself. The drink had caused it, not him. She knew in her heart it was the sights he'd seen in the war that had made him this way. He'd told her a few things: the men with loops of gut spilling from great gashes in their abdomens, the ones with limbs blown clean off, the young soldiers he held in his arms as they passed away. She could tell he was keeping a lot back. Once he admitted that he and a fellow driver used to inject themselves with morphine to get through the days: "Just a little, to take the edge off." Maybe that's why he took to booze with a vengeance as soon as he got back to New York. She should be more understanding. Surely this would pass when he got used to civilian life and the ghastly memories faded. On the other hand, perhaps it would get worse.

She lay awake till dawn was creeping around the edge of the shutters, then managed an hour's shut-eye before Eddie's alarm went off and he rolled out of bed to dress for his commute to the office. Dottie got up and went to the bathroom. As she'd expected, she had a shiner: her left eye was almost swollen shut and bruised like a ripe plum, while there was an egg on the back of her skull that hurt to touch. She was checking the damage in the mirror when Eddie appeared behind her.

She waited for him to comment, but his expression was cold when he spoke.

"I've handed in my notice at work. I'm going to Connecticut this weekend to look for a place to live, and I'll operate as a trader from there."

An icy hand gripped Dottie's stomach and twisted. "You resigned? Without consulting me?" Her mind leapt through this new scenario. If he really wanted to go, she supposed she would have to accompany him. Jeez, she couldn't face it, though. What would she do without her friends?

"I've been telling you for ages I wanted to move there, but you wouldn't listen."

"If your mind's made up, I guess I'll come and help choose a place," she said, trying to keep her tone level.

He scowled. "Don't be ridiculous! I can't possibly let Mother see you looking like *that*."

She wondered if he realized he had caused her injuries. Or had he forgotten?

"When are you thinking of moving? We need time to make arrangements. Maybe we could keep the apartment here and spend weekends in the city."

"Actually, I think you should stay here and I'll go alone," he said, and she whirled around in horror. There wasn't a flicker of expression in his eyes. Not a blink.

"What do you mean?" She scrutinized his face, trying to understand.

"We can talk later. I have to get to the office. They're insisting I work my notice." He walked out of the bathroom.

"Eddie!" She hurried after him and spoke softly, pleading with him. "What are you saying?"

If only he would meet her eyes and see that it was her, his Dottie, his girl. Instead he picked up his jacket and briefcase and left without looking back.

Was he *leaving* her? Married couples didn't live in different towns. Was it just temporary? How could he be so cruel as to lob that grenade, then leave without explaining?

She went back to finish her toiletries, but a wave of giddiness came over her. She gripped the edge of the basin and stared at herself in the mirror, feeling disoriented, as if the world were dissolving around her and all that remained was black nothingness.

# Chapter 7
# WINIFRED

**W**inifred decided to stop at the Algonquin after a busy
Saturday afternoon shift at Lord & Taylor. She'd had
several difficult-to-please customers: the season's new
cloche hats were designed for women with short, bobbed hair and
looked peculiar when crammed on top of a chignon, but try telling
them that.

Frank Case, the Algonquin's manager, had placed a large round
table in the center of the Rose Room to accommodate the crowd
of hacks and hangers-on who congregated there. As she walked in,
Winifred heard Dottie's voice first, narrating an anecdote about
baseball, of all things.

"Eddie used to fancy himself something of a hotshot back in
the day—a regular Ty Cobb—so when a kid hit a wide ball in our
street yesterday and it was coming his way, he leapt high in the air
to catch it."

Her voice had a musical quality when she was telling a story,
Winifred noticed. It contrasted with the monotone mutter she
used for her one-liners, as if she was less confident of them. She
sat down opposite, and it was only then she noticed, with a shock,
that Dottie was sporting a dramatic black eye. She hadn't seen it
before because the brim of her hat was shading it.

Alec Woollcott topped up her glass from a hip flask and Dottie took a sip, then continued her story. "He pitched it with a proper overhand throw, trying to show that he was 'one of the boys,' whereupon the kid with the bat assumed he wanted to play and whacked it straight back. Only this time, Eddie didn't catch it. I did—with my eye socket."

The laughter around the table was subdued. Dottie's eye was badly swollen.

Winifred didn't believe her explanation for a moment. She had clearly rehearsed it till she was word-perfect but it didn't have the ring of truth.

"At least he got a home run," Dottie finished, to uncomfortable titters from her listeners.

Winifred leaned over and spoke to her quietly. "Have you seen a doctor? Your eye could be damaged."

"I stopped going to my doctor after I noticed the aspidistra in his office had died," Dottie replied. "Don't worry—I'll be fine." She turned to talk to Bob Benchley, precluding further inquiry.

Winifred looked around the table. There were fifteen or sixteen people there, mostly men. A group at one side was playing a competitive word game, calling out answers with much hilarity. George Kaufman, the *New York Times* drama editor, caught her eye and smiled, so she rose and strolled over to chat.

"I hope you'll review my new show at the Bijou," she said. "It's called *The Dover Road* and it's frothy and fun. I'll adore you forever if you give it a good plug."

"Send me a pair of tickets and I'll see what I can do," he said, patting the arm of his chair and inviting her to perch there. As soon as she sat, crossing her legs, he placed his hand on her knee and began to stroke it with his thumb. "I hope you're playing the lead?"

"I am," Winifred said, steeling herself to ignore his caresses as she told him a little about the plot. It was part of the price to be paid for getting him to the show. George was a playwright himself, so she asked what he was writing at the moment.

"I'm working on a satire with Marc Connelly—do you know him?" Winifred nodded. Of course she did. "I find collaborations are a great way of getting someone else to do the donkey work."

Alec overheard this. "Why don't we all write a revue about ourselves?" He gestured around the table. "The Gonk crowd. We could have songs, dance, and jokes, with each of us playing ourselves. It would be a sellout."

Dottie murmured, "Talk about a Narcissus complex! I'm sure there are laws against loving yourself that much."

Alec replied with a grin: "Loving myself is a sign of my impeccable good taste. You should try it, Mrs. Parker."

The men started chipping in ideas about who should write it and theaters that might stage it. George joined the conversation so Winifred removed his hand from her knee and walked around to sit by Dottie.

"Have you ever thought of writing for the stage?" she asked.

Dottie shook her head instantly. "Me? After all I've written about Broadway folk? Does Chanel make a gown with a target on the back and a set of matching throw knives?" Winifred laughed. "Besides, I don't have an ear for dialogue."

"I could help you with that, by reading it from an actor's point of view."

Dottie shook her head. "If you knew how long it took me to write a four-line verse, you wouldn't be asking."

Winifred glanced across the table at the men grandstanding about how much influence they had on Broadway—all of them talking over the women present. She was fed up to the back teeth with men who thought they knew best. They might write about theater but she stood onstage and faced audiences night after night. Why not ask her opinion? Frankly, she thought their "revue" idea sounded dated. The public was used to elaborate, expensive spectacles like the *Ziegfeld Follies*, and an amateur self-congratulatory production by a bunch of hacks seemed doomed to flop.

Suddenly she'd had enough of the Gonk for one evening. "I'm heading to Neysa's," she told Dottie. "I'm meeting Peter there. Want to share a taxi?"

Dottie raised an eyebrow: "You're meeting your beau in the lair of New York's premier beau snatcher? Is that wise?"

Winifred laughed. "She's welcome to him. He's handsome, granted, but I have better conversations with my mother's poodle."

Dottie snorted. "Have you been looking for a man with conversation skills? That's where you've been going wrong all these years. My advice is kid him that you like baseball just long enough to get some decent jewelry, then buy yourself a few novels if it's entertainment you're after."

Winifred laughed, as did their immediate neighbors, but it occurred to her that it must be a strain being Dottie. She was always on show, her "friends" expecting every word that passed her lips to be hysterically funny. When did she get to relax and be herself?

"Present male company excepted, I hope," Bob said, adopting a hangdog expression.

"Of course." Dottie gave a twitch of a smile, patted his arm, and slipped her Chesterfield cigarettes into her bag. "Shall we?" she asked, scraping her chair back. "You can entertain me on the way by telling me *all* about Peter."

It wasn't far—straight up Sixth Avenue—but there wasn't much to tell. As they waited for a taxi, Winifred explained that her agent had introduced them a couple of months earlier. Peter had invited her to the premiere of Gloria Swanson's new movie, *The Affairs of Anatol*, then they started having dinner a couple of times a week. He was urging her to head out west, saying she'd be a shoe-in for plum motion-picture roles, but from what she'd heard about Holly-

44

wood, it didn't appeal. All that standing around on set, waiting for the lighting, the makeup, the whims of directors—it sounded like hell on earth.

"Hell on earth but with better weather," Dottie said, wrapping her coat around her as Winifred stuck her arm out, trying to get the attention of a passing taxi driver. "Is Peter fun in the sack at least?"

"I have no idea," Winifred said.

"You're not . . . ?" Dottie looked surprised.

"No, we're not—much to his disgust. The fizz isn't there for me. I thought maybe it would grow when I got to know him better but . . ."

She paused. Men tended to want her as a trinket to dangle on their arms and decorate their beds, in return for which they'd buy her meals and drinks and perfume. Frankly, it was a trade-off she would rather do without.

"I bet you're driving that poor man crazy," Dottie said, with a sideways glance. "He probably goes home and jerks off in front of your picture. Are you enjoying the power?"

"God, no!" Winifred protested. "What a horrible thought!"

She wondered if Dottie liked her. She'd agreed to share a taxi, and accepted her as a member of the bridge group, but did she see her as a potential friend? It was hard to tell, because the mask was almost always in place.

"I think Neysa gets a kick out of toying with men. It's her hobby. Why do they all fall head over heels with her? You're far more beautiful." Dottie waved away Winifred's objections. "I'm funnier, Peggy's smarter, but they prostrate themselves at Neysa's feet and purr like cats if she so much as glances their way. Do you think she spikes their drinks?"

Winifred laughed. "It's not that. She has sex appeal: that languid way of moving"—she curved her arm, sinuously, to imitate

45

it—"and a voice like honey that makes men imagine her reclining naked between satin sheets, her head thrown back in ecstasy. If you were a man, don't you think you would fall for her?"

Dottie shook her head. "Neysa's too smart for me. I like my partners good-looking and stupid. Haven't you met Eddie?"

Winifred thought that if she did meet Eddie, she might have trouble keeping quiet about Dottie's black eye. "No, but I look forward to it," she said, tongue firmly in cheek.

# Chapter 8
# PEGGY

Peggy took a platter of homemade molasses cookies to Neysa's salon, because her mother had brought her up never to arrive anywhere empty-handed. She put them down on the piano and immediately a swarm of hands descended and grabbed them. A tall, gasp-inducingly handsome man took the last cookie, then turned to her apologetically.

"You haven't had one yourself. Please—take this."

Peggy grinned and shook her head. "I've got another batch at home."

"If you're sure." He took a bite, then widened his eyes and licked his lips. "Delicious. You're a woman of sublime talent." He held out his hand. "Jack Baragwanath."

"Peggy Leech." They shook. "I only appear talented in comparison to most of the others here, who might as well remove the kitchens from their apartments for all the use they get."

"Where do you work, Peggy Leech?" he asked, polishing off the remainder of the cookie in one large bite, then speaking with his mouth full. "And does your boss appreciate you as much as you deserve?"

She laughed. "I work at Condé Nast, but not in a creative job. My role is to call advertisers, persuade them to book slots for their ads, then nag them to deliver copy on time. My boss is a man of meager imagination who thinks he's a sophisticate because he pronounces French and Italian words with studied affectation. I don't much care whether he appreciates me, so long as he doesn't fire me—not for now, at any rate."

"I think I can picture him," Jack said. "Does he wear a toupee by any chance?"

"How did you guess?" Peggy was enjoying herself.

"You have to hand in your notice. You can't work for a man with a toupee."

"Shall I tell you my secret, Mr. Baragwanath?"

"Jack." He had a grin that lit up his face.

He was being so attentive that Peggy began to wonder if he was flirting with her. Surely not!

"I'm writing a novel, and my dream is that when I am a published author, I can tell my boss precisely what to do with his job. In both French and Italian."

"Roll on the day. What's your novel about, if I may be so bold?"

Not many people asked, Peggy thought. Perhaps they were worried it would sound dreary and they'd have to make polite noises and lie that they couldn't wait to read it. "It's about a modern woman in her late twenties who's looking for a husband, and wondering where to find the right kind of man."

"And what *is* the right kind of man?" he asked. It definitely sounded like a flirtatious question.

"I don't know yet. So far I've been too busy ruling out the wrong kinds." He waited for her to explain. "It was easier for our parents' generation: they married family friends and settled into the same lives as *their* parents before them. Women my age are on the cusp of social change, partly because of the war, partly because more of us are working. It means we're inventing new rules as we go along, but sometimes it feels—forgive me—as if the men haven't caught up. That's what I'm trying to capture in the novel."

He nodded in agreement. "Were you part of the war effort? I heard Neysa and Jane were in France with the YMCA."

"Me too, but they were in Paris while I was out in the sticks so I didn't meet either of them till we got back."

"How did you meet? Through the Algonquin crowd?"

Peggy nodded. "Yes, that's right. But I much prefer coming to Neysa's than hanging around at the Gonk. You get the chance to make proper conversation, without all the competitive wisecracking."

"It seems there are always far more men than women here," Jack said, looking around. "Which can be disconcerting for a man."

"That's true. Men buzz around Neysa like wasps around a sugar bowl."

"Does she have a beau right now?" Jack was looking across at her, and suddenly Peggy realized it wasn't her he was interested in. He was another of Neysa's conquests. She felt a twinge of disappointment. Never mind! At least he'd been an entertaining conversationalist.

"I'm not sure," she said, and was saved from having to expand on that by the arrival of Dottie and Winifred. Peggy was shocked to see Dottie had a livid black eye.

"What on earth happened?" she asked, standing to greet them. "You need to put raw steak on that."

"Baseball accident," Dottie said, "but we were clean out of steak. All we had was dog food." She sounded a little tipsy. "I need to talk to you, Pegs. Can you give me some klutz-proof recipes to warm the cockles of a man's heart? Turns out Eddie wanted a wife who can cook but he married me by accident."

She sprawled across the couch next to Jack and picked up a half-full glass he had left on a side table, examining it, then taking a slurp.

"I'll give you some recipes at the bridge club tomorrow," Peggy offered. "We're meeting at my place."

"Did I tell you that Jane and Harold are moving to a slum in Hell's Kitchen?" Dottie continued. "As if being married to New York's ugliest man wasn't already its own version of hell." Peggy shushed her, but Dottie carried on: "You have to admit his face looks like a baseball mitt that's been chewed by a pack of bulldogs. Imagine kissing that every morning."

Jack got up and wandered over to the piano, as if he didn't want to be part of this conversation.

*Dottie's jealous*, Peggy thought, watching her drain the glass. *Jane's the only one of us who's found a decent husband*. Her, and maybe Ruth Hale, who was married to Heywood Broun, a writer at the *New York Tribune*, although rumor was they had an "open marriage"—whatever that meant.

Ruth and Jane had both refused to take their husbands' names upon marriage, and they also refused to wear wedding rings, calling them "symbols of oppression." Maybe she and Ruth were the bosses in their marriages, but that would be a rarity. Most of the married men Peggy knew had settled their wives in the suburbs and only rode home on the last train after spending the evening living it up with other women, which was not the kind of marriage she wanted.

She made a hobby out of watching other people's relationships: the unspoken nuances, the subtle glances that told you who was happy and who was decidedly not. It was research for her novel, as well as research for her life.

As she talked to Dottie, she watched Jack tinkling on the piano while trying and failing not to watch Neysa. No doubt about it—he was stuck on her. Peggy wished him luck. He would need it.

PEGGY SPENT SEVERAL hours making canapés for the bridge club meeting at her East Village tenement apartment. She felt a need to impress the group. Jane was a reporter for the country's leading broadsheet, Winifred a Broadway star, and Dottie a renowned wit, but who was she? A hanger-on?

None of the others had visited her apartment before and Winifred exclaimed at the heaving bookshelves, stretching floor to ceiling across two walls of the living room, as well as the piles of books stacked on side tables with places held by bookmarks.

"Are you sure the floor will take the weight?" she asked. "Look at all these! History, literature, philosophy, psychology . . . have you actually read them?"

"Not all of them."

"Aren't you the highbrow!" Jane exclaimed, picking up a biography of President McKinley that was lying facedown on the windowsill: "America's most mediocre president. Not exactly light reading, Pegs."

"I find you don't actually need to read books these days," Dottie commented. "Just memorize a few quotes, then nod and sigh wisely. It saves your brow getting furrowed by complex thoughts."

Peggy served them Gin Daisies, colored pink with grenadine, then dealt the cards. "This time we need to try bidding in pairs," she said. "I'll pair with Dottie, and Jane with Winifred."

The game began but Dottie's mind appeared to be elsewhere. In an early round she played a king even though Peggy had won the trick with a jack.

"Throw away your lowest card if I've already won," Peggy suggested with infinite patience. "We're on the same team."

Minutes later, Winifred took Dottie's queen with an ace.

"You should have guessed Winifred had some high spades when she chose it as trump," Peggy pointed out, "and the ace hadn't been played."

"Clearly I'm not a mind reader," Dottie said, irritably, then held out her glass. "Any chance of a refill?"

When they stopped for a break, Peggy set out her canapés—salmon mousse on squares of bread, mushrooms stuffed with cream cheese, celery and carrot sticks—and watched with pleasure as they were devoured.

"May I ask you three a question I've been pondering?" she asked. "In your opinion, how should a single girl find a husband in New York City in this day and age? I'm fed up wasting time on creeps, playboys, and married men pretending to be single."

Jane was the first to answer. "If I were you, I'd find an excuse to search through the personnel records at Condé Nast. Figure out which young men are bachelors, then stroll past their desks and check them out. If one looks promising, I'm sure you can invent a work-related reason to have lunch together. That's what I'd do."

"It feels sneaky." Peggy grinned. "But I guess that's your reporter's instinct."

"Why not join a literary or historic society?" Winifred suggested. "You'd find like-minded men there—the types you could discuss books with."

"I'm already in the New-York Historical Society," Peggy said, "and I'm the youngest member by several decades. But thanks, Winifred."

They turned to Dottie. She rearranged her feather boa—a mauve one today—and tossed her bobbed hair before speaking. "There's no great mystery. Any woman can get herself a husband if she sets the bar *low* enough."

"OK, tell us what you would do," Peggy asked. "If you weren't already taken." If she wasn't mistaken, Dottie flinched.

"Easy," she replied. "I would sit in the lobby of the Waldorf-Astoria, wearing my most seductive outfit and dabbing my eyes with a lace handkerchief. With any luck and a prevailing wind, some wealthy businessman with a kind heart would soon volunteer his services."

This was met with a chorus of disapproval. "Do you really want a man who feels sorry for you?" Jane asked. "It's not a great start to a marriage."

"That's how Eddie and I met," Dottie said. "I was wandering around the lobby of a Branford hotel late one night, after I'd lost my room key and all the staff had gone to bed. Eddie shinnied up a drainpipe and clambered into my room through a window that had been left ajar. It meant he got to feel masculine and bold and I instantly saw him in a heroic light." She took a slug of her drink. "Of course, the most heroic thing he does now is venture north of the park to buy cheap whiskey."

Peggy mused that each of them had revealed their characters in their answers. Both Jane and Winifred took charge of their own fortunes, while Dottie wanted a man to look after her. The bruising around her injured eye was fading to yellow at the edges but still lurid in the center. Her hand shook as she stubbed out her cigarette. Her collarbones were prominent in the boat-neck dress that hung from her shoulders, as if she'd lost weight. She looked fragile and insubstantial, as if a sudden gust of wind might carry her away.

Peggy gave her some recipes she had copied out, for beef brisket, glazed ham, and chicken soup with dumplings. None of them were difficult, but from the way Dottie merely glanced at them, then stuffed them in her handbag, she sensed they were unlikely to get made.

## Chapter 9
# JANE

Jane watched as Harold signed the contracts with his loopy, illegible scrawl, then she signed too, and the property at 412 West Forty-Seventh Street officially became theirs. It felt momentous. They were giggly and light-headed as they left the lawyer's office, and they stopped at Jack and Charlie's Red Head speakeasy for a lunchtime cocktail to toast their new venture.

Hawley, one of the prospective tenants, had gotten a friend to draw up architectural blueprints, and they met him at the building later that afternoon to compile a list of work to be done. There was no electricity, little plumbing, and floorboards your foot plunged straight through. It would take almost a year to complete the renovations, but now that the decision had been made, Jane was excited about the home they would create.

Hawley said he had spotted a large oak table abandoned in the street two blocks north so he and Harold set off to fetch it. They arrived back half an hour later, swearing and sweating, and only just managed to wedge it through the hallway into the area that would be a communal dining space. The three of them perched on wooden crates, and spread the blueprints in front of them.

Jane scribbled down tasks in a notebook as they dreamed of how it would look when the work was done. She could picture the way she would arrange their personal apartment, with the bedroom at the back, looking over the yard that she planned to plant with spring flowers and cherry trees.

When Jane heard a loud knocking, at first she thought it must have come from a neighboring property, but then she realized it was their front door. Who knew they were there? She went to a window and peered out to see Alec standing on the stoop, hammering with his fist. He motioned for her to let him in.

"Quick!" she said to the others, rushing to gather up the blueprints and shove them inside her satchel. "It's Alec. Don't let him see these." She didn't want him poking his nose in and interfering with their plans. He had opinions on everything and always had to be the one who knew best.

When she opened the door, Alec was leaning against the wall outside.

"Welcome to our hovel!" she said brightly. "What brings you to this neck of the woods? Have you come to see how the other half lives?" Alec came from a wealthy family and had some snobbish attitudes, which they never missed a chance to tease him about.

"Indeed." He followed her down the hall, gazing around. "Reports of its dilapidation were not exaggerated. I don't suppose there's any coffee to be had?"

"No electricity and no oil burner," Jane apologized, "so no coffee. Unless you want to build a campfire in the yard."

"I'm surprised to see you here," Harold greeted him. "Weren't you worried the poor people might infect you with their nasty diseases?"

"No one could call it a swanky neighborhood," Alec said. "But I tried not to get within spitting distance of any inhabitants. Living here seems rather . . ." He sought the right word. "Adventurous."

As he sat down on the box Jane had vacated, his foot brushed against something on the floor and he bent to pick it up. One of the blueprints had fallen from her grip.

"Aha!" he said, opening it. "I see the plans are further along than I thought. I'd better pick my apartment before you give it to some other bounder."

Jane was baffled. "I'm afraid we don't have any room for you," she said, glancing at Harold for corroboration. "We're going to be on the first floor, Hawley will be on the second, and we've offered the third to Bill Powell."

Alec turned to Hawley. "You and I could both fit on the second floor, don't you think? That back room would suit me. And the adjoining room too."

"Sure," Hawley said, looking uncomfortable.

It was directly above their bedroom. Jane willed Harold to say something, but he wouldn't meet her eye. What was going on?

"I thought you were staying in Hawley's mother's apartment," Jane said. "Why do you want to move? You'll have more space once Hawley moves out, and it's a much smarter neighborhood."

"My friends are planning an experiment in communal living and I'd hate to miss the fun," Alec said. "Am I right in thinking this is the area you want to be a dining and entertaining space?" He looked around, nodding thoughtfully. "It's a good size. We could make it a games room too. This is perfect for a poker table."

Jane was furious that Harold was letting Alec barge in and take over without comment. Why didn't he say something? "I'm afraid Harold and I decided we will only have one lodger per floor," she said. "It will be too cramped with more. Sorry!"

"Are you sure? I would, of course, contribute my fair share," he said, naming a figure that would help their finances significantly.

She looked at Harold but he was concentrating on the blueprint and wouldn't meet her eye. Hawley piped up: "I don't mind sharing. There's plenty of room."

Jane bit her lip. She didn't want Alec living with them. They were friends, and he had his fun side, but he also created discord and upset people with his forthright opinions. While it could be amusing around a table at the Gonk, she didn't want that in her home.

THEIR FRIENDSHIP WENT back several years. Jane had first met Alec when she started working at the *New York Times* in 1916, in a lowly job answering the telephone on the society pages. She found him entertaining and they started going for hot dogs in the park at lunchtime or to grab a beer after work, at a time when none of the other men there would give her the time of day. As soon as America joined the war, he volunteered for the medical corps while Jane volunteered for the YMCA. She was stationed in Tours and then Le Mans but, following the Armistice, Alec pulled some strings—she was never quite sure how—and got her transferred to Paris. By that time he was a chief reporter for *Stars and Stripes* and one night he took her to a poker game at Nini's in Montmartre, which was where she first met Harold.

She soon became an honorary member of the *Stars and Stripes* crew, sewing their torn uniforms, spending evenings dancing in Paris nightspots with them, and listening to their hair-raising stories of reporting from the front line. They started collecting contributions for a soldiers' joke book, and gradually Harold and Alec developed their double act, based on constant sparring and one-upmanship. They argued over everything from Greek mythology to grammar, and Harold made a point of never spelling Alec's surname correctly—Wolcoot, Woolcutt, Wulcotte—just because it annoyed him.

"You remind me of a coachman who used to work for my grandfather," Alec told Harold.

"And you remind me of a plump dowager duchess," Harold said, mocking his upper-class pretentiousness as well as his girth.

Jane thought they were two of the best pals a girl could wish for—but it seemed it wasn't friendship Harold was after. Instead he bombarded her with witty love letters and gifts and made it clear his intentions were romantic. Jane held him at arm's length while they were in France. What did she need a husband for? She was doing perfectly well as she was.

She returned to New York first, and was one of the organizers of an infamous "Welcome Home" party thrown for Alec at the Algonquin, featuring signs with different spellings of his name dotted around the room. Originally planned as a joke, it was such a success that core members of the group carried on meeting in the "Gonk," and it turned into a regular haunt.

In 1920, Jane finally agreed to marry Harold. She wondered if Alec's nose might be put out of joint by this change in the dynamic of their friendship, but it seemed not because he offered to plan their wedding for them. Afterward he and Harold continued with their friendly banter, just as always, but Jane felt his attitude toward her cooled. They both returned to work at the *New York Times*, but if she suggested a lunchtime hot dog, he claimed he was too busy. She wondered if it was because she was another man's wife now—or perhaps because he had fallen for Neysa and was concentrating his efforts there.

She still enjoyed seeing Alec at the Gonk, but the thought of living with him was exhausting. She couldn't cope with all that male competitiveness. But if she were the one to say that he couldn't move in, she would be making an enemy of him and she had never wanted that.

As THEY WALKED back to the Gonk later, Jane pulled Harold aside so they were out of earshot of Hawley and Alec.

"What the hell!" she hissed, turning to watch his face. "Did you *invite* Alec to live with us?" He looked shifty; she could tell it had been discussed between them. She shook her head in disbelief. "You didn't think to ask me first?"

"I didn't exactly invite him. I merely told him we were buying the building and he said he would come and look it over. It was kind of unstated."

"So tell him it was a misunderstanding. Tell him we don't have space. Tell him anything, but get him to drop the idea."

Harold scrunched up his nose. "He's seen the place now and he knows we do have space. I can't lie to him, Jane. Let's take the Woollcott family bucks to help us get the magazine up and running sooner. We'll have our own front door and we can close it whenever we've had our fill of him."

Jane shook her head. "You know Alec can't stand to be alone. He'll be down in our apartment the whole time. We'll never get any peace." She had a strong sense of foreboding.

Harold reached out for her hand and squeezed it. "Besides, Alec won't move in till everything is shipshape, and that could be a year away. Anything could happen by then. Maybe he'll marry Neysa and move in with her instead." He snorted at the unlikeliness.

"Yeah, or maybe he'll be whisked off to Hollywood as their new leading man."

"Now, that's downright cruel." Harold chortled.

"And your suggestion wasn't?" She poked him in the ribs. "You ambushed me this afternoon. I don't have any choice now."

"Think of the money," Harold said. "The rustle of crisp new dollar bills flying into our bank account." He rubbed his fingers together with a low whistle.

Jane sighed. "I suppose I have to. But make sure he understands that once we're living in our house, our rules go. And tell him it's only a short-term tenancy and we can boot him out whenever we want the rooms back."

Harold twirled her around and kissed her hard on the mouth. "Thank you, mushkins," he whispered. "That's my girl!"

At the Gonk, Dottie was horrified when she heard what Jane had agreed to. "I'm running through a list of acquaintances in my head and I swear I can't think of anyone I would *less* want to live with. Can't you wriggle out of it? Tell him you're starting a family and he'll run a mile—he loathes children." She snapped her fingers. "I have an idea! Perhaps you could borrow one from an orphanage and tell him you're adopting it."

Jane glanced across at Harold. He and Alec might be sparring partners when it came to humor, but there was a bond between them from their wartime experiences. Dodging shellfire together made them honorary brothers. She suspected that trying to get rid of Alec now that he had a foot in the door might be a battle she couldn't win.

"I'll deal with the Duchess of Woollcott, as Harold calls him," she said. "One way or another. You mark my words."

# Chapter 10

# DOTTIE

One Saturday morning, Eddie packed a suitcase while Dottie watched from the bed, clutching Woodrow on her lap. She reached for her cigarette case and extracted one, then realized she already had a cigarette burning in the ashtray.

"How long are you planning this separation to be?" she asked, her heart hammering in her chest. They'd been discussing it endlessly, and at least he wasn't asking for a divorce. Dottie couldn't bear to contemplate that. He just wanted them to spend some time apart—or so he said. "How long till you *see how it goes*?"

"Six months?" He selected two pairs of shoes and wedged them in the side of the case. "We can meet then and see how we're feeling. Go for lunch somewhere and talk it through."

A suspicion leapt into her mind. "You've got someone else, haven't you? You've got a chippy in Connecticut."

"No," he said. "There's no one else. I'm just miserable, Dottie."

The words were emotional but his tone was dispassionate, as if she were a secretary he was firing for taking overlong lunch breaks, not his wife of five years.

"What makes you think our marriage will improve with separation? That didn't work when you went to war." Her hands were shaking. She ran her fingers through Woodrow's coarse hair. *Try not to cry. He hates it when you cry.*

"We can't go on like this, Dottie. I dread coming home because I know you'll be nagging me from the moment I walk in the door. That's why I have a drink or two first, to take the edge off."

She was stunned into silence. Was she a nag? She might occasionally have suggested he should cut back on the coffin juice. Did that count as nagging? Didn't every wife the length and breadth of the land do the same?

"The bottom line is that I can't manage without you, Eddie," she said, the tears starting to leak out. "I won't be safe. I don't know how to do things like pay bills. What if the oven breaks or a pipe bursts or a window shatters? I can't even change my own typewriter ribbon. You have to stay." She hated herself for begging, but the prospect of life without him petrified her. Loneliness loomed like an abyss. She'd have no one, nothing.

He walked her through the practicalities: he'd give her an allowance so she could pay bills by writing checks from the checkbook in the drawer. The landlord would fix things that broke. He'd be on the end of the phone if she needed him.

Should she tell him she loved him? Was it true? It had been once. If she could have that old Eddie back she would love him again, but it was hard to feel love for a man who was treating her so coldly.

"Woodrow Wilson will miss you," she said, wiping her eyes. "He'll pine for you."

"I have to say, I won't miss that mutt one bit," Eddie said. "I'm fed up stepping in his mess the whole time."

"Just as well we didn't have children or you'd have hit them on the head with a rolled-up newspaper every time they pooped." She wanted him to say there was still a chance they could have children one day, but he closed his case with a click. It felt as if there was a ten-ton weight on her chest so she could hardly breathe.

He left just after noon, giving her a quick kiss, then rushing out the door to avoid the avalanche of tears he must have known was coming. Dottie hugged Woodrow Wilson so hard that he whined and wriggled off her lap. "Even you are leaving me," she accused him. *What will I do? What will I do?* ran like a Greek chorus in her head. She was almost twenty-nine years old and had nothing to show for her life. She couldn't write, couldn't keep a husband—what was she good for?

DOTTIE ALMOST DIDN'T go to the bridge group that evening, but felt guilty that they wouldn't have a four without her. Besides, what else would she do except sit at home and guzzle the half bottle of Scotch that Eddie had left behind? She layered on some makeup and chose a low-brimmed hat that shaded her puffy eyes, then walked out to Sixth Avenue to hail a cab.

For the first time, they were meeting at Winifred's apartment, just off West Forty-Fifth not far from Broadway. She lived on the top floor and when she opened the door, Dottie saw it was tiny—one room with a pull-down bed, and a kitchen sink and stove in the corner—but it was furnished like a theatrical set. A group of elephant prints hung on one wall, a tall black vase of peacock feathers stood on the floor, colorful embroidered shawls were draped over the chairs, the light came from stained-glass lamps, and swathes of crimson velvet drapes, like theater curtains, covered the windows.

Dottie accepted a gin and lemonade, then remembered she hadn't eaten all day. Her throat was so tight it was hard to swallow food, but the gin went down just dandy.

Winifred dealt the first hand and Dottie tried to concentrate, but all she could think was that Eddie had left her. Should she tell them? It was tempting. . . . But they would be sweet and caring and she would start crying and she didn't know if she would ever stop. The rest of the evening would be spent talking about the whys and wherefores and she couldn't face that; best to ignore it and carry on.

Peggy tutted as Dottie put down a card. "Don't you have any clubs?"

Dottie frowned and shook her head. She hadn't been paying attention. "Maybe you should get another gal to make up your four. It seems bridge is not one of my talents. . . . If I have any at all, I can't remember what they are. . . ."

"Says the wittiest woman in the world," Jane rejoined. "You're no worse at bridge than me. It's a tricky game to master, but we're not in competition and we're not playing for money."

Winifred noticed Dottie's drink was nearly empty and mixed her another without being asked. Tears pricked Dottie's eyes at the kindness. That's why she couldn't tell the women about her marital separation. Their empathy would finish her off.

THE NEXT AFTERNOON, Dottie telephoned Bob Benchley and told him Eddie had left. "So now I've been fired from my job and fired from my marriage too," she said. "Whatever next?"

"You could be thrown out of your apartment," he suggested. "Your friends could disown you. Woodrow Wilson could trot across the corridor and move in with Neysa."

"And you could decide you don't want to share an office with me any longer?"

"About that . . ." He paused for comic effect. "No, I hope to see you in our cubbyhole bright and early tomorrow morning. If you play your cards right, I'll even buy you lunch at the Gonk."

"You'd buy me a proper lunch? Not just pass me the free celery from someone else's table?"

"My offer is good for lunch, at one o'clock on the dot—so long as you don't order the lobster. Or the sirloin. In fact, I can recommend the soup."

*Good old Mr. Benchley*, she thought afterward. She much preferred the way men dealt with emotional crises. They didn't make a full-blown Greek tragedy out of them.

By the time she got to the Gonk on Monday she had rehearsed a "hapless Eddie" anecdote to explain his absence to the crowd. It involved him trying pathetically to ingratiate himself with his boss by agreeing to play golf with him, even though he didn't know how to play, then having to sign up for a crash course of lessons, and not realizing the ones he'd signed up for were actually in Connecticut.

"Besides, it's the new fashion for married couples to live apart," she told them. "All the best people are doing it. You can avoid the petty little uglinesses of daily life . . . like Eddie's toenail clippings."

She knew she wasn't fooling anyone, but it felt better to be herself again. If she could somehow carry on like this, burying her head in the sand and putting one foot in front of the other, maybe, eventually, the pain would lessen.

Word of the separation reached Jane, and she telephoned that evening with a string of brusque reporter's questions. "Why didn't you tell me? How long has he gone for? Where will he stay? Will you see each other in the meantime?"

"All I know is he's left his prized collection of sporting cigarette cards, so he's bound to be back," Dottie replied. "Otherwise, your guess is as good as mine."

"The shit!" Jane exclaimed. "I'm sorry."

A COUPLE OF weeks later, Alec Woollcott turned up at the Gonk with a tall, good-looking man who had naughty eyes and the most pronounced widow's peak Dottie had ever seen.

"This is our famous Mrs. Parker," Alec said, "and this"—he flung out an arm in flamboyant style—"is Charlie MacArthur, reporter for the *New York American* and budding playwright. You two should have a lot in common."

Alec had a glitter of mischief about him and Charlie was grinning widely. It was as if they'd been discussing her before they arrived, but she couldn't figure out what had been said.

"I've heard all about you, of course," Charlie said, taking her hand and bowing over it in old-fashioned style. "But I don't understand why nobody told me how incredibly beautiful you are."

It was a cheesy line, but no snarky innuendo leapt to Dottie's tongue. Instead, she gazed into his merry, dancing eyes and a little switch clicked somewhere at the back of her brain. He looked fun.

Charlie grabbed a chair and squeezed in beside her, so close their knees were touching. "I've been nagging Alec to introduce us for ages," he said.

"You have?" It was unnerving the way he was looking her up and down.

"I have an idea for you. I wondered if you might consider writing a political column for the *New York American*? A wry commentary on the follies of the great and the good. I loved what you said about Calvin Coolidge. . . ."

Dottie shook her head. "Please don't quote back to me lines I've supposedly said. I never recognize them. And I hate to disappoint you but I have no interest in writing about politics. Perhaps you should do it yourself. What kind of reporter are you anyway?"

"I'm what they call a 'roving reporter.' If a fishing boat goes missing off Maine in winter—send Charlie. If a mine collapses in West Virginia—send Charlie."

"Where have you been roving today?" she asked, musing that he certainly had a roving eye. She hadn't been so closely examined since her last full medical.

"In Little Italy. A woman stabbed her brother-in-law outside a speakeasy, and I got to interview her and ask why. To cut a long story short, let's just say she was a bitter woman." He puckered his lips and screwed up his nose, like a pig's snout.

She laughed. "What have you got against bitter women?"

Suddenly, he leaned his face close to hers, stuck out his tongue, and licked her cheek so quickly there was no time to stop him. She clapped her hand to the spot in astonishment.

"I like your taste much better," he said. "In fact, it's my favorite flavor. . . ."

"Of all the women you've ever licked?" Dottie finished. "I'm flattered, I guess." She wiped her face with her fingers.

What kind of man would lick your face within minutes of meeting you? It was extraordinary—but very sexy. The air between them was charged. His hands kept moving close by as if he wanted to touch her and was struggling to restrain himself. Dottie wanted to touch him too, but it was all so sudden she couldn't decide if she was going mad.

"May I take you for dinner?" he asked. "It's not even a question. I insist."

"Do you think we'll have enough to talk about, Mr. Mac-Arthur?" she asked, tilting her head coyly.

"I'm sure we'll find a way to pass the time," he said, with a suggestive smile. "We're both writers, we're both emerging from unhappy marriages, and we're both friends of Alec's, so in the worst-case scenario we could grouse about him."

*He's married*, Dottie registered. But "emerging from it." She guessed she was too. Eddie had only rung once, briefly, since he left. Surely that meant she was allowed to have dinner with another man?

"I'm new to New York and I hardly know a soul. Please say yes." He clasped his hands and closed his eyes as if in prayer.

They left the Gonk together, and Dottie could hear the gossip starting before they were out of earshot, whooshing around the table like wildfire in a tinder-dry forest. They wandered up Sixth Avenue, talking nonstop, and somehow ended up in Tony Soma's rather than a proper restaurant. They ordered bowls of pasta and Old Fashioneds in coffee cups and squeezed into a booth. His thigh was pressing against hers, his upper arm brushing hers, as the conversation flowed in a continuous stream.

Like her, he had lost a parent while young; like her, he'd had religion foisted upon him as a child; like her, he had married someone he scarcely knew in an attempt to find security, only for it to fall apart when they realized they wanted entirely different things. Like her, he was funny.

It was getting late and the crowd in Tony Soma's was thinning out, but Dottie couldn't bear the evening to end. She hadn't enjoyed herself so much in months.

"Do you know Neysa McMein?" she asked.

"I certainly do."

Dottie explored his face, wondering if he might be one of Neysa's conquests, but decided she would surely have met him there if that were the case. "Shall we go to hers for a nightcap?"

He didn't need asking twice. They took a taxi up to West Fifty-Seventh Street and climbed the stairs to the third floor.

"This is my apartment," she pointed out as they arrived. "And that's Neysa's."

"I'd rather see yours," Charlie said. "May I?"

She unlocked the door, and he followed her inside, then kicked it shut, pushed her against a wall, and started kissing her. Every nerve ending was on fire. She wanted to wrap herself around him, to possess him, to give herself to him completely, without reservation. She was drunk, but she knew she would have done the same thing sober. The attraction was overwhelming.

He lifted her in his arms and carried her to the bedroom, tipping her onto the bed and undressing her. It was as if they were drugged. Every movement, every touch set her skin tingling. The lovemaking was hot, intense, and totally absorbing. Nothing existed but the feel of him.

Afterward he lit a cigarette and they shared it, her head cradled on his chest. What had she done? He was only the second man she'd ever slept with. Would he tell anyone? What if word got back to Eddie? And then she decided it was Eddie's own fault for leaving. It served him right. She deserved a bit of happiness.

"Well, that's not the way I saw the evening going when I set out earlier," she commented.

"Spontaneity is my favorite virtue," he replied.

"Fornication is my favorite vice," she replied, tilting her face to look up at him through her eyelashes. "It can be murder getting a taxi at this time of night," she added, "so you're welcome to stay over."

He took the cigarette from her and stubbed it out. "Good," he said. "Because I haven't finished with you yet, Mrs. Parker." He rolled her onto her stomach and forced her legs apart with his knee, lifting her hips toward him.

"I think we've reached the stage when you can call me Dottie," she said, just before he entered her for the second time.

# Chapter 11
# WINIFRED

After the curtain came down on the first night of Winifred's play, *The Dover Road*, cast and crew went to Vincent Sardi's basement restaurant to wait for a copy of the next morning's *New York Times*. It was always an anxious time. The play was due to run for six months, but if it bombed, the doors could close after a week and they'd all be out of a job. Winifred sat back on a leather banquette beneath the walls lined with caricatures of the acting fraternity who dined there and wondered if her portrait would ever join them.

When an assistant stage manager appeared with the newspaper, the director grabbed it and Winifred watched his face, his lips moving as he skimmed it.

"Sure to be a hit!" he read triumphantly. Then: "Winifred Lenihan doesn't put a foot wrong as Anne, the brainless ingénue. She possesses impeccable comic timing and charismatic stage presence."

Winifred grinned. It was gratifying to be singled out in reviews. Letting George Kaufman stroke her knee had been galling but all actresses had to put up with a certain amount of pawing and at least he had kept his side of the implicit bargain.

When the paper was passed to her and she read the whole review, she saw that the director had omitted the negative phrases:

"insubstantial froth," "a set that was neither one thing nor another," "a bewildering host of unmemorable characters." Still, they should get a decent run if the other reviews were anything like this.

Such was the power of the press that, within days, Max received offers for her to appear in enough frothy romantic comedies to keep her busy till the second half of the following year.

"I'd rather do a serious role next," she told him. "I don't want to get typecast. But I guess I would change my mind for the right director."

A good director set the tone; he could make rehearsals and the run of the show a joyful collaboration, while a dictator who lacked imagination was the pits. Even worse were the ones who thought she was up for grabs. She felt a tightness in her chest and pushed away the images that arose, unbidden.

The curtain came down at ten-thirty each night and Winifred was always too restless to go home. The cast and crew usually congregated in Vincent Sardi's, because he stayed open as long as there were customers, didn't insist you order food, and kept good-quality booze under the counter. Winifred joined them about once a week, but on other evenings she had dinner with Peter, or dropped in at the Gonk or Neysa's salon to socialize with a non-thespian crowd. She liked a variety of conversation, not just backstage gossip.

One evening she arrived at Neysa's around eleven to see Dottie huddled on a couch in the far corner, tête-à-tête with a slim, handsome young man. She was listening to him so intently she didn't notice Winifred waving.

Winifred sidled over to Neysa, nodding in their direction, and asked, "Who's he?"

"He's a reporter, name of Charlie MacArthur," her hostess said, handing her a drink.

"Good news?" Winifred asked, and Neysa made a face, then shook her head.

"Nice but married, and with a practiced eye for the ladies. He's not what Dottie needs at all."

"Oh dear. Eddie's been gone less than a month." Winifred sipped her drink and watched. Dottie's entire body was leaning toward the newcomer and her eyes never left his face, while he had the relaxed posture of a man at ease with himself. Winifred instinctively mistrusted him.

Alec Woollcott was sitting on a couch by the window. He was also watching Dottie and Charlie, so Winifred crossed to join him.

"Is this a new romance I see before me?" she asked, sitting down.

"I played matchmaker," he said, "and it's worked rather well. Perhaps I should make a career out of it."

"But he's married, Alec—and so is she." She gave him a stern look.

"Who cares? It's just a bit of fun. Want me to find someone for you?"

"No, thanks," Winifred said quickly. "I'm spoken for." She glanced at her watch. Peter had said he'd meet her there.

"Did you hear that I'm moving in with Jane and Harold at their new Hell's Kitchen abode?" Alec asked, and began telling her about the rooms he would occupy and the housewarming party they were planning.

Winifred listened, profoundly grateful she didn't have to share her apartment with anyone. She liked closing the front door behind her, putting on some music, and running a hot tub. Her home was a sanctuary where she could relax without worrying about being on show. She cherished the privacy because she'd grown up with a huge family crammed into the one small house and had never had a bedroom of her own.

She realized Alec had asked her something and was waiting for an answer. He repeated his question: "Will you appear in our revue about the Gonk crowd? It's opening in May and it's going to be the hit of the year."

Winifred faked disappointment. "I'm afraid I'm on contract at the Bijou till June. What a shame!"

"Your loss!" He shrugged, and Winifred wondered how he figured that. She knew no one was going to be paid unless the revue covered its costs, and she couldn't imagine that happening in a month of Sundays.

The door to the studio burst open, clattering off the wall behind, and Peter appeared, looking the worse for wear. Winifred rose to greet him, and Neysa wandered over too.

"I brought you a bottle of bourbon," he told Neysa, glassy-eyed. "But it slipped through my fingers on the way up and smashed in the stairwell. A sad loss. But I would be happy to accept a drink from your establishment instead."

Neysa glared at him. "There are children living in this building. You can't leave it like that."

"Do you have a broom, dustpan, and bucket?" Winifred asked, jerking her face away as Peter leaned in to kiss her with his booze breath. She was embarrassed by him.

Neysa went to fetch them, and Winifred spoke sternly: "Go back downstairs, Peter, and don't return till you have cleared every last splinter of glass. Get a bucket of water and sluice it till the smell has gone too."

"Only if you come and help me," he wheedled.

"Not on your life," Winifred said. "It's your problem, you deal with it."

"Time to say 'so long' to Peter?" Alec asked as she sat down again. "Don't forget my offer to set you up with a new one."

"You are a darling, Alec," she said in her most actressy voice. "I'll let you know."

"YOU'RE DUMPING ME?" Peter repeated, incredulous when the message finally got through. "But I cleaned the stairs like you asked. They're sparkling now."

Winifred said that wasn't the point, and she hoped they would stay friends. It was all they had ever been, in her eyes at least.

"Friends?" he exclaimed, a little too loudly. She noticed heads turning. "But I want to marry you."

"Oh, Peter, I'm sorry! You picked the wrong girl. I'm not the marrying kind." She folded her arms, wondering why she had ever dated him in the first place. He'd seemed more interesting than he turned out to be.

"All women say that because they want the guy to pursue them. I bet you're hankering after a ring on your finger just as much as the next girl."

"Sure. Believe that if you like." She lifted her black velvet, silk-trimmed coat from the coat stand and slipped her arms into the kimono sleeves. "I hope you find an adorable woman who gives you adorable children, but it's not going to be me."

She waved to Neysa, then to Alec, who was watching the whole scene with intense interest. He loved a drama, especially the off-stage kind.

Dottie had slipped away earlier but Winifred decided to knock on her door and invite herself in for a late-night chat. She would love to hear Dottie's dry take on a man who thought all women were desperate to marry him.

She had raised her hand to knock when she heard a man's voice inside. It must be Charlie. Had Dottie invited him for a nightcap? Winifred hoped it was just a drink. All the same, best not to interrupt.

She hurried downstairs to the street but although it wasn't late—just one in the morning—she couldn't see a single taxi. The Swiss Alps restaurant at street level was closed, its shutters locked. One of the Central Park horse-drawn carriages clattered past but she couldn't afford their prices. She started to walk, then heard a street door slam and turned to see Peter lolloping after her. She felt a twinge of alarm.

"What are you doing? I'm going home," she called, scanning the horizon, praying for a taxi to appear.

He caught up with her and grabbed her forearm. "Come back with me," he said. "If we spend the night together, I guarantee you'll change your mind. All the girls do."

Winifred covered her mouth with her free hand to smother a laugh. "Peter, you're blotto. Go home and sleep it off."

"I'm not taking no for an answer," he said, twisting her arm behind her back.

It was a playful gesture, but it set off alarm bells. She looked around frantically, desperate to escape. Still there were no taxis in sight, no passersby she could ask for help.

Panicking, Winifred simultaneously yanked her arm from Peter's grip and shoved him hard on the chest so that he tottered and almost fell backward. Velvet coat flapping wide, she darted into Sixth Avenue, crossing under the elevated railway, past stores dwarfed by huge billboards advertising Chesterfield cigarettes, Ex-Lax, and Hohner harmonicas. She sprinted down a block and then swerved right at the next intersection, not daring to turn and see if he was following.

Her heart was beating like a drum and there was a rushing sound in her ears. *Help me!* a voice in her head kept shouting silently. *Help!*

She kept up the pace, zigzagging as she ran twelve blocks south, then nipped across Broadway, narrowly avoiding being hit by a bright green omnibus with its lights off. The theaters were closed and garbage collectors in white uniforms were loading their wagons. Fortunately, this was an area she knew well. A few groups of late-night revelers turned to watch as she sped past but none tried to stop her. She was so scared, she didn't know what she might have done.

At the corner of her street, she turned to check whether Peter was in pursuit and her foot slipped off the edge of the curb, her left ankle twisting over on itself. The pain made her cry out and she bent to check the damage. The bone didn't feel broken but it was tender to touch. She removed her left shoe and half-limped, half-hopped the rest of the way to her front door, then hung on the banister to haul herself up to the top floor. At least Peter wasn't following. Thank god she had never given him her address.

Once she was in the apartment, she bolted the door, soaked some towels in cold water, sank onto the couch, and wrapped them around her ankle. Gradually her heartbeat slowed, her breathing returned to normal, and the fuzziness in her head cleared.

You got a fright, she told herself. It's safe now. You're fine.

Rationally, she didn't believe Peter would have hurt her. Even if he were the violent type, he was too sozzled to have done much damage. But that single motion of twisting her arm behind her back had triggered a memory that wouldn't go away, no matter how hard she tried to forget. Maybe it would take more time; or maybe she would have to relive it over and over again for the rest of her life.

# Chapter 12
# PEGGY

Peggy took a taxi to Jane and Harold's new home for the next bridge club meeting. The whole area was run-down, but number 412 stood out as the scruffiest building in the street. She double-checked the address, then climbed the steps and knocked on the door, glancing over her shoulder. It was definitely not the kind of district where a woman would feel safe walking alone.

"Come in!" Jane greeted her. "But watch your step."

The hall was an obstacle course, with bags of cement leaning against one wall, planks of wood laid along the floor, and contractors' toolboxes dotted around. At the end of the corridor they turned into a large open space with a rectangular table in the center and wooden boxes arranged around it in place of chairs. Dottie was perched on one, drink and cigarette in hand, wearing a forest-green coat and matching hat trimmed with black astrakhan that Peggy hadn't seen her in before.

"This is it!" Jane said. "Shall I take your coat?"

"I'll keep it on for now," Peggy replied. There was no heating and she could feel the cold seeping into her bones.

"Mind you don't get splinters in delicate places," Dottie advised as Peggy lowered herself onto a box.

"Is it true you're already living here?" Peggy asked Jane, looking around at the plaster walls and concrete floor. A bare lightbulb hung from the ceiling. "How on earth do you manage?"

"We move from room to room, depending on where the men are working. It's much easier now that we've got electricity. There's a basic bathroom, and a kitchen in the basement. I feel grand having stairs in Manhattan. I shout to Harold, 'Dearest, I'm going down*stairs*'"—she mimicked an upper-class accent—"just to revel in it."

"I hope you won't drop your old friends now you've arrived at the pinnacle of high society," Dottie drawled.

A window on the back wall overlooked the yard but it was pitch-black outside. They had arranged to meet later than usual so Winifred could join them after her show. When she arrived, she hobbled down the hall with the aid of a walking stick, her left ankle encased in bandages.

"What the hell happened to you?" Jane asked, and Peggy chimed in, "Are you OK?"

Winifred lowered herself onto a box. "Last night I ran twelve blocks in three-inch heels without stumbling once, then just as I turned into my own street I tripped on a curb. The doc says my ankle's sprained, so my understudy had to go on this evening. I just hope she's not too cute in the part. Jane, I don't suppose you have another box I could rest my foot on? I'm supposed to keep it elevated."

Jane found one and Winifred bundled her coat into a cushion and lifted her foot onto it, wincing, while the others bombarded her with questions about why she had been running in the first place.

"I reached the end of the road with Peter," she explained, "but he didn't see it that way. He thought I should stay with him and even marry him. In fact, he wanted to persuade me with his sexual prowess."

78

Jane and Dottie yelled with laughter, but Peggy watched her, guessing she must have been terrified. Why else run twelve blocks?

Winifred continued: "There were no taxis for love nor money, so I set off at a trot. Peter was ossified and probably wouldn't have made it past the end of the road, but once I got going, I figured I was safer at speed. And all would have ended well but for that fateful stumble."

"It must hurt," Peggy sympathized. "You were very brave."

"Not really." Winifred wrinkled her nose. "I used to be the fastest runner in my year at high school, beating all the boys. I nearly knocked on your door late last night, Dottie, but I heard the sound of a man's voice inside. Did a certain Mr. MacArthur happen to call on you, by any chance?"

Dottie tipped her head to one side with a coy expression: "He did many things on me last night but 'calling' isn't the verb I'd use."

Peggy stared at her. Surely not! She glanced at Jane and saw she was horrified. Winifred was wide-eyed.

Jane recovered first: "Isn't it a bit soon after Eddie?"

Dottie shrugged, reminding Peggy of a petulant child. "It wasn't love at first sight, if that's what you're suggesting. It took me at least ten minutes to fall for him."

"Love already?" Peggy echoed. "Surely real love is not like the thunderbolt of Greek mythology; it's something that grows over time as you get to know a person."

"How on earth would *you* know?" Dottie asked.

Peggy gasped at the casual cruelty but persevered: "You've only just met him and . . . well, it's not uncomplicated, is it? You're married, he's married. . . ."

"We're both unhappily married and planning to get un-married, so it's entirely serendipitous, as it happens." Dottie lit another cigarette, then remembered to offer one to Jane, the other smoker in their group.

"Is he kind?" Winifred asked.

Peggy thought it was perhaps the best question of all. Had Winifred known many unkind men? Listening to her voice, Peggy suspected she had.

Dottie raved about Charlie's great qualities—kindness, wit, intelligence, modesty, compassion, stunning good looks. Had anyone else displayed such obsessive adoration, Dottie would have been the first with a sarcastic putdown, but she didn't have the awareness to ridicule herself.

"He sounds like a modern-day saint," Jane said dryly. "We wish you well, Dottie, we genuinely do, but try to keep your feet on the ground."

"That's one of the many positions we tried." Dottie grinned. "Anyway, enough of the interrogation. I thought we were here to play bridge." She put on her black spectacles and shuffled her box closer to the table.

Peggy dealt the cards and they started a rubber. Jane and Winifred took an early lead, and Jane confessed she had been reading up on bridge techniques. It was neck and neck for a while, but then Peggy got a spectacularly good hand. Examining it, she suspected Dottie hadn't shuffled terribly well after the last round, because she had clusters of high cards in every suit.

"I'm going to try for a grand slam," Peggy told them. "That means I'm bidding for all thirteen tricks. Dottie, I need you to help me by not taking any yourself."

"That shouldn't be a problem," Dottie agreed.

Peggy played a classic game, maneuvering to draw out high cards the others were holding while saving her own for the end. The entire time she counted in her head, calculating which cards each of the others had left, and she finished triumphant.

"Wow!" Jane said. "I want to learn how to do that."

Peggy grinned. "You will." Her parents had taught her to play;

80

she used to pair with her father, and they played against her younger sister and her mother. Theirs was a competitive family and games were taken seriously and analyzed afterward, but all in good spirit. It stood her in good stead at Vassar and she was admitted right away into their bridge club.

Jane got up to serve refreshments: she'd bought a platter of lox and chopped egg salad with bagels from a local Jewish baker, and she produced some gin she had distilled in a bathtub on the second floor. "Let me know what you think," she said, pouring them a tumbler each. "Harold loves it. I added juniper berries, peppercorns, and twists of orange peel to take the edge off the grain alcohol."

Peggy tasted the gin first, rolling it around her tongue. It was fragrant and aromatic, without the chemical aftertaste you got with most bootleg gin. "Did you really make this? Don't tell her I said so, but this is better than Neysa's."

Dottie tried hers and raised an eyebrow. "Dee-licious. This is the kind of drink that could get a girl into trouble. Try some, Winifred." She looked mischievous. "Oh, I forgot, you already have trouble."

Winifred took a sip. "I'm not much of a drinker, but that's divine."

Dottie rose to go to the bathroom and Peggy watched her. She had been stung by the "how would you know?" comment. She'd known Dottie for years, and was aware she had a habit of bad-mouthing friends behind their back, but she wouldn't usually do it to their face. Perhaps Peggy was oversensitive because being single was such a sore point for her. She knew she would always have regrets if she didn't have children, but she was beginning to despair of ever finding a husband. The worry that she was unmarriageable often kept her awake at night. Dottie clearly had no idea she had hurt her feelings.

"Let's call a spade a spade: that's not a bathroom, it's a hole in the ground," Dottie said on her return. "I simply can't imagine Alec living in this house, or even this area. He's far too much of a snob. He prides himself on having such 'good taste' that he doesn't permit himself to like anything."

"The area's not too bad," said Winifred, switching to a Tipperary brogue. "Bejeesus, it's me own folk from the old country. They fled the potato famine and the English rule to become hod carriers for the posh folk round Central Park."

Jane laughed. "Glad you feel at home. The neighbors are certainly friendly. They stop you in the street to tell their life stories." She turned to Peggy. "I don't suppose you know how it got the name 'Hell's Kitchen,' do you?"

"There are half a dozen theories," Peggy replied, "probably most of them apocryphal, but the goriest involves a tenement at Thirty-Ninth Street and Tenth Avenue where there had been a multiple homicide. As two cops stood outside, the rookie said, 'This place is hell,' and the older one said, 'Nah, hotter than hell. This place is hell's kitchen.'" She stopped because they were all staring at her. "What?"

"Is it official that you know everything?" Jane asked. "Christ, I wish I could take you around in my pocket. I need a personal fact-checker. If I call the ones at the office, I never know if they are playing tricks on me or not."

"Do they play tricks?" Winifred asked. "That's very unprofessional."

Jane shook her head. "It's easiest not to believe anything the guys in the office tell me. Even now, I get caught out. Last week, for example, an esteemed colleague asked me to investigate a story concerning a Mrs. Fish."

"Mrs. Stuyvesant Fish?" Peggy asked, and Jane spread her palms.

"Exactly. That's what I thought, so I didn't suspect when they gave an address which turned out to be in the East River."

"What a waste of your time!" Winifred exclaimed. "That's rotten of them."

"You're quiet, Dottie," Peggy said. It was the kind of conversation she would normally have contributed to, riffing about finding Mrs. Lake in Central Park or Mr. and Mrs. Lion outside the Public Library. Her mind seemed elsewhere.

"I have to go," Dottie said, checking her watch. "I'm meeting Charlie at my apartment."

"He can wait for you at Neysa's if you're late," Peggy suggested.

"No need. I've given him a key."

Peggy caught eyes with Jane. She half-opened her mouth to comment, but Dottie was putting her spectacles and cigarette case in her bag and preparing to leave.

"I'll share a taxi with you," Peggy suggested, thinking that would give her a chance to have a word in private. She had known Dottie longer than Jane had, and felt a sense of responsibility for her.

They said their goodbyes and wandered out into Ninth Avenue to hail one. Peggy gave the driver Dottie's address first.

"Need any supplies, ladies?" he asked, pulling back a rug in the footwell to reveal a range of bottles of booze.

"Just the ride, thanks," Peggy said, then turned to Dottie. "I'm worried about you. A woman ruled by her emotions loses the ability to use her intelligence, and I must say you seem very overwhelmed."

"You don't understand, Pegs," Dottie said, her voice soft and dreamy. "Charlie's not like the rest of them. He's . . ." She hugged herself, lost for words, and gazed out the window, her thoughts elsewhere. "He's special."

Peggy had heard the sentiment before from women wearing the

83

rose-tinted glasses of early romance. It seemed to her there was an anesthetic effect that gave them tunnel vision and made the blood bypass their brains. Even the smartest of women became gullible.

"I hope he appreciates how special you are too," she said.

"I know you think I'm crazy—don't deny it. But it will happen to you one day, then you'll see."

Peggy wondered if it would. She was too plain, too conventional, not the kind of girl to inspire wild passion. What she dreamed of was a man who would be a good companion and a responsible father for their children, while letting her be herself. Was that too much to ask?

"If you can't be good, be careful," she quipped when the cab pulled up outside Dottie's building.

Dottie replied, with merry eyes, "Careful is dull. I'm going to make sure I'm very, *very* good."

# Chapter 13
# JANE

Jane and Harold often socialized separately, but they made it a rule that they ate dinner together every evening, and they spent the whole day together on Sundays. They might catch the train out to Coney Island, or explore new areas of the city, like Chinatown, or the Lower East Side, or along the shore of the Hudson.

Once the deal was signed on 412 West Forty-Seventh Street, they spent all their Sundays working on the house. As the builders finished the structural work on each room, Jane and Harold moved in to paint and paper, put up shelves, and hang drapes. Jane loved the feeling that they were creating a home together. They chatted while they worked—about current news stories, about politics, and in particular about the magazine they planned to start.

Harold was an editor through and through. While he was in charge of *Stars and Stripes*, he'd coaxed the best from writers. No pretentious phrase or superfluous adjective got past his eagle gaze. He hid a fierce ambition behind his affable exterior and Jane had sensed from early in their relationship that he was too smart and too opinionated to work for anyone else for long. Starting his own magazine seemed the ideal way to use his talents and, once they'd agreed on this goal, they studied the market, trying to decide what form it should take.

"America needs a decent shipping magazine," Harold said as they wallpapered the living room one Sunday. "There's a gap in the market. We could charge a high cover price for a *Marine Gazette* because industrialists would pay through the nose for information on shipping lines, rates, weather forecasts, and so forth. I spoke to a sugar company boss who said they would fork out up to five dollars a copy."

Jane frowned. "It's too niche. You'd get bored publishing the same type of stories week after week." She climbed a stepladder and smoothed the top of a strip of wallpaper onto the wall. The paper had a gold geometric fan pattern against an ivory background and she'd worried it might look busy, but the overall effect was modern and warm in that north-facing room.

Harold guided the bottom of the strip into place. "Once I set up the team, I wouldn't need to be involved in the day-to-day running, and we could channel the profits into something more exciting."

"Like what?"

"Well . . . Maybe printing paperback books, keeping the cover price as low as possible. Voltaire for the masses." Jane noticed he had wallpaper paste in his hair and hoped it would wash out easily.

"We don't know anything about the printing and distribution of books. Shouldn't we stick with what we know, which is magazines and newspapers?"

"I'd love to start a new daily paper," he mused, liberally applying paste to the next strip. "One without a political bias, where reporters have the freedom to write it as they see it."

Jane descended the ladder to pick up the next strip. "Yeah, me too, but I'm told you need a minimum of five million dollars to launch a tabloid, and no one in their right mind is going to give us that kind of dough. That's why I think a weekly or monthly magazine is a better route. Something with intelligent analysis of politics and the arts, and humor too. We know lots of funny people."

Harold wrinkled his nose. "They might be funny sitting around a table at the Gonk, but that kind of oral humor doesn't necessarily translate for a wider audience. Their self-congratulatory revue was nothing to write home about."

"Oh yes, it was!" Jane grinned. "Most people who saw it probably wrote home that it had been one of the most tedious evenings they ever spent in a theater. But don't tell Alec or George I said that."

Balance was important. *Judge*, the magazine Harold was currently writing for, printed some devastating satirical cartoons with a political slant. Jane wanted their magazine to have a wider range, with serious essays, investigative journalism, and fiction and poetry too, but what would its focus be? How would they market themselves to readers?

"We know it's predominantly city dwellers who buy magazines," she said. "Why don't we make ours a sophisticated metropolitan magazine and aim it at the kind of people we know here in New York?" She smoothed down another strip of paper and leaned back to admire the effect. "Nothing about wheat yields in North Dakota, or the price of pork bellies."

"It could be a scourge of hypocrisy in whatever form it manifests, from Tammany Hall to Volstead. We could let Alec loose in an opinion column." Harold ran his fingers through his tufty hair and Jane smiled. That's how he was getting paste in it.

"I'm not sure about Alec—he can be an old curmudgeon—but I think that type of magazine would play to your strengths as an editor."

Harold started firing off ideas for articles, clearly getting excited, as Jane positioned the next strip of wallpaper, quietly pleased with herself. She was good at bringing him around to her point of view.

When they first met in France, he had told her he couldn't abide New York, but she had convinced him to try living there, and now he was as passionate a lover of the city as any. When she told him a friend was having a party, he usually tried his hardest to get out of it, then ended up having such a good time that he was last to leave. He was a man of words, an editor to the bone, a beacon of new ideas, but she was the practical one who made things happen. Together, she reckoned, they made a pretty formidable team.

ALL SUMMER THE builders were hard at work, and the first floor was completed by mid-September. Jane decided to throw a party that fall, while the weather was still mild and guests could spill into the backyard. As soon as they moved in, flyers had started appearing through the door from bootleggers offering top-quality liquor at competitive prices. She visited one and negotiated a good deal for a ten-gallon drum of pure grain alcohol so she could distill more of her own gin. She also bought bottles of Johnnie Walker, Martell cognac, Booth's gin, and Bacardi rum, with some grenadine so they could make Pink Ladies, and some crème de cacao for Brandy Alexanders, which Alec claimed—without any evidence—were named after him.

He still hadn't moved into number 412 because the plumbing on the second floor wasn't up to his pernickety requirements, but he was keen to take control of the party, and gave Jane a long list of people he wanted to invite.

Jane laughed. "Alec, you're incorrigible. You're not paying rent yet, and you haven't helped one bit with the decoration of the house. What makes you think you have a right to invite all these guests?"

"They're entertaining types who will make the party much more lively. We want to get a reputation for throwing the best parties, don't we? So we should start the way we mean to continue."

Jane noted his use of the word *we*. He clearly saw himself as one of the hosts. She bit back a sarcastic comment and replied: "Invite who you like, Alec. It's fine by me."

On the day of the party, Peggy arrived in the morning and helped Jane to prepare a buffet of cold hams and turkey, potato salad, baked beans, and chocolate cake. They even had tubs of ice cream chilling in the brand-new icebox in the basement. She set out bottles and glasses, plates and forks, with no idea how many she was catering for.

Dottie and Charlie turned up midafternoon with a fairground carousel, of all things. They'd bribed the owner to tow it across town and set it up in the street outside 412, where partygoers could have a twirl on the gaudy painted horses accompanied by tinkling music played on a windup gramophone. They seemed high as kites, Jane thought. Drunk on love. While she watched, Charlie grabbed Dottie and whisked her into a vigorous tango down the street.

Jane turned to Bob Benchley, who was standing next to her. "Long may it last," she said, nodding in their direction.

"Stranger things have happened," he said, without conviction. "Warren Harding got elected president, after all."

A crowd of Irish neighbors gathered to watch, and when Winifred arrived by taxi, there was a murmur of recognition. "Any chance of an autograph, Miss Lenihan?" one woman called. When she agreed, others ran indoors to fetch autograph books or theater programs she could sign. Winifred had played the lead in a couple of Broadway shows but she wasn't a big name by any means. Jane guessed these women were proud of her as one of their own, a girl from the Emerald Isle.

It was starting to get dark when Jane heard a familiar booming voice and realized Alec had arrived. She glanced around the dining room door to see he was holding court next to the bar area, drink in hand. Neysa had called earlier to say she couldn't make it and Jane knew he would be disappointed.

The house was packed now and, as Jane squeezed from room to room, she noticed there were several strangers she didn't recognize. Friends of Alec? Or Harold? She hadn't seen him for ages and imagined he was ensconced in deep conversation. He always found someone to pontificate with.

"I'm sorry to interrupt, but who invited you?" she asked a group of young Irishmen who were helping themselves to her Johnnie Walker.

"We heard this was a new speakeasy," one man said. "The door was open."

"I'm afraid this is my house and it's a private party," Jane said. "Time to take a walk. . . ." She held out her hand for their glasses and pointed to the exit.

"Aw, don't be a killjoy," one moaned.

Just at that moment, two men in gray trench coats and homburgs strode through the open door into the hallway. "What's going on here?" one asked.

"It's a private party," Jane told them. "For a few close friends."

"We're Prohibition agents." He held out a badge and she glanced at it with a sinking feeling. "We'd like to take a look around."

"Do you have a warrant?" she asked, but he ignored her and pushed past down the corridor and into the dining room. Why hadn't she attempted to hide the bottles? There were a dozen of them sitting in plain sight. She held her breath. Some Prohis took bribes, while others were sticklers for the letter of the law. Should she risk offering them money? Best not.

"Whose bottles are these?" the Prohi asked, picking one up and sniffing.

Without blinking, Alec pointed his finger at her. "They're Jane Grant's. That's her there."

She stared at him in astonishment and said, "Thanks, Alec."

"We'd like you to come to the station house and answer some questions," one of the Prohis said to Jane. "And we'll take these as evidence." He picked up an armful of bottles.

Harold appeared and insisted he would come with her.

"No, don't," Jane told him. "Call Carr Van Anda." He was her editor at the *New York Times*, and she knew he would arrange legal advice if she needed it.

"If you answer our questions, it won't take long," the second Prohi said, lifting all the bottles he could carry. Jane guessed he would either take them home to his family or sell them.

Harold asked which precinct they were in, and they said the station house was two blocks away.

"See you later!" Jane waved as she walked out, flanked by the two officers. "Don't do anything I wouldn't do!"

She wasn't scared. At most she'd have to pay a fine. But it wasn't the way she'd hoped the party would end, and she was still reeling from Alec's betrayal. Who'd have thought he was a snitch?

At the station house, she was led into a small room and left to stew for half an hour before a bored detective wandered in and sat down, hardly glancing at her.

"When did you open your speakeasy?" he asked.

"It's not a speakeasy. I was holding a private party and your officers shouldn't have entered without a warrant. They were breaking the law."

He ignored her. "What's the name and address of your bootlegger?" he asked, pen poised to write it in a notebook.

Jane laughed. "Which one?"

"You have more than one?"

"Doesn't everyone?"

He looked up at her now, but his expression wasn't amused. "OK, let's start with the name of the one who sold you the bottles my officers found tonight."

Jane shook her head. "Do you really expect me to answer that? I enjoy life too much to get on the wrong side of the guys who control the liquor trade."

He put his notebook down on the table and sucked his teeth. "If you don't talk, you'll receive a summons to appear in court on alcohol violations. Tell me now and you walk free. It's your choice."

"That's easy," Jane said. "Court it is. Can I go home?"

She was told to wait while the report was typed up, so she could sign it. She hadn't brought a coat and it was chilly in the room. What a mockery this law was that made criminals out of otherwise law-abiding citizens. It was enriching gangsters and undermining respect for authority, especially since everyone knew the Prohis accepted backhanders.

It was past midnight when she got back to the party, and it seemed busier than ever. Now that the good bottles were gone, everyone was drinking her homemade gin. Thank goodness the Prohis hadn't gone upstairs and found the bathtub still!

Alec was sitting in the same place when she walked into the dining room, a glass of her bathtub gin in his hand.

"Thanks for selling me down the river," she said sarcastically. "I always wanted a criminal record."

To her surprise, there was no word of apology or explanation, just a long hard stare.

# Chapter 14
# DOTTIE

Dottie and Charlie lolled on the grass in Central Park eating a haphazardly thrown-together picnic and swigging from his hip flask. A green-headed duck waddled up to them and Dottie tossed it a piece of cracker.

"Do you think he's smart?" she asked. "Is he a wise quacker?"

"I don't know. Try asking him why ducks fly south for the winter."

"I know the answer already," Dottie said, throwing another piece of cracker. "Because it's too far to walk."

Charlie laughed. "Notice he's not attempting to take any food back to his family. He's only out for himself. This one's a bachelor duck."

"Seems to me every man is a bachelor when his wife's not looking." Dottie glanced at him, a challenge in her eyes.

"I'm not letting you get away with that," Charlie cried, launching himself on top of her and pushing her backward on the grass. He held her wrists to the ground and kissed her passionately.

"Disgusting!" they heard a woman's voice say.

Dottie wriggled free to see an elderly grande dame and her male companion watching them.

"Don't worry, we're married," Dottie called, then added: "But not to each other."

"I love the way you don't give a damn," Charlie told her, with warmth in his expression.

*Love.* Dottie fixed on the word. She thought about it the entire time she was with him. He hadn't said he loved her yet so she'd held back but it was on the tip of her tongue. He filled her every thought. She simply couldn't believe her luck in finding Charlie. It was a miracle.

Unlike Eddie, he didn't criticize or try to change her. Unlike Eddie, he was interested in her work—he was encouraging her to write a play she had an idea for. Unlike Eddie, he truly wanted her to be happy. And—*my god!*—the sex! Three months and they still couldn't keep their hands off each other. It was as if they were enchanted creatures, and Manhattan was a place of color and light and bliss.

She didn't feel guilty about Eddie. He'd hurt her too badly, and he was the one who'd left. Besides, he probably had another girl by now. She felt relieved there would be no more awkward weekends staying with his parents; no more drunken abuse and black eyes. Charlie drank his fair share but he was a fun drunk, not a nasty one. He was everything she had always wanted in a man, and much more.

He had to work on weekdays, but most evenings they met at the Gonk or Neysa's, or at her apartment. One evening, when he had to work late on a story, Dottie wandered over to Neysa's, restless in his absence. Neysa fetched her a drink and led her to the couch.

"I've been wanting to have a word," she said, "but I haven't seen you alone for a while."

"What about?" Dottie sipped her drink, thinking Jane's gin was infinitely superior.

"I hope you're not getting too stuck on Charlie. He's the type of man who keeps his luggage packed. You'll never get him to settle down."

"What do you mean?" Dottie felt her stomach lurch.

"Look—I had this made for him last year." Neysa pulled an object from the pocket of her painting smock and handed it across. It was an ink-smudged rubber stamp, with the words "I love you" carved on it. "We joked that it would help when he couldn't remember the name of the girl of the month."

"Why are you telling me this?" Dottie shivered and handed it back.

"How long have you been together? Three months perhaps?"

Dottie nodded. "Just over."

"That's longer than most girls get." Neysa slipped her arm through Dottie's. "Enjoy yourself, but don't take it seriously."

Dottie's cheeks colored. "He told me that what we have is special and he's never known a girl like me."

"I'm sure that's true," Neysa said. "But he's not a one-woman kinda guy." She listed several women of their wider acquaintance who'd had a fling with Charlie at one time or another, and Dottie listened with mounting alarm.

"You don't know what you're talking about," she said defiantly when Neysa had finished. "Even if he was with all these women in the past, he's a changed man now."

Suddenly she didn't want to hang around there a moment longer. It made her feel sick to think of him in bed with anyone but her. "I'm going home. If Charlie comes by, please tell him where I am."

Neysa reached out to squeeze her arm. "I'm sorry," she said. "I had to tell you. I couldn't forgive myself if I hadn't."

Back in her own apartment, Dottie telephoned Jane and told her what Neysa had said, then added, "Do you think she's in love with Charlie herself? Otherwise, why would she try to spoil things for me?"

Jane paused before answering. "I think she's trying to protect you, Dottie. Anyone with eyes can see that Charlie is smitten but it might be better to take things more gradually. I kept Harold hanging on for a year from the first time he proposed until I said yes, and I've got a collection of wonderful love letters to show for it. Men like to be the pursuers."

"Playing games with the man I love is not my style," Dottie replied. "You know me, Jane—I'm an all or nothing kinda girl."

NEYSA'S WORDS LODGED in Dottie's brain like shrapnel, and when Charlie told her he couldn't see her one evening because he was working, her imagination ran riot. Could he be with another woman? Was she losing him?

"It wasn't fair of your editor to keep you so late," she said the next day, keeping her tone casual. "Where was the roving reporter roving this time?"

His answer was so detailed and convincing, she told herself she had nothing to fear. She trusted him; she was only suspicious because she couldn't believe her luck in finding such a wonderful man.

A week later, he told her he had to stay late at the office, but when she called, the receptionist said he'd left at the normal time. She wouldn't have thought twice about it if only Neysa hadn't planted doubts in her head. Now, anxiety scorched her brain as she had visions of him out on the town with another girl. She kept dialing his apartment until he finally answered past eleven o'clock.

"It's good to hear your voice," he said. "I'm beat. The editor sent me to cover a meeting at the International Chamber of Commerce. Don't ask what it was about, because I didn't understand a word, but somehow I have to conjure up a story by tomorrow morning." He yawned. "Christ, I wish you were here. Tired or not, I'd love to throw you on the bed and ravage you."

"I could be there in twenty minutes by the magic of New York

City taxicabs . . ." she suggested. "Wearing peach silk underwear and a naughty smile."

He yawned. "I just can't, Dottie. Save it for tomorrow, will ya?"

Two days later, she checked the *New York American* and, sure enough, there was a story about international commerce with his byline. He'd been telling the truth. She could trust him. She should relax.

One evening she went for a drink with Bob Benchley at the Fifty-Fifty Club, a speakeasy she didn't normally frequent, and her worst fear came true: there, in a corner booth, she spotted Charlie sitting with a girl. A young blond girl with an eager-to-please look. Her stomach twisted and a wave of giddiness washed over her.

"Look who it is!" she cried, her voice rising to a squeak as she waved at them.

"Let's stay by the bar," Bob murmured in her ear, but she ignored that and tugged him across the room by the arm.

"Hi!" she cooed to Charlie, trying to appear nonchalant. "Fancy meeting you here! Mind if we squeeze in?"

Charlie grinned and said of course not, introducing the girl as Alice.

Dottie launched into a stream of gay chatter as if she hadn't a care in the world. God knows what she was talking about; she couldn't remember afterward. Her stomach was clenched so tight she thought she might throw up all over Alice's dainty pale-blue frock. Bob pressed his elbow against her side, as if to restrain her.

"Bob, is that real coffee you're drinking?" Charlie asked, looking incredulous. "Not so much as a slosh of brandy to liven it up?"

"He's teetotal," Dottie explained. "I guess someone's gotta be."

"It's a family thing," Bob said. "We're pacifists."

"You can drink without getting in a fight after," Charlie replied. "I manage it most nights. You don't know what you're missing— does he, Dottie?"

"Maybe we should corrupt him," she said with a mischievous sideways glance. "Drinkers are more fun. Don't you want to be fun, Mr. Benchley?"

"Fun?" he repeated. "Isn't that one of the seven deadly sins?"

"It was where I grew up," Dottie agreed. Suddenly it seemed imperative that Bob have a drink. She rallied the others: "Let's choose Bob's first-ever alcoholic drink for him. What's that you've got, Alice? It looks innocuous enough for a beginner."

Alice said it was an Orange Blossom, a cocktail with gin, vermouth, and orange juice. "I like it because you can't really taste the alcohol," she said.

They took a vote and agreed that Bob should try an Orange Blossom, and Charlie went to the bar to order one. The other three watched, enthralled, as Bob took his first-ever sip of booze.

"It's not unpleasant!" he pronounced, wrinkling his nose. "Kind of like mouthwash."

"A convert!" Dottie cried, throwing her arms around him. "Welcome to our world."

Charlie reached across to shake his hand, then glanced at his watch. "Look at the time! Alice and I have to go." He stood up and took her hand. "I promised to get her home by eleven."

"You could put her in a taxi and come back to join us," Dottie suggested.

"Better not risk it," he said. "I'll see you tomorrow, Dottie."

Once they were out of sight, she burst into tears.

"How can he go out with another girl? Do I mean nothing at all to him?"

Bob fumbled in his pocket and passed her a crumpled and none-too-clean handkerchief: "I'll give you my best advice, but only if you promise not to sock me in the eye."

Dottie blew her nose noisily before agreeing she wouldn't.

He took a deep breath, his eyes kind. "Men like Charlie relish

98

a challenge and you have to let him do the chasing. Be busy some nights when he wants to see you. Answer mysteriously when he asks where you've been. When you talk to him next, don't even ask about Alice. You are an independent creature who doesn't need him and he's lucky to have you. Remember that."

"Can't a gal just be honest about her feelings in this darn town?" she wailed.

"Best not," Bob advised. "You might scare the horses."

The telephone was ringing when she got home that night and, to her immense relief, it was Charlie on the line. Alice was the daughter of a friend of his mother's, he explained. He had promised to take her for a night on the town, but Dottie mustn't think it was a romantic date; the girl meant nothing to him. Besides, shouldn't he be worried about the amount of time Dottie spent with Bob Benchley? They had seemed very chummy earlier. But jealousy was a poison in relationships, he said, and he didn't want it to affect theirs. They were better than that.

Dottie brooded on it for days afterward. Her love had begun to seem like an illness that befuddled her brain. She didn't feel herself at all. Every morning she woke up as thickheaded as if she had a humdinger of a hangover, even when she had hardly drunk a drop. She fell asleep over her typewriter most afternoons and she was tired to the point of dizziness by ten p.m. It must be because Charlie was keeping her awake at night with all the sex.

"You look peaky," Peggy told her. "Are you eating properly? Maybe you should see a doctor."

Dottie didn't, because she was sure it was vast insecurity about Charlie that was causing her malaise and there was nothing any doctor could do about that.

ONE AFTERNOON SHE dropped by the Gonk and had a drink with Marc Connelly. As they talked, she began to feel a curious giddiness, as if a fog were descending on her brain. She pushed her chair back and rose to go to the bathroom, and her legs collapsed under her.

She came around to the acrid scent of smelling salts, like needles in her nostrils. Frank Case, the hotel manager, was crouched beside her, along with a man in a white coat who introduced himself as the hotel doctor.

"Take my arm," he said, "and we'll go somewhere quieter."

Frank Case led them to an unoccupied guest room and Dottie lay on top of the bedcover, still feeling woozy.

"What happened?" she asked.

"That's what I aim to find out," the doctor said.

He took her temperature and blood pressure, checked her pulse, and listened to her heartbeat.

"When was your last monthly?" he asked, palpating her abdomen.

Dottie racked her brain. It seemed ages. "I'm not sure," she said.

"Have you put on weight recently?" he asked. "Any tenderness around your breasts?"

"I'm not sure." Charlie had names for her breasts—Ethel and Annie. That's all she could think of.

"Well, Mrs. Parker, I suspect you may be pregnant. I suggest you go to your regular doctor and . . ."

The rest of his words were lost as Dottie reeled in shock. It was impossible. They were careful—most of the time, at any rate. Oh god, was it true? What would happen now?

She'd always wanted a baby. If she and Charlie had a child together, maybe she wouldn't feel insecure anymore. Sure, it was too soon—way too soon—but perhaps it was meant to be.

"Your husband will be delighted," the doctor told her, glancing at the wedding ring she still wore.

Dottie wandered back to the Rose Room in a daze but didn't tell any of the crowd at the Round Table. The news burned inside her like a red-hot ember, but it seemed only fair that she tell Charlie first.

Her brain whirred over practicalities. They'd have to get their divorces post-haste to avoid the little one being born out of wedlock. She was sure she could make Eddie agree, but what if Charlie's wife tried to stop them? It was sooner than they might have chosen, but otherwise it was everything she wanted. She flushed at the thought of becoming Charlie's wife and mother of his child, and tried to still the nagging feeling of self-doubt.

She visited her own doctor the next morning. After examining her, he agreed with the diagnosis, so she called Charlie and asked him to meet her at her apartment that evening. All day she rehearsed ways of telling him, like "Do you think this baby makes me look plump?" Jokes didn't seem appropriate though.

He seemed to sense something was up. "Are you sick?" he asked, his expression full of concern. "I heard you fainted at the Gonk."

She took a deep breath. "No, not sick, but I . . . I appear to have a little one on the way." She bit her lip as she scrutinized his face for a reaction.

His mouth fell open. He was genuinely shocked. "Honey, I'm sorry," he said, pulling her into his arms so her face was squashed against his shoulder. "I was so careful. . . . Oh Christ, I want you to know you're not alone in this."

*Not alone?* That sounded odd. She pulled her head back and looked up at his dear, handsome face, asking, "What do you mean?"

"I'm not going to abandon you," he replied. "Of course not. I'll pay whatever it takes for you to have an abortion at the very best place in the city. Nothing but the crème de la crème for my girl."

She twisted out of his arms and turned away so he wouldn't see how devastated she was. Of course they couldn't have the baby. All her plans and dreams came crashing down. *Don't cry. Men hate women who cry. Don't beg either.* She bit her lip hard.

*Poor Dottie*, she thought as she turned to face him. What a deluded fool she had been. What a sad little patsy.

# Chapter 15
# WINIFRED

Winifred draped herself across Neysa's chaise longue, wearing an ankle-length mauve satin gown held up by shoestring straps and clutching a coupe glass. The fabric clung to her figure. It was cold in the high-ceilinged studio with its skylight windows, and she worried that her nipples were poking through.

"They are, but I won't paint them," Neysa promised.

She crouched to position the hem of the gown so it flowed onto the floor like a spilled cocktail, then she arranged Winifred's hand around the stem of the glass till she was happy with the effect.

"Whatever you do, don't move a muscle," she instructed, walking back behind her easel, then turning for a critical look at her subject.

"How long will it take?" Winifred yawned. It had been a late night, but Neysa had insisted she get to the studio by ten. It was an honor to be a *McCall's* cover girl, but she felt self-conscious being scrutinized so closely and she already had a cramp in her left foot.

"Most of the day," Neysa said, "but we'll break for lunch." She held up her pencil and squinted, measuring perspective, before making a couple of sweeping strokes on the paper in front of her. "How's the show going?"

Winifred made a face. "It's getting near the end of the run and

I have a co-star who thinks it's hilarious to play tricks onstage by altering his lines, or introducing new moves during our scenes. Juvenile humor. He claims he's trying to keep things fresh, but I think he's trying to upstage me."

"Don't you get bored saying the same lines night after night?" Neysa asked, her pencil scraping the paper.

"It can certainly get repetitious after a while. I prefer the rehearsal period. That's when you make a family with your colleagues and work to create something interesting together. It's the fun time."

"Do you know what your next show will be?" Neysa asked, but before Winifred could answer, the door clicked open and Dottie wandered in, shoeless and disheveled, the remains of last night's dark blue eyeshadow smudged beneath her eyes.

"Oh, *you're* here!" she said rudely, on seeing Winifred. "I was hoping to talk to Neysa alone."

"Can't stop—I'm working!" Neysa said, without turning around.

Winifred could tell Dottie was upset about something. She slumped into a chair and slid down, like a child in a huff.

"What if Neysa makes you look plug-ugly in an attempt to sabotage the competition?" she asked Winifred. "Aren't you worried about that?"

Winifred laughed: "Neysa's too gorgeous to have to worry about me. I'm from Irish stock, with peasant bones and a body built for tilling the fields, so I've never relied on my looks to get by." It was true. She'd been an ugly duckling as a child but somehow in her twenties she'd grown into those heavy bones and knew she was rated a beauty now. It helped to get parts, so it was useful in that way, but she didn't take it seriously.

"I've always preferred the company of peasants," Dottie said. "Is there coffee, Neysa?"

"In the kitchen. Help yourself." Neysa's pencil was moving fast across the paper.

Dottie wandered through and there was a clatter of dishes before she returned holding a cup and sank into the chair with a grunt.

"You don't seem your usual sparkling self this morning," Neysa said, glancing her way. "How's Charlie-boy?"

Dottie wiped an eye with the back of her hand, smearing the eyeshadow further.

"That man has so many sterling qualities, I never thought I'd find another," she replied. "But now he has proved himself the most generous of men."

There was a sharpness in her tone that alerted them both. Neysa put down her pencil.

"Not only did he manage to get me knocked up . . ."

They both gasped out loud and Neysa said, "Oh, Dottie . . ."

". . . but he is gallant enough to offer to pay whatever it takes for some high-society butcher to un-knock me. 'Only the crème de la crème for you,' he said. Wasn't that swell of him?"

Neysa ran over to her, turning to caution Winifred. "Don't move!"

Winifred felt desperately sad for Dottie, and embarrassed to be there. She didn't know her well enough to be party to such a secret. She would have crept out to give them time to talk in private if it hadn't been for Neysa's firm instruction.

"Anyway," Dottie said, "I came to ask if you have any advice on finding such a butcher." At the word *butcher* she started to cry and Neysa wrapped her arms around her.

Winifred shivered. When she spoke, her voice was low. "I know exactly where to go. Not to a backstreet abortionist but to Lenox Hill Hospital, where you can get what they euphemistically call a 'therapeutic abortion.'"

"They'll do it in a hospital?" Dottie perked up. "But I thought it was illegal?"

"An actress friend of mine had it done at Lenox Hill," Winifred explained. "You have to argue that your mental health depends on it. Say your husband left you, that he's not paying any alimony, and that you won't survive if you have to care for a baby on your own. Hint that you might do something foolish. Don't mention Charlie. As far as they're concerned, you're all alone."

Neysa produced a handkerchief and Dottie dried her tears and sat up straight. "Will they definitely help me? What if they say no?"

Winifred reflected how peculiar it was to be posing on a chaise longue in a revealing evening gown while giving advice about terminating a pregnancy. She rested the glass on her stomach.

"When was your last monthly?" she asked, businesslike now.

Dottie shrugged and shook her head. She had no idea.

"If you're over sixteen weeks gone, they won't do it, so say your last monthly was in August," Winifred advised.

"What happened to your friend?" Neysa asked. "Did the baby's father not want to know?"

"She couldn't see his heels for dust." Winifred used two fingers to mime running into the distance. "I'm afraid there are some men who think actresses are a step up from prostitutes and try to treat us that way. If worst comes to worst, we look out for each other." Winifred stretched her cramped foot, pointing the toes, then bending them backward. Neysa frowned at her.

"Was she alright afterward?" Dottie asked. "Your friend, I mean. No long-term side effects?"

Winifred paused. It had been traumatic for Nora, but she didn't want to scare Dottie with tales of bleeding and cramps, plus the emotional scars caused by grief and guilt. "She was fine," she lied. "It had to be done."

"How much does it cost?" Dottie asked, and Winifred told her it had cost Nora twenty-five dollars.

"Ask Charlie for two hundred," Neysa advised, "and treat yourself to a fur coat with the change. He owes you."

"I wouldn't dream of cheating him," she said. "It wasn't his fault. It's just one of those things."

Neysa wandered back to her easel. "Besides, are you sure you want to get rid of the baby? You told me you wanted children. You could call Eddie in Connecticut and say 'Guess what, honey? Surprise!' He'd surely come back once there was a nipper involved and he needn't ever know it wasn't his if you fudge the dates."

Winifred was surprised at Neysa's cynicism. She spoke as if letting a man bring up a child that wasn't his own might be a pragmatic course of action, without any moral transgression involved.

Dottie shook her head: "Eddie would most definitely know it wasn't his, since there have been no incursions of his appendage within the last nine months. He may be an idiot, but he can count to nine."

Winifred spoke softly. "Charlie was probably shocked when you told him the news and he reacted in panic. Maybe once he's had time to think it over, he'll get used to the idea." She gave a half-smile. "It's not ideal, I grant you, but he could get his divorce, you could get yours, the two of you could get married and have the baby. . . ." Her voice trailed off at Dottie's wretched expression.

"We've been talking most of the night," Dottie said. "Let's just say it's not in the cards."

Winifred and Neysa caught eyes. "The bastard," Neysa mouthed.

Winifred's heart went out to Dottie. What a dreadful situation to be in with a man you'd fallen hard for. "Do you want me to come with you to Lenox Hill?" she asked. "I took my friend, so I know how it works."

"Oh god, would you?" Dottie breathed. "I couldn't manage on my own. I'd surely mess it up somehow. Thank you." She kissed her fingertips and blew the kiss in Winifred's direction.

Winifred felt a heaviness at the prospect of going there again, but she wanted to help. Dottie was as vulnerable as a gaping wound and anyone with eyes could tell that Charlie was a player. Strange she was so astute in her writing, yet couldn't see what was right in front of her nose.

# Chapter 16
# PEGGY

Peggy nudged the sturdy street door of Dottie's apartment block with her shoulder while balancing a platter of muffins in one hand and clutching her handbag with the other. The door was stiff, but fortunately Winifred appeared and held it open while Peggy edged sideways into the hall.

As they climbed the stairs, heels clicking on the stone, they chatted about Winifred's show. Peggy had seen it during the week and praised Winifred's acting but said she found the leading man talentless. Winifred said she was glad it was ending soon; it had gotten tedious.

Dottie looked tired when she answered the door, Peggy thought. All those late nights cavorting around town with Charlie must be taking their toll. She went to the kitchen to lay down the muffins, and couldn't help overhearing a whispered conversation in the next room.

"What should I bring with me to the hospital?" Dottie asked Winifred, and Peggy frowned. *What hospital?*

"Your checkbook, of course," Winifred replied. "And some loose comfortable clothing for afterward. They give you a gown to wear during the—"

"Are you going into the hospital?" Peggy asked, walking into the living room. "I hope it's nothing serious."

Dottie and Winifred caught eyes, like guilty co-conspirators.

"I'm having a little growth removed," Dottie said, then took a puff of her cigarette and exhaled loudly. "Oh, all right, I suppose you may as well know. The growth is in my womb. Turns out I'm knocked up. But please don't tell Jane."

"No!" Peggy sat down hard, feeling shocked. "I'm so sorry, Dots. Can't Charlie—?" She broke off. Clearly that must have been discussed and a decision reached. "When is the operation?"

"Wednesday. Winifred is coming with me. I'll be back here by evening, so long as they remove the right bit." She sucked on the cigarette as if gasping for breath.

Peggy sought the appropriate words. Her instinct was to try and talk Dottie out of the abortion. She wanted to argue that it wasn't a growth, it was a miniature human being—but she stopped herself. It wasn't her business. As a friend, she should support Dottie's decision. Besides, it was impossible to imagine her coping with a baby. "Give me a key and I'll have a hot meal waiting for your return," she said. "You'll need someone to keep an eye on you for a couple of days."

She was about to ask why Dottie didn't want Jane to know, but there was a knock on the door and Jane appeared, clutching her battered leather satchel, her hat askew, and her boots caked in mud.

"I've just run across the park," she said, kicking off the boots and leaving them by the door. "The mud is so deep it's like Flanders Fields. Can someone pour me a drink? Or, even better, inject it directly into my veins."

She sat down and Dottie handed her a whiskey, topping it up with soda from a pretty turquoise lacquer siphon—a gift from Charlie, she told them. "You been working?"

Jane nodded. "Way too boring to explain." She took a gulp of the drink.

"Any news on your alcohol violation?" Peggy asked. She had

been there when Alec told the Prohis that Jane was the owner of the bottles, and it made her blood boil. She had berated him later but he was unrepentant.

"Can you be*lieve* Alec did that?" Jane asked. "What is *wrong* with the man?"

"I have a theory that it's a side effect of sexual repression," Dottie said, pouring drinks for the rest of them. "All that unused semen surges the wrong way around his system and swamps his brain cells."

"Have you never known him to have a girlfriend?" Winifred asked, sipping her drink.

"Never. The story is that a bout of mumps in childhood left him impotent," Peggy told her, "but I don't believe it. My cousin had mumps and the doctor said it might lower the number of swimmers in his sperm, but it wouldn't stop his equipment standing to attention." She glanced at Dottie, hoping this mention of fertility wouldn't upset her under the circumstances.

"Perhaps he has a secret love life," Winifred suggested. "I knew a director once who could only perform if he paid for it. Freud would say it had to do with guilt."

Jane shook her head. "Harold lived with him in France and Hawley lived with him in New York, and they both say there's never been any sign of a bedfellow."

"Do you think he might be homosexual?" Peggy asked. "I mean, I hear he's in love with Neysa, but it doesn't seem a very carnal kind of love. He wouldn't have a clue what to do if he got her between the sheets."

They laughed at the improbability of that vision.

"How on earth are you going to live with him, Jane?" Dottie asked. "Whatever possessed you to say yes?"

"Don't," Jane said, burying her head in her arms. "Just don't."

Peggy guessed she must have agreed in the spirit of marital

compromise. Jane was normally no slacker when it came to standing up for herself, but it seemed Harold had won this round. She wondered again why Dottie didn't want Jane to know she was having an abortion. Jane was a firm believer in a woman's right to birth control and was bound to be supportive. Besides, wasn't she Dottie's closest female friend?

Now that Peggy had gotten over her initial shock, she was upset about the abortion but not entirely surprised. Dottie was careless with her health, never eating proper meals but living off snacks grabbed on the run. She had that "poor little match girl" look, with her round soulful eyes, as if pleading with the world to rescue her, which made for an odd combination with her guillotine sense of humor. For her to get pregnant accidentally was entirely in keeping; and for her to do it with a philanderer was par for the course.

Dottie had no concentration at all when they played bridge that evening, seeming to throw down cards at random. Previously, when she gave the game her full attention, she had shown the odd flash of talent; but on this evening, Peggy mused, she might as well have been partnering Woodrow Wilson.

TWO DAYS LATER, Peggy went to the Public Library after work to return some books and pick up a new one she'd ordered. She was a regular there, and the cheerful woman at the front desk greeted her by name. She signed for her book—T. E. Lawrence's *Seven Pillars of Wisdom*, about which she had heard great things—then left through the exit that led into Bryant Park.

It was a bitterly cold evening. Frost twinkled on the paths, her breath misting the air, so it was a surprise to see a young couple sitting on a bench, entwined in each other. As she got near, the man turned and she recognized the distinctive widow's peak: it was Charlie MacArthur. And the girl certainly wasn't Dottie. She felt a surge of anger. How *dare* he?

The path she was walking along led past the couple, so she stopped and said a tart "Hallo."

"Peggy!" Charlie exclaimed with artificial cheerfulness. "Fancy seeing you here."

The girl was young—maybe in her early twenties—with a white fur hat and a nose reddened by cold.

"This is Alice," Charlie said. "We've got tickets for a show but we're early so we stopped to pass the time."

The girl giggled, as if "passing the time" meant something saucy.

"How nice for you," Peggy remarked, with sarcasm. "I hope you have a good evening," she said, the words sticking in her craw.

She walked a few steps farther, then halted. She wasn't going to let Charlie off the hook. She couldn't.

She turned, called his name, and beckoned him toward her.

He hesitated momentarily, then rose, leaving Alice on the bench.

When he was close enough, Peggy spoke in a low voice. "I wonder if you know what Dottie is going to do on Wednesday?" He looked stricken. "Yes, I can see from your face that you do. In that case, I'll give you the benefit of the doubt by assuming you don't realize how traumatic the procedure is for women."

Charlie stared at the ground. "I can't tell you how rotten I feel about it," he mumbled.

"And yet you are out with another woman tonight? Actions speak louder than words, Charlie. What if Dottie were to see you with young Alice? She's already devastated and that would destroy her."

"It's not what you think," he said. "She's the daughter of a friend of my mother's."

Peggy glared at him, angrier than ever. "I don't care if she's your sister and has taken vows of chastity in a holy order. Listen to me, and listen hard. If you upset Dottie by parading other girls around town over the next few weeks, you will have the entire

Gonk crowd to deal with. Don't forget that Dottie's friends know the great and the good in journalism. A word in the right ear and we will end your career."

"I won't, I promise," he said quickly. "I feel awful the way things turned out."

Peggy glanced back at Alice. The girl clearly sensed there was tension and looked worried. "I'm going to be at Dottie's on Wednesday evening," Peggy said. "I'm preparing dinner for her return from hospital, and I think it would cheer her if you were to drop around. Bring flowers. Say the right things. Do you need coaching on that?"

He shook his head. "I'll be there, I promise."

"You need to pay more attention to women's feelings," Peggy told him, still cross. "And grow up. The boyish charm is wearing thin—like your hair."

She wanted to say more, but he looked so penitent, she left it at that.

As she pounded the pavement back to her apartment, she mused that his easy charm had made his life fall into place without too much effort. He couldn't understand why some people struggled. Men generally got off scot-free in these situations—but not this time. She planned to make sure that Charlie suffered at least a small part of the consequences of his actions.

# Chapter 17
# JANE

When the women talked about Alec at the bridge club, Jane didn't mention that the morning after the house-warming party she and Harold had discussed him while they lay in bed with coffee and toasted bagels.

"I don't think Alec likes me anymore," she had said, "which is not a good omen considering he is due to move in with us soon. Can you have a word with him for the sake of domestic harmony? Tell him he has to be a team player when he's living here."

Harold put an arm around her and kissed her temple. "You can't blame him for being a tad peevish after I snatched you from under his nose. He thought he was in with a chance back in France."

Jane was puzzled. "What do you mean? Alec and I were only ever friends. I don't see why we can't remain friends now that I'm married to you."

Harold touched the tip of her nose with a finger. "He was in love with you. We all were at *Stars and Stripes*. We agreed it was a case of 'let the best man win'—and, to my eternal gratitude, you chose me."

"You're kidding!" Jane was genuinely surprised. "He never made a pass at me, or anything resembling one." It didn't add up. She remembered hearing speculation that he might be homosexual. "Are you sure it's not *you* he's in love with?"

Harold guffawed, accidentally overturning the plate of bagels. She grabbed them to stop the butter and cream cheese smearing into the bedcovers.

"Of course not! He's in love with Neysa now," Harold said. "That's hardly the act of a man with homosexual tendencies."

"Perhaps falling for women who are never going to return his ardor is a way of avoiding his true nature. Perhaps he's lying to himself."

Afterward she wondered: was it true Alec's nose was out of joint when she married Harold? He had claimed to be happy for them, and they were delighted when he offered to take care of the wedding arrangements. It seemed an act of genuine friendship. He'd booked City Hall, bought the rings, organized a celebratory lunch, and even arranged a honeymoon—but then he spoiled the gesture in Jane's eyes by presenting them with a bill that included a hefty fee for his time. At first she'd thought it was a joke, but Harold paid up. Was Alec sore with them for getting married? Had that been a sign?

Now that they were all going to be living together, she decided the best course was to win back his friendship. She hadn't told the women at the bridge club about Harold's theory that Alec used to be in love with her because Dottie was notoriously indiscreet. If Alec heard they were talking about him that way, his revenge would be swift and remorseless. He could dish it out but he couldn't take it.

The day Alec moved in to 412, Jane prepared fried chicken with cornbread and all the trimmings for a welcome dinner. She helped carry his belongings upstairs to his apartment, and ran up some drapes on her sewing machine when it transpired he hadn't brought any. Alec seemed genuinely grateful, and he complimented her chicken recipe, but after the meal she noticed he didn't offer to help clear the dishes. Neither did Harold or Hawley. It seemed that was going to be part of her role.

Most evenings, Alec was out at the theater, and he usually dropped in at Neysa's afterward, coming home in a taxi long after Jane and Harold had gone to bed. If he saw their light on, he knocked on the door and asked if they fancied a nightcap. Invariably, Harold would join him in the communal dining room for a whiskey and sometimes Jane joined them, but not for long, as she had to get up for work much earlier than either of them. It was perfectly convivial but Alec never tried to stop her when she announced she was going to bed; she sensed he preferred having Harold to himself.

One night she and Harold were in the midst of lovemaking when a drunken Alec banged on the door asking if they would join him for a drink. They ignored him at first but he knocked so loudly and for so long that their passion dissipated and Harold pulled on a dressing gown and went to join him. It got so that Jane listened for the sound of taxis at night and quickly switched off their light if she heard one approaching, in an attempt to keep some time with her husband to herself.

Still, she tried to be sweet as pie. If she bent over backward to be nice to Alec, surely they could all be friends together?

CARR VAN ANDA summoned Jane to his office one morning and motioned for her to sit down. She had huge respect for this titan of the newspaper industry, who had taken her under his wing and promoted her at a time when others on the paper wouldn't take her seriously because of her sex. He wouldn't hesitate to criticize if she handed in a substandard piece of work, but she never minded because his detailed critiques had helped her to become a better reporter. She trusted his instincts. In 1912 he had been the first editor to print the news that the *Titanic* had sunk, while its owners were still trying to claim it was merely "missing." His coverage of the war in Europe had been second to none. As a result he had Jane's loyalty; whatever assignment he gave her, she accepted without question.

"We know some speakeasies never get raided because they are paying protection money to gangsters, and the gangsters are paying Prohis," he said that morning. "I want to run a story about the corrupt finances of Prohibition, and I thought you could talk to Arnold Rothstein and Larry Fay and see how much they spill."

Jane blanched. They were well-known bootleggers, with gangs of armed hatchet men at their beck and call. You didn't mess with guys like that.

"They both have an eye for the dames," he said, "and I think they'd be more likely to open up to you than a male reporter. They'll also be less likely to kill you if you say the wrong thing." He grinned at her alarmed expression. "Don't worry! I bet you'll find them keen to make a good impression on our readers."

Jane knew that Carr Van Anda wouldn't send her if he thought there was any risk, but still she was rattled. She decided not to tell Harold because she was pretty sure he would try to stop her. She would do her research first, and prepare her questions with the greatest care.

When she was ready, she approached Tony Soma, reckoning he must buy his stock from Rothstein, and asked him to make the introductions. He called the very next day, saying that Mr. Rothstein would meet her at Lindy's on Broadway and Forty-Ninth at eleven in the morning, and that he insisted she come alone.

Why say that? Jane wondered. Was he planning to flirt with her? Or bump her off?

She didn't normally pay much attention to clothes, but that morning she wanted to look businesslike and not at all sexy. She chose a baggy tan suit, a cream blouse that buttoned all the way to the neck, and an unadorned tan cloche.

Lindy's was only two blocks north of 412, and easy to spot for its large sign beckoning above picture windows. Outside, half a dozen hoods with slicked-back hair were hanging around the street corner, blocking the entrance. "I'm meeting Mr. Rothstein," she told them and one searched her satchel before waving her inside.

The restaurant was almost empty, a lone waiter setting tables and folding white linen napkins into cones. Rothstein was sitting at a table near the back with three other men, who rose as she approached and moved to a table close by.

"Do I call you Miss Grant or Mrs. Ross?" he asked as he rose and shook her hand. "I hear you're sensitive on the subject."

It was unnerving to think that while she had been researching him, he had also done his homework on her. "Jane will do," she said, and sat in the chair he indicated.

He was wearing a red satin bow tie and looked almost like a jovial uncle, but for a glint of steel in his eyes. This was the man who had fixed the 1919 World Series and who ran successful horse-racing scams long before becoming a bootlegger. Rumor had it he was also peddling narcotics, but Jane didn't plan to mention that.

He offered her a drink and she asked for black coffee, opening her notebook to the list of questions she'd compiled.

"A few ground rules first," he said. "You can quote me by name, but you should know that if questioned I might deny ever meeting you. Anything I say can be printed, but if you invent quotes or slant things to make me look bad, you'll have me to answer to. Are we clear?"

Jane shivered involuntarily, and shifted her notebook in an attempt to disguise it. She had a feeling his sharp eyes took in everything. There was an ink stain on her cuff and she saw him noticing it.

She took a deep breath. "I never make up quotes; that's not how I operate. I'll take down your replies in shorthand, for the sake of accuracy."

He nodded, and she took that as permission to proceed.

"Do you want to start by telling me your opinion of the National Prohibition Act?" she asked.

He waited for the waiter to give Jane her coffee before he began.

"It's obvious that alcohol supplies a legitimate public need." He spoke succinctly, keeping an eye on the movement of her pencil on the page. "Where there's a need, there's money to be made, so I've taken advantage of a business opportunity. Some of the temperance mob might claim I'm a villain pandering to the lowest form of humanity . . ."—he paused to let her catch up—". . . but if it wasn't me, it could be someone with far fewer scruples. There are scum out there selling moonshine that makes you blind. My associates work hard to keep those types off the streets."

Jane glanced around at the associates in question, who were playing a card game she didn't recognize. Two of them were smoking and the smoke drifting across made her long for a cigarette, but Mr. Rothstein wasn't smoking. A lot of men disapproved of women smoking and he might turn out to be one of them, so it wasn't worth the risk.

"It's been suggested that you have contacts within the Bureau of Prohibition, and can arrange protection from prosecution for the city's speakeasy owners." She bit her lip, wondering if she'd gone too far.

"As I said, I provide a public service," he replied. "And that extends to the business community. Who do you buy your liquor from?"

"I would never dream of naming my sources," Jane told him. "The Prohis tried to force me after they raided a party at my house recently, but I told them they were wasting their time."

"Are they pressing charges?" he asked.

She nodded. "I guess so. They said I'll receive a summons."

"The whole thing is lunacy," he said. "Arresting decent folk like you, when they should be out looking for murderers."

Jane glanced again at the card-playing associates, who looked as if they probably had several murders apiece under their belts.

"Do you remember the names of the agents who nabbed you?" he asked and nodded when Jane told him. "They're a thorn in the flesh, those two." He drummed his fingers on the table and Jane noticed he had unusually large hands, easily twice the size of hers. Suddenly she had visions of them wrapped around a victim's neck.

She looked down at her notes for the next question. "I read that you're worth ten million dollars. Would that be an exaggeration?"

"Are you trying to bring the tax authorities down on my head?" he replied. "Next question."

They chatted about the changes in New York society since Prohibition. Jane told him that a friend of hers, Bob Benchley, had been a confirmed teetotaler until he was persuaded to try an Orange Blossom, and now he'd swung too far in the other direction and got staggering drunk most nights. They chatted about Tony Soma and other speakeasy owners they knew, who occasionally got fined by the Prohis but managed to continue trading undaunted.

In a pause in the conversation, Rothstein asked a personal question. "Say, why does your husband let you work? Is he short of dough? No wife of mine would ever be allowed to work."

"No husband of mine would ever be allowed to tell me what to do," Jane retaliated, and he laughed at that.

"She's a handful, right enough," he remarked to his associates. "Have you met the guys?" He introduced them: Legs Diamond, Meyer Lansky, and Lucky Luciano. Jane had heard of them, and felt uneasy as she shook hands with these men who often cropped up as suspects in crime stories in the paper. They were friendly, smartly turned-out guys, like Arnold. If she had met them at a party, Jane might not have realized they were gangsters, but for an unnerving sense they were assessing her carefully.

When she had asked all her questions, she thanked Mr. Rothstein for his time, packed her notebook in her satchel, and stood.

"Want someone to give you a lift back to 412 West Forty-Seventh Street?" he asked.

Jane might have guessed he would know her home address, but it was chilling to hear him say it all the same. She tried to sound breezy as she replied, "No thanks, I'm heading downtown to the office."

"To 41 Park Row? We can give you a lift there too," he offered, but she said she would get the subway. He looked at her as if she were crazy. "A dame who gets the subway on her own? Your husband must be quite a guy for letting you."

"He is," Jane said, with a smile.

She left, and started striding down Broadway toward Times Square. On the whole she thought she had stayed fairly calm and professional throughout the interview but now that it was over, she realized her shoulders and jawbone were tight as bowstrings. She kept glancing around to see if she was being followed. When she opened her purse and pulled out a nickel for the subway, her hand was trembling so hard she dropped it, and it bounced down the stone steps and through a grate, before disappearing from sight.

LARRY FAY WAS less forthcoming than Arnold Rothstein. He arranged to meet her at the headquarters of his taxi company, and it soon transpired that he had a hidden agenda for agreeing to the interview. He was married to Broadway showgirl Evelyn Crowell, and wanted Jane to include a plug for her new show in the article.

"Say that my Evie is the best thing about it," he insisted. "Make sure you mention her by name."

"I'm not a theater critic. I came to ask about your involvement in bootlegging," Jane persisted. "That's what my article is about."

"You've got the wrong man," he said. "I'm a respectable businessman and I've never committed a crime in my life."

"You've been arrested forty-six times in the last three years, according to police," Jane said. "Can you explain that?"

He shrugged. "They've got it in for me. What can I say?"

He gave her a look so ice-cold that she felt the hair stand up on the back of her neck, and she decided to draw a line under the interview right there.

# Chapter 18
# DOTTIE

Dottie asked Winifred to collect her from her apartment on the morning the abortion was scheduled. She'd hardly slept the night before, as she went over the decision in her head. Could she possibly keep the baby and bring it up alone? Her friends would help. Maybe Charlie would change his mind once the child was born, and they could all live happily ever after. But then she heard Woodrow yapping and remembered she hadn't walked him the previous day. She couldn't take care of a dog, never mind a helpless infant. It was a ridiculous idea.

What if she had the baby adopted? Lots of girls who got caught out did that. The nurses would whisk it away and find it a good home with a nice couple in the suburbs. But it would be unbearable to know her child was out there somewhere and she couldn't see him or play a part in his life. She couldn't say why but she had a funny feeling it was a boy.

There was another thing preying on her mind: she was terrified of hospitals. Bad things happened whenever she went near them. She still felt traumatized from her father's harrowing death almost a decade earlier. The doctor had been called out on Christmas Eve, but her father wasn't admitted to the hospital till two days later and he died of a heart attack on the twenty-seventh, with Dottie and her sister, Helen, by his side. He'd been terrified and in a lot of pain, and there was nothing they could say or do to calm him.

"I don't think I can go through with it," she greeted Winifred at the door. Her stomach was churning. "I'm not brave enough."

Winifred wrapped her arms around her. "I know it's a horrible decision to have to make, but what's the alternative?"

Dottie leaned her head on Winifred's shoulder, one hand on her belly, and tried to picture a crib beside her desk. She could type with one hand and rock it with the other. But the picture wouldn't come into focus. Her brain hurt from trying to figure it out.

Winifred looked at her watch. "Six hours from now it will be over and you'll be back home again. Try to focus on that."

Dottie struggled to pull herself together. "I'm glad it's a proper hospital and not the back parlor of some witchy woman with hairy warts."

She was glad, too, that she wasn't alone. If it hadn't been for Winifred, she knew she would never have managed to get herself to the appointment. She'd have gotten lost or been late or somehow messed it up.

"Fetch your coat," Winifred said. "Let's get it over with."

Out in the street, random snowflakes were drifting horizontally across the sidewalk. Winifred hailed a taxi and gave the address. In the back seat, Dottie slipped an arm through hers and watched the people outside going about their normal days: working, shopping, women wheeling baby carriages into Central Park.

"How's your friend?" she asked. "The one you took to the hospital before."

"Nora?" Winifred said. "She's fine now. It was the right thing for her." She squeezed Dottie's arm. "And it is for you too."

Once at the hospital, Winifred knew which way to go. She led Dottie by the hand, like a child, and came into the room with her for the consultation with a doctor, answering questions when Dottie didn't know what to say. The story they gave was that Eddie had disappeared two months earlier, without leaving a forwarding address, and he wasn't sending her any money.

"Couldn't you go to Eddie's parents?" the doctor asked, and Dottie was stumped.

"They're dead," Winifred said quickly. "And so are Mrs. Parker's. She has no one to turn to. Her friends are very worried. She's been in a terrible state. . . ."

Dottie glanced at Winifred and wondered why she was doing this. In truth, they scarcely knew each other, but for a few bridge club evenings. She was five years younger than her, but seemed mature and reassuringly self-possessed.

The doctor agreed to perform the operation. Dottie signed all the forms and paid the twenty-five dollars, counting out the notes Charlie had given her. His treat. On the whole, as gifts went, she preferred the turquoise soda siphon.

"Now you need to change into a hospital gown," the doctor said. "Your friend can keep your personal items and sit in the waiting room."

Dottie's heart lurched. "Can't she stay with me?" she begged, clutching Winifred's arm, but the doctor said, "Not in the operating room, no."

Winifred put an arm around her, and whispered, "It's alright. They'll take good care of you and I'll be right outside. It will all be over soon."

Dottie tugged her sleeve. "What if I die?" She'd heard of women bleeding to death after abortions, or catching horrible infections that left them sterile.

"I promise you won't die," Winifred said, and kissed her forehead tenderly, like a mother kissing her child.

Dottie was left alone to change into the cotton gown, and a few hot tears trickled down her cheeks. If she was being her normal self, she would have prepared some quips to lighten the atmosphere—but she was sure the medical staff would find abortion humor in bad taste. Best not.

A nurse came and told her to lie on the narrow bed. She filled a syringe, tapping it with her fingernail. "This will make you feel woozy," she said.

"I'd rather have a whiskey, if it's all the same to you," Dottie replied.

"This stuff's much better," the nurse said, and Dottie wondered if it was morphine, like Eddie used to take in Italy.

The injection took effect quickly, making her brain fuzzy. She panicked when she remembered there were still some questions she had to ask. Should she change her mind and scream at them to stop?

"Will I still be able to have children later?" she asked when she was wheeled into the operating room and the doctor appeared. She could hear her words were slurred, like a drunk's. He frowned and said, "Probably," which wasn't exactly the reassurance she had sought.

She lay back, tears rolling silently down her cheeks, as the doctor and nurses arranged her legs in stirrups and draped a sheet over her knees, talking among themselves as if she wasn't there. The paint was peeling on a pipe that ran along the edge of the ceiling and she wondered what was flowing through it. The blood of murdered infants, perchance?

She gasped at a sudden pain deep inside, then felt a gush of liquid as if she had wet herself. It was humiliating, and unutterably sad. A line had been crossed. It was too late to change her mind.

What felt like a tug of war ensued, with a nurse holding on to her shoulders and a doctor down below wielding barbaric instruments. He seemed to be struggling to yank the baby out of her, while it didn't want to come. Poor thing was clinging to life.

Dottie wondered how it had been for her mother when she gave birth. She had only the vaguest recollection of her, and she wasn't sure if it was a true memory or one taken from the single photograph that survived. What would she say if she could see her now? She'd be disappointed, for sure. Her ultra-religious stepmother would scream that she was going to be consumed by the fires of hell. Her father would be furious. She could picture him shouting at her, rage distorting his features. She was an evil person.

"Mrs. Parker," the doctor said sternly, "you lied when you said you were fourteen weeks gone, didn't you? This fetus is much further along."

"Can I hold it?" she asked, trying to sit up, but no one answered. She didn't deserve to hold it. She had killed it.

"Is it a girl or a boy?" she asked, and when the doctor said "Boy" it confirmed her instinct. *Charlie's son.* He didn't have any children. Would this boy have been like him? At that thought, she started sobbing so hard her chest hurt. *Oh shit! What had she done?* The doctor and nurses ignored her.

Maybe she could still give him a son, as soon as they were both divorced, if her insides weren't too mangled. They could do it properly, get married first. She forced herself to think of that. But maybe she had ruined it by killing their son.

The doctor was stitching her up down below, giving her instructions that she promptly forgot. When he finished, she closed her eyes and dozed for a while, all cried out for now.

She woke to see Winifred sitting beside the bed. "Hello," she said gently and stroked Dottie's hair with soft fingers. "I'm here. And you have another visitor too."

Dottie turned to see Bob Benchley, hat on his lap, awkward

128

and unsure where to look. She wished Charlie had come, then remembered she'd told him not to. She was dying to see him, but not here, not like this. She must look a fright.

"Well, Mrs. Parker," Bob said. "I never thought I could be enticed to wander into a women's gynecological ward, but here you are—so here I am."

"I made the mistake of putting all my eggs in one bastard." She scrunched her mouth comically to one side.

"Is that how it works? I leave that business to my wife, and am planning to be introduced to our children once they reach their teens." He took her hand and squeezed it. Good old Mr. Benchley.

"The nurse says you're doing well," Winifred said. "You can go home soon. They're going to give you a bottle of morphine and a sheet of instructions, god help us. Peggy's back at your place getting everything ready for your homecoming."

"Is she throwing a party?" Dottie asked. "A bye-bye baby party? That sounds swell."

She was beginning to feel herself again with Bob there. Women always wanted to ask about feelings, as if sharing your deepest emotions would somehow smooth them into a more manageable shape. If you had to have an abortion, there's no question Winifred was the person to take along. Dottie considered telling her this, then decided against it. She'd been wonderful, but on the whole she preferred the company of her male friends. With Bob, she could riff and play with words, and he didn't force her to think too much about the terrible thing she had done.

# Chapter 19
# WINIFRED

Winifred had been surprised when Bob Benchley appeared—Dottie hadn't mentioned that she'd told him about the operation—but it was just as well he came because the patient was wobbly on her feet. Once she was dressed and ready to leave, they borrowed a wheelchair to get her to the front door, then Bob helped her into a taxi. Getting up to her apartment at the other end would have been a nightmare, but he scooped her into his arms and carried her up all three flights of stairs, while Winifred followed with her handbag.

"You're quite the he-man, Mr. Benchley," Dottie said.

"And you're heavier than you look, Mrs. Parker," he puffed.

Winifred used Dottie's keys to unlock the door and swung it open, to be greeted by the sound of Woodrow Wilson barking, and the smell of fresh-baked bread. Bob carried Dottie into the living room and laid her on the couch. A bowl of crimson camellias sat on a table alongside. Peggy appeared from the kitchen, and then Winifred noticed a movement in the chair by the window and realized Charlie was there too.

Charlie rose and walked over to Dottie, then knelt on the floor beside her and buried his head in her chest. Winifred heard a sound like a muffled sob. Dottie's face softened and she ran her fingers through his hair, murmuring, "It's alright, I'm fine. Don't . . ."

"We should leave them alone." Winifred nudged Bob. "Let's help Peggy in the kitchen."

They crowded into the tiny space. There was steam rising from a golden-crusted apple pie on the table, and a pot of soup simmering on the stove.

"I'm starving," Bob said. "There was no catering in that hospital. I don't suppose . . ."

Peggy ladled some soup into a bowl for him and cut a hunk of bread. Winifred said no, thank you, she wasn't hungry. She couldn't get the smell of rubber and disinfectant out of her nostrils. The whole experience had been traumatizing.

There was a knock at the door and Peggy went to answer. Winifred recognized Neysa's voice and looked out to see her walking into the apartment bearing a bottle of gin in one hand, whiskey in the other. Behind her came Alec Woollcott. Dottie must have invited them to drop around. She should be resting, not entertaining.

Peggy laid the soup and bread and pie on a table in the living room, then returned to the kitchen to chat with Winifred.

"This feels inappropriate," Winifred said, gesturing toward the guests. "As if she's turning today's event into a melodrama, like a racy episode of *The Perils of Pauline*."

"I know, I share your discomfort, but it's the way Dottie copes with difficult situations: invite a gang and make a joke out of it." She frowned. "You look a bit ropey. Are you alright?"

Winifred shook herself. "She got cold feet this morning and I talked her into it. Now I keep asking myself if I did the right thing."

"Of course you did. Dottie's in no fit state to have a baby."

"It's my Catholic upbringing. I thought I'd left it behind long ago, but while I was in the waiting room today, I couldn't get rid of the nuns in my head chanting about sin and guilt and shame."

"Goddamn nuns!" Peggy exclaimed. "I'm not Catholic but I know what you mean. Rationally, it's clear to me that religion is just

131

man's compromise with a hostile environment, but it still troubles me at times, like a sharp stone in my shoe."

Winifred admired the way Peggy could express herself so succinctly. "Did you force Charlie to come or did he volunteer?"

Glancing toward the door to make sure no one was eavesdropping, Peggy explained that she had seen him with another girl just two days earlier and had given him an earful. "We've had quite a chat while we've been waiting here this afternoon, and I'm sorry to say the future is not looking bright for their relationship."

"Oh god no!" Winifred gasped. "Why not?" She knew Dottie was clinging to the prospect of a future with Charlie. She would fall apart if he left her.

Peggy shook her head. "He said he fell for a woman who was smart and witty, a great dancer, a 'sexy little minx'—I quote—and it felt to him as if she could be the love of his life. They never ran out of conversation, they had a great time in the sack, and they had dozens of interests in common. He said he can't pinpoint what went wrong, but after a few weeks Dottie became demanding." Peggy made a face, as if to imply she knew that side of her. "She wanted to know where he had been on nights he hadn't seen her. She wanted to know when he would divorce his wife and dropped heavy hints about their future together."

"He needs to reassure her," Winifred said. "Did you tell him about her background? All it would take is a bit of kindness and he'd get that carefree, witty girl back again."

"I'm not so sure. Charlie said he's baffled about it, and he's trying to be nice, but he doesn't feel the same way anymore."

"Did you not want to bash him over the head with a frying pan? After what she's been through, she deserves better." It made Winifred furious to think he might go straight on to the next girl and do the same thing all over again.

"I have verbally bashed him over the head," Peggy promised.

"Those camellias in the living room are from him. He knows we're watching. But you can't force a man to love someone he doesn't love."

By the time Winifred left, there were eight guests in the living room and Dottie was holding court. She kissed her goodbye and Dottie clung to her for a moment and whispered, "Thank you." She looked very young, Winifred thought. Young and innocent.

She had taken a day off rehearsals for a new play called *Will Shakespeare* that was due to open at the National Theatre on West Forty-First Street on the first of January. It was at the stage when it felt as if it would never come together. She had learned her lines as Anne Hathaway, Shakespeare's wife, but the same couldn't be said for the actor playing Will. Otto Kruger was a blond matinee idol who always had hordes of adoring fans waiting at the stage door. It seemed he had never performed blank verse before and needed careful coaching by the director, which made rehearsals slow and tedious.

She took a book so she could sit in her dressing room and read when they were rehearsing a scene she wasn't part of. Today she had the new Edna Ferber short story collection, *Gigolo*, which she was enjoying immensely. Edna was part of the Gonk crowd so Winifred knew her to say hello to, but they had never had a conversation. In truth, she found her a little intimidating, with her deep voice and brusque manner.

She remembered Dottie being rude about Edna's novel *The Girls*: "I couldn't have read it all the way through to save my mother from the electric chair," she had quipped. How could you reconcile that ruthless humor with the frailty of the woman Winifred had taken to hospital?

Someone knocked on the door and she opened it to see an assistant holding a box of roses. Winifred groaned, wondering if it was from Peter—he still pursued her from time to time—but the name on the card was altogether more chilling: Arnold Rothstein, a well-known bootlegger.

"I am a big fan of yours," he wrote, "and would be honored if I might have the pleasure of your company over dinner this evening."

Winifred bit her lip. She knew what these guys were like. Growing up in Brooklyn, she'd watched them turn from the street bullies who threw stones at stray dogs and put spiders down girls' dresses into men who would kill you as soon as look at you, then dump your body in the East River like a bag of trash. She couldn't have dinner with Rothstein. What if he fell for her? She would never escape his clutches.

"Is someone waiting for a reply?" she asked the assistant, and when the lad nodded, she said, "Please pass on my apologies and say many thanks for the roses but I have a beau who doesn't like me dining with other men."

She sat down at her dressing table and exhaled. With any luck, that would be the end of it. Her week had been tough enough.

# Chapter 20
# PEGGY

I n mid-December, Peggy organized a bridge club meeting at her apartment, and prepared a buffet of festive canapés: baked ham sandwiches, roasted chestnuts, mincemeat pies, fruitcake, and eggnog. She placed a Christmas tree in one corner of the living room and festooned it with colored paper garlands. Underneath she placed a gift for each of the women, tied in festive bows, then stood back to survey the effect. "Red and green should never be seen" was the old-fashioned maxim, but those were the colors that summoned up Christmas.

She glanced in the mirror over the fireplace, admiring the corn-flower blue jersey dress with tan piping on the collar, pockets, and cuffs that Winifred had persuaded her to buy in Lord & Taylor. It was simple but very flattering to her figure.

Unusually, Dottie arrived first. Physically she looked frail, with a pale complexion and shadows under her eyes, which were ac-centuated by her purple felt cloche with a spray of osprey feathers on the side.

"How are you?" Peggy asked as she took her coat.

"Grim," Dottie replied. "I haven't stopped bleeding since the operation, and I get cramps so agonizing it's as if God is reaching down and twisting my womb to punish me."

"The Holy Father is probably too busy with church matters at this time of year, but I'm sorry you're in pain," Peggy said. "Talking of fathers, is Charlie being kind?"

Dottie shrugged. "Kind enough, but his work is busy and he just announced he has to spend Christmas with his wife in Chicago. Why that should be, I don't know, since he told me they were separating. . . . But so it is. Do you have any whiskey? I could murder a highball."

Peggy poured her a drink and watched, alarmed, as Dottie drained half a glass in one gulp. "I'll get you some water if you're thirsty," she remarked, but Dottie ignored her and wandered over to gaze out the window at the dark streets glistening with rain.

"Here come Jane and Winifred, huddled under the same umbrella. I wouldn't have thought they'd have much in common, would you? Beauty and the Feminist."

Peggy laughed. "I don't think Jane's brand of feminism excludes those who are pleasing to the eye." She went to the door to welcome them.

"Your tree is beautiful," Winifred exclaimed, walking in. "My room is too small for one, but I do adore the Christmassy scent of pine."

"We have a huge tree at 412," Jane said. "Alec insisted on it. Every detail of Christmas has to be exactly the way his dear mama used to do it, from the menu to the décor." She smiled indulgently. "Harold and I are going to make him a Christmas stocking with childish gifts like marbles, a slingshot, and a joke book."

"How many will you be feeding on Christmas Day?" Peggy asked.

"The biblical five thousand," Jane replied. "All the waifs and strays of our acquaintance who don't have anywhere else to go are welcome."

Peggy noticed Dottie flinch at the description, which clearly touched a nerve.

"I guess that's me," she said. "I'm Waif of the Year. What are you doing, Winifred?"

Winifred switched to her Tipperary brogue: "All the aunts and grandmas and cousins-twice-removed turn up at me ma's for Christmas dinner, so it's standing room only, and even then we're spilling into the street. I'd much rather be at yours, Jane, but I'd be hung, drawn, and quartered if I missed it."

Peggy guessed that the 412 celebration would turn into a day-long bacchanalian feast with much booze consumed, which was not at all what Dottie needed. Without thinking, she asked, "Dottie, why don't you come to Newburgh for Christmas with my family? My mother always says I'm welcome to bring a friend. It's very casual, food will be plentiful, and there's real countryside around about."

Dottie looked at her thoughtfully. "The proper all-American family experience? Will there be stockings on the fireplace and candy under the tree? Cookies and milk for Santa Claus?" It sounded as if she was building up to one of her wicked one-liners, but instead she said, "I think I'd rather like that. It sounds *whole-some.*"

When they started playing bridge, it became clear that Winifred and Jane had devised a set of signals—winks, head scratches, earlobe tugs, crossing and uncrossing legs—which they used to communicate their cards. Perhaps that's what they had been discussing in the street outside.

"I'm sure that's cheating," Peggy said with a grin, but it seemed to work because when they stopped to eat, they were in the lead.

Peggy served the food and the others tucked in, but Dottie scarcely ate a morsel. She crumbled a mince pie and moved the crumbs around her plate with a finger, while gulping highballs as if her life depended on it. She was quiet too, not contributing to the conversation unless asked a direct question. After supper, she started hiccupping and it was clear she was too pickled to play another rubber.

Peggy handed out her gifts—she'd gotten them each a leather-bound diary with a day to the page. "These are for your hopes and dreams," she said. "May they all come true in 1923."

"You are the kindest of friends," Winifred said, hugging her. "I need to think hard about my hopes and dreams instead of just drifting from one acting job to the next. I'll use this diary to help me focus."

"Harold and I are getting closer to our dream," Jane said. "Maybe next year will be the one when we launch the magazine. How about you, Dottie?"

They all turned to her. "I'm dreaming of another highball," she said, raising her glass. Her elbow slipped off the edge of the table, and whiskey sloshed onto her new diary. Peggy rushed to get a towel to mop it up, whisking away the glass at the same time. She was beginning to regret the Christmas invitation. If Dottie was drinking with such determination, it could be a disaster.

WHEN THEIR TRAIN pulled in to Newburgh, Dottie and Peggy saw that the town was knee-deep in twinkling snow, and crusty ice lined the shores of the Hudson, just leaving a narrow channel of water flowing in the center. Streetlamps were surrounded by fuzzy haloes and they could see their breath in the air. Peggy's father met them at the station and greeted Dottie like a visiting celebrity, insisting she take the front seat in their Ford Model T and placing a plaid rug across her knees.

"It was clever of you to arrange such picture-perfect snow for us," Dottie said, and he laughed as if it were the funniest thing he'd ever heard. Peggy cringed in the back seat.

Her mother greeted them on the porch and hugged Dottie

warmly. "I know we've never met before but you're family now that you're joining us for Christmas," she said, "so please make yourself at home."

Peggy noticed a glint of tears in Dottie's eyes, and swept her upstairs to show her to her room.

"There will be drinks in front of the fire in the living room as soon as you're ready," her mother called after them.

Peggy's kid sister, Rose, brought a beau for dinner, a conventional type who worked in a bank and spoke at length about the best fishing spots in the vicinity. Peggy worried that Dottie would mock him; in front of the Gonk crowd she would have been ruthless, but she made only one mild quip: "I don't know much about fishing, but I believe good things come to those who bait."

It was strange seeing her family through the eyes of a sophisticated New York friend: her parents' conversation seemed mundane, her sister's plain silly, but Dottie remained polite and appreciative, quite unlike the urbane wit of the Round Table.

"You're lucky," she told Peggy later as they sat in front of the crackling log fire clutching highballs. "I've never had anything like this. My stepmother thought Christmas should be spent on our knees worshipping Jesus."

"What about your father? Was he religious?"

"Not so as you'd notice, but he was grateful to my stepmother, the divine Eleanor Lewis, for bringing up his children after my mother died, so he humored her. I remember one year she gave me a Bible as a Christmas present. You can picture my gratitude." Dottie made a comic face, crossing her eyes.

"I'm glad you came here," Peggy said. "I hope you won't find it dull."

"Your mother's a peach, isn't she?" Dottie looked wistful. "I wonder if my mother would have been like that? And I wonder what I would be like now if she'd lived? I guess we'll never know." She held out her glass with a wink. "Any chance of a quick refill while the grown-ups are out of the room?"

NEXT MORNING, THE family decided to go for a snowy walk in a nearby wood, but Dottie announced the only boots she had brought were high-heeled lace-ups. There was good-natured teasing about "city folks and their ways" before Peggy's sister found some snow boots she could borrow.

The Leeches were a tall family, who strode along, but Dottie's short legs couldn't keep up, so Peggy held back and walked beside her, pointing out the spots where she used to play as a child.

Dottie was quiet, keeping her innermost thoughts to herself, and Peggy hoped she was beginning to recover from her recent trauma. She wasn't wisecracking much, but maybe that was a good sign, because it meant she was relaxing and didn't feel she had to "perform."

On Christmas Day evening, after a few drinks, Dottie's composure slipped. She took Peggy aside, close to tears.

"I need to speak to Charlie," she sniffed. "He told me not to ring in case his wife answers but I have to hear his voice. I miss him too much."

Peggy frowned. It seemed he was more solidly married than he had let on to any of them if Dottie wasn't even allowed to call him at home.

"Will you call for me, Peggy dearest? If she answers, tell her you're ringing from the news desk at the *New York American* to check a detail on one of his stories. Say it can't wait."

"Me? I couldn't carry it off. Besides, they've probably got guests around." It was a terrible idea, Peggy thought. It would only end in more tears.

"I'm begging you." Dottie clasped her hands in prayer. "The silence is killing me. I can't bear it a moment longer."

That's why she had been distracted; she was pining for Charlie. Peggy wished she could take the pain away, but didn't know any cures for heartache. "Oh, Dottie, don't you see that you drive him away when you're like this? Please don't bother him at home."

Dottie's mind was made up. "If you won't ring, I'll do it myself. I'm sure your mother will allow me to use the telephone."

Peggy did her best to talk her out of it, but nothing worked, so finally, with heavy heart, she agreed to place the call. She dialed the operator and gave the Chicago number then, when a woman's voice answered, she asked, "Is Charlie there? It's the news desk calling. We need a quick word." She waited till Charlie's voice came on the line, then handed Dottie the receiver and left the room. She had a bad feeling about this. A very bad feeling.

A few minutes later, she heard the sound of Dottie running upstairs. Peggy followed, knocked on her bedroom door, and entered the room. Dottie was sitting on the window seat gazing out across the moonlit snow, her face shiny with tears.

"What did he say?" Peggy asked, sitting down and passing her a handkerchief.

Dottie dabbed her eyes and blew her nose. "Oh, you were right, of course. He was mad at me for calling. His wife was listening so he had to keep up the pretense that I was someone from the office, and he told me I had a nerve disturbing him on Christmas Day. It was a disaster. Why am I so bad at this?"

"You're better at it than me," Peggy said. "You and I are both going to be thirty next year but at least you've been married and had a serious love affair, whereas I'm still a virgin and fast becoming a confirmed old maid."

"Ah, but you're a wise old maid, wiser than I'll ever be. I can't imagine you humiliating yourself over some dumb married guy on Christmas Day." She sniffed.

"Never say never," Peggy replied. "I'm sure my turn to be a fool in love will come."

She looked out across the snowy garden. Maybe it wouldn't. Maybe it was her destiny to write about love, and counsel her friends on love, but never to experience it for herself.

# Chapter 21
# JANE

Seventeen "waifs and strays" turned up for Christmas dinner at 412, most of them Gonk habitués. Jane had decorated the communal dining room with holly and ivy and squeezed a huge Christmas tree into one corner. She hired three women who worked in a local Chinese restaurant to roast a suckling pig over a spit in the yard and prepare a menu that included candied sweet potatoes, diced turnips in hollandaise, cranberry-apple sauce, and three different desserts. All morning, the women kept coming to Jane to query the unfamiliar recipes and she realized she would have been better off asking them to cook Chinese food, but Alec had planned the menu and wanted it just so.

The men dominated the conversation over the dinner table, just as they did at the Gonk. There were competitive word games and Christmas riddles to be solved, which Jane didn't find restful or particularly festive. She sat back and listened, keeping half an ear out for the cooks calling from the kitchen or the yard.

"I saw your bootlegging article in the *Times*," Marc Connelly said. "It's a good piece. Has there been much reaction?"

"A flurry of comments on the letters page," she said, "but so far neither Rothstein nor Fay have sent their hatchet men to bump me off." She knocked on wood.

"I wondered how it might affect your court case for alcohol

violations. Might the Prohis treat you more sternly because you've criticized them?"

"On the contrary," Jane said, glancing at Alec. "Carr Van Anda called the precinct and found that charges against me have been mysteriously dropped. We've got no proof, but we wondered if Mr. Rothstein might have pulled some strings." She could tell Alec was listening, but he made no comment. Perhaps he had a guilty conscience.

Jane had been relieved to hear she wasn't about to acquire a criminal record, but it was creepy to think Rothstein might have helped her. She didn't want to be in his debt.

"Sounds as if you've made a conquest," Marc said. "Are you sure he knew you were married? You don't wear a ring so maybe he thinks his luck is in. Perhaps you should be worried, Harold."

"Oh, he knew everything about me," Jane told them. "Hell, he probably knows what brand of tooth powder I use."

"You must be awfully brave," Helen Hayes, an actress friend of Alec's, commented. "I wouldn't have dared meet him. Do tell us what he's like."

A chorus of voices urged her, so Jane described the strange meeting in Lindy's and the hatchet men in smart suits and slicked hair shaking her hand with great politeness. She described details, like Rothstein's huge meaty hands, the two-tone shoes Legs Diamond wore, and Lucky Luciano meticulously cleaning under his fingernails with a toothpick.

"Shall we invite them for dinner sometime?" Alec suggested. "I'm sure the conversation would be riveting."

"Christ, no!" Jane exclaimed. "I escaped unscathed this time but twice would be pushing it."

Desserts were brought in and everyone groaned that they were too full, yet when the plates were passed around, they all took one.

"Where's Dottie?" Marc asked. "It's not the same without her caustic commentary."

"Dottie's been banished to the country for bad behavior," Alec said, shoveling plum pudding into his mouth.

"Has she slipped off somewhere with Charlie?" Helen asked. "Is that what you mean by bad behavior?"

"Don't listen to him," Jane intervened. "She's spending Christmas with Peggy Leech's family."

"Charlie's in Chicago with his wife," Alec said, unfastening the lower buttons of his waistcoat. It was stretched so tight around his middle that they were threatening to pop off. "Our Dottie's lying low while she recovers from aborting Charlie's little bastard a couple of weeks ago."

Several people gasped.

"Alec!" Jane rebuked him. "That's not true!"

He regarded her with a triumphant expression. "Oh, but it is. She invited me for a party at her apartment the evening she got back from the hospital. Neysa was there. And Peggy and Winifred. How odd they didn't tell you."

Jane looked around the table, horrified. From the expressions on her guests' faces, she could tell some of them had already known. Why hadn't Dottie confided in her? She realized they hadn't seen each other alone for weeks. She'd been tied up with work, and she'd assumed Dottie was spending all her spare time with Charlie so she hadn't even called.

"True or not, this is hardly suitable conversation for a Christmas dinner table," Harold interrupted. "Let's change the subject. Marc, how confident are you that the founding of the Irish Free State will end hostilities on the Emerald Isle?"

Jane got up to clear the dishes, almost knocking over her chair. She was seething that Alec had tossed such private information into the gathering like a ball to be kicked around for sport. Was he drunk? Even still, there was no excuse. She no longer felt sociable and wished the guests would leave, but it was only six o'clock and there was a long night of hard drinking ahead.

Poor Dottie. She must be devastated. Jane decided to invite her for lunch just as soon as she got back from Peggy's.

THEY MET AT Barbetta's on West Forty-Sixth, where an extremely good table d'hôte could be had for seventy-five cents a head. A waiter led them to a dimly lit corner table. Tired festive decorations drooped from the salmon-pink walls and little gold lamps stood on each table.

"How was your Christmas?" Jane asked once they were seated. "What's it like at Peggy's?"

"Twee and suburban," Dottie replied. "Nary a surface was unbedecked with holly and even the birds in the trees were jolly."

Jane cackled. "You look well on the country air. And I loved your story in *Smart Set* this month—'Such a Pretty Little Picture.' Harold laughed out loud all the way through." It was about a man in a dull marriage who was trimming his front garden one afternoon when suddenly he put down his shears and walked out. "We think it's based on Bob Benchley and his wife. Are we right?"

"I couldn't possibly comment," Dottie said with a wink.

"Will *Smart Set* buy more from you? It would be good to get a regular commission from them."

"Yeah, but they only pay fifty dollars a story and it took so many drafts that I doubt I earned a dime a day," she drawled. "I love *having* written. It's the actual *process* of writing I can't stand."

The waiter came to ask what they wanted to drink and Dottie was disappointed to learn they didn't serve alcohol: "I shan't be coming back here in a hurry if it's run by killjoys who let a little law get in the way of customer satisfaction."

146

"I hear the meatballs are good," Jane said, and they pored over the menus. The waiter took their order and, once he had gone, Jane stretched her hand across the table and took hold of Dottie's.

"How are you feeling?" she asked. "Are you alright?"

"Why?" Dottie asked, sounding suspicious.

"Because I heard about your operation. I'm sorry. That must have been an ordeal."

"Who the hell told you?" She cupped her face in her hands, elbows resting on the table.

"Alec blurted it out over Christmas dinner, of all things. I was furious with him. So was Harold." Jane sighed. "I just wish you'd told me first and I could have dealt with him better. As it was, I was stunned."

Dottie's voice was almost inaudible. "I couldn't tell you. I was too ashamed."

"You dope! You're my best friend! Why on earth were you ashamed to tell me? I would never judge any woman for ending a pregnancy. It's an incredibly brave decision to make, and certainly the right one in your circumstances." She peered more closely at Dottie. Had she really thought Jane would condemn her? Was that the impression she gave? "I'm hurt that you confided in Winifred, Peggy, and even Alec, of all people, but you didn't tell me."

Dottie's eyes filled with tears. "I don't care about their opinions, but I've always wanted you to think well of me. You once said to me that women from Kansas have backbone, and it made me wish I came from there too because I seem to have a spine made of jelly. You would never get yourself into the scrapes I do. That's why I couldn't tell you."

"Don't be ridiculous!" Jane said. "I'm always getting into scrapes. Being arrested by the Prohis was a scrape. Interviewing Arnold Rothstein felt like a scrape. Living with Alec is one continuous bloody scrape."

Dottie sighed. "And yet you survive them."

"And so will you," Jane said firmly. "Of course you will."

"The baby was a boy," Dottie said, her voice flat. "I called him Jacob, after my father. A good Jewish name."

"Oh, Dottie." Jane felt sad for her, and worried too.

"I wish I had kept him, even without Charlie's support," she continued. "That's what you would have done, isn't it? You would be capable of bringing up a child on your own, but I knew I wasn't."

"I'm not sure what I would have done," Jane said. "As you know, I'm not wild to have children. But I'm sure you will have more one day. Jacob won't be the only one. Until then, why don't you come to Margaret Sanger's clinic with me and get a diaphragm to save any more accidents?"

"No need," Dottie said. "Charlie hasn't come near me since the operation. I guess the thought makes him squeamish."

"He'll get over it," Jane said. "Men's anatomy is ruled by biological instinct, not rational thought."

The waiter brought their meals, and she could tell from a slight twitch of his lips that he had overheard her.

Dottie changed the subject while they were eating. "Is Alec still abusing your hospitality, and does Harold stand up for you?"

"You know Harold," Jane said. "Frankly, I don't think he's aware of any tension. It goes right over his head. My current tactic is to smother Alec with kindness and try to appeal to his better nature."

"Good luck with that," Dottie said. "With him, everything comes down to status. He wants to be kingpin and won't accept a woman being in charge, even of something as inconsequential as the brand of toilet paper in his bathroom."

"I'm fed up to the back teeth with men's egos," Jane said. "I'm forever tiptoeing around them: at work, at home, at the Gonk, and at Neysa's. We mustn't ever upset them because they're such sensitive, delicate creatures." She noticed Dottie was just playing with

148

her meal, pushing it around her plate without eating, and guessed her thoughts were back with Charlie and the baby. "Did Charlie apologize for getting you knocked up?" she asked.

Dottie nodded slowly. "He did. He paid for the operation, brought flowers, and said all the right things. I think Peggy had given him fifty lashes first, but they worked a treat."

*Good for Peggy*, Jane thought. To meet her, you would never think she was fierce but there was a core of steel beneath the friendly exterior. "I'm sorry you didn't think you could turn to me. I feel as if I've failed as your friend. But I hope we can see more of each other next year, just the two of us."

"Sure," Dottie said, without enthusiasm. "Let's do that."

She didn't seem herself, Jane thought. Not sad or tearful; just flat. "I've been too busy with the job and the house, but I'll resolve to be a better friend, if you'll resolve to write more wonderful stories—and take better care of yourself around dangerous men."

"All work and no playboys makes Dottie a dull girl," she said with a wan smile. "But I'll try."

# Chapter 22

# DOTTIE

On New Year's Eve, Dottie realized her telephone hadn't rung for three days. Charlie must be back in New York by now. Why hadn't he called? Was he still cross with her for calling at Christmas? Neysa popped across the hall to say she was having a party later, but apart from her, Dottie hadn't spoken to a soul since her lunch with Jane. She could have called someone—Bob, maybe—but couldn't bring herself to make the effort. She felt dull and boring, and it wouldn't be fair to burden anyone else with her mood. All she could think about was Charlie. Where was he? How could she make him love her?

She jumped at the sound of knocking on the door and rose slowly to answer it. There, with a wide grin, was the man who had filled all her thoughts of late: he was holding a gift-wrapped box in one hand and a bottle of Veuve Clicquot in the other.

"There you are!" he cried. "I've been trying to call but I don't think your telephone is working. Can I come in?"

All Dottie wanted to do was throw herself into his arms and sob, but she resisted the urge and instead led him in. "Ah, that old line about telephones not working . . ." She picked up her phone and listened. Sure enough, it was dead.

"Have you paid the bill recently?" Charlie asked, and threw

himself onto the couch. "Get a couple of glasses for this, will you?" He held up the bottle. "It's time to start the New Year's party."

Dottie got the glasses and he popped the cork, which ricocheted off the canary's cage. Onan fluttered and squawked in protest.

"Happy New Year," Charlie said, handing her a glass. "I brought you a Christmas present."

Dottie untied the bow and opened the box to find a chartreuse green velvet devoré scarf. It was pretty, but it felt like an afterthought. She couldn't imagine him walking into a store and spotting it and thinking, "That's perfect for Dottie." She had bought him a hideously expensive midnight-blue smoking jacket, but it was too generous a gift to give in exchange for a scarf; better to keep quiet.

"How was your Christmas?" she asked. "Sorry for phoning you at home that time. I was pickled."

"My parents-in-law were listening, so it was awkward," he said, "but no harm done. We haven't told them we're separating yet so we had to act like the 'ideal married couple.'" He made a face, as if to imply they were anything but, then began chatting about some art projects his wife was working on, about ice-skating on Lake Michigan, about catching up with old friends. Finally, as if it were of no consequence, he mentioned that his editor was sending him back to Chicago for a few months to cover for a colleague.

Dottie's stomach lurched as if she were on an elevator plunging down through a skyscraper. "Chicago? Did you say you would go?" She knew the answer. Of course he did.

He said it was a promotion and a great opportunity for him. He would miss her and all his New York friends, but the months would pass in no time. A quote came into Dottie's mind: "Absence, that common cure of love." Was it Shakespeare? She couldn't remember. Would Charlie's absence cure her of loving him?

"Don't look so crestfallen!" he said in a teasing tone. "Come on, let's head over to Neysa's and welcome in the New Year. Irving Berlin is going to play and I don't want to miss him. Then I want to pop by Ruth Hale and Heywood Broun's party later."

"I'll see you at Neysa's," Dottie said. "I have to get changed and put on my party face."

She stared at her pale complexion in the bathroom mirror. Charlie hadn't even kissed her. She'd hugged him in thanks for the scarf, but only briefly. Should she wear it tonight to please him? He probably wouldn't notice either way. She sprayed on some scent and took the top off her tube of wine-red lipstick.

Charlie was leaving her. She knew in her heart that men would always leave her. She drove them away because she needed more than they could possibly give. She hated herself for it but couldn't seem to change. She'd been unloved as a child, and she was unlovable as an adult too. That's just how it was, how it would always be.

STRAIGHT AFTER NEW Year, winter storms buffeted Manhattan, leaving deep snow on the ground, but unlike the snow in Newburgh it didn't stay pretty for long. This snow was soon churned to gray slush by thousands of feet trudging on sidewalks and cars skidding along roads. It matched Dottie's mood. Charlie had left New York without spending another night with her, and that stung. Was she so unappealing now? What had happened to the giddy rush of love and lust that had swept them off their feet last year? Clearly it had been a mirage.

She tried to focus on work, as Jane had suggested. Bob Benchley got her a commission to write a poem for *Life* magazine, and she produced a cynical little ditty called "One Perfect Rose." They loved it and asked for another, but she couldn't come up with an idea. The deadline came and went, like a freight train steaming into the distance. *Smart Set* wanted another story too but she felt utter terror when she contemplated the blank page. She was well and truly blocked.

Meantime, she was in a panic over money. Somehow she kept spending all her monthly allowance from Eddie on clothes and cocktails and cabs and now she was behind on the rent and had to lie to the landlord that she was waiting for checks in the post. The phone still didn't work, and then the oil burner conked out, as if to spite her. It had plenty of oil in it and the settings seemed correct, but it wouldn't produce heat. She kicked it in frustration. Fortunately the oven still worked, so she could turn it on and open the door and that warmed the kitchen just enough for her to sit at her typewriter, wrapped up in woolens. She should ask the landlord to come and fix the burner, but didn't feel she could contact him till she caught up on rent. If only she and Bob still had their little office! It would have been heated, and he'd have been there for company, but they'd given it up to save money and now he was working in the offices of *Life* magazine.

"Hell, just write something, for crying out loud," she yelled at herself. But what did she have to say? Her work was trite and bleak—about cheating men and desperate women and the impossibility of love. She had said it all before.

Occasionally Neysa came to drag her across to the studio for some company, but Alec was often there and she couldn't bear to be around him since hearing he had told everyone at Jane's Christmas dinner about her abortion. And then Neysa went on vacation to Florida for the rest of January, so that was that. Dottie stopped answering the door because she couldn't face company. Peggy sent her a note asking where she was and what was up with her phone, and reminding her that she had agreed to host a bridge club meeting on the last Saturday of the month. Winifred mailed her two tickets for her new show, *Will Shakespeare*, but she didn't go.

The days passed, each the same as the last: cold, dark, and lonely. One afternoon she was flicking through the new issue of *Smart Set* when she came across an article by the poet Elinor Wylie, who had just won the Poetry Society prize for a collection called *Nets to Catch the Wind*. Elinor wrote that an appreciation of death was essential for a poet, because it was the ultimate human experience against which all else was measured. Dottie read that Elinor had lost three close relatives to suicide: her brother had asphyxiated himself in her apartment, her first husband shot himself after she left him, and her sister also killed herself after an unhappy love affair. Elinor claimed in the article to have lost eight babies through miscarriage and stillbirth—*eight!*—and said she often considered suicide. She said all true poets considered it from time to time.

Dottie could understand what she meant. She too had known loss, although not through suicide; she too had lost a baby, although that had been at her own hand. She bought a copy of *Nets to Catch the Wind* and sensed a wish for death in its descriptions of the passing seasons: "Go burrow underground . . . hold intercourse with roots of trees and stones . . . and disembodied bones"; "sleepy winter, like the sleep of death."

It infected her mood the way only the best writing could, seeming to offer an escape from a world that was heartless and stale. Gradually, an idea for a story took shape in Dottie's brain: a blond woman of a certain age, living penniless in a shabby hotel room, who has given herself to men and been used up and left by them, and who is contemplating suicide.

With the story in mind, Dottie began to research methods of suicide. Should her heroine have a pistol? Where would she have obtained it? There would be no gas oven in a hotel room. What about pills? You'd have to be very sure which kind to take so you didn't just make yourself ill, because then you'd be accused of

154

a cry for help. No, her heroine truly wanted to die. What about hanging? What would she tie the rope around in a hotel room?

The subject preoccupied her, and she could feel the story springing to life in her head, but she couldn't face starting to write the words. Everything she wrote was a failure. The initial idea seemed worthwhile, but the words on the page never captured it. Maybe when the snow melted and the sun came out, she would be able to write again. In the meantime, she was spending too much time stuck inside her own head. She felt as if she had shrunk, as if her body was getting smaller and so was her mind. If she kept shrinking like this much longer she might simply disappear.

ONE EVENING, WHEN Dottie hadn't been out all day, her stomach growled and she realized she was starving. There wasn't a scrap of food in the apartment, except half a bag of dog biscuits. She shook them into a bowl for Woodrow Wilson and he gulped them down in record time, making her feel a pang of guilt. When had he last been fed? Or walked, for that matter? The birdcage stank when she went to top up Onan's seed and water. Cleaning it was another chore she'd have to find the energy for, but the thought defeated her.

The Swiss Alps restaurant downstairs was the closest source of food. They had walls painted with twee alpine scenes and served dubious Swiss specialties, but at least they delivered so she wouldn't have to hang around. She ordered raclette, a cheesy potato dish, and went back upstairs.

She poured a whiskey and soda, took a gulp, then looked in her purse for money to pay the delivery boy. Her heart plummeted. There were only a couple of cents left, and she remembered she'd paid her bootlegger earlier and that had wiped her out. Eddie's allowance wouldn't be in the bank for another week, and there weren't any checks left in the checkbook. She buried her face in her hands. She wanted to cry but didn't have the energy. It truly was rock bottom when you couldn't afford a carton of potatoes.

She had another gulp of Scotch, but it made her stomach clench as if she were going to throw up. She rushed to the bathroom, bent over the bowl, and heaved. Nothing came, but the sensation of nausea remained, along with a nagging pain in her temples—like a hangover, but she hadn't drunk enough for that. She was all out of aspirin. Was there any morphine left from the operation? She opened the bathroom cupboard. The brown glass bottle was still there but when she shook it, it was empty. Could things get any worse?

On another shelf she noticed a folding razor blade Eddie had left behind. Was it really only last summer he'd gone? It felt like it had been a lot longer than six months. He had promised they would meet after six months to see if the marriage could be salvaged but she had never believed him. He had walked out that door with a sigh of relief and never looked back.

She opened the blade and touched the edge of it, pressing her finger down till a bead of blood appeared. Strangely, she couldn't feel it, as if all the nerve endings had gone numb. She looked at her left wrist, with its pattern of blue veins beneath the surface, like tributaries of a river. Where were you supposed to cut?

Suddenly she swiped the blade across, pressing down hard. It stung so much she cried out and hopped up and down. *Ow, ow, ow.* At first the blood just appeared as pinpricks along a thin red line, but then it began to ooze and drip. Should she do the other wrist, for symmetry? It was harder to hold the blade handle with her left hand, especially with the blood making it slippery. The cut she made on her right wrist was ragged and so painful she thought she was going to pass out. Blood was dripping everywhere. She grabbed a towel and slid to the floor, leaning back against the tub, her brain all jumbled.

She should have brought the Scotch. Might as well get drunk while she bled to death. But now that she was sitting down, she didn't have the strength to get up and fetch the bottle.

Was she really going to die? Was this what she wanted?

"I want my papa," she murmured, and that made tears come. *Papa!* She began to sob so hard she could scarcely catch her breath: she cried because she was an orphan who had lost everything; she cried because now she would just be remembered as a lousy suicide.

Someone was knocking at the door. She stopped crying. The sound was insistent but if she ignored it, she hoped it would go away. She wasn't capable of speech, and certainly couldn't get up.

Then she heard a voice calling: "Mrs. Parker? I've brought your order."

It was the delivery boy, and from the way Woodrow was yapping it sounded as though he was inside the apartment. *Oh, hell.* She must have left the door on the latch.

She closed her eyes and pretended to be unconscious when the boy came into the bathroom, so she didn't have to see the expression on his face.

# Chapter 23
# WINIFRED

**W**ill Shakespeare got middling reviews. It wasn't a great script, but a couple of critics singled out Winifred's performance for praise. The cast and crew were a friendly crowd and normally she would have enjoyed the run, but a pall was cast over it by the boxes of roses that kept appearing from Arnold Rothstein. He was clearly a man who didn't take no for an answer.

As she signed autographs at the stage door one night, Winifred became aware of a fancy car idling behind the crowd, with a man in a dark suit and hat at the wheel. He caught her eye and beckoned her over, but she pretended not to notice. After a while he got out of the car and came closer.

"Mr. Rothstein asked if you would join him tonight," he said, in a Philadelphia accent.

Winifred affected a gaiety she didn't feel. "That's very kind, but my beau would have a blue fit," she replied. "Do send my apologies."

"We know you're not with Peter Costello anymore," the driver said, "so who's the lucky guy?"

Winifred shivered. How did they know about Peter? What else did they know?

"It's a secret," she replied, touching a finger to her lips. "We want to keep it out of the papers. I'm sure you understand." As soon as she could, she ducked back inside the stage door. A fellow actress was standing in the corridor and Winifred confided in her.

"What the heck am I supposed to do?" she asked.

"Let him buy you a few fancy meals but keep him at arm's length," the actress suggested. "That's what I would do. Maybe you'll get some jewelry out of it. I hear he's minted."

But Winifred knew you didn't play games with types like Arnold Rothstein. He wouldn't like to be taken for a fool.

Next evening, another box of roses arrived, with yet another invitation. She decided she would ask advice from the bridge club girls when they met at Dottie's on Saturday. Peggy and Jane were bound to have an idea.

WINIFRED CAUGHT A taxi to Dottie's straight after the show and hurried up the stairs, conscious the others would be waiting. She was surprised when Peggy opened the door with a warning expression on her face as if she was trying to communicate something. Glancing over her shoulder, Winifred saw Dottie lying on the couch, a blanket draped over her.

"Oh no, are you ill?" she asked, walking into the room.

It was freezing inside, a penetrating icy cold, and it smelled like a bad drain. Peggy and Jane had kept their coats on and she did the same.

Dottie looked paler than ever, her dark eyes sunk deep in their sockets. It was the first time Winifred had seen her entirely without makeup. Even at Lenox Hill, right before the abortion, she had touched up her lipstick, checking her reflection in a compact mirror.

Dottie held up her wrists, which had ostentatious black bows tied around them, then peeled back one bow to show Winifred the bandaging underneath.

"What happened? Did you have an accident?" She glanced at Jane, whose expression was grim, then back at Dottie.

"I never could trust Eddie to get anything right," she said, her voice low and husky. "He left behind one of his razors but it was too blunt to cut deep enough. He truly was the most useless of husbands. . . ."

"You cut your wrists? But why?" Winifred breathed hard, so shocked she couldn't think.

"I didn't plan to," Dottie related. "But the oil burner is broken, the rent is overdue, the phone's been cut off, I can't write anymore, the love of my life has left me, and then I ordered some raclette from the restaurant downstairs and found I didn't have enough to pay for it. It was all too much." She gave an exaggerated shrug. "I was bleeding all over the bathroom floor when the poor delivery boy arrived and I guess he called for help because I woke up in the hospital."

Winifred perched on the edge of the couch and wrapped her arms around her, careful not to touch the damaged wrists, then kissed her forehead. Dottie felt fragile, like a little bird whose bones would break if she hugged any tighter.

"You must come from a tactile family," Dottie said, with an attempt at a smile. "My stepmother didn't believe in hugging, but I could get used to this." She laid her head on Winifred's shoulder, and Winifred held her close, patting her back and rocking gently.

"I wish you had called me," she said. "You could have used Neysa's phone. I'd have been around in a flash." She looked at the others. "Any of us would."

Dottie wouldn't meet their eyes. "Neysa's away, and it turns out when you decide to die, last thing you want is an audience. Anyway, I failed at suicide, just like I fail at everything else. Talking of which, who wants to play bridge?" She reached for a pack of cards.

160

The women looked at each other, and Jane shook her head.

"We can't just play bridge as if nothing's happened." She stood up. "Look at the state of this place! No wonder you were depressed."

Winifred looked around. Magazines littered the floor, empty bottles and overturned glasses sat on stray surfaces alongside over-flowing ashtrays, and Woodrow Wilson appeared to have used the entire carpet as a toilet.

"I think you should move in with us at 412," Jane said. "We've got a spare room on the third floor."

Dottie gave a mock shudder. "The only way I could live in the same place as Alec Woollcott would be if he were dead and buried in the backyard."

"You can stay at mine," Peggy offered. "I'll sleep on the couch."

"No, I'm fine," Dottie insisted. "Stop fussing. I'm not going to cut my wrists again. Frankly, I had no idea how much it would hurt!"

Jane began tearing up strips of newspaper and using them to pick up dog turds. Peggy started collecting glasses, and Winifred joined her. She was badly shaken that Dottie had tried to take her own life. Was it her fault for helping her get rid of the baby? In the Catholic church, suicide was a grave sin, just like aborting a baby.

Five years younger than the others, she felt out of her depth, as if anything she said would be inadequate. She shouldn't be there. Jane and Peggy knew Dottie better. On the other hand, it seemed as if Dottie lived her entire life in the public arena, and nothing was sacred.

Peggy filled a kettle and put it on the stove to heat water. "Oh god, how was she living like this?" she whispered to Winifred. "She could have died of cold."

"It smells awful too," Winifred agreed. "But cleaning alone won't solve her problems."

"We'll put our heads together and come up with a plan," Jane said. She had disposed of the dog waste, and Winifred was glad to hear that at least the toilet flush still worked.

Jane went through to talk to Dottie: "I'll call the landlord first thing Monday morning and explain that you've been ill and that's why you're behind on rent. I'll ask him to fix the oil burner too." She ran through a list of things to do, ticking them off on her fingers as if somehow she could fix this problem if she only applied enough energy.

*You can't bring Charlie back*, Winifred thought, with a flash of insight. *That's all she really wants.*

She emptied the ashtrays into the garbage pail and began folding magazines into a pile. If only there was more she could do.

Peggy brought out a homemade cake, flavored with cinnamon, nutmeg, and cloves. She said it was one of her grandmother's recipes. They all had a slice with a cup of coffee, and Winifred noticed it was midnight already. No bridge was going to be played that evening, and no booze consumed.

"Come back to mine," Peggy urged Dottie. "At least till your oil burner is fixed. The temperature is set to drop below freezing most of next week."

"What about Woodrow and Onan? I can't leave them."

Winifred glanced into the corner. "If we give the bird some food and water he'll be fine for a couple of days."

Peggy grimaced. "I suppose the pooch will have to come with us. I'm simply not leaving you alone until we have figured out how we can make your life better."

Dottie caved in. She packed a few items of clothing and they left together, four of them plus the dog. Peggy and Dottie took the first taxi, after successfully pleading with the driver to bend his no-animals rule. Winifred and Jane shared another cab, and on the journey they discussed ways they could help Dottie. Jane volunteered for all the practical tasks, and Winifred predicted she would complete them the following morning. She was a person who got things done.

It was only after she jumped out at her apartment that Winifred remembered she hadn't asked advice about Arnold Rothstein. *Damn!* The moment hadn't been right. She supposed she could call Jane or Peggy during the week, but her problem seemed insignificant in comparison to Dottie's. Maybe it would just go away on its own.

# Chapter 24
# PEGGY

D ottie slept late, the covers pulled so high that only a mop of dark hair was visible on the pillow. Peggy spent the morning baking a loaf of bread, making lentil soup, and preparing a meat pie for dinner. It wasn't a day for cross-examining Dottie about the whys and wherefores of her suicide attempt; it was a day to feed and cosset her.

When Dottie finally woke, Peggy took her a cup of coffee and a slice of fresh bread and black currant jam, then drew a hot bath for her, tipping in some gardenia-scented bath salts. She took Woodrow Wilson outside to do his business, stepping cautiously on the sidewalk, which was layered with a treacherous sheet of ice. On her return, she put a jaunty Paul Whiteman record on the phonograph, and stoked the burner so it was toasty in her apartment.

"Did your mother do all this for you when you were growing up?" Dottie asked, coming into the living room wearing Peggy's robe, her hair wrapped in a clumsy turban. She gestured around the room, taking in the heat and the cooking aromas.

"Yes, I was lucky."

Her mother hadn't been perfect. She was a little too pushy when it came to marrying off her daughters, and a little too inclined to favor Peggy's younger sister, Rose, who was a more easygoing character, but she was intensely "maternal." Peggy never had any doubt that she was loved.

Dottie curled up on the couch, tucking her feet beneath her. "I wonder if I would be saner if I'd had a mother? Maybe that's why I'm doomed to failure: I drive men away with impossible demands that they prove their love, like a princess in a fairy story challenging them to fight dragons."

"It might help next time if you choose a man who's not already married," Peggy suggested, her tone kind. "Value yourself enough to insist that if they want to be with you, they can *only* be with you."

"Sounds easy when you say it like that." Dottie laughed, with a bitter tone. "You mean you don't approve of my technique of choosing someone unavailable, then hurling myself at him?" She looked pensive. "But Eddie *was* available and I even got him to the altar before he ran off into the sunset."

"Maybe you need time away from the opposite sex. I wish you would get back to writing. Having more work published would boost your self-confidence in a wholesome way, unlike fancy compliments from some fella who wants to get you in the sack." Peggy was speaking personally; the boost she got from writing a chapter of her novel that she was happy with outweighed anything else.

"I had an idea for a story . . ." Dottie said, and told Peggy about the blond woman who had been used and abused by men and was considering suicide. "I might write it one day if I ever get my energy back."

"I hope you do," Peggy said, although privately she thought it might be better for her to write something that lifted her spirits rather than dragging them down again.

DOTTIE STAYED WITH Peggy for a week, while Jane appeased Dottie's landlord, got her oil burner fixed, and cleaned her apartment from top to bottom. Her phone was reconnected after Peggy wrote a check to the telephone company. They went to inspect the place one morning and Dottie suggested perhaps it was time for her to move back.

Peggy was wary of leaving her alone there. It seemed too soon, and she was still frail. She had an appointment at the hospital later that day to have her stitches removed, so Peggy took the afternoon off work to accompany her, hoping to get advice from the medical staff. How could they stop Dottie from trying it again?

They were seen by a junior doctor named Alvan Barach, a smooth-complexioned, very clean-looking man in steel-rimmed glasses who, at a guess, was roughly their age. He cradled Dottie's arms with the utmost gentleness, then told her to look the other way while he used tweezers to ease out the ugly black stitches crisscrossing the length of her wounds.

Peggy winced at the sight of the zigzag scars. Dottie's wrists looked as skinny as a child's.

"These will fade in no time," he said. "I'm more concerned about the internal scars, Mrs. Parker. I wonder if you have considered psychoanalysis?"

"Certainly not," Dottie replied. "I don't want to give away all my best lines and, what's more, have to pay for the privilege."

He laughed politely. "In my studies of analysis I've seen dramatic results in cases not dissimilar to yours." He pulled out the last stitch and put his tweezers down, still holding her wrist in the palm of his hand. "Sometimes depression is caused by repressed emotion from traumatic incidents in childhood—incidents you may not even recall because the memory is stored deep in the unconscious. Analysis can help to unlock the past and thus change entrenched patterns of behavior in the present."

"Isn't it true that anyone who goes to an analyst needs his head examined?" Dottie asked.

Typical of her, Peggy thought: using humor to deflect attention. "Are you a Freudian or a Jungian, Dr. Barach?" she asked. "Is it the parents' fault, or the universe's?"

"A mixture of both." He turned to her. "Freud makes many good points, but he's perhaps overobsessed with sex."

Peggy agreed. "I like the Jungian theory about a collective unconscious influencing whole cultures, but he loses me when it comes to his beliefs on the paranormal."

"You sound as if you have studied the subject." He gave her a quizzical look. "Do you work in the field?"

"I've read a few books," she replied. "It's an interest of mine, but I'm not qualified. I work in the advertising department at Condé Nast."

"Isn't this supposed to be *my* consultation?" Dottie asked. "Or are you going to tell me I sound like a petulant child who seeks attention because she was weaned too early?"

They both laughed. "I think that's Freudian analysis in a nutshell," Peggy agreed.

Dr. Barach tidied his instruments, packed his bag, and shook Dottie's hand. "Let me know if you change your mind about analysis. And try to take better care of yourself," he said. "I hope we won't see you here again."

*Was that it?* Peggy jumped up and followed him out of the room.

"Dr. Barach, can I ask your advice?"

He stopped and said, "Of course," but she saw him glance at a clock down the hallway.

"Is there anything Dottie's friends can do to help? Any signs we should be listening for to prevent a recurrence?"

He regarded her for a moment. "Encourage her to set goals for the future, and keep checking in to ask about her progress," he said. "Don't let her spend too much time alone. If you feel her withdrawing, arrive on the doorstep and force her to connect." He

167

gave a close-lipped smile. "It looks as if you're doing a good job at the moment, Mrs. Leech. The key is keeping it up as the weeks and months go by."

"It's Miss Leech," she told him. "And thank you. Several friends are doing their best for her. We're all very shocked."

"I'm sure you are." He patted her quickly on the arm. "I wish you the best of luck, Miss Leech. And to Mrs. Parker as well." He turned and hurried down the corridor without looking back, as if he were late for something more important.

"SHALL WE GO to the Gonk?" Dottie suggested after they left the hospital. "Mr. Benchley will be there, and Jane is stopping by after work. It's time I started mixing in society again."

Peggy had misgivings, thinking of the backstabbing atmosphere at the Gonk, but she persuaded herself that Dottie needed the company of friends.

The Round Table was busy that afternoon, with regulars crammed elbow to elbow. All conversation ceased and everyone turned to watch as Dottie and Peggy walked in. Bob Benchley leapt to pull up chairs for them.

"To plagiarize Mark Twain," Dottie announced to the room, "rumors of my recent demise were much exaggerated."

"Good to see you, Dottie," Harold said gruffly, and there was a chorus of greetings and good wishes.

"Have the doctors passed you fit for human company?" Bob asked.

"What makes you think you're human, Mr. Benchley?" Dottie sat down beside him and let him fill a glass for her from a hip flask. Peggy was surprised. When did Bob start drinking?

Dottie had a sip of her drink, then continued: "I saw a doctor this afternoon who urged me to try psychoanalysis. I'm sure he could tell at a glance that I'd be a lifelong meal ticket for some lucky head doctor. Hell, not just meals—I'd probably pay for his vacation home in Florida and his children's educations."

"I've always fancied trying analysis," Helen Hayes said. "It must be such fun to lie on a couch and tell your secrets to a mysterious bearded man. They all have beards, don't they?"

"It's not Dottie I'm worried about," Bob said. "Think of the trauma that poor delivery boy from the Swiss Alps restaurant went through. You should be paying for *his* analysis."

"Nah," Dottie said. "He'll be fine. I'll bet he sat and scoffed my raclette while he was waiting for help to arrive."

Peggy watched as Dottie fielded their questions with a kind of hyper-liveliness. She had once seen a group at Neysa's salon snort cocaine, and they were the same: chatty, wide-eyed, and wildly overexuberant. It didn't seem natural, somehow. She was putting on an act.

Jane arrived and squeezed in beside them. "How's the patient?" she whispered to Peggy.

Peggy told her about the stitches coming out and Dottie wanting to go back to her apartment that evening.

"I'll stay with her," Jane said, putting an arm around Dottie. "You've done your bit, Pegs."

Peggy was glad Dottie wouldn't be alone in the apartment where less than two weeks earlier she had attempted to take her own life. She looked vulnerable among the Round Tablers; too many of them didn't care about her, but were simply poised to laugh at her next witticism or to revel in her next melodrama.

When Peggy got home that evening, she was relieved to have her apartment to herself again, but still fearful for Dottie. She thought about what Dr. Barach had said and decided she would telephone every day and rush around at any signs of backsliding. At least some of Dottie's problems had been caused by her feckless attitude toward money, and she wondered whether Eddie might shoulder more of the responsibility. He was still her husband, for goodness' sake.

On the spur of the moment she rang the operator and asked for the number for Edwin Pond Parker in Hartford, Connecticut. The operator didn't have a listing for him, but Peggy remembered once meeting Eddie's parents and knew their names were Harris and Dora. She got the operator to connect her to them.

Dora answered the telephone and told her that Eddie was staying there for now, in his old bedroom; she would just call him.

"It's Peggy," she told him when he came on the line. "I've got bad news, I'm afraid. Dottie's not been coping very well on her own, and she did something rash." She told him the story, quick to assure him that Dottie had recovered, physically at least.

There was silence on the end of the line. Was he angry with her for calling? Did he not care?

"I know some of the worries that overwhelmed her were financial," Peggy continued, "and I wondered whether you could take care of bills for her in the short term? Or perhaps increase her allowance? Just till she is able to work again."

Peggy paused, wondering if she had overstepped the mark, and then she heard a gasping intake of breath, followed by another. The noise was odd, not like normal breathing.

"Oh, my poor Dottie!" His words burst out with a choking sound, and Peggy was astonished to realize he was sobbing. "I should never have left her. This is all my fault."

"No one thinks that," Peggy hastened to assure him. "Everything got on top of her." She told him about the rent, the oil burner, the telephone, but she didn't mention Charlie. He didn't need to know about him.

"Where is she now?" Eddie spoke in a rush. "I'll get the train to Manhattan tomorrow morning. I'll call and see if I can get my old job back."

170

Peggy bit her lip. She wasn't sure if that was the best idea, but he was still Dottie's husband so she supposed she couldn't stop him.

When she came off the line, she called Dottie's apartment to confess what she had done. If Dottie wanted to stop him, she should do it right away, before his plans were too far advanced.

Instead, she seemed quite taken with the idea. "Are you sure he was actually crying? Isn't that sweet?" she said. "Gosh, who would have thought a suicide attempt was the way to rescue a marriage?"

Peggy lay awake in bed that night, mulling it over, not at all sure if she had done the right thing or if she had added a whole new overture to the tragic opera of Dottie's life.

# Chapter 25

# JANE

A couple of days after Eddie's return, Jane telephoned Dottie to ask if all was well.

"Suicide must be an aphrodisiac," Dottie purred. "He's being *very* attentive."

"I'm glad to hear it," Jane said. "But is he drinking as much as before?"

"He only had one whiskey last night. I think he's realized he has to rein it in."

*Long may it last*, Jane hoped. When drinkers cut down, it generally didn't last long in her experience. She decided she would be keeping an eye on him.

"Now that he's back, we should try to include him more in our social set," she said. "He used to complain he didn't feel part of it, but we can welcome him and make a fuss. You want him to stay for good this time, don't you?"

"If he's going to maintain the standard he's set so far, I certainly do," Dottie said.

Jane thought she sounded like a different person. Feeling loved made all the difference. "Am I right in thinking that Eddie likes dancing?"

"He does! We used to dance all the time when we first met. Back in the ragtime years when everything was light and fun." She paused. "Now the dance styles have gotten more complicated, and so have we."

"But we can still have a fun night out. Harold doesn't dance, but I'll find someone to make up a four. Ask Eddie when he's free."

Jane came off the telephone pondering whom she could ask. Her male colleagues were either married or they were dullards she couldn't face spending an evening with. She thought about the Gonk crowd. Maybe Bob Benchley? He was always up for an adventure and he adored Dottie, but she felt badly for his wife that he was hardly ever at home. And then she thought of Alec.

Alec was an enthusiastic dancer. In Jane's opinion he hopped around like a beetle with springs in its feet, but he was always one of the first on the dance floor and last to sit down. It could be part of her campaign to win him over. Dottie had been cross with him for his indiscretion at the Christmas dinner table, and she was cross with him for denouncing her to the Prohis, but maybe it was time to bury the hatchet.

A doubt nagged: might he try to make trouble between Dottie and Eddie? Jane dismissed it. Alec could have a mean tongue but only with those who could take it; he wouldn't harm someone so fragile.

She asked Alec, Dottie asked Eddie, and a date was set.

THEY DECIDED TO go to Connie's Inn, a new nightclub in Harlem run by a bootlegger called Connie Immerman. Tables were clustered around three sides of a long dance floor, and on the stage, Wilbur Sweatman, composer of the hit song "Kansas City Blues," was playing with his band. It was energetic, syncopated jazz, the type that made your feet tap and your head bob. Jane was glad she'd booked a table because it was standing room only at the back.

A waiter asked for their orders and Jane asked if he had any "imported ginger ale," which was the universally recognized code for highballs.

Dottie and Eddie leapt straight onto the floor, launching into a lively foxtrot. Jane had never seen them dance together, and it was like watching entirely different people. Their feet moved in unison, their arms were held elegantly aloft, and Dottie's head tipped back as she called something over the music that made him laugh out loud. Their heights, their posture, their movements—they looked every inch the perfect couple.

"How's work?" she asked Alec. "Any shows you recommend?"

He made a face. "The gems amidst the dross grow ever scarcer. I sit through the direst piffle most nights. It's no wonder I drink."

Jane gave a sympathetic cluck. "Have you seen Winifred's new play, *Will Shakespeare*?"

"I almost lost the *will* to live," he said, with a shudder. "Pun intended. Casting Otto Kruger was a blatant attempt to bring the out-of-town housewives flocking to coo at his floppy blond locks, thereby ruining it for the rest of us."

"What did you think of Winifred?" Jane had been mesmerized by her performance. Sometimes when you saw a friend onstage, it just looked like them playacting, but Winifred transformed into someone else entirely.

"She's in a league of her own," Alec agreed. "I'd love to see her in a more challenging role. She could play any part she turned her hand to. But on a personal level, I find her very reserved—as if she has secrets. Don't you agree?"

"She doesn't shout about her personal life, like some people I know."

Thinking about it, Jane realized she knew very little about Winifred, despite their bridge evenings. She was beautiful and talented, but she didn't flaunt either quality. She answered direct questions but rarely volunteered information. Jane didn't believe she had se-

174

crets, though; she wasn't sly or devious, just self-contained. Unlike most of the rest of their crowd, she didn't try to be the center of attention.

Dottie and Eddie waltzed over, urging them to join the dancing.

"In a minute!" Jane called. "We're waiting for the drinks."

"It won't last," Alec said, leaning sideways to talk in her ear. "Those two. They're too different. She's Little Nell crossed with Lady Macbeth, while he's boring old Bob Cratchit."

"You're such a cynic," Jane chided with a smile. "I think Eddie's drinking was the cause of their problems before. He needed time to recover from the war. But he's livelier tonight than I've ever seen him."

"Lively as a sloth. I think she's the one leading."

Their drinks arrived, and Alec paid the waiter. Jane took a sip. It was good-quality gin, praise the lord.

"You're mixing your metaphors tonight, Mr. Woollcott," she said. "You claim Dottie is dominant and ruthless and at the same time a helpless creature from Victorian melodrama. Surely both can't be true." She clinked glasses with him. "Chin chin!"

"And yet our Dottie is precisely that contradiction, don't you think? There's the cutting wit and then there's the pathetic side." He adopted a falsetto voice and impersonated her: "I didn't have enough money to buy food. What else could I do?"

Jane slapped his knee. "Alec, you're evil. You totally cross the line sometimes."

"And who leaves the front door open when they're committing suicide?" Alec continued. "Interesting, don't you think?"

Jane had thought the same thing: that Dottie had subconsciously wanted to be found and rescued, but it didn't make her despair any less real. There was no point having that conversation with Alec in his current mood. "Come on," she nudged him. "Let's dance. I love this band."

The floor was crowded but folks stepped back as Alec started his bouncing beetle routine. He had no self-consciousness, and Jane admired that. He liked music and enjoyed moving his body in time to it. They used to have a great time dancing together in Paris in 1919. Alec was once a good friend of hers, and she wished she could see this side of him more often.

Some couples were tangoing, others were doing the Black Bottom or the foxtrot, and there was general anarchy on the dance floor, with frequent collisions. Jane had trained as a dancer before she worked at the *New York Times*, and was good at picking up new steps. She loved dancing. It put her in a mellow, relaxed mood, so Alec's next words caught her totally off guard.

"You and Harold will never last the course either," he said. "No man wants to come home to a virago who scolds and harangues him from dawn till dusk."

Jane broke away from his hold. He had a glint of meanness in his eyes that she recognized. Harold had once described him as an overfed Persian cat with its claws extended, ready to pounce. But she had done nothing to deserve this attack. "What on earth are you talking about?"

"I hear you set a five-dollar limit on Harold's spending at the poker club, as if you were his mother and he was still in short pants." He tipped his head to one side, challenging her.

"That's just prudent," she replied. "We both agreed on it because we're saving for the magazine."

Alec stopped dancing, so she did too. "Oh, the magazine, yes. Whose idea is it exactly? Because Harold says you are taking over and changing the entire concept so it's no longer the one he wanted to produce."

Jane was annoyed. "That's simply not true, and I don't believe Harold said that. Stop stirring up trouble, Alec."

"He told me he had no idea when he married you that it was

going to mean a lecture on feminism at every meal, and that he doesn't even get any peace in bed unless he pretends to be asleep." He turned, walked back to their table, and picked up his drink.

Jane knew he was simply in a petulant mood, but she couldn't stop herself responding. She followed him to the table. "What about you, Alec?" she countered. "When are you going to find a woman? Everyone knows you moon over Neysa, so why don't you put your cards on the table and see if she reciprocates? Are you scared of what she might say?" She held his gaze, challenging him.

He didn't blink as he replied: "There might be news on that front, sooner than you think."

Jane laughed, harshly. "I can't wait. You'll make a lovely couple." She had a gulp of her drink, then turned to survey the dance floor, reluctant to sit down at the table with Alec in case he continued his rant.

Dottie and Eddie danced over and Jane asked if she could cut in.

"Sure!" Eddie said, holding out his arm. Dottie grabbed Alec's arm and pulled him to his feet, just as a new number struck up.

It was fun dancing with Eddie. He was light on his feet and good at maneuvering through the crowd. They danced up close to the band, cheering as Wilbur performed his signature trick of playing three clarinets at once, while the other five band members accompanied him on their saxophones.

"I'm glad you're back," she told him. "You and Dottie are great together."

"I think we are too," he said.

On a whim, Jane decided to invite them to a friend's house for a vacation. "We're going to Herbert Swope's mansion in Manhasset Bay in June and he told Harold and me to bring our liveliest friends. It would be great if you and Dottie could come."

"Why I'd love to—and I'm sure she would too." He seemed pleased. "I'll take the time off work."

After dancing with Eddie, Jane danced a couple of numbers with Dottie. They messed around, miming taking a phone call and putting on lipstick as they quick-stepped across the floor. Dottie pulled up the beads around her neck like a hangman's noose and stuck her tongue out as if being throttled, without once losing the beat.

For the rest of the evening, Jane made sure she wasn't left alone with Alec. His words had stung but she didn't want to get into a fight with him. They took separate taxis back. He was going to Neysa's so he shared Dottie and Eddie's cab, while Jane headed for 412.

Harold was reading at his desk, and she rushed in and threw her arms around him from behind, kissing his dear shaggy head. He smelled of coffee and printer's ink.

"Did you have a good time?" he asked, taking off his glasses.

"It was OK," she said. "Segregated. Black musicians and white customers, but that's par for the course. How about you? Good book?"

"Not really." He rubbed his eyes. "Did Alec come back with you?"

"No, he was in a tricky mood," she replied. "He said a few things about you that bothered me."

"Like what?"

"He said you feel as though I'm taking over your magazine idea and making it my own, and that you are bored with me talking about feminism." She watched his face, to see if there was a flicker of recognition.

Instead he threw his head back and laughed, then pulled her onto his lap. "You know what Alec's like. He's a snake who has to spit out venom from time to time or he'd choke on it. Don't pay any mind."

Jane was reassured. Thinking about it rationally, she couldn't imagine Harold saying any of these things to Alec. That's not the kind of relationship they had. Alec had simply put his own poisonous thoughts into Harold's mouth in order to make trouble. She should have known better than to let him get under her skin.

# Chapter 26
# DOTTIE

D ottie watched Eddie reading the financial pages of his newspaper over breakfast, frowning slightly at one of the stories. His dark hair was still ruffled from sleep, and he was wearing a maroon dressing gown she'd given him two Christmases ago. His toast was spread with his favorite brand of orange marmalade, which she'd bought from the store. She was making an effort to keep food in the apartment, even to cook occasionally. It was nice looking after him.

"Would you like some eggs?" she asked. Peggy had taught her how to scramble or boil eggs; she'd only known how to fry them before.

Eddie laughed. "You *have* changed," he said. "I'm fine with toast, thanks." He turned back to his paper.

"What stocks are doing well?" she asked.

"More or less everything," he said. "It's what they call a bull market. The economy is booming."

"I guess paper will always be stationery," she said.

Eddie looked up, puzzled, and then light dawned in his eyes as he got the joke.

"Pencils will probably lose a few points, but I predict knives will be up sharply," she said, then paused to see if Eddie would join the game. Charlie would have been throwing in his own suggestions by now, but Eddie just sniggered at hers.

"The market for raisins has probably dried up," she continued. "And balloon prices are inflated. While toilet paper has touched the bottom. Aren't I a good wife giving you all this market advice?"

"Very useful. I'll be sure to tell the guys in the office," he said, then returned to his paper.

Dottie got up to clear the dishes. *I don't know him*, she thought with a sudden stab of insight. The man sitting opposite felt like a stranger. They were both being polite and kind to each other but she would have to learn about him from scratch, and he her.

When they were dating, he'd been gallant and attentive, surprising her with little gifts or theater tickets or bookings at restaurants he knew she liked. That's the man she'd thought she was getting when she married him. Then there had been the bad-tempered drinker who came back from France and picked fault with everything. That Eddie had been cruel, and inside she had a little nugget of worry that he could turn cruel again. She knew he was capable of it.

Why had he come back? Did he love her, or was it a guilty conscience? Maybe he couldn't face being labeled as the guy who abandoned his wife and drove her to suicide.

"What did your mother say about you moving back in with me?" she called. "Was she hoping we would divorce so you could marry another more palatable girl, preferably a non-Jewish one?" Dora Parker came from a line of Anglican clergymen and deplored Dottie's Jewish blood on her father's side.

"She's over the moon," Eddie said. "She wants us to visit. She was very upset by the separation. I know she didn't tell any of her friends. I heard her on the telephone saying, 'Oh, it must be so

181

hard for Eddie and Dorothy having to live apart while he's working in Connecticut.'"

Dottie imagined Dora was trying to save face. She would hate the disgrace of a divorce in the family. "Can we leave it awhile before we visit?" she asked. "I'm enjoying having you to myself for now. It's like we're finding each other again. Do you know what I mean?"

"Of course," he said, but he looked slightly baffled. She sensed he wasn't analyzing every last utterance the way she was. He'd come back, and that was that.

She should stop questioning things. She felt a million times more stable with him here. It wasn't just that he made sure bills were paid and he fixed things that broke; he also anchored her emotionally. The sense she'd had of teetering on the edge of a precipice was less acute, although she worried that it wouldn't take much for her to topple back into blackness.

If Eddie's kisses didn't set her on fire the way Charlie's had, if his bedroom skills weren't so imaginative, these were areas they could work on. Charlie was a hard act to follow, but she mustn't let him spoil her for other men. Their relationship had never been real.

NEYSA KNOCKED ON Dottie's door one afternoon with a proposal.

"I'd love to paint you," she said. "Would you sit for me?" .

"Me?" Dottie was astonished. "I'm not one of your willowy cover girls. My legs are so short I barely reach the counter in stores and have to stand on tiptoe to get my change."

"It's for my own collection, not a magazine cover. I'd love to see if I can capture the essence of Dottie. Will you let me try? It would just take a couple of hours a day. . . ."

Dottie agreed. Was it vanity? Or curiosity? Or an excuse to get away from her typewriter?

Peggy had taken to ringing her every afternoon and she always asked how the writing was going. Dottie was embarrassed when she had to report she had written twenty-seven words all morning and scored out thirty. Now at least she could blame Neysa for her lack of productivity.

Neysa looked through her wardrobe and chose a rather girlish navy frock with a white Peter Pan collar and elbow-length sleeves. She didn't want Dottie to wear much makeup, and asked her to sit on a chair and look as though she was deep in thought. That wasn't hard; the tough bit would be staying still longer than five minutes.

At her first sitting, she was surprised when Jack Baragwanath, the miner, wandered out of the bedroom and kissed Neysa on the lips. "Shall I make coffee for you girls?" he asked, heading for the kitchen.

"Just me," Neysa said. "Dottie's not allowed to move."

Dottie raised her eyebrows in question, but Neysa smiled, sphinx-like. Once he'd made the coffee, Jack sat watching them for a while.

"Found any gold recently?" Dottie asked.

"I certainly have," Jack said, gazing at Neysa, his voice throaty and masculine. "I'm just back from Brazil, where there are some very lucrative mines in the Amazon basin."

Dottie asked him about life in the Amazon, and he chatted pleasantly enough, but she sensed he would rather have been alone with Neysa. It was clear she'd cast her famous spell over him.

When he left for the office, Dottie said: "If you threw a stick for him in Central Park, he'd rush to pick it up in his mouth and bring it back for you to throw again, tail wagging."

Neysa laughed. "Don't be so sure. Jack's the philandering type. I'm not the only girl he's seeing."

"You don't mind that?" Dottie remembered the crippling jealousy she'd felt when she came upon Charlie with another girl at the Fifty-Fifty Club.

"Not at all." Neysa sounded carefree. "The minute you start trying to cage a man is the minute they start eyeing the door."

"Is that true? Isn't marriage a cage of sorts?"

"It needn't be," Neysa said. "It depends on your attitude. Some folk have open marriages: Heywood Broun and Ruth Hale, for example."

"They *say* they have an open marriage," Dottie replied. "But I wonder if that's just because they want to appear modern and liberal-minded. I've never seen either of them with anyone else."

"No, me neither," Neysa agreed.

Dottie couldn't imagine how an open marriage would work. Did they tell each other about their conquests? Make love in hotel rooms on stolen afternoons? Or even have threesomes in the marital bed? Her heart tilted at the thought. Thank god Eddie was too prudish to suggest such a thing.

She was far too insecure to allow him to have other lovers. And look what happened when she slept with someone else! She fell madly love with Charlie and now she couldn't get him out of her head, no matter how hard she tried. She had to stop comparing Eddie and Charlie or she'd end up in a straitjacket.

She had asked Eddie if there had been another girl in Hartford while they were separated and he'd said no. She waited for him to ask her the same question, but he didn't seem curious. She decided not to volunteer the information about Charlie in case it risked upsetting their cozy marital harmony.

If only she were confident in her own skin, like Neysa. Neysa would never expect a man to rescue her, because she didn't need rescuing. She never chased men, but let them chase her. Maybe that's why they all fell for her, like dominos toppling in a row.

Maybe that's why she always had the upper hand in her relationships, while Dottie never did.

NEYSA UNVEILED HER portrait of Dottie at a party in her salon the week after Easter. There was a chorus of cheers followed by appreciative murmurs. It was a stunning likeness, all agreed.

"It's clever the way it captures your intelligence as well as your fragility," Jane said. "What do you think, Eddie?"

He glanced around to check Neysa wasn't in earshot before he answered. "She looks like a fifteen-year-old girl rather than a married woman. But she has captured the expression well. I know that look of yours, Dottie."

"It brings out your Jewish side," Bob commented. "Perhaps you should learn Yiddish and buy a sheitel."

"I have an announcement to make," Neysa said, raising her voice. "My salon will be closed in May and June because I'm sailing to Europe for a vacation, but I'll be back in July and the bathtub gin still will be in operation once more."

Dottie looked around to see Jack watching with a guarded smile. "Are you going with her?" she asked.

He ran his fingers through his sleek hair. "No, I'm heading back to the Amazon. Neysa's staying with some old friends in Paris, so it will be one long party with people I don't know in a language I don't speak."

He didn't seem at all put out, Dottie thought. If her lover had been leaving for a two-month vacation, she'd have been beside herself with doubt and suspicion. Jack knew that Neysa attracted male admirers wherever she went. Why wasn't he worried about that?

A week later, Dottie was sitting next to Alec at the Gonk. "I expect you'll miss Neysa when she's away," she said.

*"Au contraire,"* Alec confided. "I'm going to France with her."

"You're kidding!" Dottie exclaimed. It was a riddle she couldn't figure out. "Did she invite you?"

"She doesn't know yet, so don't tell her, but I've booked a passage on the same ship. We'll have five days alone together on the crossing and I plan to surprise her with a marriage proposal."

He was so delighted with his plan that Dottie didn't have the heart to tell him she didn't think it had a cat in hell's chance of success. Did he know she was having an affair with Jack? He must. Neysa always had a lover on the scene.

"What if she doesn't accept?" she asked.

"I will marshal my arguments and use the time to persuade her. Don't you think a proposal at sea is romantic?" His eyes were shining behind his round specs, and his cheeks glowed. Dottie couldn't bear to disillusion him.

"Very romantic," she said, "but don't go overboard."

She mulled it over, and when she bumped into Jane in the bathroom she couldn't resist confiding in her.

"It's doomed to fail," Jane agreed, "but he would hate us if we told him that. I hope Neysa will let him down gently."

"He must have an inflated opinion of himself if he imagines a goddess like Neysa, who could have her pick of the men in New York, would choose him. Do you think he ever looks in a mirror?"

"Dottie!" Jane chided. "If you can't say something nice . . ."

". . . say something funny," Dottie finished the sentence for her.


ON THE EVENING the *Olympia* set sail, Dottie got home to find a note had been pushed under her apartment door. She recognized Neysa's copperplate handwriting.

*"Guess what?"* she wrote.

*"Jack and I slipped off and got married yesterday in Peekskill, with only his startled parents as witnesses. Before you come to the conclu-*

186

sion that your friend has taken leave of her senses, I should add it's not going to be a conventional marriage—as shown by the fact that I'm spending our honeymoon in Paris without him! Will write from there with more details, but wanted you to be the first to know. In haste, Neysa."

Dottie stared at the sheet of paper. No wonder Jack hadn't been worried about her leaving; he knew he would already have his ring on her finger. But whoever heard of anyone spending their honeymoon on a separate continent from their new spouse?

She sat down to telephone Jane.

"Oh hell." Jane sighed. "I wonder how Alec will take the news?"

"Like a dose of salts administered simultaneously with an enema," Dottie suggested.

"I do feel sorry for him," Jane said. "It's rotten luck to be in love with someone you can't have. I wonder if he'll write to us about it?"

"I doubt it somehow," Dottie said. "He'll be licking his wounds in a Parisian bordello, once he gives up trying to persuade Neysa to get an annulment."

"You don't think he'd do anything silly, do you?"

Dottie didn't understand what she meant at first, then it dawned on her. "You mean like my blunt razor trick? No, Alec likes himself *far* too much for that."

THERE WAS NO word from Alec right through May, and the whole saga slipped Dottie's mind. The weather in Manhattan was glorious: sunny with a fresh breeze. Birds were trilling and flowers were blooming like crazy, as if trying to outdo each other with their splendor. She and Eddie went for walks in Central Park, and rowed around the lake like a courting couple. Her work was going well. She finished a play she had started, about a husband who has an affair with his next-door neighbor, and felt rather pleased with it.

In June they caught the train with Jane and Harold to Herbert Swope's house on Manhasset Bay, Long Island. Swope was editor of the *New York World* and a member of the Thanatopsis poker club with Harold, but he clearly came from old money, Dottie thought, when she got the first glimpse of his sprawling seafront mansion. There were dozens of windows blinking along the façade, looking out over lush gardens that led to a strip of white beach fringed by sparkling water.

Herbert greeted them at the entrance, shaking hands and saying he was honored and delighted they could come.

"Do you hand out maps to guests?" Dottie asked, gazing around and noticing a swimming pool and some tennis courts off to the side. "Or provide tour guides?"

"I'll arrange both if you like," he promised. "The staff have been instructed to fetch whatever you want, so just ask if you are hungry, thirsty, or need anything from a tennis racket to a cocktail."

"I don't know much about being a millionaire," Dottie told him, "but I have a feeling I'd be darling at it."

They were shown upstairs to a huge bedroom, with bay windows on two sides, both with sea views. The bed was a four-poster with hangings, as if transported directly from an English stately home.

"I'm going swimming," Jane called from the room next door. "You coming, Dottie?"

She pulled on her navy striped bathing suit and grabbed a towel, then raced Jane down through the house to the water's edge. It was bracing, but once she'd gotten over the initial shock of immersion, the effect was refreshing after the stuffiness of the train. Dottie wasn't a strong swimmer so she stayed close to the shore, floating on her back and gazing up at the cloudless sky.

Almost exactly a year earlier, Eddie had left her. Now, here they were, together in paradise. What was she to make of that?

She decided not to think about it while she was there. Maybe her problem was that she thought too much. Perhaps she should just relax, take a deep breath, and indulge.

IT DIDN'T TAKE long to slow down to the rhythm of the house: lazy mornings, lunch on the terrace, swimming in the ocean, or tennis, croquet, or card games, then cocktails before dinner. There was a party most nights, with guests driving up from New York for the evening. Dottie was much in demand, and she rolled out witticisms to entertain the crowd; it seemed the least she could do in exchange for the lavish hospitality. She could reuse some of her best lines in this new company, where only Jane, Harold, and Eddie might have heard them before.

They'd been there a week when a car drew up during luncheon and out stepped Alec, wearing a straw Panama hat and clutching a suitcase.

"You're back!" Jane waved. "Come and join us!"

He sat down, accepted a drink, and talked about Paris: the shows he had seen, the restaurants he had dined in, the people he'd met. He seemed quite unruffled. Nothing was mentioned about Neysa and her unexpected marriage. Dottie glanced at Jane and decided she wouldn't be the one to bring it up.

Later that afternoon, Dottie and Eddie were sitting on a swing seat looking out over the bay when Alec sauntered across to join them, pulling up a lawn chair.

"You two look very settled," he said.

"I ad-*ore* it here," Dottie said. "I want to persuade Herbert to adopt me. Do you think he will?"

"Why didn't you tell me about Jack and Neysa?" he demanded abruptly.

Eddie looked puzzled; Dottie hadn't told him the story.

189

"I had no idea Neysa was planning to marry him," she said, feeling her cheeks redden. "It was as much a surprise to me as it must have been to you."

Alec leaned toward her. "I received a telegram from Harold on the ship, warning me not to propose because Neysa was already married—but by then I had done the deed and humiliated myself. It's the timing of it that interests me. I've thought about it a lot. You see, Harold told me that he'd heard about it from Jane, who'd heard about it from you before we even set sail." His tone was crisp. He was clearly livid. "What I don't understand is why *you* didn't tell me first? You knew I planned to propose. You knew Neysa had married Jack. I thought you were a friend of mine, but clearly I was mistaken because you were happy to let me make a fool of myself. Perhaps you were all laughing behind my back."

"Steady on there, Alec," Eddie intervened. "I'm sure it's a misunderstanding."

Dottie took a deep breath and tried to explain the exact sequence of events, but Alec was incandescent and looking for someone to blame.

"I confided in you and you betrayed me," he accused her. "It's not the action of a friend. Since you had that abortion, you've been selfish as a fox."

Dottie whirled around to look at Eddie, whose eyes widened with shock. This could ruin everything.

"What abortion?" Eddie asked, frowning.

"Hadn't she told you?" Alec looked taken aback, then shrugged. "In that case, I'd better leave you two to talk." He rose and padded away across the lawn.

Dottie gulped hard before she took Eddie's hand and opened her mouth to explain.

# Chapter 27
# WINIFRED

Winifred was relieved when *Will Shakespeare* finished its run. Seven shows a week for thirty weeks was more than enough. She couldn't imagine how vaudeville actors toured the same show around the country, year after year, the only changes being a new dressing room in a different town in front of a fresh audience.

Another reason she was glad to finish the run was to escape the attentions of Arnold Rothstein. She had begun sneaking out the side door of the theater after shows to avoid the hoodlums waiting in idling cars at the stage door, but still the boxes of roses turned up. She hated the fragrance that lingered in her dressing room, and started doling them out to other members of the cast and crew, just to get rid of them.

She had planned to take a long summer vacation but when her alma mater, the American Academy of Dramatic Arts, invited her to teach a class to some drama students in June, she agreed. It seemed an interesting challenge, but as the first class grew closer she got nervous. What did she know that she could pass on to students only seven or eight years younger than she was? They would see through her in a flash.

She spent hours preparing her classes but still felt like an impostor when she stood in front of the class for the first time, clutching a list of notes. It was scarier than any Broadway premiere. To her astonishment, once she started talking they seemed to be in awe of her, scribbling down her words as if they were gospel.

As her confidence grew, she particularly enjoyed teaching movement classes, showing the students how to stand onstage, how to use space, and ways of working with props. The types of movement could vary depending on the period in which the play was set: they would walk, gesture, and greet one another differently in a Shakespearean play than in a modern one, for example. Acting was a craft, she explained, through which they pursued authenticity and truth. The students asked intelligent questions, and she felt moved that they were so fresh and green in their hopes and ambitions, with little sense of the harsh reality of the profession they were trying to enter.

Finally, toward the middle of July, the course ended and she caught a train to Rhode Island to share an apartment with some actress friends. They spent their days swimming, playing tennis, sailing, and drinking cocktails with suave young men at yacht clubs. Winifred hadn't felt so carefree in a long while. She let her skin tan, and put on a few pounds with all the lobster and crab dinners.

The vacation was interrupted by a telegram from Max asking if she could return to the city the Friday before Labor Day because an influential playwright was in town and wanted to meet her. Who could it be? she wondered. Eugene O'Neill? Paul Eliot Green? She knew the main New York–based playwrights already, so it couldn't be one of them. Her friends suggested names, but Max would give her no clues.

"This had better be good," she said, when she called him on her return to the sweltering heat of New York.

"Come to the Plaza Hotel at twelve noon," Max said. "Dress to impress."

Winifred had a lucky suit she kept for auditions, a black silk Directoire one by Lucile, with a matching tricorn hat. It was elegant but not overly feminine or sexy. It was a suit that meant business.

As the maître d' showed her to the table, the playwright had his back to her and all she could make out was that he was elderly, with longish white hair and a bushy beard, and he was wearing a tweed jacket, which was crazy for New York in late August. Definitely not a local! Max waved her across.

"Forgive me for not standing," the playwright said, in an accent that was polite and English, with a musicality to it. "I have terrible trouble with my knees."

Winifred gasped, recognizing him right away. It was George Bernard Shaw, in her opinion the world's greatest living playwright. She hadn't dared to hope it could be him.

"It's an immense honor, Mr. Shaw," she said, extending her hand, and bending toward him in a movement that almost became a curtsey. "Max didn't tell me who I was meeting. I'm overwhelmed."

"Please sit." He gestured to a chair. "And call me Bernard." He gazed at her face for a moment, his expression kind and jovial. "You certainly have the Irish look," he told her. "Max explained your heritage. I'm a Dubliner myself."

Winifred could hear the Irish lilt now. "Dublin South, I'm guessing," she said, because that was the smart bit, and he gave a quick smile. "*My* folks hail from the peat bogs of Tipperary."

He asked which area and it transpired they had relatives in the same part of the county. They could even be related, he speculated, way back in the distant past. She couldn't wait to tell her mother, who would swoon with pride.

"I'm not sure if you're familiar with my plays," he began, and Winifred snorted.

"Well, of course I am, Mr. Shaw, like every other actress the world over."

"If you could choose a role in any of them," he asked, "which would you choose?"

She didn't have to think for long. "I'd love to play Major Barbara." She adored the jolly moral character of the Salvation Army worker who spoke from the heart.

"Not Cleopatra?" he asked, raising an eyebrow. "You're beautiful enough."

"Why, thank you, kind sir." She made an actressy face.

"Have you heard of Joan of Arc?" he asked. "The fifteenth-century French girl who was recently canonized."

"I read about her in the papers," Winifred said, racking her brain to remember any details of the story.

"I've written a play about her and I'm looking for an actress to open in it on Broadway. That's why I invited you here today."

Winifred listened, spellbound, as he explained his vision for Joan, the teenage girl convinced she was seeing visions and hearing voices from God. The voices told her the French could overthrow English rule, and inspired her to lead an uprising before she was captured, tortured, then burned at the stake at the age of nineteen.

Winifred felt a tingling in her bones. She knew she could play the role. She had been schooled by nuns who believed with every fiber of their being that they were brides of Christ; she could channel that passionate conviction in her performance. When he asked if she would like to read for it, she said yes without a moment's hesitation.

JANE WAS HOSTING a bridge club at 412 the weekend after Labor Day and Winifred looked forward to telling the women her news. When the door opened, she gasped to see that Jane had had her brown hair cut into the shortest of short bobs.

"The hairdresser kept asking 'Are you sure?'" Jane said. "But it was practical and cool for the summer."

"It suits you," Winifred said. "I love it!" Privately, she thought she looked like a boy and an inch or so longer would have been more flattering, but she would never say so.

Dottie was already sitting in the communal dining room and started telling Winifred about Alec dropping her in the mire by blurting out about the abortion in front of Eddie.

"I hadn't even told Eddie I'd had a lover while he was away, so that came as somewhat of a surprise," she said. "He asked lots of questions—what does Charlie look like, what does he do for a living—and I could tell he wanted to ask that question all men dwell on—'Is his bigger than mine?' But fortunately, he stopped short, because the answer would have been yes."

"What did he say about the abortion?" Winifred asked. She hoped Eddie wouldn't blame her for her part in it. She'd been the one who'd told Dottie about Lenox Hill and persuaded her to go ahead when she got cold feet the morning of the operation. She still felt guilty about it.

"He was hopping mad at me for being such an idiot as to get caught out." Her eyes darkened for a moment and she took a quick sip of gin. "But I suppose he thinks I made the right decision, because if I'd kept Charlie's baby we couldn't have given our marriage another chance. I'll never know what goes on beneath the surface with Eddie, but I suspect he doesn't feel things as deeply as I do. If our situations were reversed and he had knocked up some chippy while we were separated, I would never let him hear the end of it. And if I met said chippy in the flesh, I wouldn't be able to resist a spot of verbal assassination."

"Has Eddie met Charlie yet?" Winifred asked.

"No, but he's back in town so they're bound to bump into each other. I hope it will be a civilized handshake rather than pistols on the lawn."

"Good grief, why does your life always lurch from drama to

crisis?" Jane asked. "You should take a leaf out of the book of the little old lady from Dubuque and lead an uneventful existence."

"Who's she?" Peggy inquired, with furrowed brow.

"She's hypothetical," Jane said. "Harold and I were dreaming up marketing slogans for our magazine, and we came up with one that goes: 'Not for the little old lady from Dubuque.' Do you like it?"

"You may get a large postbag of complaints from ladies in Dubuque," Dottie said. "But I love it."

"Is Dubuque a real place?" Winifred asked.

"It's in Iowa," Peggy told her. "There's a big Irish community, and German too. It's a Mississippi port town so it has a thriving economy."

"Probably thriving on bootlegging these days," Jane murmured. "How was your summer, Peggy?"

"Uneventful," she shrugged. "I spent a couple of weeks with the family, but most of the time I was in the city, trying not to get heatstroke. Did you hear the thermometer topped a hundred and the asphalt was melting? You had to walk quickly or your heels sunk in."

"You should have taken more vacation," Jane said. "Everyone does. Harold and I spent most of the summer in Long Island."

She looked very tan and healthy, Winifred thought. She suspected Jane was the type who spent vacations swimming, hiking, and water-skiing, rather than lazing around on the beach. She never seemed to sit still for long.

"I enjoyed having the city to myself and plenty of time to think," Peggy said. "There were no lines, not even for Luigi's ice cream stall in Central Park."

"Sounds kind of lonely," Dottie said. "Too much thinking is my downfall. I spend more time wondering what Eddie and Charlie are thinking than they do actually thinking."

"But you're done with Charlie, aren't you?" Jane said, narrowing her eyes. "You're not holding out for a reunion?"

"I know, I know." Dottie took another sip of her drink. "I was pleased to have him come, but I'm not sorry to see him go."

*She's lying*, Winifred thought. *She'd leap into bed with Charlie in a split second, given half a chance.*

"How was your summer, Winifred?" Peggy turned to her. "You look tan and happy."

"The tan is from Rhode Island, and the happiness is from a call with my agent this afternoon." She smiled and paused for effect. "I've just been cast as the lead in the world premiere of a new George Bernard Shaw play opening at the Garrick in December."

It felt amazing to say the words out loud. When she got the news, she had telephoned her mother first, and had to hold the receiver away from her ear so she wasn't deafened by the shrieks of excitement. Next she had telephoned a couple of actress friends, who had been delighted for her. She knew deep down they had a twinge of "Why not me?" envy, but they hid it well. Winifred still couldn't take it in. Her exhilaration was mixed with nerves: Was she good enough? Could she pull it off?

Jane was the first to react. "That's wonderful! It's going to take you into a whole new league."

"Congratulations." Peggy leapt up to hug her. "What's the play about?"

"Joan of Arc. It's called *Saint Joan*. I'll have to buy some rejuvenating face creams because she's a teenager. . . ."

"So you'll be burned at the stake onstage," Dottie commented, "and then burned at the stake metaphorically in the reviews if it's a flop."

"I know. I'm terrified about taking such a high-profile role, but flattered that Mr. Shaw trusts me." She got a flutter in her stomach just thinking about it.

"You've met him?" Peggy shrieked. "What's he like?"

Winifred described their meeting, their bonding over Irish ancestors, and the audition piece she'd read, then Max's triumphant telephone call. "The best thing about it was that I didn't have to sit on his lap, lift my skirt, or let him run his hands over my figure to 'check how the costume would fit.'" She put on a male voice to indicate a director speaking that last line. "Mr. Shaw was a gentleman and he thinks I'm right for the role, so I'll do my best not to let him down."

"You won't let him down," Jane assured her. "This will make your name."

Winifred laughed. "I hope it won't make my name mud. . . . Come on, let's play bridge."

She was uncomfortable being the center of attention. It was strange for an actress, but she'd always been reserved. Jane dealt the cards and Winifred fanned hers out, thinking about what they had said.

It was true the play was likely to bring her a whole new level of fame. There would be press interest and crowds milling outside. Might Arnold Rothstein renew his pursuit? She hoped he had found himself another woman over the summer and that little problem would be off her plate. She'd had stage-door creeps chasing her before, and she knew how to deal with them, but he was a different ball game entirely.

# Chapter 28
# PEGGY

Since Dottie's suicide attempt, Peggy had taken to telephoning her every day, usually around two in the afternoon. They chatted about what they had done the previous evening, they gossiped about mutual acquaintances in the Condé Nast empire, whom Dottie knew from her time at *Vanity Fair*, and most days they talked about their writing.

Dottie was producing stories and poems for a range of magazines, and her play was set to go into rehearsals. It was reassuring that she was working so hard. Peggy had set herself a deadline of finishing her novel by her thirtieth birthday, on November seventh. She was starting to wrap up each character's story, and was enjoying the sense of neatness as it neared completion and plot strands fell into place. She confided to Dottie that she found it harder to write about her character, Vergie, finding happiness in love than it had been to describe all her failed relationships.

"Happy ever after is a myth," Dottie said. "Happy till the bottle is finished, perhaps. Happy till his secretary leans over revealing she has far better cleavage than his wife."

"I need a happy ending," Peggy said. "But what does it say about me that I find it easier to describe a bad kisser than a good one?"

Dottie's answer surprised her: "Charlie's back in town and he's an excellent kisser. You should try him out—purely for the sake of research, of course."

"Don't be daft—you would rip my throat out if I kissed Charlie!" Peggy retorted. "Have you seen him yet?"

"He came to Neysa's a couple of days ago. I introduced him to Eddie and they chatted politely, then moved apart. I'd flattered myself there might be fireworks, but neither seemed especially interested in the other."

"Did it upset you to see him?"

Dottie paused for a long time before she answered. "I'll get used to it. He's leasing an apartment with Bob Benchley so they can be married bachelors together. Can you imagine the action those mattresses will see?"

Peggy shook her head. Why did their wives put up with it? It was beyond her.

Dottie's thirtieth birthday had been on August twenty-second, while she was at the beach with Eddie. They had stayed at the Branford hotel where they'd met seven years earlier.

"It's a landmark birthday," Peggy said, "and I think you should make this the year you get a book deal. You have more than enough poems for a collection. Why not offer them to a publisher? It would be easy money, since they're already written."

"Ah, but where are they?"

Peggy wasn't surprised when Dottie admitted that, living up to her reputation as a scatterbrain, she hadn't kept copies of her work. She'd typed each poem and sent it to the editor in question without making a carbon; sometimes she'd kept the printed version from the magazine, but more often not.

"You can remember the publications you've written for, presumably?" Peggy asked. "Call the editors and request copies. It'll keep the office juniors busy. I'll round up any Condé Nast ones for you."

Every lunch hour for the next week, Peggy tramped down to

the basement archive and copied out Dottie's poems by hand, thankful that they didn't tend to be longer than eight lines each. She delivered them to Dottie, who promised she was gathering the rest, like a sheepdog trying its hardest to corral a wayward flock.

PEGGY FINISHED HER novel two weeks before her birthday, typing the words *THE END* with a sense of trepidation. She spent the weekend reading it through and decided it was the best she could make it.

Her mother wanted to host a party for her birthday, but she turned it down. To be unmarried at the age of thirty meant you were a failure in the marriage market and was not a cause for celebration as far as she was concerned. Peggy didn't care to have all the family friends turning up with sympathetic expressions to cross-examine her about her spinsterhood while quaffing her father's liquor. Her sister, Rose, had gotten married to the fishing bore, and their wedding had been painful enough, with old biddies asking when it would be Peggy's turn and offering to introduce her to their spotty grandsons. Her mother told her she scared men by being too intellectual, but she didn't want to snare a husband by playing dumb. How long would you have to keep it up? What if you forgot and quoted Euclid over breakfast?

Finishing the novel gave her a sense of achievement, as if her twenties hadn't been entirely wasted. She felt anxious about showing it to anyone, though. What if they said she was devoid of talent and should give up all hope of being published? Edna Ferber was often at the Gonk so she could have given it to her and asked an opinion—but Edna was notoriously forthright and wouldn't spare her feelings.

"For god's sake," Dottie chided, "just send it to Tommy Smith at Boni & Liveright. He's got an eye for bestsellers and he won't soft-soap you either."

Peggy was apprehensive. It was one of New York's biggest publishing houses. "What if he rejects it?"

"Approach him with courage, not with awe. If he doesn't have the good sense to fall in love with your book, try someone else," Dottie replied. "I promise I'll do it with my poems if you venture out first to test the water."

On the morning of her birthday, Peggy dressed smartly, wearing a new dove-gray turban-style hat and matching cinched-waist suit that Winifred had urged her to buy. The shade was flattering, warming her skin tone and somehow—she wasn't sure how—making her blue-green eyes stand out.

She wrapped her manuscript in brown paper and tied it with string, then walked across Midtown to the Boni & Liveright office in an old brownstone on West Forty-Eighth Street, feeling simultaneously excited and terrified. Glass doors led into a lobby where three intimidating women sat behind a long desk.

"I brought this for Tommy Smith," Peggy told one of them, laying it on the desk. "There's a letter inside with my details."

She waited for the woman to ask more but she just said, "Thank you, I'll see he gets it."

That was it. Peggy hesitated, then turned and left, her hands trembling and palms sweaty. It felt as if her entire future happiness rested on a stranger's opinion.

On the way home she stopped with a jolt of panic. Should she have made a copy of the manuscript? What if they lost it? They must get dozens delivered to the office every day and if her letter became separated, they would never know it was hers. She couldn't possibly re-create the whole thing from scratch. Why hadn't she used a carbon? What an idiot!

Fretting about that at least stopped her from fretting about whether Tommy Smith would like it. Dottie had told her it could take a couple of months before you heard back from busy editors, so she tried to relax and start making plans for Thanksgiving and then Christmas.

The telephone rang when she was at the office the following afternoon, and an unfamiliar voice said, "Miss Leech? It's Alvan Barach."

The name rang a bell. Was he one of the advertisers? She shuffled through her memory banks.

"I wanted to ask how your friend, Mrs. Parker, is getting along."

In a flash, she remembered that he was the doctor who had removed Dottie's stitches. How odd he should call.

"She's doing well," Peggy said. "Her husband came back and that seems to have made her more stable. She's working too, which always helps her mood."

"I'm very glad. I was thinking of her recently when I read a paper on suicidal ideation. She mentioned that she'd been reading a lot about suicide in the weeks leading up to her attempt, but I didn't get a chance to ask if there is a family history. Do you happen to know?"

"Not of suicide, no," Peggy told him. "But she lost many family members at a young age."

"Adverse life events are certainly a risk factor," he said. "The author of the paper is developing a scale for estimating suicidal intentions in an individual, and assessing through a simple set of questions whether they are acute or chronic cases. It may help in early identification of risk."

"I would be fascinated to read that," Peggy said. "None of us had any idea Dottie was considering it. She didn't seem the type at all."

"Perhaps there isn't a type *per se*," he replied, "but unhappy childhood experiences plus a susceptibility to anxiety can predispose. . . . Tell you what, shall I lend you a copy of the paper?"

"I'd like that," she said, glancing at the clock. "I'm afraid I can't talk any longer because I'm at work."

If her boss wandered out of his office and realized she was on a personal call, he would raise his eyebrows and tap his watch. The gesture never failed to irritate her, since she often heard him making long jovial calls that were clearly not work-related.

"Perhaps we might have dinner sometime?" Dr. Barach asked. "This Friday perhaps?"

Peggy blushed. "I'd like that."

They arranged to meet outside her office at five-thirty on Friday. She put the phone down feeling stunned. Was it a date? No, of course not. It was just so that he could lend her the paper. But why dinner? How very odd.

PEGGY WASN'T SURE whether a doctor would drink or not, but right away Alvan said he knew a speakeasy just a couple of blocks down Madison Avenue. He gave the password through a grille in the basement door. It was a classy place with dark paneled wood, chandeliers, and discreet booths. You could imagine Upper East Side ladies meeting there for martinis after shopping.

"Have you tried a sidecar?" Alvan asked. "It's one of my favorites: Cognac, Cointreau, and lemon juice in a sugar-rimmed glass."

"It sounds rather alcoholic . . . ," Peggy said.

"Try one," he insisted. "I'm a doctor, you're safe with me."

She laughed. "Do you often use that line?"

"Never fails," he said with a grin.

She asked about his interest in psychoanalysis and he explained that it was a sideline. His main specialization was pulmonary medicine, in which he had undertaken postgraduate studies at Harvard. He was fascinated by analysis, though, and was currently seeing a couple of patients in a consulting room he shared with a colleague.

"You have a calm, authoritative voice," Peggy said. "I suppose that helps patients to have faith in you."

He was a good listener and she found herself telling him about finishing her novel and waiting to hear from an editor whether it was any good or not. He said he was sure it was, and promised he would be first in line to buy a copy.

After two sidecars, she felt the world sway when she stood up. Alvan took her arm and whisked her to a little restaurant around the block, where he ordered steak for both of them, and two glasses of champagne so they could toast her birthday, albeit belatedly. She wasn't a fan of either steak or champagne, but felt she shouldn't complain since he was paying.

At the end of the evening he walked her home and thanked her for a very enjoyable time. She paused, wondering if he would try to kiss her, but he made no attempt, and nor did he ask if he might see her again. Were his intentions strictly honorable? He had lent her the psychiatric paper, so she supposed he would have to see her again if he wanted it back. Peggy very much hoped he would.

She confided in Dottie on the phone next day, saying, "I would flirt with him but I don't have a clue how to go about it."

"Flirting is the gentle art of making a man think he's a swell guy," Dottie replied. "Most of them are off to a flying start."

Peggy tried to imagine how she might do that, but guessed if she tried, she would be so self-conscious she'd sound more of a fool than a flirt.

Alvan called again the following Monday to ask if she was free on Wednesday. "Apologies for the short notice," he said. "I have to wait and hear which shifts I'm working before I can make plans."

Yet again they had an entertaining evening, but Peggy searched in vain for a sign of his intentions. Did he find her conversation stimulating? There were no soulful glances or fingers brushing her knee. She didn't know what to make of it.

The following week he called and asked if he might cook dinner for her at his apartment near the hospital. "I'm rather proud of my culinary skills," he said. "My grandmother taught me when I was a boy."

Peggy was curious to see his apartment, and to test his cooking. It was the most personal invitation yet. Surely men didn't ask a girl to their home if they didn't have designs on them? And a man who could cook was a rarity.

He made brisket with herbs and vegetables, in a sauce that was thick and slightly sweet. There was a bottle of Bordeaux to drink, and some honeyed pastries for dessert.

"I'm impressed," she said, licking her lips. "My compliments to your grandmother."

"She would like you," he said. "Perhaps I'll introduce you sometime."

Before Peggy could speculate on what that might imply, he rose abruptly from the table, pulled her to her feet, and began to kiss her. There was no warning, and Peggy worried that she had a shred of beef between her teeth. Would he notice?

Still kissing her, he guided her through a door to his bedroom and began unfastening the buttons at the back of her dress. He obviously saw her as "that kind of girl." Peggy didn't try to stop him. Her heart was beating fast, her legs felt like liquid, and she was shaking with nerves, but she wanted to do this. She knew she would regret it if she refused.

"It's my first time," she murmured, her cheeks burning.

"Don't worry—I'll be gentle," he said, as he slipped off her dress and kissed her bare shoulder, before removing her undergarments and lowering her onto the bed.

She closed her eyes and succumbed to the sensations as he made love to her with ardor, touching her with expert fingers and kissing her in places she had never imagined being kissed. When he pushed inside, Peggy hardly felt any pain, just a sensation of deep fulfillment. He clearly knew what he was doing. As they lay side by side afterward, she decided it had been a very good idea to choose a doctor for her first experience.

"Can we do this again, please?" she asked.

"Of course." He grinned, and kissed the tip of her nose. "I'll bring you a diaphragm next time so we don't have any accidents."

And that was it: Peggy was no longer a virgin. As she hurried home the next morning to change before work, she felt deliciously naughty. *This* was what it was all about. *This* was why people got their hearts broken. At last she had joined the club.

She and Alvan slid into a routine of seeing each other two or three times a week, depending on his shifts, and the sex was so addictive that they usually leapt into bed first and had dinner later. It all happened so fast that she sometimes felt giddy, but she was having the time of her life. She felt blood coursing through her veins and she walked around the city with new energy and aware-ness of her body, as if she had never been so fully alive. There was no sense of shame that she was having sex out of wedlock; instead, she couldn't imagine why on earth she had waited so long.

Was she falling in love? She couldn't tell yet, but whatever was happening, she sure as hell didn't want it to stop.

# Chapter 29

# JANE

Jane opened an envelope that arrived for her at 412, and found a ticket to the dress rehearsal of *Saint Joan*.

"I've invited Dottie and Peggy too," Winifred wrote in a note. "I'm so nervous, I need moral support, and it would mean the world to me if you are able to come."

It seemed odd that Winifred was nervous when she had so much talent, but Jane thought her modesty was one of her many likable qualities.

She took the afternoon off work to go to the Garrick, arriving just before the rehearsal started and sneaking along the row to sit beside Dottie.

In the opening scene, Winifred played a young peasant girl convinced she hears the voices of the saints speaking in her head. She tells a French noble that his hens will resume laying if he assists her in lifting the siege of Orléans by the English, and she claims she will put the French Dauphin back on the throne. Winifred's performance was chilling; she completely transformed into young Joan. Watching her, you were convinced she was hearing those voices. There was no breast-beating declamation; it was a performance of subtlety and conviction.

Jane was mesmerized throughout as Joan's position grew increasingly perilous. The scenes of her torture and then burning at the stake were harrowing. Jane shivered with emotion during the final parts.

As they waited for Winifred in the foyer afterward, even Dottie couldn't fault her performance, saying, "She's so convincing, Catholics across the land will write asking her to send them her nail clippings as holy relics."

Winifred floated out from backstage and seemed overwhelmed by their congratulations. "Are you sure?" she repeated. "You definitely think I'm not too bad?"

Jane squeezed her hand. "You're phenomenal."

"God, I hope so," she said. "I feel as if this is my swan song. I'm never going to get such a great role again. I'm twenty-five years old and it's all downhill for actresses after that."

"Really?" Dottie said. "You don't look a day over forty."

Jane poked her in the ribs. "I'm sure directors will be falling over themselves to hire you after such a tour de force." She found it charming that Winifred was so lacking in ego. Most other actresses of her acquaintance had it in spades.

As they walked to a speakeasy farther along West Thirty-Fifth Street, Jane wanted to ask Winifred more about how she had prepared for the role, but Dottie changed the subject.

"Peggy has some scandalous news," she announced, with a grin. "Are you going to spill the beans, or will I?"

Peggy blushed to the roots of her hair. "It's nothing much . . . just that, to my astonishment, I appear to have a beau. Can you believe it?"

"That's exciting!" Jane said. "Who is he? Do we know him?"

"Here's the odd thing," Peggy replied. "He's the doctor who treated Dottie back in January. Dr. Alvan Barach. He called and asked me for dinner."

"What's he like?" Winifred asked.

"He's smart and easy on the eye," Dottie replied, "but he's clearly

Jewish so I can't figure out what's he doing with a WASP like our Peggy."

Peggy grinned. "I have absolutely no idea either, but I'm not complaining."

She was glowing, Jane thought. She hoped Dr. Barach would prove worthy of her.

IT WAS FIVE-THIRTY and the speakeasy was crowded with office workers having a quick sharpener. The four women clustered in a spot by the bar and ordered drinks, having to shout to make themselves heard. Christmas was only a few weeks away, and Jane asked Dottie what she was buying for Eddie.

"I asked what he wanted for Christmas and he said 'a divorce'— but it turns out we can't afford one."

"Is that a joke?" Jane asked. She couldn't tell from Dottie's deadpan delivery.

"Yeah, but not a very funny one."

"Are things not OK at home?"

Dottie paused, before replying: "I'm sure there's a law of physics that says that when you glue together a broken clock, then wind it up again, the pendulum will eventually come back to rest at the lowest point. It seems that's also true of broken marriages. But we're still slapping on more glue."

Jane was worried, remembering what had happened the last time Eddie left. Dottie needed him. They had to try and make him stick around this time.

"All marriages go through tough patches. Harold and I have weeks when we scarcely see each other and we feel like strangers when we bump into each other in bed."

"His gambling losses must be a sore point," Dottie said. "I heard he's the biggest sucker at the Thanatopsis table."

210

"Harold? No, you're mistaken. We have a deal that he walks away if he's down by five dollars."

Dottie gave her a shrewd look. "I heard about that deal. I told him he'd never stick to it, but he bet me ten dollars he would."

Jane tensed. He wouldn't lie to her, would he? It was their dream to start the magazine. She'd been hoping next year might be the year they'd have enough for the launch. Dottie must have heard wrong.

WHEN JANE GOT back to 412, Harold wasn't home. She glanced at the clutter on his desk: spectacles with broken arms and missing lenses, dried-up ink bottles, bits of string he had carefully removed from packages, abandoned notebooks, and umpteen scraps of paper on which he had jotted down ideas for articles and jokes. Tidiness had never been his strong suit. She was looking for statements from the bank account his salary was paid into, just to set her mind at rest. She opened the desk drawers one by one but most were stuffed with old magazines he'd decided to keep, for reasons best known to himself.

After searching the desk, she looked in his bedside table, where a pile of books he was currently reading tottered precariously. Next she searched his bureau drawers, and then his wardrobe. The statements had to be somewhere.

Finally she found them in an old briefcase at the back of the wardrobe. She pulled them out and flicked to the most recent one, and her heart skipped a beat. The balance was only a few hundred dollars when it should have been at least thirty thousand. Her stomach twisted. Where was that money? Had he moved it elsewhere and not told her?

Mounting anger fueled her as she began a forensic search through his suit pockets. Several slips of paper emerged, detailing what appeared to be debts: FPA $175; Fleischmann $350; Alec $402.

She was boiling with rage by the time Harold arrived home to find the statements and slips laid out on the bed, but she controlled herself as she spoke. "Can you explain these, please? I don't understand."

Harold sat down hard, burying his face in his hands, and she felt the twisting in her stomach get worse.

"Tell me," she urged.

"I've been an idiot," he said, unable to look at her. "I made the classic mistake of chasing my losses because I couldn't face telling you. I'm sorry."

"How much?" she demanded. "There's thirty thousand dollars missing from your account. Please tell me you haven't lost it all."

He looked as though he might be about to cry. "I'm not sure. Alec is the treasurer so we could ask him."

Jane swallowed hard, thinking of all the sacrifices she had made for their magazine fund: the clothes she had denied herself, the rushing home to cook instead of eating out, walking instead of taking taxis. Why the hell had she bothered?

"What do you plan to do about it?" she asked, her tone icy. "And don't tell me you can win it all back, because we both know that's nonsense."

"No, you're right. I mustn't gamble anymore. I've stopped already."

"Are there any debts outstanding?"

He hesitated. "I think there might be. I'm sorry, mushkins. I guess we'll have to postpone the magazine until I've gotten on top of this."

"Absolutely not!" Jane said. "I'll find a way around this. Tomorrow morning you ask Alec for a list of all unpaid debts and we will work out a repayment schedule. I'll keep your bankbook so you can't even access your salary from now on. And somehow, I will raise the magazine money myself." She was thinking fast, running through options.

"But how? You can't pluck it from thin air."

Jane looked at him, all crumpled and boyish and consumed with guilt, and she felt a twinge of sympathy. "I guess we'll have to bring in private investors. It means we won't own the magazine outright, but it will still be ours in practice."

Everyone had weaknesses and this was his; the pity was it had turned out to be a bigger flaw than she had suspected. This was a body blow, but they would get around it.

"Are you coming to bed now?" he asked, his voice pleading.

Jane knew she was too wound up to sleep. "No, I'm going out for a walk," she said. "I'll see you later."

As soon as she was outside, she lit a cigarette and inhaled to the bottom of her lungs. Putting the pack in her coat pocket she turned right and pounded all the way down West Forty-Seventh to the Hudson, walking off her rage and disappointment, and ignoring the sidewalk drunks who called out to her. It was dark, with a cold wind whipping up from the river. As soon as her cigarette was finished, she lit another from the butt.

A man approached and before she could stop him he plucked the cigarette from her mouth. "Filthy habit for a woman," he said, flicking it into the gutter.

"Goddamn you to hell, you son of a bitch," she yelled. "Take your goddamn morals and get out of my goddamn way."

He leapt back as if she had hit him, his shocked reaction almost making her laugh. It was good to blow off steam. She felt better afterward.

When she got back to 412, Alec's light was on upstairs. She toyed with the idea of marching up to give him a piece of her mind. Why hadn't he tried to stop Harold? As treasurer, he could have pulled the plug at any time. Or at least he could have warned her there was a problem. He knew they were saving to launch a magazine. He had a vested interest in it since Harold had offered him a column, but it was almost as if he wanted them to fail. Could that be true?

She shook herself. All was not lost. Tomorrow was another day. She would go to her own bank and see what could be done. She would manage all their money from now on and she'd make this magazine happen, come hell or high water.

# Chapter 30
# DOTTIE

When Dottie and Eddie talked about the future, he still insisted he wanted to raise his children in Connecticut.

"I know what happens to wives in the suburbs," she objected. "Bob Benchley never sees his from one week to the next. Let me tell you now: I ain't that kinda girl." She had never understood how Bob's wife, Gertrude, put up with his absence, but guessed her life was invested in the children.

"The schools are better, there are fields where they can run around in fresh air, and the neighbors would be other couples in the same situation as us," Eddie argued. "You'll need help when we have children, and Mother would be nearby."

Dottie shuddered at the prospect of his mother interfering. "There are schools in Manhattan, and there's Central Park. Here is where our friends are. They'll help."

But Eddie didn't have friends. There was no one he would keep in touch with if he left the city.

"We all have to grow up, Dottie," he said. "You're thirty years old. It's time to settle down and stop leading the life of a flapper. Frankly, it starts to look desperate at your age."

"Growing old is inevitable, but I believe growing up is optional," she replied, fully aware they were never going to agree on that.

Once he'd gotten over the initial shock of hearing she'd had an abortion, he didn't want to discuss it any further. "It was appropriate in the circumstances," he said when she pushed him for an opinion, and that word haunted her. Killing a child was "appropriate"? What kind of person could say that? He'd reacted with more emotion when they found Onan dead in his cage one morning.

Dottie often thought of little Jacob. She knew she would always consider him her first child. In the future, if she had more, she would look at them and wonder if that's what Jacob would have been like. She yearned for children, but was it the right thing to do when their marriage felt so strained?

Since Eddie had come back, they hadn't used contraceptive measures. Dottie thought she would let Nature decide: if she got pregnant with Eddie's child, that was a sign she should stay with him; if she didn't, well. . . . And so far, she hadn't.

He wasn't a bad husband, now that he'd cut back on the booze. Why couldn't she just make do? Lots of women put up with worse.

It was getting harder, though. There were long silences at the dinner table because Dottie couldn't think of a single thing to say that would interest him. She stored up titbits she'd read in newspapers, tried to plan conversations in advance, but her tactics failed because he didn't bat the conversational ball back at her.

Their "second honeymoon" in Branford had been dull. Their home life was tedious. She almost wished Eddie would meet another woman and have an affair, because at least it would make him more interesting.

Sometimes Dottie wondered if her marriage would have worked if only she hadn't had the affair with Charlie. The four months with him had been so joyous, they had spoiled her for anyone else. How could she accept second best? How could she love a husband who was ordinary, and—let's face it—boring?

There was no explosive confrontation. Instead, the end of their marriage crept up on them gradually. Jack and Neysa invited Dottie to spend the month of January at a house they had rented in Miami Beach, but Eddie said he didn't want to join them, not even for a week.

"You go," he said. "I'll stay at Mother's."

"Can we spend Christmas together?" Dottie asked. "We don't have to stay with your parents, do we?" She pulled a face like a motion-picture actress confronted by a monster.

"Let's have Christmas here, just the two of us," he said, "then you go to Florida and have a wonderful time."

He didn't say it, but they both knew that he wouldn't be there when she got back.

MIAMI BEACH WAS paradise. It was wonderful to feel warm sun easing the knots in her neck and shoulders, to walk barefoot along the beach with waves lapping her toes. She thought back to the previous January, when she had tried to take her own life, and decided the grim, wintry weather had been partly to blame. Maybe she should come to Florida every January; somewhere warm, at least.

Jack was often tied up with business, so she had plenty of time to chat with Neysa. They were trying for a baby, Neysa told her, and planning to buy a house in upstate New York. It was the life Dottie couldn't imagine with Eddie, but Neysa seemed content; she'd gotten what she wanted. Dottie could see no signs of the "open marriage" she had talked about; if Jack had other women on the go, he was discreet about it.

When she thought about her return to New York, Dottie couldn't face living alone in the Fifty-Seventh Street apartment. It was a dark place, noisy with the clatter of trains going past on the El, and it evoked too many bad memories. But where would she go? Jack came up with a solution over dinner one evening.

"Forgive me for saying, but I've noticed you're not a fan of housework," he said with a grin.

"What a waste of time it is!" Dottie said. "You sweep the floors, wash the dishes, and six months later you have to do it all again."

They laughed. "Why not live in a serviced apartment," Jack suggested, "and let someone else do it for you? I believe they have some at the Gonk. You could call for room service when you wanted food, and wander downstairs when you wanted company."

"Isn't that expensive?" Neysa asked.

"The manager is sweet on Dottie," Jack said. "I bet he'd cut her a deal."

"Are you sure they'd have me?" Dottie asked. "What about Woodrow Wilson?"

"It's worth asking. Just don't mention he's not house-trained," Neysa advised.

AS SOON AS they got back to Manhattan, Dottie went to see Frank Case and asked about serviced apartments. By chance, one was available and he took Dottie upstairs for a look.

The door opened into a tiny hallway with a coat stand and mirror, then she walked through into a bright high-ceilinged living room. There was a couch and two armchairs with beige velvet upholstery, beige drapes, a desk and chair, a blue rug—everything about the décor was bland and inoffensive. The matchbox-sized bedroom had a bed, a dressing table, and a wardrobe—just enough and not too much. There was a large tub in the bathroom, and the tiniest kitchen nestled in an alcove, with a refrigerator where she could make ice for drinks. Who needed more?

Frank told her the rate he normally charged for the apartment and she said she could only pay him half.

"Alright," he said, with a shrug. "Let's give it a try."

Dottie didn't mention Woodrow Wilson. For the first week or so after moving in, she smuggled him upstairs under her coat, and gave him cookies to shush him if he started barking. There were a few unfortunate accidents and the couch would never be the same again, but Frank pretended not to notice and, all in all, the arrangement worked well. Every afternoon, Dottie wandered downstairs to see who was at the Round Table, and when she came back, her bed had been made and everything cleaned, as if by magic cleaning fairies.

Bob Benchley and Charlie MacArthur were at the Gonk most days. They had become best buddies and secretly Dottie felt aggrieved at Bob's disloyalty. Wouldn't a true friend have given Charlie a wide berth after the way he'd treated her? Still, she went downstairs to fraternize with them when the words weren't flowing, trying to ignore the fresh-faced young girls who tagged along.

"This is our new office," Bob told her. "Have you met our secretaries? This is Delphine and that's Clara."

Dottie still felt a tug on her heart when she saw Charlie with another girl. She wasn't immune to him yet, although she hoped to be one day soon. On the beach in Florida, she had noticed a tall, white-feathered bird wading through the shallows looking for fish. Jack told her it was a great egret, and Dottie immediately named it Charlie MacArthur. That's how she thought of him now. One day she would tell him she'd named a bird after him, but not quite yet. Not while it still hurt.

Peggy called every day and Dottie told her about the girls Bob and Charlie hung around with, most of them numbskulls. "Their pooled intellect wouldn't fill a teaspoon," she said. "I didn't realize Charlie was a player. Neysa warned me and I didn't listen."

"You live and learn," Peggy said. "Next time maybe you'll spot the signs and choose differently."

Dottie sighed: "I doubt it. I'm the contrary type. When men are sweet and unmarried and keen on me, I go off them in a trice; if they're cruel and unavailable, I fall headlong in love. Maybe your Alvan could cure me after years of intensive psychoanalysis, but otherwise I guess I'm doomed to keep repeating the same mistakes."

ONE AFTERNOON WHEN Dottie wandered down to the Round Table, she found the *New York World* columnist F. P. Adams talking to a thin, attractive woman with tawny hair wearing a purple velvet gown and a scarf in a burnt orange and moss green Art Deco pattern. The colors shouldn't have matched but somehow they did. She had an unusual accent that slid from English to upper-class East Coast, and she gesticulated as she spoke. Curiosity got the better of Dottie and she wandered over.

"This is Elinor Wylie, the poet," Frank introduced her. "Elinor, this is the renowned Mrs. Parker. You two have a lot in common."

"I'm sure we do," Dottie said, shaking her hand. She decided not to tell Elinor that her interview in *Smart Set* had been one of the triggers that made her slash her wrists.

Elinor was gazing at her so intently it was almost rude, and still hadn't let go of her hand. "When FP invited me to the Gonk, I told him it was one of my dearest wishes to be introduced to you, and here we are. I'm quite giddy to meet you, my dear."

"In that case, it's fortunate you're sitting down," Dottie said. "May I join you?"

"Of course. Oh, I'm so glad you dropped by." Elinor was still staring with her intense witch-hazel eyes. She had an ethereal movie-star beauty, like Mary Pickford, although Dottie guessed she must be older than her—in her mid to late thirties perhaps.

"I live here," Dottie said. "So strictly speaking I dropped down, not by. I have a copy of *Nets to Catch the Wind* upstairs. It's one of my favorite anthologies."

"Oh, you darling girl. I'll sign it for you, shall I? Please let me. And when will we be seeing an anthology of your poems? I'll be first in line, I swear. I'm such a fan!"

"I'm working on it," Dottie told her. "But I can't decide on an order for my poems. Yours have a narrative logic, but mine jump around like jelly beans."

Elinor laughed. "I can't decide if you mean the candy or the promiscuous young men of this town, whom I've heard called by that name."

"Precisely," Dottie agreed, thinking of Bob and Charlie. The term could have been coined for them.

They talked about the arrangement of poetry anthologies they admired, and then they shared their writing methods, from the first glint of an idea, through the torment of searching for each perfect word, to the finished work. Dottie was encouraged to hear that Elinor also found writing torturous.

"I know my poems are just rhyming ditties, but I find them excruciating," she confided.

"They're not ditties!" Elinor insisted. "As a fellow poet, I can see the craft in them, although you make it seem effortless. Your lines balance perfectly and your word choices are exquisite, while, unlike me, you can also make readers laugh."

"But my themes are so limited. You run the gamut of human experience."

"I have oodles of material to draw on," Elinor said, waving an arm dismissively, "from all the tragedies in my life."

"I've read about them," Dottie said, thinking of the article. "I've had a few myself, with parents dying young, a marriage breakup, and a bruised heart, but you certainly take the cake."

Elinor clasped Dottie's hand between hers, her face so close that Dottie could see face powder clogging the pores on the sides of her nose. "I strongly believe that everything happens for a reason. Tragedy makes us more spiritual, giving us sustenance for our poetry and feeding our souls. All of us have a purpose here in this life. Most people never find theirs before they pass to the next world, but you and I are women who think deeply and uncover profound truths about human nature." She leaned back. "We need to spend more time together and get to know each other. May we do that?"

Dottie blinked at her intensity. The moment felt charged with importance, like a turning point from which there would be no return.

"Of course," she said. "We certainly must."

# Chapter 31
# WINIFRED

Winifred arrived at the theater early on opening night, dressed smartly in her black Directoire suit, because there were press photographs to be taken outside. She posed arm in arm with George Bernard Shaw, and was astonished to realize he was more nervous than she was. He jumped at each whoosh of the magnesium flares, as if he'd never been photographed before. Backstage he couldn't sit still, but wandered from room to room, muttering to himself and stroking his beard obsessively.

Winifred got into costume and sat quietly in her dressing room until she was called to the stage. She knew the lines backward, she knew all her cues, but she needed stillness to steady her nerves. *I can do this*, she said in her head. *I've done it before.* But she hadn't starred in the Broadway premiere of a George Bernard Shaw play before. It was the biggest moment of her career.

Her stomach was in knots as she waited in the wings to make her entrance, but as soon as she stepped out onto the boards in her bare feet, the blue scarf tied around her head and the apron around her waist, it was as if her cells knew how to be. Her voice became girlish, her gestures simple and pious. She could hear nothing except the voices of the saints telling her how to save her country.

She wasn't one of those actresses who spotted friends sitting in the stalls; she lived completely in character.

The time flew past in a blur till curtain call. Winifred had no idea if it had gone well or not, but the audience was on their feet, applauding. She glanced around and saw that George Bernard Shaw was beaming in the wings.

There was an opening night party in the foyer, where she circulated, accepting congratulations and making the usual small talk. She had invited her mother and her aunt, and they stood together whispering about the glamorous folk in their swanky clothes.

"You're my Joan," George Bernard Shaw said, kissing Winifred's hand. "I knew it from our first meeting. You breathed life into the creature of my imagination, and I'm in your debt. This is a small token to express my gratitude."

He handed her a box tied in blue ribbon, and when she opened it she found a pretty stone sculpture of a girl in peasant costume, her head tilted back to look at the skies.

"It's beautiful," Winifred said, feeling very touched. She would treasure it always.

She gestured for her mother to come and be introduced, but Mrs. Lenihan was so overawed in his presence she could barely stutter her own name, and it was left to Winifred to keep the conversation going.

Just after midnight the first newspaper arrived, the all-important *New York Times*. She held her breath as she scanned it. John Corbin liked the play but reserved the majority of his praise for Winifred: "A truly ground-breaking performance," he wrote. It seemed it was a hit!

THE FOLLOWING DAY, there were half a dozen photographers outside the theater when Winifred arrived, and some journalists were waiting to interview her. She agreed to chat with them, one at a time, expecting to talk about Mr. Shaw's drama, but was taken by surprise at the personal nature of their questions. Did she have a regular beau, what did she do in her spare time, favorite recipes, favorite designers, her beauty regimen, all about her family background. . . . As she answered, Winifred realized her cherished privacy was about to be invaded and life would never be quite the same again.

By the end of the first week the crowds at the stage door had grown unmanageable, and the stage manager had to set up a barricade that Winifred could stand behind to sign autographs. Some fans stood in the freezing cold and snow for over an hour just to save a place at the front of the crowd. She found it alarming to be the object of such idolization. Look what had happened to poor Joan when she became famous overnight! She had to give up her shifts at Lord & Taylor and stop frequenting speakeasies, after being spotted by fans in both locations.

Letters began to flood in from women asking who styled her hair and which perfume she wore, from men who wanted to ask her for dinner or propose marriage, and from a handful of religious nuts too, as Dottie had predicted. Flower deliveries were commonplace, but when a distinctive box of red roses arrived before the show one evening with a note tied on top, Winifred felt goose bumps on her arms.

She tore open the envelope and her eyes skimmed the note: "Arnold Rothstein invites you for dinner at Lindy's, 11 p.m. this evening. His car will collect you from the stage door at 10.45." It was an order, not a request.

She ran down the corridor to the stage door and asked the doorman if anyone had waited for a reply, but he shook his head. What should she do? Stand him up? Or go to Lindy's? She couldn't decide which was more terrifying.

As she took a bow at the end of that evening's performance, she glanced out into the auditorium, wondering if Arnold Rothstein might be there. Was he watching her right now? She shivered.

A young assistant stage manager brought a jug of fresh water to her dressing room as she took off her makeup, and she had an idea. "I don't suppose you could deliver a note for me?" she asked, with her most winning smile. "I'd be ever so grateful."

The boy actually blushed as he agreed. It baffled Winifred that people reacted to her so differently now, all because of one role. She wrote a note, apologizing to Mr. Rothstein, saying she had a previous engagement and life was terribly hectic at the moment, as she was sure he would understand. She instructed the boy to go outside at ten forty-five and give it to the driver of a car waiting at the stage door. Before then, she sneaked out a side entrance with the director and a couple of fellow actors, and scurried to an Italian restaurant around the corner.

Winifred requested a table in an alcove at the back and they sat down and ordered, but she couldn't touch her food. Every time the door opened, she jumped, thinking it might be Rothstein. The actors treated it as a grand joke, but she was alarmed by the tone of his note. It was more insistent than before.

"I'll make sure you get home safely," the director promised. "You can share my taxi and I'll get the driver to wait till you're inside."

Maybe she was being silly, Winifred thought. Past experience had made her wary, but there was no reason to think Rothstein meant her any harm. Rich men liked to date actresses, the more famous the better, but they couldn't force them.

Her apartment wasn't far. She glanced out the back window of the taxi but there was no sign of anyone following them. She took out her keys, ran to the heavy wooden street door, and unlocked it, before turning to wave to the director and slipping into the hallway. The door slammed shut and she turned to flick the switch for the lights. Only one bulb was placed on each floor, so it wasn't bright but there was just enough light to negotiate the stairs.

She screamed when she saw the bulky shape of a man in a dark suit standing by the foot of the stairs, blocking her way.

"Good evening, Miss Lenihan," he said, tipping his hat. She noticed he had a Philadelphia accent. "Mr. Rothstein was upset you couldn't dine with him tonight and he wants you to join him for a cocktail. I've got a car outside."

She couldn't make out his features, which were shaded by his hat, but she saw he was wearing two-tone shoes, cream with brown tips, and a brown suit.

"I'm afraid it's too late for me," she said, trying to disguise the tremor in her voice. "I'm tired and I've got a show tomorrow." She wondered if she could slip back out into the street and run, but dismissed the idea. He was bound to run faster than her, and he probably had a gun.

"It's not a question," he said. "My orders are to take you to him now." He stepped toward her and Winifred backed against the door, feeling behind her for the handle.

The neighbors in her walk-up kept themselves to themselves. There were three elderly couples, one family, and a tenant on the first floor whom she had never met. If she screamed at the top of her voice, would anyone come?

As he got close Winifred turned to open the door but he was too fast for her, and he grabbed her arm. "Come, now," he urged. "It's just a friendly drink."

Winifred screamed instinctively and fought to shake his hand off. "Leave me alone! Help!"

He clapped his free hand over her mouth, pushing her back against the door, and Winifred panicked. She lashed out with her

227

fists and fought with all her strength to push him away, but he was solid and immovable as a statue. She tried kneeing him in the groin, but he dodged out of the way.

"Calm down, will ya?" he said. "I don't wanna hurt you. What's the big deal?"

Her brain was working overtime, trying to figure out how she could escape. If he had a gun, could she grab it? What other weapon might she be able to use? Then she remembered her hat. She reached up to remove the long pearl hat pin holding it in place and lashed out at his face, feeling the pin make contact.

He yelped in pain and let go of her to touch his wounded cheek. "Why d'ya do that? You could have taken my eye out."

She tried to shove past him toward the stairs but he blocked her with his shoulder, pinning her against the wall so she couldn't raise the hand holding the hat pin. In desperation, she jabbed the pin hard at the only bit of his body she could reach, which was the groin area. It sank all the way in, right up to the hilt, and his high-pitched guttural shriek made it clear she had hurt him. He bent double.

Winifred seized the moment to sprint down the hall and leap up the stairs two at a time, her heart pounding so hard it felt like it might burst from her chest. She fumbled with the keys to her door, dropping them once, before she finally got them in the lock and hurled herself inside. She'd had extra bolts fitted and she pulled them across, then dragged a chair beneath the door handle. Next, she fetched her sharpest knife from the kitchen drawer and waited for him to pound on the door, trembling so violently she could hardly think.

Downstairs she heard the street door slam. Had he gone to get backup? She ran to the window and saw a bent figure limping toward a car. He got in and drove away. She considered calling the cops, but everyone knew the gangsters paid them off. Besides, he was the one who was injured. Perhaps he could charge her with assault.

She couldn't call her mother. The only person she could think of who might be able to help was Peggy, the smartest person she knew.

PEGGY SOUNDED GROGGY but she woke up quickly as Winifred stuttered out her story.

"You need to call Jane," she said. "She interviewed Rothstein for the *New York Times*. She'll think of something."

"But he's probably on his way back here already," Winifred wailed. "They could smash my door down at any moment."

"Hail a taxi and come to mine," Peggy suggested, but Winifred said she couldn't leave in case they were waiting outside.

There was a pause. "OK, I'll come and pick you up. Watch from the window and when my taxi arrives I'll get the driver to beep the horn twice, then I'll step out and wave. Run down and we'll be watching for you. Can you manage that?"

Winifred was petrified by the thought of setting foot outside her own door, but the alternative was waiting to see if a gang of hoodlums arrived to overpower and kidnap her. "I'll manage," she said.

"Pack what you need in an overnight bag. I'll be there in ten minutes," Peggy promised.

They were the longest ten minutes of Winifred's life. She stood with her coat wrapped around her, bag in hand, and watched the street outside, wondering who would come first: Peggy or the gangsters. When a taxi pulled up and beeped its horn, then she saw Peggy step outside, she sprang into action.

She was trembling as she undid the bolts, and stepped out onto the landing. She stopped and listened hard but there was no sound in the hallway. She flicked the lights on, locked her door, and ran down at breakneck speed, flinging the street door open and hurling herself into Peggy's taxi.

Peggy put an arm around her and she burst into hysterical tears. "Th-thank you," she tried to stammer but beyond that words failed her. What would happen now? She twisted around, looking out the back window. There didn't appear to be anyone following them, but what would happen tomorrow? And the day after? She wasn't safe in New York. She'd have to leave the city—and soon.

BACK AT PEGGY'S apartment, Winifred rang Jane and told her story, slightly more coherent now that she was temporarily safe.

"What did the man look like?" Jane asked.

Winifred described his suit, his bulky shoulders, his Philadelphia accent. She remembered he had been clean-shaven, with dark hair, but she hadn't seen his face clearly. "Oh, and two-tone shoes," she finished.

"That's Legs Diamond, one of Rothstein's hatchet men," Jane said. "He's not going to be happy."

Winifred wailed. "I've handled this so badly. I'm such an idiot. I'll have to leave town." *But what about the play?* The understudy would have to take over. She hated to let Mr. Shaw down, but there was no choice.

"Did you try telling Rothstein you've got another beau?" Jane asked.

"I did, but they knew I had broken up with Peter. I think they must have been tailing me so they know I'm not seeing any other men. I've only been socializing with women for the past year or so."

"That's it!" Jane cried. "That's the answer. I'll tell Rothstein you're a lesbian, but that you didn't want to admit it in case the press got wind of it. It's the only reason he'll accept for you turning down his advances. Men are arrogant that way."

Winifred gasped. "Will he believe you?"

"We need to make it plausible. First thing tomorrow you should make a date with a well-known lesbian—one of the Tallulah set—and arrange to meet in a public place. I'll talk to Arnold Rothstein. I'll also send your sincerest apologies to Legs Diamond, and explain that he scared the bejeesus out of you. You lie low at Peggy's until I call."

Peggy made up a bed for her on the couch, but Winifred couldn't sleep. She sat, wrapped in a blanket, listening to the creaking of the building and the wind blowing outside, terrified that any moment the door would be broken down by a bunch of gangsters who had followed their taxi and were seeking bloody revenge. If they were going to kill her, she hoped it would be quick—a shot to the head—and that they spared Peggy, who had only been trying to help.

# Chapter 32
# PEGGY

When Peggy rose next morning, she found Winifred had drifted off to sleep huddled in the corner of the sofa, her neck cricked at an uncomfortable angle, a blanket bunched around her knees. Peggy knew she'd had very little sleep; she'd heard her pacing in the early hours. Keeping her voice hushed, she telephoned the office and lied that she had an upset stomach and wouldn't be coming in. She made some coffee, then sat reading in a chair by the window.

When Winifred finally awoke, rubbing her neck and yawning, Peggy fetched a cup of coffee for her and offered to draw a bath.

"Maybe later, thank you. Any news from Jane?"

"Not yet. But I had an idea. Have you met Eva Le Gallienne? You would remember. She used to turn up at the Gonk wearing skintight evening gowns that made Alec's eyes pop out."

Eva had had an affair with Tallulah Bankhead before she left for England two years earlier. Peggy had an inkling she and Winifred would hit it off because they were both smart and glamorous but not remotely entitled.

"I've seen her onstage, but we've never been introduced."

"You'll like her," Peggy said. "Let's wait to hear from Jane. If we are proceeding with her plan, I'll give Eva a call and I'm sure she'll agree to pose as your new 'lesbian lover.'"

Winifred was too knotted with nerves to eat, but she had a quick bath to freshen up, then she sat, trying to make conversation with Peggy.

"How is Alvan? It must be interesting dating a doctor."

"His schedule makes it challenging," Peggy said. "You can bet that if I cook a special dinner, he'll get called back to the hospital just as we're sitting down to eat. But he has his compensations."

She grinned, expecting Winifred to ask more, but her attention was wandering. She kept glancing at the phone, as if willing it to ring.

The truth was that Alvan was a tender lover and an entertaining conversationalist. They had fun when they were together, and he had bought her some thoughtful gifts. One evening, as they strolled down Fifth Avenue on the way back to her apartment, Peggy had stopped to admire some emerald drop earrings in a jeweler's window. Next time she saw him, Alvan presented her with them.

"I hope you didn't think I was hinting," she said, embarrassed.

"Not at all," he replied. "But you deserve them."

Was she in love? Was he? It still felt like early days. Even after they had been lovers for three months, she didn't feel she truly knew him. Dottie had fallen in love with Charlie in ten minutes—or so she said—and look how that ended up. It must be better to take your time in affairs of the heart.

Peggy served ham and cabbage soup for lunch, and Winifred was washing up when the call from Jane came. Peggy spoke to her first.

"I've been to see Arnold Rothstein," she said. "He was very cross, but I think I've smoothed things over. How's Winifred?"

"Jumpy," Peggy said, glancing at her. "Did he buy the lesbian story?"

"He did, but he's annoyed that Winifred kept him dangling for so long instead of telling him right away."

Peggy nodded at Winifred to reassure her. Winifred sank onto the couch as if her legs had given way, clasping a hand over her mouth.

"I'm going to set her up with Eva Le Gallienne," Peggy told Jane. "I'm sure she'll play along."

"Good choice. They'll have to make it convincing. If Arnold ever thinks he's been duped, I'm not sure I can protect Winifred. And I don't want him thinking I'm a liar either."

"What about Legs Diamond? Was any serious damage done?"

"It's just a flesh wound. Legs won't seek revenge if Arnold tells him not to, but he needs some kind of recompense for the sake of his pride. I suggested that Winifred could arrange complimentary tickets for him and his friends to see *Saint Joan*. Will you ask her if that's alright?"

Peggy relayed the request.

"He can have as many as he likes," Winifred said right away. "Any night. Best seats in the house."

Peggy handed her the telephone. Winifred was trembling as she thanked Jane repeatedly, promising she would use every ounce of her acting talent to convince Arnold that she was a lesbian. She certainly wouldn't be seen with any other men, not for a long time.

"Doesn't that bother you?" Peggy asked when she came off the phone. "What if you meet a man you like?"

Winifred shook her head vehemently. "There's no place in my life for men right now. Things are so much easier without them."

Easier maybe, Peggy thought, but not so much fun. She felt as if she was making up for lost time when it came to men and she wanted as much of Alvan as she could possibly get.

WHEN WINIFRED LEFT, Peggy wandered down to check her mailbox in the front hall. Her heart leapt when she saw an envelope printed with the Boni & Liveright colophon. It was bound to be a rejection letter. She tore it open and skimmed the words, then stopped and read them again, unable to believe her eyes.

"You have a keen eye for the nuances of social interaction," Tommy Smith wrote, "and I warmed to your characters immediately." She read further, looking for the *but*. It wasn't there. Instead he said he would like to publish her book and wondered if she could contact him at the first opportunity to arrange a meeting.

Peggy raced upstairs as fast as she could, reread the letter one more time to check she wasn't misinterpreting it, then rang the telephone number given.

"Actually, it so happens I'm free this afternoon," she told Tommy Smith's very friendly secretary, and an appointment was made for four-thirty.

When she hung up the phone, Peggy crouched on the rug, hugging her knees to her chest and waiting for her heartbeat to settle. She couldn't take it in. Was it a mistake? Had the letters gotten mixed up and he meant to write to someone else? She checked the letter again: he mentioned her title, *The Back of the Book*. It must be right.

*Oh golly*, she kept thinking. *Oh my!*

She dressed for the meeting in her dove-gray suit and hat, and applied a dash of scarlet lipstick. She took a taxi so she wouldn't be out of breath or disheveled on arrival, but as a result she got there so early she had to walk around the block.

Tommy Smith's secretary was all smiles as she led her upstairs to a plush-carpeted suite of offices, and asked if she would like a coffee while she waited. Before long, a lean figure emerged to shake her hand and wave her into a huge office with a window overlooking a dentist's practice opposite. Tommy Smith was younger than she'd expected, and quite handsome, with a high forehead, round spectacles, and slicked-back dark hair.

"Miss Leech, I'm not sure where you stand on such things, but it seems to me the time of day when one might respectably have a martini."

"That's a wonderful idea," she said.

"I had a feeling you'd be a drinker." He grinned. "All the best people are."

As he mixed her drink, he said: "You know we publish the Modern Library: T. S. Eliot, James Joyce, Ezra Pound? We believe in bringing a range of new voices to the American public, and yours is certainly an original."

*He's trying to win me over,* Peggy realized with astonishment. He didn't know she was so grateful to him she would have knelt and kissed his shoes if he'd asked.

"We'd like to publish your book next year," he said. "And I hope you're already working on a new one. Are you?"

He handed her a martini and she could tell from the first sip it was made with top-quality gin. "I am, as it happens," she said, and began to tell him about the new novel she had started, which was called *Tin Wedding*. It was about a beautiful woman named Lucia reaching her tenth wedding anniversary and reflecting on her life and her choice of husband.

Tommy sat behind his big oak desk, listening intently, occasionally asking questions, and finally said he loved the idea. "I can tell it's exactly the type of subject you will excel at. You have a real talent for getting deep inside your characters' heads and making readers care about them. How far along are you? Is there anything I might have a look at?"

Peggy blushed. "Not quite yet. I'm still feeling my way."

"No matter," he said, with a wave of his hand. "I'm confident enough of your talent to offer you a deal for both books. I'm afraid we can only pay an advance of two hundred dollars each, but you will get royalties on every copy sold."

*Only two hundred?* That was more than she earned in a month.

She mumbled that she'd be delighted to accept, her hand knocking her glass so a few drops spilled onto the polished surface of his desk. She felt like leaping up and hugging him but that seemed a step too far.

After the meeting, she floated out of the office, giddy from the combination of two martinis and the extraordinary news. She was seeing Alvan that evening, so they could celebrate together. First, she couldn't wait to get home and telephone her mom. Peggy may not have found a husband yet, but she had a beau and a book deal, and it felt as if she had the world at her feet.

THE BRIDGE CLUB was meeting the following Saturday at Dottie's apartment in the Gonk. Jane telephoned Peggy beforehand.

"I wanted to warn you not to tell Dottie about Winifred's brush with Arnold Rothstein and Legs Diamond. I can just imagine her jokes about gangsters' triggermen with pearl hat pins decorating their genitalia. The Round Table would lap it up but I'm afraid word might get back. . . ."

"Yes, Dottie can be rather indiscreet," Peggy said, remembering many secrets she had divulged over the years. "Have you told Winifred not to mention it?"

"I have."

Peggy's news of her book deal was on the tip of her tongue, but she decided to save it and tell all three women at once, in person.

She was the first to arrive on Saturday, carrying a tray of cheese pastries. It was unspoken but taken for granted that she provided food for their gatherings, while the hostess of the night supplied the hooch.

Dottie greeted her, wearing a dramatic Art Deco–patterned scarf in shades of terra-cotta, cornflower blue, and dusty pink that hung almost to her knees. Woodrow Wilson was snoozing in his basket, gray whiskers the only sign of his advanced age. The room was tidy and fresh-smelling, and Peggy mused, not for the first time, that moving to the Gonk had been a great idea for Dottie.

"How's the work going?" she asked, nodding at the typewriter on a table by the window.

"It's going," Dottie said. "Somehow I appear to be meeting deadlines, despite the crowd from downstairs knocking on my door at all hours of the day and night. And my play's opening next month. You must come to the first night."

Winifred and Jane arrived together, saying they had bumped into each other in the lobby. Peggy noticed their arms were linked and thought it was a nice side effect of the Rothstein drama if it made them closer.

She waited till everyone was sitting with drinks in hand before saying, "I have an announcement!" She beamed, still unaccustomed to saying the words out loud: "Tommy Smith at Boni & Liveright wants to publish my novel."

Jane was the first to shriek, then jump up and hug her, followed by Winifred.

"It's all thanks to Dottie," Peggy said. "We've been egging each other on. I wouldn't have been brave enough to send it to Tommy if she hadn't forced me."

"I told you he had an eye for a bestseller," Dottie said. "I hope you negotiated a tough deal, to show him you're no pushover."

Peggy laughed. "He fed me martinis and pushed me right over. He also wants another book next year so I need to get my head down. But remember we had a deal, Dottie? It's your turn to get a book published next. I can feel it in my bones. Your poems will make your fortune."

Dottie mumbled, "Well, of course, I'd like to be a good writer, and I'd like to have money, but if I can't have both at the same time, I'll take the money." She eyed Peggy. "I guess you won't be needing extra dough if you marry that Jewish doctor of yours."

"Not a word has been uttered about marriage." Peggy blushed, thinking how annoying it was that she still blushed now that she was in her thirties. She clearly was never going to grow out of it.

Just at that moment, the door opened and a tall, attractive woman walked in, wearing a frock printed with a peacock feather pattern. Peggy was surprised she hadn't knocked first, but Dottie rose to greet her without batting an eye.

"Dottie told me about her *little* bridge club and I've been simply dying to come and meet you all," the woman said. "I'm Elinor Wylie."

She shook hands with each in turn and they introduced themselves, while Dottie mixed Elinor a drink. There were no free chairs so she perched on the arm of Dottie's, crossing her slender ankles.

"Just you ladies carry on and don't mind me," she said. "What were you talking about when I interrupted so rudely?"

"Peggy's beau," Dottie told her. "He's a doctor with an interest in psychoanalysis—"

Without letting her finish, Elinor burst in: "Dottie, you should absolutely get him to analyze you! Think of all the material you'd get for your poems and stories. It would be priceless. Do say you'll do it!"

Peggy thought it was a terrible idea. She glanced at Jane, and could tell from her grim expression that she had taken against this newcomer. They caught eyes.

Dottie seemed enamored of her, though. "You're quite the expert, aren't you, Elinor? How many analysts have you been through?"

"Dozens. I drove them all crazy. I don't think it's supposed to work that way around, is it?" She laughed at her own wit. "Every time they thought we were making progress, someone else close to me died or some other disaster happened. All my analysts washed their hands of me in the end. I've had so many tragedies in my life. Dottie's probably told you."

Jane answered in a crisp tone. "Dottie hasn't mentioned you at all, as it happens."

There was an awkward pause.

"It's been a while since our last bridge club," Dottie said. "Elinor and I have been spending time talking about poetry and getting acquainted."

"How nice," Jane said, and the cool way she said it sounded rude.

Peggy jumped in to change the subject. "Winifred, I hear from Neysa you've had another honor heaped on you recently, on top of your triumph in *Saint Joan*."

They all asked what it was, and Winifred looked sheepish. "Oh that! It's so silly."

Peggy turned to the others. "*McCall's* magazine asked readers to vote on the ten most beautiful women in the world and Winifred was chosen as one of them. In the *world*!"

Winifred pulled a face to signify she didn't take it seriously.

Elinor stood up abruptly, her expression stony. "Well, they can't have cast the net very wide," she said. "If you'll excuse me, ladies. I have another appointment I must get to."

She swept out of the room, and Dottie hurried after her. The remaining three looked at each other in disbelief.

"What was that about?" Peggy asked.

"I don't think she minded being left off the list at all," Jane quipped. "Not one little bit."

"What an uncongenial new friend Dottie has found for herself," Winifred remarked.

Peggy snorted. "That's the first time I've heard you say a negative word about anyone, Winifred. But I completely agree. What has Dottie gotten herself into now?"

# Chapter 33
# JANE

"Elinor has had a *most* extraordinary life," Dottie said on her return. "She's clairvoyant and claims she is visited by the spirit of an ancestor, Lizzie Wylie, who was hanged as a witch in the seventeenth century. Lizzie told her she is going to die young so she tries to pack in as much experience as she can, just in case it's true."

"Utter hogwash!" Jane snapped. "You should know better, Dottie."

She felt unreasonably annoyed. Dottie could be so gullible sometimes.

"Keep your hair on, I didn't say I believed her." Dottie sat down and gulped her drink. "But it's refreshing to talk to people whose points of view are different from your own, especially when she's a poet whose work I admire." She produced a pack of cards. "Shall we play, ladies?"

Jane partnered with Winifred, Dottie with Peggy, and they started the first rubber. Jane was in a grumpy mood she couldn't shake, and it distracted her. She made a couple of rookie errors that swung the result in the other team's favor.

"Oh, bad luck," said Winifred, not at all concerned that Jane had let their side down.

They played a few more rubbers, but Peggy and Dottie prevailed.

All evening, Jane couldn't shake her mood. She was happy to hear Peggy's news, pleased to have been able to rescue Winifred from her scrape, but annoyed with Dottie for launching herself into a new friendship with that self-obsessed woman. It wasn't that she was jealous of Elinor Wylie, Jane told herself; it was irritating to see an otherwise smart woman like Dottie being taken in by her. Clairvoyant indeed!

There was something else: since Dottie had broken the news that Harold had run up debts at the poker club, she hadn't so much as telephoned Jane to ask if things were alright. She knew about Jane and Harold's dream to start a magazine, but it seemed to have slipped her mind that they were trying to save money for it.

In fact, Jane didn't feel like discussing Harold's gambling debts with her women friends. She was ashamed of him, and didn't want them to think badly of him. The knowledge weighed heavily on her that she had married a man she couldn't trust with money; a man who had broken the deal they made to save his salary while living on hers; a man who kept secrets from her.

When he had gotten the full list of his debts from Alec, it transpired that he had lost almost the entire thirty thousand dollars that should have been in their savings account. Thirty thousand! It was an unbelievable amount of money. She was furious with all the so-called friends who had let him keep digging himself deeper into debt at the poker table, and she was especially furious with Alec. But the real blame lay with Harold. He was the one who couldn't control himself.

At least he was penitent, and happy for her to take over their joint finances. If she respected him a little less, she was doing her best not to show it. But maybe that's why she was in a grumpy mood and unable to relax that evening.

Before she left Dottie's, she mentioned that they were producing a prospectus for the magazine to tout to potential investors.

"Will you let us list you as a member of the editorial board?" she asked Dottie. "We can't pay anything yet, but we'll give you stock in the magazine in return for your advice."

Dottie agreed cheerfully. "I'll make sure my advice is worth every cent."

"Do you have a title yet?" Peggy asked.

There was one piece of positive news at least. A man called John Toohey, one of the Gonk crowd, had come up with what Jane thought was the perfect title for a stylish, metropolitan magazine.

"We're going to call it *The New Yorker.*"

The reaction was instant enthusiasm, and Jane smiled for what felt like the first time in ages.

BACK AT 412, Jane and Harold pored over other magazines on the market, trying to make the all-important decision on a design for their front cover. Most artists they briefed came back with a stylized sketch of the New York skyline, which seemed a cliché. One of them drew a curtain rising to reveal skyscrapers behind, but Harold hated that over-literal interpretation and threw it back at the disappointed artist.

Months went by with no cover design agreed on, and finally he asked Rea Irvin, then art editor of *Life*, for advice. Rea drew a sketch they both fell in love with at first sight: an epicurean dandy in a top hat peering through a monocle at a butterfly. Jane liked the subtlety and style, and was also keen on the sophisticated typeface Irvin suggested for the title. It felt like a giant leap forward.

If the cover took months of deliberation, the content took even longer. Harold had always been a perfectionist, but the problem was that he had difficulty explaining what he wanted. He knew what he *didn't* like, but only when he saw it, and writers and designers had to keep pitching ideas till they got his thumbs-up. There were going to be stories, poems, profiles of leading figures, a "Talk of the Town" column with insider gossip to make readers feel as if they were "in the know," theater and book reviews, and a feature on fashion called "On and Off the Avenue." Many other column ideas were pitched and rejected because Harold said they didn't get his "juices flowing."

Once the cover and prospectus were ready, Jane asked Carr Van Anda's advice on drawing up a list of media investors. He reckoned fifty thousand dollars was the bare minimum they needed to launch, and cautioned they would run out of cash if they didn't break even within six months. That was the danger point, when they could find their funds had sunk so low that it was impossible to print the next issue. It didn't give them long to make their mark. They would simply have to be a success by then.

First, Jane had to raise that fifty thousand. She started by going to her own bank, and persuading her bank manager to give her a loan of twenty-five thousand, backed by her salary at the *New York Times* and her share of number 412. Next, she started visiting potential investors, fitting in meetings around her job.

"Interesting, but too high risk for me," the first one said. "There are hundreds of magazines on the market, and most of them fold after the second or third issue."

"I admire your spirit, but I'm not a charity," said another.

Jane pointed out the credentials and experience of their editorial panel. As well as Dottie, they had Alec Woollcott, Edna Ferber, Heywood Broun, and George Kaufman, among many others. Surely that counted for something?

But the answer was no at every turn. She was exhausted, mentally and physically. Every morning she wrote a list of tasks to achieve during the day: telephone calls to make, stories to file, contacts to approach, as well as food to buy for dinner, and other domestic arrangements at 412. It felt as if she was carrying the whole weight herself, and she had to swallow her irritation when she came home, laden with bags, to find Harold, Alec, and Hawley drinking whiskey in the communal dining room.

"We've run out of coffee, Jane," Alec complained, and it was on the tip of her tongue to tell him he should buy his own since he had a forty-cup-a-day habit, but she didn't want to clash with him. They needed his help with *The New Yorker* and couldn't afford to pay him—couldn't pay any of the contributors to start with—and that made it tricky.

One evening she was invited to a party thrown by Raoul Fleischmann, the baking heir, and his wife. Jane got to chatting to him in the corner and asked how the bread-making business was going.

"Fleischmann's Yeast ticks along nicely, but the business is deadly dull," he told her. "I envy you literary types, using your brains creatively. The most creative I get is choosing between two different advertising campaigns."

"Why don't you join our team?" Jane suggested, in a flash of inspiration. It hadn't occurred to her to approach him because he didn't work in media, but she told him about their plans for *The New Yorker*.

"We're looking for another twenty-five thousand. If you are able to invest the whole amount, you could be the publisher and have a say in the running of the magazine. I'm sure you'd find it more stimulating than yeast."

"Only twenty-five thousand? I like that idea," he said, thoughtfully. "Get Harold to visit me tomorrow with the prospectus and we'll see if we can hammer out a deal."

Jane managed not to whoop out loud. Keeping her expression businesslike, she agreed that Harold would visit his office at eleven the following morning.

She couldn't wait to get home and tell him the news. He already knew Raoul through the poker club. Surely it was better to work with a friend than a stranger? It benefited everyone. And if he came on board, they could launch the magazine soon. She felt a bubble of excitement at the prospect.

JANE LEFT FOR work early the next morning, well before Harold set off for his meeting with Raoul. She was researching a story about the murders of dozens of Osage Native Americans in Oklahoma, thought to have been committed on the command of some prominent local cattlemen who wanted to sink oil wells on their land. It was a distressing tale, involving low-life contract killers and intricate family feuds. Jane had a contact from the Osage community feeding her inside information, and she felt strongly that the case deserved national attention.

At twelve noon, she glanced at her watch and wondered how Harold and Raoul's meeting had gone. Were they shaking hands on a deal even now?

When she finally got to her office at three o'clock, she rang Harold, bubbling with excitement, and asked how it had gone.

"Naw, he's not interested," Harold said right away.

Jane was crestfallen. "What do you mean? Why not? He seemed keen last night."

"Maybe he was drunk last night, and thought better of it in the cold light of day. I don't know. We'll find someone else, mushkins. Never fear."

Jane hung up and stared at the telephone. Raoul hadn't seemed the flighty type, and he certainly hadn't seemed drunk. What made him change his mind?

She called the operator to get his office telephone number and asked to be put through.

"I got the impression you were keen to be involved with *The New Yorker,*" she said. "Was there something about the prospectus you didn't like? Because we can change things if it would make you come on board."

"It wasn't *The New Yorker* Harold pitched to me," Raoul said. "It was a shipping magazine called *Marine Gazette*. He seemed very passionate about it, but I'm afraid I couldn't get excited."

"*Marine Gazette*?" Jane clutched her head. Was he still harping on about that old idea? "I'm sorry, I think Harold got the wrong end of the stick when I told him to meet you about the magazine. *Marine Gazette* is a project on the back burner, but it's *The New Yorker* we want to raise funds for. Can I swing by and bring you the prospectus?" She glanced at her watch. "I could come later this afternoon if you have time."

Raoul agreed that she could drop by at five. Jane took a well-thumbed copy of the prospectus she kept in her satchel, along with a mock-up of the magazine with its stunning cover, and got to his office by five on the dot.

She sat on the other side of Raoul's huge boardroom table, chewing the inside of her cheek as he read through the pitch.

"'Not for the little old lady from Dubuque.'" He grinned. "I like that."

When he got to the end, he nodded thoughtfully. "I like it a lot. Are you sure you're asking for enough money though? You don't want to be penny-pinching when you launch a new magazine."

"A lot of our writer and artist friends are not charging for their work," Jane said. "The main costs in the early days will be printing and distribution."

"Uh-huh," he nodded, holding the cover at arm's length. "Where's your office?"

Jane smiled. "It's currently our dining room. The swanky offices can come later."

"That doesn't seem very professional." He played an arpeggio on the desk with his fingertips. "I've got some office space sitting empty at 25 West Forty-Fifth Street, and you're welcome to use it."

"Are you kidding?" Jane said. "That would be wonderful if—"

She stopped to breathe. "Does that mean you are interested in investing?"

"I sure am. As I said to you at the party, I've been looking for something more stimulating to do with my time." He grinned. "When were you thinking of launching?"

Jane dug her fingernails into her palms to quell her excitement. "Carr Van Anda said early in the year is best. We were thinking next January or February perhaps."

"Great. Just tell me when you need the money, and when you want to move into the offices." He stood up to shake her hand. "*The New Yorker*, eh? This is going to be a fun ride."

Jane looked at her watch. It was after six. Harold was probably at the Gonk. She would rush over and break the good news.

The Round Table was crowded: Harold was sitting with George Kaufman, Dottie was with Bob Benchley, and Helen Hayes was at the other end of the table, sandwiched between Charlie and Alec, who appeared to be competing for her attention.

She kissed Harold in greeting and sat on his lap before giving him a quizzical look. "I hear you tried to get Raoul to invest in *Marine Gazette*?"

"Yes, I thought it would complement his baking interests. Help with exports, and so forth. But, like I told you, he didn't go for it." He shrugged.

"That's because it was *The New Yorker* he was interested in." Jane's face broke into a grin. "And we've got ourselves a backer. We can launch early next year."

A twitch of puzzlement crossed Harold's brow before he responded. "That's my girl!" he announced to the table, putting an arm around her. "Never takes no for an answer. I knew you would find the money."

There was a chorus of congratulations and a clinking of glasses containing clear liquid.

"Will you write a story for the launch issue, Dottie?" Jane asked. "Any subject you want."

"I'd be honored," she drawled, "but give me plenty of time. To say I'm snail-like would be an insult to snails."

Jane ducked under the brim of Dottie's hat and kissed her cheek. "I know you won't let us down."

At the other side of the table, she heard Alec talking in a low voice to Helen Hayes. Jane clearly wasn't intended to overhear but she'd always had especially acute hearing.

"I used to know Harold back in the old days when he was still a man, before he let himself be pushed around by a skirt," Alec said, and Helen tittered.

Jane felt her temper flare and considered snapping at him to keep his opinions to himself. But it would only cause an argument and she wanted this evening to be a celebration. She stored it up, though. Alec's barbs were like fishing hooks that got under the skin and were hard to dislodge.

# Chapter 34
# DOTTIE

Dottie's play got terrific reviews—hardly surprising since she was friends with most of the theater reviewers in town—but tickets didn't sell. In the third week, when box office takings amounted to just ninety dollars, the producers decided to pull the plug. Dottie put a brave face on for the Gonk crowd—"Ninety dollars! Drinks are on me!" she cried—but it dented her confidence to be associated with a failure.

She had come to a standstill in selecting poems for a collection too. Her work wasn't good enough; they were silly rhymes, nowhere near as profound as Elinor's poems.

Elinor urged her not to compare herself with other writers. "Each of us has our own unique voice," she said. "You can't compare Mozart with Beethoven, or Rembrandt with Da Vinci. Readers love your poems. They speak to our age."

"Yes, but their only message is that love doesn't work and I am a terrible poet," Dottie replied. Nothing Elinor said cured her of the feeling that she was not in a good frame of mind to write. Words were not flowing, the muse was not with her.

Dottie fully intended to write a story for *The New Yorker*'s launch issue. She asked Harold if he had any guidelines, but he told her to write what she wanted, so long as it was set in New York. That didn't help much. She toyed with one idea, then another, talking them through with Elinor, but nothing seemed right and the deadline was creeping up fast.

"Sharpen your tongue and write about pretentious literary types who believe in spirits and past lives," Bob suggested, in an obvious dig at Elinor. But Dottie couldn't do that; Elinor felt like her only ally.

She'd had periods before when she couldn't write. "It will come back," she told herself, wrestling with the familiar, stomach-clenching terror of staring at a blank sheet of paper. She busied herself with cleaning her typewriter keys, rearranging her closet, and grooming Woodrow, trying not to let panic take hold.

ELINOR INVITED HER to her apartment at number 1 University Place, near Washington Square, to meet her third husband, Bill Benét, who was the editor of the *Saturday Review of Literature*. Bill was an elegant man with eyes that crinkled with warmth as he greeted her.

"Come in, make yourself at home," he said, clutching her hand. "I've been urging Elinor to invite you."

Dottie looked around. The apartment was small but tastefully furnished with a mixture of antique and modern furniture in a color scheme of black, pink, and silver. Above the fireplace hung a huge silver mirror with sirens decorating the frame. A set of black-painted shelves in an alcove showcased a collection of fine porcelain painted with peonies. The couch and chairs were in an old-fashioned style but upholstered in hot pink velvet.

Dottie sat in an armchair, marveling at how comfortable it was.

"They're Louis Quinze," Elinor said, "but I modernized them. Will you fetch some coffee, child?"

Her husband disappeared down the hall.

"I call him 'child,'" she confided. "He calls me 'lamb' or 'falcon,' depending on my mood." She adopted a confiding tone. "We adore each other, but it's not a sexual marriage. We had been friends for a long time, and he came back into my life at a very low point, after my second marriage failed. Our companionship suits us."

"Don't you miss the joys of conjugal sheet-dancing?" Dottie asked, taken aback by the flow of confession.

"I have affairs when I feel the need," she said. "The last one was with a young reporter called Ernest Hemingway. Perhaps you've heard of him?"

"Of course I have," Dottie said, with a twinge of curiosity. She had met Hemingway and found his earthy masculinity very attractive, but he'd seemed devoted to his wife, Hadley.

"He was a dear boy. Used to call me his lecherous cat." She giggled, as if pleased with the description. "Child and I are having a soiree for our literary set next week. You must come! Edmund Wilson will be there, and Edna St. Vincent Millay. . . ." She was still listing names when Bill appeared with a tray of coffee and a ginger cake. "I've invited Dottie to our soiree," she told him.

"You absolutely must come," he agreed. "There are lots of people I want you to meet."

"Some old friends are traveling up from Washington, DC," Elinor said. "I haven't seen them for over ten years because I was persona non grata in DC after all the scandal surrounding my first marriage. I think I told you about it."

"The marriage to the lawyer?" Dottie remembered.

"Philip." Elinor pursed her lips. "He wasn't a bad person, but life was humdrum. I had a son with him, of course, but then there were all those miscarriages and I simply couldn't *breathe*." She clutched her chest dramatically. "So when I met Horace, I *fell* into his arms."

"Your second husband?" Dottie was struggling to keep up.

"Eventually," Elinor said. "You wouldn't believe the trauma of my divorce from Philip. President Roosevelt had attended our wedding, and we were establishment figures. Everyone in high society snubbed me when I ran off with Horace. That's why we decided to sail for England. And then Philip shot himself and I got the blame, even though I was on the other side of the ocean."

"What about your son? Did he join you in England?"

"No, the poor dear stayed in Washington with Philip's family. It broke my heart clean in two, as you can imagine. I haven't been allowed to see him since." She paused to sip her coffee, looking pained, as if telling the story was distressing her.

"You don't see him at all?" Dottie was horrified. "How can they stop you?"

Elinor shrugged in a wide gesture. "There's nothing to be done. It's a sorrow I have learned to live with, along with the suicides of my brother and sister. That was a dreadful time. I carry my grief in a sack on my back as I stumble through the days."

It sounded like a line from one of her poems but Dottie couldn't recall which one.

When she left several hours later, she realized that Elinor and Bill hadn't asked a single thing about her. Elinor liked to be the center of attention and Bill indulged her. It was a quality Dottie would have scorned in anyone else, but Elinor intrigued her. She was talented and sure of herself in a way that Dottie envied. She had been through tragedy and survived. Perhaps by being around her, some of her strength would rub off, like pollen falling from a lily and leaving its stain.

ELINOR AND BILL'S soiree was packed with New York literary types, who were far too intellectual and far too busy ever to appear at the Gonk. There were Harvard professors, a range of literary editors, and many of the top writers of the day—people who actually wrote rather than sitting around talking about it.

Champagne flowed, and delicate canapés were passed, along

with jars of caviar and tiny silver spoons. In the corner, Dottie noticed a group using the spoons to snort cocaine, but she was too much of a coward to join them. She had never tried it and was wary of being out of control. Instead she kept refilling her glass with champagne, feeling intimidated among such highbrow types. If only Peggy had come! She would have been in her element.

Halfway through the evening, Dottie realized she was ossified. Not just tipsy in the normal way, but staggering drunk and liable to fall over if she moved away from the wall she was leaning against. She put her glass down, wondering what to do. Should she try to make her way home?

Bill spotted her dilemma. "Are you feeling tired?" he asked kindly. "Come and rest in our spare bedroom and you can rejoin the party when you perk up."

He took her arm and led her down the hall, holding on firmly as she wobbled and tripped over her feet. In the bedroom, he removed her shoes and draped a blanket over her. Dottie fell asleep instantly.

She had no idea how much later it was when she was shaken awake. "Dottie!" Elinor's voice called. "Wake up! We're missing you."

Dottie clutched her head. Her temples were pounding and her heart was aflutter. Getting up was the last thing she felt like doing, but Elinor was insistent. She pulled herself to her feet, checked her reflection in the mirror, wiped a smudge from under one eye, then staggered along the hall. The soiree had thinned but there were still around a dozen guests, drinking and talking, while a phonograph played jazz in the background.

"Here she is!" Elinor announced. "My wonderful newfound friend." She turned to Dottie. "We were just talking about suicide and I wondered if you would mind showing everyone your scars. They're so impressive."

Dottie was taken aback. She had told several of the Gonk crowd

254

about her suicide attempt, but not the world at large. She didn't want it to get in the papers.

"Don't be shy," Elinor urged, pulling her forward. "We're all friends here."

Dottie couldn't refuse without appearing a bad sport. She rolled up her sleeves and held out her wrists to show onlookers the jagged scars, now silvery-white, that snaked across the delicate veins and tendons beneath her skin.

"Cheaper than Tiffany bracelets," she told them. "And definitely more of a conversation starter."

"I consider them badges of courage," Elinor cried. "And I'm proud to consider myself your friend."

BACK IN HER apartment at the Gonk the following day, nursing a bilious hangover, Dottie felt very alone. Neysa and Jack had recently had a baby, a little girl they called Joan, and Neysa had disappeared into the misty realms of new motherhood. Bob was neglecting her now that he had Charlie to play man about town with. Jane's spare time was devoted to the magazine, Peggy was absorbed by Alvan, and Winifred always seemed busy with work.

Before she left that morning, Elinor had said, "*Mi casa es tu casa.*" If she ever felt lonely, she should come to their apartment to write, to chat, or just to sit and gaze out the window drinking tea.

"Perhaps we should adopt her," Bill suggested to Elinor. "Is it legal to adopt a thirty-year-old woman?"

"I don't see why not," Elinor replied. "Let's look into it."

It was nice to feel as though she had surrogate parents. Dottie's spirits had been sinking as fall slid toward winter and the days got dark almost before she was out of bed. She wasn't a winter person. She yearned for warm sunshine on her bones. Neysa and Jack weren't going to Florida this year because of the baby. Perhaps she would ask Elinor and Bill if they'd like to go. . . .

255

When she telephoned later to thank them for the soiree, she asked Elinor about Florida, but she replied straightaway that she couldn't go without Bill and he couldn't leave New York because of his job.

"I understand. It's just that I tend to get very blue in winter," Dottie said, swallowing back tears.

"I've told you before," Elinor replied, "that you should start psychoanalysis. I'm sure that beau of Peggy's would agree to analyze you. I swear, it will change your life."

Dottie came off the telephone mulling over the idea. It had a certain appeal. Peggy had been against it when it was mooted before, but she hadn't given a specific reason.

Dottie suspected she would find analysis fascinating, but there was no way she could afford to pay the fees of a Park Avenue analyst. She wasn't earning any money to supplement Eddie's allowance, and she had fallen behind on rent at the Gonk. Perhaps Alvan wouldn't charge her; he'd said he wanted to gain experience.

She picked up the telephone and left a message at the hospital asking him to give her a call.

WHEN ALVAN CALLED back, he said he would be delighted to analyze Dottie free of charge and they made an appointment for the following week. He gave her the address of a consulting room he shared with another analyst, not far from the hospital.

The night before the appointment, Dottie sat in her room drinking gin and feeling desperately alone. She was scared about what might happen at their session, but she also knew she had no choice. She had to do something before she sank too low.

The first thing she noticed when a receptionist led her into Alvan's consulting room was a richly colored Persian carpet. Then she spotted a chaise longue with a brown blanket thrown over it. Alongside was a low table with a jug of water and a single glass.

His desk was positioned behind the chaise. It seemed odd that she wouldn't be able to see him as she spoke, but perhaps that's how he worked.

Alvan came into the room wearing his doctor's white coat, with a stethoscope around his neck.

"Dottie," he said, shaking her hand. "I'm very glad you came. Please lie down and make yourself comfortable."

"Normally when young men ask me to lie down on couches I insist they kiss me first," she said. It was a line she'd thought of the night before. He didn't laugh, but she heard the rustling of paper. She poured herself a glass of water. "I don't know what I'm supposed to do. I'm an analysis virgin. Will you be gentle?"

She heard the faint scratch of a pen on paper. "I understand that you use humor as a defense," he said. "Perhaps you're not aware of it. But the more honest you are able to be in our sessions, the faster we will proceed."

Dottie felt chastised. Already she wasn't doing it properly. Maybe she wouldn't be any good at this.

"Why don't you start by telling me a memory from your childhood," he said. "The first one that comes into your head. Describe the scene to me."

Right away, Dottie thought of the time her father introduced her to the woman who would become her stepmother. They were in the drawing room of a new house near Central Park. Dottie was six years old, and her mother had died just over a year earlier.

"This is Miss Lewis," her father said. "Shake hands."

Dottie remembered the bony fingers that crushed hers. A clock was ticking in the room, sounding louder than usual, and she got a sense that her life, which had already changed completely in the last year, was about to change again, and that everything familiar was going to be ripped away.

"Did you feel as though she might steal your father's love from

257

you?" Alvan asked, and Dottie frowned. She couldn't remember her father as a loving parent in that period, only a distant, bad-tempered one. Looking back, he was probably grief-stricken, and panicking about being left with four children to raise.

"As a stepmother, Miss Lewis considered it her main role to force religion down our throats till we gagged. My siblings were teenagers and old enough to stand up to her, so I became the main target of her religious zeal. She was convinced she could force me to love God, so help her."

Layer by layer Alvan got her to work through the memories from that period, and Dottie tried to lighten the atmosphere.

"I got religion on all sides," she said. "At school the nuns scolded me for referring to the Immaculate Conception as the Spontaneous Combustion. And as soon as I got home, Miss Lewis—by then Mrs. Rothschild—asked, "Dorothy, how much have you loved Jesus today?" There was no escaping it. . . . Then she died too, three years after marrying my father. First Mother, then her."

"How did that make you feel?" he asked.

Dottie blinked. "Do you know Oscar Wilde's play *The Importance of Being Earnest*?" She didn't wait for his answer. "There's a line in it: 'To lose one parent may be regarded as a misfortune; to lose both looks like carelessness.' Well, I've actually lost three. That begins to look like parricide."

"I suspect you feel guilty about it," Alvan said, "because you wanted your stepmother to die and then she did."

Dottie was stunned into silence. It was true. She remembered praying in chapel for Miss Lewis to be struck down, and feeling as if she was an evil person when it happened.

"I think we've explored enough for your first day," he said after a while. "But before you go I'd like to try some word association. I'm going to say a word and I want you to respond quickly with the first thing that comes into your head. Are you ready?"

Dottie's throat was parched. She took a sip of water, her hand shaking. "OK."

"Family," he said.

"Loss." She blinked.

"Home."

"Where I hang my hat."

"Love."

"Betrayal."

When his list of words came to an end, Dottie felt as though she had revealed too much, as if his questions had peeled her raw. She tried to speak with a light tone. "So do you think I am crazy enough to make a good subject for analysis?"

"Not crazy, no, but I think we can achieve a lot if you are prepared to commit to three sessions a week. Can you do that?"

She shivered. "I'll try."

"I want you to stop drinking alcohol while we are working together," he said.

That was an unexpected shock. "But I can't get to sleep without drinking," she told him.

"Your sleep will improve after a few days off the booze," he promised. "I suspect alcohol might be part of the problem and I need you clearheaded if we are to make progress."

She gave a deep sigh. "I can try. But I may have to wear a badge with my name on it or none of my friends will recognize me."

When she walked down the street afterward, she spotted a cordial store. Although they were only supposed to serve soft drinks, most of them kept booze under the counter and sold it disguised in soda bottles. Alvan's words about not drinking rang in her ears, but she decided to buy a quart of Haig & Haig, just to get her through the rest of the day. Tomorrow, when she felt stronger, she would try to give up drinking, although she didn't think she had an alcohol problem. It wasn't as if she passed out in speakeasies like some people she knew; she always managed to get herself home.

Maybe she could get her hands on some veronal to help her sleep. Alvan hadn't said anything about not taking veronal. It was prescription-only in Manhattan but available over the counter in pharmacies in New Jersey. The next afternoon she took a train to Hoboken and bought up as many packs as she could find from every pharmacy in walking distance, so she had a good supply to see her through a winter of analysis and no drinking.

Alvan had warned her that analysis would be hard. Underlying conflicts that had been causing her depression would be brought to the surface. He said the losses she had suffered in childhood had felt to her young self like rejection. These feelings had been buried deep in her psyche but as an adult they made her become dependent on others, especially the men in her life, and to fear rejection so much that her anxiety made her drive them away. Unless these issues were resolved, she would be caught in a vicious circle and would never be free.

Dottie understood what he was saying, and wanted to get better, but at the same time she couldn't shake a feeling of dread. Was she strong enough for this? Could it break her?

That evening, the telephone rang and she was overjoyed to hear Jane's voice: her good friend Jane. She was on the point of confiding that she was depressed, and that she had started analysis and was nervous about how it was going to affect her. Before she could say a word, though, Jane began to harangue her.

"You promised us a story for *The New Yorker*, Dottie, but the launch issue is going to press soon and there's no sign. Is it nearly ready?"

"I'm sorry," Dottie said, her voice barely more than a whisper. "I can't write just now."

"You've had *six months*!" Jane exclaimed. "I asked you ages ago, and you agreed. Now I'll have to find someone else to fill the space. You have no idea the pressure we're under, without you adding to it."

"I'm sorry," Dottie said. "Truly I am. I just can't write."

"Probably because you're too busy swanning around cocktail parties with Elinor Wylie. Thanks for nothing!"

Jane hung up and Dottie burst into tears, crying so hard that her chest ached, her eyes stung, and her jaw felt as if it had dislocated. Jane had never spoken to her like that before. She felt as if she'd lost a friend, just when she needed her most.

# Chapter 35
# WINIFRED

Winifred arranged to meet Eva Le Gallienne in Lorber's, a late-night haunt popular with operagoers, which had photographs of famous singers on the walls and a grand piano at the far end. She wore a black fedora that shaded her face and, after sitting down, she glanced around the room, checking the clientele. No matter how much Jane reassured her, she was still nervous walking into public places in case Arnold Rothstein or Legs Diamond might be there. Only once she was sure the coast was clear did she remove her hat.

There was a jar of celery sticks on the table and an oily dip, as well as a jug of water. Winifred poured herself some water. Peggy had promised she would like Eva, so she wasn't worried about that, but how far would they have to go to appear convincing as lovers?

Eva turned up ten minutes late, tall and striking in an ankle-length black coat with a raccoon collar, and a smart boyish bleached-blond haircut, which was all the rage that season. Winifred liked the cut, but so far hadn't been brave enough to part with her wavy shoulder-length bob, which had been the height of fashion the previous year.

"Hi!" Eva said with a grin, taking off her coat to reveal a scarlet dress, accessorized with several strings of crystal beads. Winifred stood to shake hands.

"Aren't you lucky you can wear that color!" she said. "With my pale skin I look like a ghost in red. You look majestic and scary, like a siren luring sailors to their deaths on a rock."

"I think that's a compliment, so thank you. We met before," Eva reminded her as she sat down. "Back in 1920, at a dance class at the Academy."

"Did we?" Winifred scanned her memory but couldn't remember. "I can't tell you how grateful I am for you coming to meet me. You're doing me a huge favor."

"Of course I came!" Eva replied, pursing her lips in a moue of sympathy. "It must have been terrifying having a run-in with those gangster types. Shall we order martinis?"

She signaled across the room to a waiter, miming tipping a glass into her mouth, then drawing an M in the air with her finger.

"They know me here," she explained. "It should be champagne to celebrate your triumph in *Saint Joan*, but they don't serve it. I've seen your performance three times and I learn something new every time."

"Three times! Goodness me!" Winifred was surprised. "It *is* a great play."

"*You* are the great thing about it. Seriously, I'm in awe of your talent." Eva ran her fingers through her short crop and Winifred noticed she wore several rings studded with large colored gemstones, clearly fake. "What are you doing next, after *Joan*?"

"I haven't committed to anything," Winifred said. "There have been offers but *Joan* is a hard act to follow. My agent is getting frustrated with me but right now, to be frank, I'm not even sure if I want to carry on acting." Certainly, she didn't plan on accepting any more high-profile roles, much to Max's chagrin.

"You can't give up! Wouldn't you miss it?" Eva crunched on a celery stick.

Winifred shook her head. "I love theater, but I haven't enjoyed the limelight one bit. I'm teaching classes at the Academy, and I'm directing a student production for them, which is fun. After that, I'll see . . ."

The waiter brought their martinis and they clinked glasses and took delicate sips.

"I'm trying to place your accent," Winifred said. "I consider myself an expert on accents but with you I'm detecting a mixture: English, American, and a hint of something European . . . Perhaps French?"

Eva laughed out loud. "Spot-on!" she said. "Born in London, spent my childhood between there and Paris, and came to New York at the age of sixteen, where I instantly picked up American vowels. So my accent is pure melting pot."

"That's exotic." Winifred smiled. "I would love to go to Paris and London one day. The theaters sound superb."

"They can be. They can also be dire, just like here. I wanted to be an actress from the age of eight when Sarah Bernhardt signed an autograph for me after I watched her in *The Sleeping Beauty* in Paris."

"Isn't it strange how your life can change on a dime?" Winifred mused. "I decided I wanted to be an actress after an aunt took me to see *Peter Pan* on Broadway. I wanted to be Tinkerbell, of course. If it hadn't been for that aunt, perhaps I would have been a schoolteacher, or a secretary. Who knows?"

"That would have been a great loss to theater," Eva said.

Winifred felt uncomfortable with all the flattery. "What are your ambitions?" she asked. "Any roles you're itching to play?"

Eva shook her head. "I like acting, but my burning ambition is to start my own repertory theater with a group of like-minded thespians." Her eyes were glowing. "It would be like one big hand-picked family. I would take on different roles as required, from writing to directing to acting. What do you think?"

"It sounds like a marvelous plan. Will you stay in Manhattan?"

"If I can find the right theater at the right price. I want to stage plays I believe in—interesting, thought-provoking dramas aimed at women, rather than the unrealistic romances that are standard fare on Broadway." She stared at Winifred as if an idea had just occurred to her. "Why don't you join us? It would be wonderful to have you on the team. I couldn't afford—"

"I'd love to," Winifred interrupted her. "If there's a chance to direct, even better. I've had enough of male directors telling me what to do onstage when most of the time I know better."

Eva grinned and held out her hand: "You've got yourself a deal," she said.

THE THEATRE GUILD had been a sponsor of the *Saint Joan* production and Winifred got to know its founders, most of them august literary types with theatrical connections. When she mentioned that she was interested in spreading her wings into directing, they began showing her scripts by aspiring young playwrights. Winifred enjoyed reading them in her spare time, and imagining ways they could be staged: what kind of set would work, how to cast the roles, and tricks for grabbing the audience's attention.

If Winifred read a script she liked, she passed it to Eva, and they soon found their taste in plays was similar. In particular, they liked stories about unconventional women who stepped outside the norms of marriage and motherhood. They began meeting once or twice a week to exchange ideas for Eva's repertory theater— and, of course, to prove they were romantically involved should any associates of Rothstein be watching.

That winter Winifred accepted a minor role in a comedy by a new young playwright named Stephen Vincent Benét. She had admired the script when she read it and only later found out the writer was the brother-in-law of Dottie's new friend, Elinor Wylie.

Dottie, Elinor, and Bill Benét turned up at a rehearsal one

afternoon, and Winifred could hear them whispering in the front stalls. Afterward, Elinor accosted her in the foyer.

"It was simply marvelous of you to take a role in Stephen's play, hot from your extraordinary success in *Saint Joan*," she said. "The director thinks it will increase our audience tenfold."

"I'm sure it won't make much difference," Winifred murmured modestly.

Elinor carried on as if she hadn't spoken. "That's why I wondered if you could play up the role a little more. Your performance is very understated from what we saw today. I didn't get a sense of *who* Peggy Thatch is. Do you follow me?"

"It's a supporting role," Winifred explained. "Putting more emphasis on her would upset the balance of the play."

"Yes, but with *you* playing it, the audience will want more." She clutched Winifred's arm. "Have a think. Maybe you could put more emotion in your lines. Move to the front of the stage more. Be a star!"

Winifred smiled politely and glanced at Dottie, but she was chatting with Stephen and hadn't heard Elinor's advice. "I'll mention your concerns to the director," she said. "I'm sure he'll be most grateful." She pulled on her coat. "Now I'm afraid I must leave you. I have another commitment."

Elinor protested, saying she simply had to join them for cocktails, but Winifred didn't think she could stand another minute of patronizing advice.

"I have a taxi waiting," she called. "Bye, Dottie. See you soon." She waved and hurried off without looking back.

What did Dottie see in that woman? It was hard to understand the attraction.

ONE EVENING, WINIFRED and Eva emerged from a restaurant near Penn Station and looked around for a taxi. It seemed a busy train had just pulled in and there was a long line of people with suit-cases at the taxi stand. Eva persuaded Winifred to walk instead; she was joining friends at a speakeasy just a few blocks north and Winifred was heading home.

Winifred scanned the crowds as they went. It was early by New York standards—shortly after eleven—but the theaters had come out and the streets were thronged. She was wearing her black fedora to shade her face, but still she was anxious that someone might recognize her, or they might bump into one of Rothstein's mob.

Eva pointed to a quieter street. "Shall we cut down that way to avoid Times Square?"

They were only three blocks from Winifred's apartment now. She knew the area, and had often walked that way in the past, although she would normally have avoided it after dark.

They turned down the side street, aiming to head north at the next intersection, when suddenly a young man leapt in front of them. Winifred heard a metallic click before she saw the flash of a knife. Instinct took over and she grabbed Eva's arm and turned to run, but another man was standing behind them, blocking their way.

"Give us your purse and you won't get hurt," the first one said, waving the knife close to Eva's face. She jerked back and Winifred screamed at the top of her voice. The sound seemed to reverberate in the air.

The second man thrust his knife toward her. "Shut up, if you want to keep that pretty face."

Something snapped in Winifred. In a play long ago, a director had trained her to fend off an attacker and she did it now. She used her left arm to block the hand holding the knife and swung her right fist at his face, connecting with his cheekbone and following up with a vicious kick to the shins. He yelped and hopped backward.

"What the hell are you doing?" Eva hissed.

Winifred barely heard her, she was so consumed with rage. She turned on the first knifeman, fists raised like a boxer.

"Give him your purse!" Eva's voice was hoarse with panic.

Instead Winifred shoved the man hard on the shoulder, screeching, "Get outta here! Leave us alone."

There was a moment when the situation could have gone either way.

"She hurt my leg," the second attacker complained, bending to rub his shin.

"These broads are maniacs," the first one said. "Total lunatics."

Winifred swung her foot as if to kick the second one again and he scuttled backward, then they both turned and dissolved into the shadows.

"Jesus Christ, Winifred! Have you never been robbed before?" Eva yelled. "They could have killed us."

Winifred rubbed her right knuckle, the one that had connected with cheekbone, puzzled by her own reaction. "I'm sorry—I wasn't thinking straight."

Eva shook her head in disbelief. "Next time, forget about playing Jack Dempsey and give them the goddamn money. You're a danger to yourself—and others."

Winifred knew they could both have been stabbed. She felt shaky now that it was over and the surge of rage was wearing off. How could she have been so stupid? What was she thinking? She apologized to Eva repeatedly, but could tell she was still furious when they parted. She kept giving Winifred sideways looks as if she suspected she might be insane.

Winifred made her way back to her apartment and sat curled in an armchair by the window, looking out at the blank windows of the office block opposite. It was almost a full moon and ghostly white rays bathed the room.

She had to stop letting her rage against men get the better of her, or one day she would find herself in trouble she couldn't get out of. She shivered and wrapped her arms tight around her shoulders as her thoughts took her back to a place she couldn't bear to remember, and a time when she was still young and innocent and full of hope.

THE SMELL CAME to her first: freshly painted scenery, leaning against the wall, showing a Bavarian castle with mountains behind. She'd been waiting for forty-five minutes, sitting on a hard chair in a dusty props room, looking at that mountain scenery, and feeling surprised there wasn't a line of other actresses waiting. It was an audition for a speaking part in a Broadway show and she couldn't believe she was there. The director had spotted her on a visit to the Academy, where she was a student, and asked her teacher to send her to read for him on Monday at five o'clock.

Perhaps it was a mistake and he'd forgotten all about it. How long should she wait before she wandered out into the corridor and found someone to ask? She decided to leave it a bit longer.

Just before six, he came in carrying an armful of scripts and put them down on a wide leather-topped desk. He was a tall man, with silver hair, tanned skin, and a diamond-white smile, probably about forty, well dressed.

"You came. Wonderful!" he said, looking her up and down. "You have the right look for the part: beautiful, tough, and sassy at the same time."

She smiled, modestly, and asked, "Would you like me to read for you?"

"Not yet. Could you walk over to that wall and back?" He sat on a chair to watch.

What kind of walk did he want? She decided on a confident one because he'd said "tough and sassy."

"Perfect!" he said, his tone impressed. "Now lift your skirt so I can see your knees and do the same walk again."

She did as he asked, excitement bubbling over. She wanted this so badly. Imagine getting her first Broadway role at the age of seventeen, before she had even finished college! It was more than she had ever dared dream of.

"Now I want you to flirt with me, without speaking," he said, sitting back. "Show me how you would do that."

She paused, thinking of a plan, then sauntered up to him, a suggestive look in her eyes, and bent to rearrange his necktie, letting him catch a glimpse of cleavage and a whiff of her scent.

He didn't move. It wasn't enough.

Throwing caution to the wind, she sat on his lap and circled her arms around his neck, giving him what she hoped was a seductive look: coy, yet daring.

"Very good," he breathed. "You're a natural temptress. Do you know how to kiss a man? Have you ever done it?"

"Of course!" She laughed. She'd had a boyfriend for almost a year, and they'd done a lot of kissing.

"Show me!"

She didn't hesitate. She cupped his chin in her hands and leaned in, slowly and deliberately, making eye contact until just before their lips touched. She could feel him harden in his pants and felt pleased. That meant she must be doing it right.

She pulled back to watch his face. He was breathing hard, his eyes half-closed. She loved that power women had over men. Her boyfriend complained it wasn't fair that she got him all hot and bothered, then didn't follow through, but he clearly didn't mind too much because he kept coming back for more.

"Stand up and turn around," the director said, his voice hoarse.

She stood and turned slowly, winking at him over her shoulder.

Next moment, the breath was knocked out of her when he

pushed her down hard on the desk. At first she thought it was another test, just part of the audition, but she could feel his hands lifting her skirt and fumbling with her undergarments.

"Stop!" she said feebly, and tried to lift herself. "No, please don't."

His hand slammed down on the back of her head, squashing her face into the desk. She couldn't breathe. She started struggling to get free but between the desk and his masculine strength she could only twist her head sideways, which allowed her to catch her breath. That's all she could think about: breathing. Her neck was at an odd angle and she was scared it might snap.

And then he thrust inside her, hard, and the pain was like nothing she had experienced before. It shocked her so badly she stopped trying to get away, stopped everything but breathing and enduring. That Bavarian castle was in her eyeline so she focused on that. Time stood still as she let him rape her.

When he was finished, he stooped to pick up the scripts, which had gotten knocked to the floor. Winifred pulled down her skirt.

"You're adorable, sweetheart," he said, his eyes cold, his lips unsmiling. "I'll be in touch."

And she never heard from him again.

WINIFRED DID NOTHING about the rape. She broke up with her boyfriend because she couldn't bear to have him near her anymore. She counted the days till her next monthly to make sure she wasn't pregnant. Then she locked the memory away deep inside. It had been her own fault, and she would bear the shame alone. But next time she would be damn sure to protect herself better.

Only, given what had happened that evening with Eva and the knife-wielding robbers, that strategy didn't seem to be working out so well. Overreaction could be more dangerous than not reacting at all. Sitting in her armchair, looking out on the moonlit street, she wondered what on earth she could do now.

# Chapter 36
# PEGGY

It had been months since the bridge club met, and Peggy missed the women. She had other friends, of course, but they tended to be quiet bookish types, without the verve of the bridge girls. She decided to try and round them up, which was never an easy task these days. First she rang Winifred, to find out whether she was still appearing onstage every night.

"I've just finished the Stephen Benét play and I'm not taking on any more acting roles for now," came the answer.

"Good! That means we can start a bridge evening early, without waiting for you to dash over from the theater in greasepaint and an eccentric hairstyle."

"I'm sure it's my turn to host," Winifred said. "Let me know when everyone's free and I'll find a new cocktail for us to test."

Next Peggy telephoned Jane.

"Sorry, Pegs, no can do," she said brusquely. "*The New Yorker* is launching soon and I'm working all day, every day. Maybe we can get together in March."

Peggy rang Dottie last. She'd been annoyed to hear that Alvan was analyzing her. It was odd to think of her friend confessing intimate secrets to the man she was sleeping with, and she was sure it was unprofessional of Alvan to analyze someone he knew socially.

She told him quite strenuously that she thought it was wrong, but hid her reservations from Dottie.

"Jane can't make it for a bridge evening, but I wondered if you would like to come to Winifred's with me?" she asked her on the telephone. "Just the three of us for a change."

"I'm not sure," Dottie said, her voice sounding low and slurred.

"Did I wake you?" Peggy glanced at the clock. It was two o'clock, the time she normally called. Dottie should be at her typewriter by then.

"I've not been sleeping well. I must have overslept." She yawned. "I'm not sure about Winifred's. Jane might be upset if we met without her."

"I'm not suggesting we bring in another bridge player," Peggy said, "but we three could meet for a cocktail and a chat."

"I'd better not risk it," Dottie said. "Jane's cross with me already. And Alvan says I'm not allowed to drink."

No argument Peggy produced would persuade her. Perhaps she would have to forget about the bridge group until they were all less busy—or give up on it entirely, which would be a shame. She had enjoyed spending time with these women—but if they were moving on, she supposed she must too.

TOMMY SMITH OFFERED Peggy some editorial notes for improving her novel. He felt the mother was unsympathetic and asked that her portrayal be more nuanced; perhaps she wanted the best for her daughter but came from a generation who had quite different views. He thought the suitors were too universally hapless, in particular the one who was seeking a wife to look after his obnoxious hypochondriac mother. Peggy laughed and told him that this character was based on someone she had stepped out with in her late teens.

After the meeting, she read through the novel again, revisiting every word with a critical eye, attempting to make her descriptions fresher, and questioning the decisions she had made the first time around. Why had she called the main character Vergie? Was it too obvious a reference to virginity? Tommy said he liked the name and she should stop worrying, but she felt very exposed now that her private thoughts were going to be read by the world—or at least by anyone who bought her novel.

Would her sister, Rose, object to the portrayal of the spoiled younger sister she had named Pet? Would her parents mind that the parents in the novel were staid and unimaginative?

She discussed it with Alvan, and he reassured her.

"Few of us would recognize ourselves seen through another's eyes," he said. "Our self-image dominates because we think we know ourselves better than anyone else. Of course, that may or may not be true. When you look in a mirror, the image you see is reversed left to right, but when you look at a photograph of yourself—the photographer's view—you see yourself as others see you."

"Are you suggesting that other people can know us better than we know ourselves?" That seemed odd to Peggy.

"It varies from person to person. I know myself better than you know me, and I'm sure the reverse is true."

Peggy nodded in agreement. After six months of sleeping together, she still felt she didn't know Alvan in a profound sense. She knew his body, she knew the music he liked and the books he read, she knew he rarely suffered self-doubt, but she didn't feel she understood the heart and soul of him.

"However," he continued, "I know your friend Dottie better than she knows herself. For such a smart woman, she has very limited self-knowledge because she is blocked in so many areas."

Peggy gave him a disapproving look. "Alvan, I asked you not to discuss Dottie with me. I don't want her worrying that you might have passed on confidences from the therapy couch."

He didn't seem to think there was an issue. "I've only told you the most general insights. Nothing specific."

"All I want to know is that you are taking good care of her," she said. "You of all people should know how fragile she is."

"Of course I am," he assured her, his face serious, his glasses reflecting her own face in their round lenses.

ON SATURDAY EVENING Peggy went to Winifred's on her own, taking some homemade Irish soda bread and a hunk of cheese.

Winifred mixed French 75s—a cocktail with gin, champagne, lemon juice, and syrup—and handed Peggy a glass. "Cheers!" she toasted.

Peggy took a sip and smacked her lips appreciatively. "This is the cat's meow," she said, then made a purring sound. "I could lap up buckets of these."

Winifred laughed. "I've got plenty of ingredients. Let's make a night of it!"

They chatted about work, about *The New Yorker*, about Dottie and the Gonk. Winifred mixed more drinks and Peggy felt herself getting uncharacteristically tipsy.

"I bumped into Eva last week," she remembered, "and she told me you fought off some armed robbers. She seemed quite shaken up about it."

"I know. I'm afraid I lost my temper." Winifred relayed the story. "Fortunately, they decided we weren't worth the trouble."

"Did you have lots of cash with you?"

"Less than five dollars. It would have been stupid to die for that, but I saw red."

Peggy had never been robbed in the city. She was careful where she went after dark and certainly wouldn't have been walking in the Times Square area, which was notorious for pickpockets.

"Do you often lose your temper?" she asked. "I'm curious. You fought back against Legs Diamond too. And I'll never forget you slapping Peter's friend in Tony Soma's. Are these lessons from your Brooklyn upbringing?"

Winifred took a sip of her drink, and gazed out the window. "No," she said eventually. "I had elder brothers so I had to defend myself as a kid, but that's not what it's about."

Peggy waited to see if she would explain.

"Something happened to me eight years ago when I was at college. I've never told anyone." She picked up her glass, then put it down again and shifted her legs, curling them under her, and fidgeted with her bracelet. "It makes me lash out in panic whenever I feel threatened by men."

Peggy could sense Winifred wanted to talk. She just needed urging.

"You don't have to tell me if you don't want to, but I know Alvan would say that buried traumas can cause us to act irrationally and unpredictably. If the emotion attached to the experience has never been expressed, it lies dormant and can burst out at unexpected moments in response to triggers in everyday life. Do you think that's what happens with you?"

"Yes. That's exactly what it is." Winifred was silent for a while, then sighed. "The truth is . . ."

As she told the story, she clutched her throat with one hand, and Peggy guessed it was a subconscious gesture of self-protection. She listened without comment, feeling increasingly upset on Winifred's behalf. Peggy had once met the director she named at a *Vanity Fair* party, where he had appeared suave and charming. She would never have suspected him capable of such a callous attack. He clearly hid his dark side well.

"Why didn't you go to the cops?" Peggy asked when Winifred stopped speaking.

"It was his word against mine and he would have said I led him on. He would have been right: I *did* lead him on."

"He was the one in a position of power and you just did what he asked you to. It wasn't your fault." Peggy tried to imagine Tommy Smith molesting her. They were often alone in his office, but she knew he wouldn't dream of it, even if she were as beautiful as Winifred. He was too much of a gentleman. "Is this kind of behavior common in your profession?" she asked.

"Oh, sure. Pretty girls and powerful men are a volatile combination, and the theater is full of both." Winifred paused. "But I wasn't smart enough to read the signs. I could have stopped him if I hadn't been so preoccupied with trying to win the part."

"Was it your first time?" Peggy asked quietly.

"First and only," Winifred whispered. "I've dated since then but I can't bring myself to go to bed with any man."

Peggy was surprised to learn she had more sexual experience than her glamorous, beautiful friend, who could have had any man she wanted. But it was understandable she was wary, given all she'd been through. She felt fury that the director had caused so much harm yet had walked away as if nothing happened.

"So that was it? Afterward he just picked up his scripts and left without a backward glance?" she asked.

"He even got me to hold the scripts while he . . ." Suddenly Winifred frowned and clasped a hand to her mouth. "I'd forgotten that." She turned to Peggy, open-mouthed. "The door was locked. He had to unlock it before he left, and I held the scripts for him. Which means he must have turned the key in the lock when he arrived. I didn't notice. I suppose I was so nervous . . ." Tears filled her eyes.

Peggy understood immediately. "That means he'd planned it all along. Your actions were nothing to do with it. You don't have to blame yourself anymore."

She put her arms around Winifred and held her as she sobbed.

LATER, PEGGY TOLD Alvan what she had heard about the theater director's behavior, without mentioning that Winifred had been the victim.

"He sounds like a classic narcissist," Alvan said. "He has a grandiose sense of his own entitlement, and a lack of empathy for others. These types are virtually impossible to treat in therapy. They are incapable of change."

"In novels, such behavior would be punished," Peggy said. "I wish the same were true in life. I bet she's not the only girl he has raped."

"What do you think would become of us in a novel?" Alvan asked. "I hope if you ever write about a psychoanalyst, you'll give me a good report."

Peggy paused. He had changed the subject so quickly, he clearly didn't realize how upset she was. He didn't know it had been someone very close to her who had been raped, and she couldn't tell him without betraying Winifred's confidence.

"Us in a novel? Now there's an idea," she said. "An analyst who is a talented lover and a great cook. . . . He sounds too good to be true. I'd have to give him a flaw. Perhaps he snores, or his laugh is like the braying of a donkey."

Alvan smiled, and it occurred to Peggy that she couldn't imagine ever having an argument with him. He would sit with that knowing smile instead of yelling back. She wondered what she would have to do to rattle him—and whether she would ever find out.

# Chapter 37
# JANE

Jane heated some beef stew in the kitchen at 412 and packed it in a tin pail with a lid, picking up plates, forks, and a fresh loaf of bread before she left. For once she allowed herself to take a cab to *The New Yorker* offices, so that the food would still be warm when she got there. Harold had been working all day without a break, and she knew he would have forgotten to eat.

She discovered him in his office, scarcely visible behind a desk that was piled high with stacks of paper, discarded pens, overflowing ashtrays, and unwashed coffee cups with mold growing inside.

"I can't find the cartoon for page nineteen. The 'wages of sin' one." He scratched his head, and she saw his fingers were stained with his favorite red ink.

"Eat first, and I'll find it after." She dished up a plate of stew, cut a hunk of bread, and handed him the plate, then helped herself. The only other chair had papers piled on it so she perched on top of them.

"I expect you will," he said, devouring his stew in rapid forkfuls. "Do you understand how frustrating it is that I could comb through every scrap of paper on this desk without finding it, while you will probably lay your hands on it in seconds? Is it a form of witchcraft?"

Jane smiled. She was simply observant. As she walked around

the house, she made a mental note when Harold had left his keys on the arm of his favorite chair, his wallet by the sink where he had been shaving, and his notes for the first issue of the magazine in the laundry basket underneath the shirt he had worn the previous day. He was hopelessly absentminded when it came to everyday essentials, laying them down wherever he happened to be, then wandering off.

Inside the magazine's offices he was similarly disorganized, but what stood out was his extraordinary talent. He was a brilliant editor, who could take a story from the most experienced of writers, cross out a couple of sentences, scribble a few notes in the margin, and magically transform it into an infinitely better piece. It was the same with cartoons: by changing a single word in the caption, he could convert something mildly funny into a satiric masterpiece. He had the knack of finding the heart of any piece of work.

The fact that few people apart from Jane could read his handwriting added to the many challenges of working for him. Whenever she arrived at the office, she was mobbed by staff members asking her to translate his marginal scribbles, saying they didn't like to disturb him. Truth was, he often couldn't decipher his own writing—but Jane could.

Harold gobbled down the stew so fast she could tell he had been ravenous. She scraped half her portion onto his plate and cut him another hunk of bread. He'd lost weight; his shirt was loose and his bony shoulders jutted beneath the fabric. His eyes were red-rimmed from reading without glasses, most likely because he had mislaid them. His hair stuck up in unwashed clumps. He looked like a caricature of himself, Jane thought fondly.

It was nine in the evening but the office was still buzzing with sub-editors, typesetters and designers, marketing assistants, and advertising sales staff. The team was all dedicated types, prepared to work for pin money until *The New Yorker* was established.

"Is that the cartoon?" She pointed to the corner of a sheet of paper protruding from a precarious pile on the far side of his desk. She eased it out, admiring the inked artwork.

"Definitely witchcraft," Harold muttered, laying it on top of a file tray marked "Urgent."

Jane walked around the desk and swung her leg to sit astride his lap, facing him. She combed her fingers through his hair and kissed him on the lips. "I haven't seen you for ages, Mr. Ross. Are you still the same adorable husband I married almost five years ago?"

"Less adorable and more bad-tempered, but I believe we're still married—unless you know something I don't."

"We need a vacation," she said. "Later this year, once the magazine is a rip-roaring success. Where shall we go? How about Europe?"

"Right now, I'd settle for Coney Island. Remember our day trips there, eating Nathan's hot dogs, then feeling queasy on the Wonder Wheel?"

"One of the highlights of my life," Jane said, arching an eyebrow.

"Alec has invited us to Neshobe Island," he said. "He's forever nagging me to set a date, but it doesn't sound as though there are many amenities. It would mean sleeping in tents, cutting our own firewood, and casting a line in the lake to catch dinner."

The previous year, Alec had clubbed together with five friends to buy some land on an island in a lake in Vermont, where he was building a house.

"It doesn't appeal in the slightest," Jane replied. "Not even remotely." She couldn't think of anything worse than being trapped in the wilderness with Alec acting lord of the manor. One day, when the magazine was making a mint, she and Harold would buy their own house by the sea, where they could hold weekend parties for their friends.

The mention of Alec killed the intimacy of the moment. She climbed off Harold's lap. "Shall I get you a coffee, boss?" she asked, and he grunted assent, his attention already back on the story he'd been reading when she arrived.

As she walked out the door, she glanced back, and her heart lurched with love. The money problem was ancient history; everything had worked out just fine and their dream was on the cusp of becoming reality. She felt as if she had never loved him as much as she did in that precise moment.

LAUNCH DAY, FEBRUARY TWENTY-FIRST, rolled around fast. The magazine nearly wasn't printed on time because of Harold's last-minute fiddling with typography and fretting over a comma in the opening article. It was Jane who told the printer to start the presses, and when she woke in the morning of the twenty-first, her first thought was that thousands of magazines should already have landed on newsstands across the city.

There were stories by F. P. Adams, Fairfax Downey, and Ernest F. Hubbard; there were poems, cartoons, and columns, including one by an aptly named Van Bibber III, talking about the way that the quality of liquor a host served had become the new mark of social status in New York. Readers of *The New Yorker* would definitely not be dries!

Jane was annoyed that Alec, Edna Ferber, and Heywood Broun hadn't contributed. She knew some writers of their acquaintance had held back because they didn't want their names in a magazine that might sink without a trace. Dottie had written a few theater reviews but hadn't supplied a story. Jane had hoped for a little more loyalty. Still, she was determined not to let them spoil the excitement of the day.

She got dressed in a hurry and dashed out, leaving Harold to sleep longer. On her way to work she checked every newsstand she passed. Their distributor had done a good job; she couldn't find a single one that didn't have at least a few copies. The cover, with its top-hatted dandy in a monocle, stood out from its competitors. Overall, the design was knockout.

"Do you think it will sell?" she asked one vendor, after introducing herself.

"Cover price of fifteen cents is decent," he said. "Depends what's inside."

"Will you push it for me?" she begged, with a smile that she hoped was winning. She shifted the pile to the front of his stall. "I'd be ever so grateful."

"Anything for a lady," he agreed.

She watched as a business-suited man picked one up, flicked through, read one of the cartoons, chuckled, then put it down again.

"Are you not going to buy it?" she asked.

He turned, surprised to be accosted. "I like magazines, but I seldom have time to read them. My wife gets cross when they pile up in the living room."

"If you only read one magazine a week, make it this one," Jane urged. "I guarantee you'll love it."

"In that case, how can I refuse?" He pulled some coins from his pocket and handed them over, tipped his hat, and walked off with *The New Yorker* under his arm.

Jane was excited to have made a sale, but she couldn't spend all day doing this. She had to get to the *New York Times* by ten for the editorial meeting. Harold wasn't earning any money from *The New Yorker* for now, so it was imperative she didn't get fired.

AT THE END of the first week, the returns were depressing: more than a third of the copies they'd printed came flooding back to the warehouse.

"That's not bad," Carr Van Anda told her. "You sold two-thirds of your print run. Now you have to work harder at marketing the next issue because you don't have novelty on your side anymore."

He was right: the second issue didn't sell as many, and the third even fewer. Raoul Fleischmann began hosting a weekly meeting where the heads of each department threw in suggestions to boost sales, and Jane always tried to attend. One of the best ideas to emerge was starting a weekly column in which celebrities endorsed selected products, from ties to cold cream. These would raise a useful side stream of income from the manufacturers, who had to buy the endorsements, and engage readers who wanted to know which cold cream the likes of Winifred Lenihan used.

"The content has to keep getting better with every issue," Carr Van Anda advised Jane. "The minute standards slip, you'll lose readers and it will be a hundred times harder to get them back again."

She and Harold lay in bed late at night tossing out ideas for features, stories, and profiles until they couldn't keep their eyes open. Their sex life went out the window because they were too frazzled. It was all about the magazine for now.

ONE EVENING WHEN Jane arrived at *The New Yorker* office, Harold was nowhere to be seen and no one seemed to know where he'd gone.

"Try the Gonk," Lois Long, the pretty young marketing manager, suggested.

It was just around the block, on West Forty-Fourth. Jane hadn't been for weeks, not since before Christmas. She found a few clusters of people at the Round Table. Dottie was alone at one side, slumped over a glass of amber liquid. She was wearing an expensive-looking moss-green dress with multiple tiny pleats and a matching hat trimmed with silk lily of the valley.

"Howdie, stranger!" Jane greeted her with a grin. "I don't suppose you've seen Harold?"

Dottie looked up without smiling. "Has your errant husband gone astray? You should tighten the matrimonial reins." Her voice was slow and slurred, and Jane guessed it wasn't her first whiskey. Peggy had mentioned that she wasn't supposed to be drinking while Alvan was psychoanalyzing her, but she was clearly disregarding that.

"Can I join you?" she asked, sitting down. "I've been on my feet all day."

"I'm waiting for Elinor," Dottie said, "but feel free to warm the chair." She lit a cigarette. Jane noticed she had switched from her normal brand, Chesterfield, to Herbert Tareytons.

Close up her face was puffy and her eyes pink. Jane wondered whether to comment on her drinking, but they hadn't seen each other for a while and she didn't want to be a nag.

"Shame about *The New Yorker*," Dottie slurred. "It seems traffic didn't stop, crowds didn't gather, attention generally was not paid. What will you do now?"

Jane felt as if she'd been punched in the stomach. Her first reaction was defensive. "It's doing perfectly well for a new magazine. We always planned to give it six months to break even."

"You said you wanted to set the world of magazines on fire, but it's hardly created a spark." Her dark eyes glittered.

Jane's temper flared. "Maybe it would be faring better if we'd had more support from our so-called editorial board. Were you planning on writing a story for us anytime soon?"

"Rats don't usually leap *onto* sinking ships, do they?" Dottie dragged deeply on her cigarette and blew out a long trail of smoke.

"What's got into you?" Jane snapped. "I thought friends tried to support each other's new ventures, not trash them." Dottie seemed like a different person. It was as if she was turning into a

285

mirror image of Elinor Wylie, complete with the haute-couture dress, fancy cigarettes, and supercilious attitude.

"Touché! I haven't had any support from you in ages. You claim you've been too busy with the magazine—but it's not even yours, it's Harold's. He's the one with his name on the masthead. You're just the editor's wife."

Jane gasped out loud. "If that's what you think, you have no idea what you're talking about."

"Don't I?" Dottie gave her a knowing look, as if to imply she was aware of far more than she was letting on.

Jane fought her corner: "I came up with the idea for a New York humor magazine; I raised the money to make it happen; and I work there every single evening and weekend. The only reason I'm not on the masthead is because of the clash with my *New York Times* job." She paused, a few choice comments on the tip of her tongue, but held back. Dottie was clearly not in a good frame of mind. Maybe she was drunker than she appeared, and that's what was causing the belligerence.

"I'm sure your husband appreciates all the sacrifices you make for him," Dottie said, her tone thick with sarcasm.

She was jealous of their happy marriage, Jane knew that, but it hadn't gotten in the way of their friendship until now. Before she could stop herself, she hit back: "At least I know how to hang on to a husband."

Instantly the words were out she regretted them.

Dottie scraped back her chair and stood abruptly. "I'll wait for Elinor upstairs," she said. "Goodbye, Jane."

Jane considered rushing after her, but she was still too furious. She certainly didn't want to be there when Elinor arrived. She strode out of the Gonk, heading west toward 412, pounding the sidewalk to burn off her anger.

She would telephone and apologize later. She'd say she was under a lot of stress, then ask if Dottie was OK. She hadn't seemed herself at all. Could it be the psychoanalysis that was making her such a bitch?

She unlocked the front door of 412 and called out: "Harold? Anyone home?"

The dining room was empty but the door to their apartment stood ajar. She glanced in the living room, then the bedroom, calling Harold's name. It was then she heard a groaning sound coming from the bathroom.

The door was blocked by Harold's legs. She pushed to make enough room to poke her head around, and saw him lying on the floor, clutching his stomach. There was vomit splattered around the toilet bowl.

"My stomach," he whispered, retching. "It's excruciating."

Jane knelt on the floor beside him and touched his forehead with the back of her hand. His skin was gray and clammy. "Do you think it could be food poisoning?" she asked.

He shook his head, and winced at a spike of pain. "My father gets the same thing. It's ulcers, the family curse."

Jane sat on the edge of the bath, feeling as if the rug had been pulled from under her. Harold was too young for ulcers. Was it serious? She needed him to be hale and hearty so they could live to a ripe old age together. If he got ill, who would take the reins of the magazine?

"Shall I get a taxi to take us to the hospital?" she asked.

He shook his head, breathing heavily. "I'll see a doc tomorrow. He'll give me some medicine and tell me not to drink or smoke, or eat rich foods. It's time to start being sensible. I guess my youth ends here."

He wiped his mouth and she helped him to stand up and stagger to bed, fetched him a glass of water, then came back to clean up the vomit around the toilet bowl.

His words "youth ends here" echoed in her head. It was a long time since she had felt young. Maybe the last time was in France in 1919, before she was married. Since then, she'd had to grow up fast. She was only thirty-two but felt at least twice that age.

# Chapter 38

# DOTTIE

Dottie instantly regretted her argument with Jane. She was drunker than she'd realized and had lashed out saying mean things about the magazine. It was true she didn't think it was brilliant. The quality of the humor was mediocre with only occasional flashes of genius, but she shouldn't have criticized Jane's baby.

She let herself into her apartment, and the scent of dog mess reached her nostrils. She had completely forgotten to take Woodrow Wilson outside to do his business. She hadn't fed him either. What an abysmal dog owner she was!

"Woodrow!" she called as she filled his bowl. She frowned at the silence. Normally he would be yapping at her legs with excitement when he heard the cupboard door open and the bowl clatter to the floor.

She had moved his bed into her bedroom because she found his snuffling a comfort if she wakened in the night. She walked through to find him sound asleep. That was odd. He would usually wake at the slightest sound.

She crouched to stroke him, then snatched her hand back with a scream. He was cold, unmoving, and stiff as taxidermy. She wailed: *"Wood-row!"*

Tears flowed as she rushed to the telephone. What should she do? Who could she call? She rang Bob's number first but his wife answered and said he wasn't home, her tone cold and unfriendly. The next person she thought of calling was Jane, but she couldn't, not after their argument.

She glanced at the clock. Where was Elinor? She should have been there by now.

She dialed Elinor's number, expecting Bill to answer, but instead Elinor's voice came on the line.

"Woodrow Wilson died!" Dottie sobbed. "He's in the bedroom. I don't know what to do."

Elinor gasped. "Oh, my darling, I know how much you loved that dog. He was old, though, and now he is at peace. You'll meet him again in another life."

"I thought you were coming over," Dottie said, tears streaming down her cheeks, her words indistinct with sobbing. "I need you."

"Did we arrange to meet? I'm completely drowning in the proofs of my new collection and can't even remember my own name." She paused and Dottie detected a sigh. "You're welcome to come here, if you can entertain yourself while I work. Stay for dinner."

"I'm on the way," Dottie said, filled with gratitude. "Thank you."

Before leaving, she stood in the bedroom doorway and whispered her goodbyes to Woodrow. She couldn't bear to touch him or go anywhere near him.

On the way out she asked a maid to get Frank Case to deal with the body. Maybe there should be a funeral but she couldn't think about that now. First of all, somehow, she would have to find a way to cope with the loss, which felt so overwhelming she didn't know how she'd survive.

Bill wasn't at home when Dottie reached University Place. Elinor let her in and gave her a warm hug.

"You were the best of mothers to Woodrow. He had a happy

life and a peaceful end. You must remember the good times and not dwell on his passing." She stroked Dottie's cheek. "Come, let's make tea, then I must get on with my work. The fella who set the type for my new collection had clearly never encountered a poem before."

Dottie trailed in her wake as she prepared a pot of tea, laid out a plate of cookies, and carried them through to their sunny living room.

"Would you like something to read?" she asked, but Dottie shook her head. She had no concentration for reading. She would have liked to talk but Elinor clearly didn't have the time.

"Why not try a jigsaw?" Elinor suggested. "I have a fiendish one that took Bill and me several days to complete. It's a map of Paris with pictures of all the sights. Have you ever been to Paris? You simply must go. Perhaps you can come with us next time."

Dottie sat at the table in the window and opened the box. Images filled her head of Woodrow snuggling on her lap and licking her face; lying on her feet while she worked at her typewriter; jumping up and down with unreserved joy whenever she arrived home. She hadn't appreciated how much affection he gave her till now, when he was gone forever. She pulled a moist handkerchief from her pocket to dab at her eyes. Elinor was hard at work across the room and ignored her sniffles.

Dottie turned to the jigsaw. She hadn't done one since she was a child. She began to hunt for the corners and then the edges. If only the search for the towers of Notre-Dame Cathedral could help to drown out the insistent clamor of her darkest thoughts.

DOTTIE STAYED OVERNIGHT at Bill and Elinor's. The thought of sleeping in the room where Woodrow had died was too much for her. She couldn't contemplate being alone just yet.

The next day she sensed she was outstaying her welcome. Elinor paid her scant attention, busy asking Bill's advice on her proofs and scribbling notes on the pages, but it was a comfort simply to be there, with other human beings in the room. Dottie carried on with the jigsaw, eating meals when they were served, drinking tea when it was put in front of her, most of the time managing to achieve a state of numbness. She would have loved a whiskey or two but Elinor and Bill didn't keep alcohol in the house unless they were throwing a party. Besides, Elinor knew that Alvan had told her not to drink while she was being analyzed, so she couldn't buy some and drink it there.

On the third morning of her stay, Elinor was a little tetchy. "Don't you think you should go home and do some work, Dottie? If you're not earning, you'll run out of money, and then where will you be?"

Dottie didn't confess that she hadn't been able to write for weeks. Far from analysis providing material for her writing, it seemed to have dried up her creative juices entirely. She had no idea how many months she was behind with rent at the Gonk, but it was a lot, and her bills for room service were mounting. Eddie was still giving her an allowance but she couldn't stop buying new clothes; it was like a compulsion. If she told Elinor she was broke, it would feel as if she were holding out a begging bowl, and she didn't want to put them in that position.

"I have a session with Alvan later," she said. "I'll go home afterward. I've imposed on your kindness long enough."

She yearned for Elinor to say, "No! Please stay as long as you like." But instead she said, "Perfect," and glided off to work.

AS SHE TOLD Alvan about Woodrow Wilson dying, Dottie sobbed so hard the words were barely coherent. "I hadn't walked him that morning," she cried. "Or fed him. I can't even remember if I had the day before. Do you think he starved to death?"

Alvan usually didn't answer when she asked direct questions. It had taken her some time to get used to that; he left them hanging in the air till she answered them herself. This time, he replied: "He was an old dog, Dottie. He would have gone soon, one way or another. But I'm interested in what this new loss is bringing up for you. You feel guilt? Abandonment? What else?"

Dottie blew her nose. Her eyes stung. She tried to define the aching chasm she felt inside. The loneliness. The terror that depression would suck her down into its depths. The fear that she would never be able to climb out again. Alvan didn't comment but she heard his pencil scratching on the page.

There was a crack in the ceiling above the couch—rather a serious-looking one—and she pictured the roof falling in and crushing her. Would it be a quick death or might she be trapped beneath the rubble? If rescued, would she be wheelchair-bound? That idea appealed. If only she could be injured badly enough that someone would have to look after her. Perhaps she could stay in a sanatorium where nurses brought her meals and tucked blankets around her knees.

"I need someone to look after me," she told Alvan. "I'm not capable of being on my own anymore." It was a terrifying thought.

Alvan listed her career successes, as if that should cheer her up. She couldn't tell him she was no longer able to write; couldn't tell him she was drinking more than ever despite his instruction; couldn't tell him she was broke. Maybe she should, though.

"Time's up," he said. It seemed he always said that just when she was ready to open up with him. She had asked once why he didn't have a clock in the room where she could see it, but he claimed patients would blurt out all their deepest anxieties in the last five minutes and not leave him time to address them. He didn't seem to sense how desperate she was when he ushered her out of the office, as if his mind was already on the next patient.

As she walked home afterward, she paused at the corner of Park Avenue, watching the traffic rumbling by. What if she stepped out in front of a truck? How would she time it so that she would be injured but not too badly? A broken leg would be perfect but she didn't want her face to be disfigured. Eventually she decided it was too risky. She'd probably get it wrong, like she got everything else wrong.

She stopped at the cordial store and bought a quart of Haig & Haig, telling herself it was just to get her through the first night alone without Woodrow. She unlocked her apartment door and sniffed a disinfectant smell. When she ventured to the bedroom door, she saw that someone had removed Woodrow's bed entirely and she was glad. It would have been a constant reminder.

She set the whiskey and a glass on the table, wondering who was downstairs at the Round Table. Bob might be there, and it would be wonderful to see him, but he was almost always with Charlie and she couldn't face that. She certainly didn't feel resilient enough to deal with Alec. If anyone made a joke about her dog dying, she would lose it.

She lifted the telephone and dialed Peggy's number but it rang and rang. It was early evening. She was probably meeting Alvan. He wasn't supposed to discuss what they talked about in therapy but perhaps he would mention Woodrow's dying. She was sure Peggy would ring as soon as she heard.

Next Dottie tried ringing Winifred. She had rescued her once before, by taking her to Lenox Hill Hospital. Might she come to her aid again? The telephone rang and rang. Dottie tried to remember if she was appearing in a play right now. If so, she'd already be at the theater having her hair and makeup done and getting into costume.

More than anyone else, she yearned to talk to Jane. She'd said she spent every evening at *The New Yorker* offices. Perhaps

Woodrow Wilson's dying gave Dottie an excuse to extend an olive branch.

She called the operator and asked to be put through to *The New Yorker*. The telephone was answered by a cheerful-sounding woman who identified herself as Lois Long.

"I haven't seen Jane or Harold all day," she told her. "Are you a friend?"

Dottie said she was.

"Between ourselves," Lois continued, "I think Harold's got a bad stomach and she's nursing him. We're pretty sure he'll be back tomorrow to sign off on next week's issue. He'd have to be at death's door before he'd miss that."

After Dottie hung up, the phrase *death's door* rattled around her brain. What did death's door look like? How did it feel to know you were close to death? Was there a sense of peace at last, even if there were no angels and heavenly choirs?

She poured herself a stiff whiskey and gulped half of it, feeling the familiar fuzziness descend. Lines from Elinor's poems about death filled her head: "Your sky is riven like a tearing veil," and "The dead leaves are varnished with color like blood."

She finished the whiskey and poured another. She couldn't work, couldn't earn money, and her friends were too busy to see her. Woodrow had been the only one who truly loved her and now he was gone. She drank more, hugging a cushion to her chest. The pain was physical, as if her heart truly were broken. She needed help. How could she make someone help her?

After a while she had to go to the bathroom. It was cool in there. A maid had left the window open to air the place. The breeze had blown the cabinet door slightly ajar and inside she spotted her stockpile of veronal. Almost without thinking she swallowed a couple. One stuck in her throat, so she fetched her whiskey to wash it down, then she swallowed more. Another stuck in her throat, making her retch, but she persevered until she had lost count of the number she'd taken. There was a bitter, powdery taste in her mouth.

And then she felt wooziness descend terrifyingly fast, and knew she was going to pass out. The bathroom was wobbling, the walls no longer vertical.

Panic gripped her as she hit the tiled floor. This wasn't clever. She wanted to be ill enough so someone would have to look after her but she didn't want to die.

"Shit!" she moaned. "Oh shit!"

There was a whooshing sound in her head. The whiskey glass was still in her hand. With the last of her strength she hurled it out of the bathroom window and then she lost consciousness.

# Chapter 39
# WINIFRED

Winifred was window-shopping on Fifth Avenue when she heard someone calling her name from the other side of the street, and turned to see Bob Benchley weaving through traffic toward her. She waved and called a cheery "Hallo!" but as he got close she realized his expression was grim.

"Have you heard the news?" he asked.

"What news?"

"It's Dottie. She's in the hospital. I'm sorry to be the bearer of bad tidings but she—" He choked as if close to tears. "She took an overdose last night."

"Oh god no!" Winifred clutched a hand to her throat. "Is she going to be OK?"

"She is. I've just been to visit. I told her if she doesn't stop this sort of thing she'll make herself sick. She said that was kind of the point." He shook his head in despair.

"Is it too late to visit today?" Winifred glanced at her watch. It was almost five.

"Visiting hours are over, but why don't you go tomorrow? She's in the Harkness Pavilion at the Presbyterian Hospital."

"I will. I'll call Jane and Peggy too." She hesitated. "Are you alright, Bob? You look devastated."

"I'm as well as can be expected when one of my closest friends has decided she doesn't want to be alive anymore. I just can't . . ." He hung his head, and Winifred put her hand on his arm.

"I know. I can't either."

She was used to putting herself into the shoes of the characters she played and imagining what it felt like to be them . . . but she couldn't begin to imagine what might have made Dottie try to end her life. The concept was entirely beyond her.

Winifred abandoned her shopping and rushed home. First, she tried Jane, ringing *The New Yorker* and the *New York Times* offices before finally catching her at 412.

"No!" Jane shouted on hearing the news. "Oh, Winifred, it's all my fault. We fell out. I was cross with her for not writing a story for *The New Yorker*, and she accused me of neglecting our friendship—and she was right."

"It's not your fault, Jane. It's no one's fault. . . . Let's go and see her tomorrow and figure out how we can help." They arranged to meet at the front door of the hospital at two o'clock.

Next Winifred rang Peggy.

"I just heard from Alvan," she said. "He's going to talk to her this evening. Did you hear what happened?"

"Not the details."

"Frank Case was in the alley out back of the Gonk when a glass came hurtling through the air, narrowly missing his head, and shattering at his feet." Peggy's voice was shaky. "When he looked up, he saw Dottie's window open and sprinted upstairs. If he hadn't seen that glass, she probably wouldn't have survived."

"Oh Jesus!" Winifred choked on a sob. "So she'd taken a serious amount of pills, had she?"

"Enough to fell a mule, Alvan says."

"What are we going to say tomorrow?" Winifred asked.

"I don't know," Peggy replied. "Truly I don't."

THE THREE WOMEN linked arms as they walked along the corridor to Dottie's hospital room. She was propped up in bed, her face as white as the pillows behind her.

"I didn't realize it was a bridge night," she said, her voice frail and scratchy. "Did someone bring a deck of cards? Because I'm afraid it slipped my mind when they were carrying me out of the Gonk on a stretcher."

"I don't think any of us are in the mood for bridge," Jane said, bending to kiss her cheek. "I'm sorry about our fight, Dottie."

"What fight?" She shrugged. "I don't recall one."

"How are you feeling?" Peggy asked. "How's the room service?"

"I haven't tested the catering yet. For some reason I've been off my food, but I'll let you know when I get my appetite back."

Winifred glanced at the cabinet by her bed, where a sick bowl had been left within easy reach. She wondered if they had pumped her stomach. The thought made her queasy.

"Is there anything we can bring you?" she asked. "Grapes? Magazines? I can rush to the nearest shop."

"I'd love a quart of Haig and Haig," Dottie said, "but my doctor is a killjoy who seems set against me imbibing anything stronger than water for the foreseeable."

"That sounds sensible," Peggy said. "In the circumstances."

"Are they being kind?" Winifred asked. She had heard that medical staff could sometimes be brusque with attempted suicides, considering self-inflicted injuries a waste of their time.

"They're just peachy," Dottie said. "And the other patients are friendly too. The girl in the room opposite has offered to teach me rug weaving, and there's a French viscount down the corridor who gave me an anthology of poetry—in French, of course."

At first Winifred wasn't sure if she was making this up, then she saw the volume sitting under the sick bowl: Baudelaire's *Les fleurs du mal*—*The Flowers of Evil*. What an odd choice!

"Have they said how long you have to stay?" Jane asked.

"I don't think they know what to do with me yet, but I'll keep you informed."

"Why did you do it, Dottie?" Jane asked, her voice infinitely sad.

Tears leaked out of Dottie's eyes and her face crumpled. "Woodrow Wilson died. It felt like he was all I had left."

Winifred felt her own eyes well up. Her family had a dog when she was a girl, a scruffy sheepdog called Conal, whom she had loved with her heart and soul. She had mourned for months after Conal died.

"I'm sorry. I know what it's like to lose a pet," she said, and bent to wrap her arms around her.

Dottie clung to her: "One of Winifred's famous hugs. Doctors should prescribe these rather than pills."

"You can have one anytime," Winifred promised. "Call me in the middle of the night and I'll race across town."

Dottie started to sob noisily, and reached for a handkerchief to cover her face. "I'm so fed up with crying," she said. "Who knew one undersized human being could produce so many tears?" She closed her eyes.

Her face was puffy, but her skin was smooth and unblemished. Her dark hair was tangled and needed a wash. The scars on her wrists were shiny, like snail trails. Winifred thought she looked like a child of maybe ten or eleven. A very sad child.

After their visit, the women went for coffee. Winifred felt low and she could tell the others did too.

"I blame Elinor Wylie," Jane said, lighting a cigarette. "Dottie was attracted to her hocus-pocus, life-after-death shit like a kitty to catnip. If she's persuaded her that there's a sunny afterlife where we meet our loved ones again, death doesn't seem so final. It might even sound appealing."

"I blame Alvan," Peggy said. "He's supposed to be protecting her, but I think he underestimated how fragile she is when he started delving into her past and making her confront traumatic memories."

"Is he going to continue the therapy after this?" Winifred asked.

"Sure! He wants to, at least." Peggy sounded cross. "He claims there is often a breakthrough in therapy after a trauma, so he believes they can start to make real progress now. We argued about it last night. I told him she is not some 'case' for him to experiment on for the sake of research. Of course, he claims he has her best interests at heart, but he doesn't care about her, not the way we do."

"It must put you in a difficult position," Winifred said. She hoped it wouldn't damage the relationship. Peggy was desperate for a husband to have children with, and Winifred had wondered if he might be the one. "Try not to let it get in the way of your happiness. Alvan seems a good man."

"It's always useful to have a doctor among your close acquaintances," Jane said. "If you marry him, we could call and get advice without paying medical bills."

Peggy gave a halfhearted smile. "Good point. If he ever proposes, I'll bear that in mind."


WINIFRED MET EVA for a drink at Tony Soma's later, for the first time since their encounter with the knife-wielding robbers. She had telephoned to apologize profusely for her rash behavior and Eva had said she forgave her, although she insisted she wouldn't walk the streets at night with her ever again.

They picked Tony's because it was one of the speakeasies under

Arnold Rothstein's protection so he would be likely to hear they'd been there. Winifred still felt nervous going out in public, but there was no way around it if she were to convince him she and Eva were together.

She arrived first and managed to grab a side table when a couple stood to leave. It was thronged, with a noise level like the crowd at a baseball game, and she wished they had chosen somewhere quieter. She felt emotional after seeing Dottie, and not remotely in the mood for gaiety.

All heads turned when Eva swept in, six foot tall in heels and her raccoon coat. Winifred waved and stood to embrace her.

"I'm guessing you've heard about Dottie?" Eva said, sitting down.

"We've been to visit her this afternoon," Winifred said. "She was frail and wan, but alive at least."

"I heard from Alec Woollcott. I don't think I've ever seen him so upset."

"All her friends are beside themselves. You know she tried before?" Eva nodded. It seemed everyone knew. "I guess we didn't help her enough after that. It's so hard to talk about, you end up sweeping it under the carpet. She seemed fine on the surface. But what if she had succeeded this time? It doesn't bear thinking about."

"You look very shaken. Let me get you a drink." Eva glanced at the crowd that was three deep around the bar.

"I'd love a gin rickey, but won't it take ages to get served?"

"Watch me!" Eva said. She slipped off her coat to reveal a black backless dress dripping with sequins, then shimmied to the bar, head held high. "Pardon me," Winifred heard her say in an aristocratic English accent as she pushed through. "Thank you! Terribly kind." In no time at all, she was at the front and summoning a waiter with a curl of her finger.

She returned, carrying their drinks in Tony's trademark white coffee cups.

"How did you do that?" Winifred asked, awed.

"By acting as if I have the God-given right," Eva said. "I swear no one ever challenges me."

They clinked glasses. Winifred took a sip and felt it burn away some of the heaviness she'd been feeling since she heard the news about Dottie.

"Did you finish that play?" she asked, referring to a script she had given Eva to read.

As Eva opened her mouth to answer, the door swung wide and a new bunch of customers came in, shouting and screeching with laughter. Winifred pressed her hands to her ears.

Irritatingly, the crowd decided to stand right next to their table. Eva glared, but they didn't take the hint to move.

Winifred sipped her drink and grimaced. "You know what?" she shouted over the din. "The booze here is dire and we can't hear ourselves speak. Why don't we go to my apartment? I have a bottle of French wine."

"So long as we can take a taxi," Eva said, with a wary look, and Winifred agreed straightaway.

It was the first time Eva had been to Winifred's apartment and she twirled around, taking it in.

"It's enchanting! I love your elephant prints. And those lamps. And the jewel colors."

"It's tiny," Winifred said, "but it suits me." She was glad Eva liked her taste.

She fetched the wine and two glasses and set them on a low table by the couch, then opened the bottle and poured. They both kicked off their shoes and sat with feet curled beneath them.

"That's more like it," Winifred said, taking a sip of wine and enjoying the peace and comfort of her own home.

They talked about the play they had both read, called *The Mongrel*, and Winifred announced her news: she was going to direct it in a tiny theater a few streets from Broadway. It would be a low-key first step into directing. No big names, no fancy set, just a strong story produced on a small budget.

Eva was delighted. "This is exactly what New York theater needs," she said. "Women directors bringing a fresh approach to new plays. I'm so fed up with the tired old formulas."

They talked about a show they had both seen on Broadway recently, and then they got on to directors they had worked with. Winifred was feeling emotional after visiting Dottie, and light-headed from two glasses of wine, and she found herself confiding in Eva about the director who had raped her eight years earlier. It was easier to tell the story the second time around. Now that she had brought the memories to the surface, they didn't give her the choking sensation she'd had when she'd confided in Peggy.

"That's truly horrifying," Eva said, frowning, "but I have to say it doesn't surprise me. I've heard stories about him before." She reached across to squeeze Winifred's hand. "Was it your first time?"

"Yes . . ." Winifred whispered. "First and only."

"But that was years ago! You can't lock yourself away forever, or he will have won. I'm sure some poet said living well is the best revenge."

"I've dated other men, and thought about going to bed with them, but the idea of being alone and vulnerable with someone physically stronger than me. . . ." Winifred shuddered. "It makes me panicky, so I avoid it."

"It's rotten luck no one warned you about him before the audition," Eva said. "I hope you're telling the students you work with to be wary."

Winifred furrowed her brow. "I couldn't. What if word got back to him? He'd be furious."

Eva was indignant. "Are you *scared* of him? What's the worst he could do?"

"It's not just him—although he was the worst. Lots of other directors have taken liberties, one way or another. You must have found the same."

Eva nodded emphatically. "God yes! Have you ever worked with Gilbert Harris? *'Just a little kiss . . .'*" She mimicked his whiny voice. "And Tony Moncrieff ran his hands all over me, saying he was measuring me for a costume. I told him I'd chop off his fat fingers if he did it again."

Winifred shook her head. "It's infuriating that we have to put up with their behavior if we want to appear on Broadway."

"We should get Dottie to write a poem about it," Eva suggested. "Can you imagine? She'd put them firmly in their place."

Winifred smiled. "It's a tempting idea, but she's not known for her discretion. And I don't think she's in the best frame of mind right now."

"Do you have some paper and a pen?" Eva asked. "Let's write our own."

She topped up their glasses while Winifred found both, then they started suggesting lines and Eva scribbled them down. They giggled at each new idea, interrupting each other to call out suggestions.

The finished poem was clumsy and amateurish, but it made them laugh till their sides ached. Winifred read it aloud in her best upper-class diction:

**The Actresses' Guide to Directors**
*Gilbert Harris will try to steal a kiss*
*Daniel O'Neal is a legs man*
*Tony Moncrieff has wandering hands*
*And so do Messrs. Cornell and Lawrence and Brand.*

*Watch out for Ambrose—he'll tear at your clothes.*
*Wriggle free if Simms pulls you onto his knee.*
*And if a famous lech says he wants a private word,*
*Kick up your heels and flee.*
*A role is a role, and our work can be fun,*
*But we don't want our ovens containing a bun.*

"I don't think we'll be nominated for any poetry prizes," she finished.

"We could show it to our acting friends at least," Eva suggested. "We're all in the same boat. I'll make a fair copy."

"I'm astonished to hear you've had trouble too." Winifred shifted her knees. "You seem indomitable."

"Me?" Eva looked incredulous. "You're the one who stabbed Legs Diamond in the gonads and attacked armed robbers in the street."

Winifred made a penitent face. "I'm amazed you agreed to see me again after that."

"Of *course* I wanted to see you again," Eva said, her voice low and husky. She gazed at Winifred with a tender expression.

Winifred realized their feet were touching on the couch. *I should move*, she thought, but didn't. She felt close to Eva, and didn't want to spoil the moment. "I'm very glad Peggy introduced us," she said.

"Mmm, I'm glad too." Eva put down her glass. She leaned over and tucked a strand of hair behind Winifred's ear, then kissed her cheek. When Winifred didn't move away, she kissed her temple, then let her lips brush downward to kiss her on the lips.

Winifred could smell her jasmine scent. She tensed. *Did she want this? Would it ruin their friendship?*

"I'm not a lesbian," she whispered, pulling away slightly.

"Me neither," Eva replied, then kissed her again.

Winifred felt a tug in her stomach and a tingling in her breasts, and let herself relax into the sensation. It felt as natural as breathing, and as essential.

Sometime later, she pulled down her foldaway bed and they undressed each other and climbed between the sheets.

*So this is what sex with a woman is like*, she thought afterward, as they lay with their limbs entwined and faces close. There was a delicious throbbing between her legs and her mouth was swollen with kisses.

"Are you OK?" Eva asked.

"Better than OK," Winifred breathed. "Infinitely better."

She felt as if a door had been unlocked and she had been set free.

# Chapter 40
# PEGGY

After Dottie was discharged from the hospital, Peggy began visiting her at the Gonk for lunch several times a week. It was only a short walk from her office and she reasoned that she could catch any signs Dottie was feeling suicidal more clearly in person than on the telephone. She took homemade soup and sandwiches so they could eat together. At first they chatted about friends and current news stories rather than anything personal, but one day Dottie began to talk about the overdose.

"I slipped," she said, "from a place of light and possibility to a dark place without hope. It was like being at the bottom of a deep well and the sides were so steep it didn't seem I would ever be able to climb out again."

Her voice was flat, Peggy thought, as if she had entirely run out of zest. "And now? Are you still in that deep well?"

Dottie had to think about that. "No, but I feel untethered, like a balloon drifting across the rooftops."

"What can we do to tether you?" Peggy asked. "What's the answer? Friends? Work?"

"I'm working," Dottie said. "It's not easy but I'm forcing myself." Since coming out of the hospital, she said, she had completed an indifferent story and several poems. "They're all deeply cynical, of course. There is no chance of redemption in my fictional worlds."

She handed Peggy a poem entitled "Resumé." "Perhaps this is the darkest of the lot," she said. "What do you think?"

It was short—just eight lines, with three or four words in each. She listed the drawbacks with each method of suicide, from drowning to gas, guns to hanging, and concluded that you might as well live.

"Golly!" Peggy exclaimed, startled. "That is the most depressing poem I've ever read, but it's powerful too. You must include it in your collection. Are you getting close to having it ready?"

"Perhaps," Dottie said, chewing her lower lip. "But I'm nervous about sending it out. I'm not robust enough for rejection."

"I'll introduce you to Tommy Smith at my book launch party next week," Peggy said. "You are coming, aren't you?"

The party was to be in the Boni & Liveright offices. She made a mental note to warn Tommy to be encouraging. She didn't want to be responsible for tipping Dottie back down into that dark place without hope.

PEGGY'S PARENTS AND her sister drove into Manhattan for the party, while Alvan collected Peggy in a taxi. They picked up Dottie on the way so she wouldn't have to arrive on her own.

Peggy was jittery with nerves, but at least she knew she looked good. Winifred had helped her to choose a striking cocktail dress in black crêpe de chine with a green velvet collar and elbow cuffs. Her hair had been cut and styled into a wavy chin-length bob, and she wore the emerald earrings Alvan had given her. All she had to worry about now was the first reviews of the novel, which should be appearing any moment—that, and introducing Alvan to her parents.

Her father shook hands with him so enthusiastically it was as if he were pumping water from a well. Her mother was gushingly polite, keen to know where his folks were from and where he was raised, while her father quizzed him about his work on lung disorders. Alvan began telling him about his design for a new type of oxygen tent that would help patients with breathing difficulties. He seemed to be coping well with the parental interrogation, so Peggy took the opportunity to guide Dottie through the room and introduce her to Tommy.

He clasped both of her hands as he spoke. "It's a great honor to meet you," he said. "I know your work, of course, and I'm sure our poetry editor, Horace Liveright, will be delighted to publish anything you care to submit. Even your laundry list."

"Be careful what you promise," Dottie warned. "My anthology is called *Enough Rope* and its themes are grim. Whoever publishes it should include a free razor blade so readers can slash their wrists after reading." She glanced coyly at him through her lashes. "At the very least, they can get rid of unsightly facial hair."

Tommy grinned, still holding her hand. "I'll introduce you to Horace just as soon as you're ready. And perhaps we can invite a representative from Gillette."

Dottie laughed—a rare sound these days.

Peggy left them chatting and wandered around the room greeting her guests. There were lots of congratulations and people asking her to sign their copies, while Boni & Liveright assistants kept pressing cocktails into her hand. Piles of her book, with its blue cover and gold lettering, were stacked on tables. Every time she opened a copy and flicked through, she was amazed to see her words inside, and her name—Margaret Leech—on the front. It didn't feel real, not yet.

Tommy Smith tapped his glass with a fountain pen to get the guests' attention, and began his speech. He said that as soon as he read the first pages of Peggy's book, he knew he had to publish it—and he was delighted to announce that the *New York Times* book critic agreed with his judgment. He pulled a review from his pocket with a flourish and began to read: it called Peggy "a powerful and original novelist, a keen psychologist and deft observer, with an unusual gift for vivid characterization."

Peggy felt as if her entire face was on fire. Had Tommy invented that quote? She couldn't believe such a prestigious paper would pay attention to her little book, never mind rave about it. She gulped the rest of her cocktail, and someone took the empty glass and handed her another without asking.

Dottie was watching her from across the room with a wistful smile. Was she thinking that could be her one day? Or wishing she could have a drink? She still wasn't allowed alcohol. Peggy raised a glass to her, in a silent toast.

PEGGY'S PARENTS HAD booked a table for dinner in a nearby restaurant and they invited Dottie and Tommy to join them. Alvan was working a late shift at the hospital so he had to take his leave.

Peggy linked arms with her mother on one side and Dottie on the other as they walked to the restaurant.

"What do you think of Alvan?" she asked her mother. "Is he respectable enough for you?"

There was a pause. "I like him," her mother said. "But I had a chat with him about his background, and it's clear he's going to marry some nice Jewish girl one day. I hope you're not holding out for him to propose."

Peggy kept walking. Her footsteps sounded unusually loud. She knew it was true. Why did her mother always have to be right about everything?

"I'm glad he's a friend of yours," her mother continued. "But he's not going to put a ring on your finger, so I'm sure you're being smart enough not to let him handle the goods."

Dottie snorted, and Peggy nudged her in the ribs.

"That's like trying to squeeze an omelet back into the eggshell," Dottie murmured and Peggy hoped her mother hadn't heard.

They arrived at the restaurant and were shown to a circular table. Dottie sat next to Tommy Smith, and they were soon deep in conversation. They were so animated that Peggy worried Dottie was flirting with him. She would have to find a quiet moment to warn her he was married.

Her father had arranged for the restaurant to provide champagne, which was served in opaque tumblers, and Peggy was especially touched when he rose and made a short speech about how proud he was, then asked them to toast his clever daughter.

After they ordered their food, Peggy's sister, Rose, leaned across.

"I have some news of my own," she said, with a shy smile. "A little delivery due right around Christmas."

It took Peggy a moment to catch on. "You're expecting a baby? Rose, that's magnificent news! Why didn't you say earlier?"

"This is your night," Rose said, an arm cradling her belly. "But I thought you should know."

Peggy got up and walked around the table to embrace her. "Becoming an auntie is the best gift you could ever give me. I'm so happy."

It was true. She was happy, of course she was. But she had to pin her smile in place while the news was relayed around the company. She wasn't jealous of Rose, was she? Yes, perhaps she was. She didn't resent her being pregnant, but she wished with all her heart that she could be too.

A COUPLE OF nights later, Peggy cooked dinner for Alvan in her apartment, and they discussed his meeting her family.

"They're good people," he said. "Your father is a fine man. I'm not sure what your mother made of me though. She asked a lot

312

about my religious beliefs." He grinned as if in mockery of the older generation who still set store by such things.

"She told me I shouldn't let you handle the goods if you're not going to put a ring on my finger," Peggy told him, with a conspiratorial smile.

"What goods are those?" Alvan asked, reaching out to fondle her breasts. "These goods?" He slid a hand up her skirt. "Or these ones? Perhaps I should telephone her and ask for clarification."

"You're a wicked man," Peggy said, pushing his hand away and standing up to clear the plates. She spoke over her shoulder, as if it were of no consequence. "Mother seems convinced that you'll have a traditional marriage to a nice Jewish girl someday, complete with signing of the ketubah and smashing of the glass."

"I probably will," Alvan said, and the words fell like stones. "But for now, I'm having a very good time with a world-famous author, who's sexy and smart and a terrific cook too. Why would I want to change anything?"

Peggy nodded to herself as she dished up their dessert. Deep down, she had known he wouldn't marry her. Truth be told, she wasn't in love with him. But her mother's words and Rose's news had reminded her that she couldn't delay any longer. Having children was one of her dearest wishes and she had to start looking for a father for them before it was no longer biologically possible. She was going to be thirty-one soon and she didn't have time to waste.

That night, when they had sex, she felt wilder and freer than ever before. Alvan thought it was her new status as a published author that made her so ardent, but it was because she knew it would be the last time they would make love and she wanted to make the most of it.

The next morning, after he left, she wrote him a letter thanking him for the months they had spent together and wishing him happiness but saying she didn't see any future in the relationship, so she'd be grateful if he would not call her anymore.

Right after she mailed it, she wondered if she had made a mistake. He had been her first lover and, if she didn't find anyone else, he might be her only one. The sex had been delicious and the conversations fascinating. What had she done?

She moped around for the next few days, wondering how he would react to her letter. Perhaps he would try to win her back? If he did, she would be tempted. She missed being part of a couple, and she was sad to think he might have been her sole chance at having children. Maybe she could have persuaded him to marry her if she had stuck it out, religious issues notwithstanding.

Would she have said yes if he had asked her? Could she have married someone she didn't love in order to have children? She knew lots of women did, but were they happy with their choice? What if she never found someone else? She wasn't prime marriage material at her age, and she certainly wasn't swamped with suitors.

And then a letter arrived that was polite but entirely lacking in passion. He said he understood her reasons and wouldn't attempt to change her mind. It was the kind of letter she might have written to an advertiser who had decided to pull their business from Condé Nast publications. He clearly hadn't been in love with her either.

She was still sad, but at least the letter confirmed she had done the right thing. Alvan was far too self-absorbed to be the kind of husband she wanted to find.

# Chapter 41
# JANE

ane bounded up the stairs to *The New Yorker* offices. It was eight o'clock and Harold should already have given the order to print the next issue, so she hoped he would come home for dinner. Instead, she heard raised voices coming from his office and recognized Alec's pompous tones. She paused for a moment to eavesdrop.

"It's nonsensical," Harold was saying. "It wrecks the flow of an otherwise well-argued piece. Removing it improves the article immeasurably."

"Removing it is not an option," Alec replied. "If you insist, I'll pull the entire piece and you'll be left with a blank page. Your choice."

Harold ran his fingers through his hair, tugging on it. "Why does this happen every time, Alec? Your eleventh-hour ambushes are unprofessional and hardly the act of a friend."

"Mangling my article is also not the act of a friend." Alec folded his arms, entrenched.

Jane popped her head around the door. "Trouble?" she asked lightly. "Need an impartial adjudicator?"

Alec growled at her: "It's none of your business. Get the hell out of here."

Jane gasped at his rudeness and opened her mouth to retaliate, but Harold raised his hand. "Truce!" he said. "The sentence stays, but don't ever do this to me again, Alec. I mean it." He turned to her. "Jane, I'll be with you in two minutes." He picked up the telephone to call the printer.

Alec swept past Jane without a word. She stuck out her tongue at his departing back.

Over dinner at 412—a bland dish of creamed chicken and boiled rice that wouldn't exacerbate Harold's ulcers—she asked him about Alec's behavior.

"Now that he's decided to get involved in the magazine, he's switched from bystander to bully," Harold complained. "He tries to dominate editorial meetings, but fortunately Raoul keeps him in check. And get this: he's keeping a tally of how much we owe him, even though I've told him we're not paying contributors yet." He wrinkled his nose. "Cash is running out and Raoul is suggesting that we cease publication over the summer, because fewer copies are sold then, and resume in the fall."

Jane was horrified. "We can't do that! Not when we are starting to grow the readership little by little. The public has short memories. No one would remember us by fall, so all the work we've put in would be wasted."

"That's what I said. I've asked Raoul to look at the numbers again." He laid down his fork, as if the effort of lifting it to his mouth was too much for him, and rested his head on his hand, eyes closed.

"Did Dottie turn in a story?" she asked, in an effort to distract him from money woes.

Harold raised a smile. "She did, and it's brilliant! About a hungover man asking a friend if he'd made a fool of himself the night before and she keeps insisting, 'You were perfectly fine,' but through the course of the story it's clear he wasn't. Classic Dottie!"

Jane laughed. "Perfect! I can't wait to read it."

She made a mental note to call and thank Dottie. To date she had written three stories and a poem for them, as well as regular theater reviews in a column titled "Last Night." She seemed to be in a period of intense productivity, although there was something frenetic about it, as if she were trying to distract herself from her troubles.

Dottie's name on the cover of the magazine would help sell copies but, as far as Jane was concerned, Alec was dispensable. She wished Harold would stop commissioning him. It would relieve at least part of the unremitting pressure he was under.

ONE SCORCHING AFTERNOON in late July, Jane rushed back to 412 to pick up some notes for a story she was working on. She was surprised to find the door to their private apartment ajar and her first thought was to wonder if Harold had fallen ill at the office and come home to rest. Instead, she walked into their living room to find Alec sitting in an armchair reading a letter, for all the world as if it were his own living room and his own chair.

"Hello!" she said in surprise. "Did Harold let you in? Is he here?" She glanced around.

"No, he gave me a key a while ago so I could borrow books when I wanted." He put down the letter he'd been reading and stood up. "I guess I'll go back upstairs."

He ambled toward the door. Jane bent to pick up the letter, thinking he'd forgotten it, and saw it was addressed to her. It was from a friend, Janet Flanner, who lived in Paris. Jane had written asking if she would be interested in contributing a "Letter from Paris" feature for the magazine, and this must be her reply.

She gasped at the audacity of Alec reading her letter. Had he opened it himself, or had Harold opened it earlier and Alec chanced upon it? Either way it was a shocking breach of her privacy. It was creepy to think of him coming into their apartment and snooping through their possessions. Something had to be done.

She telephoned Harold at the office and asked if he had opened the Janet Flanner letter. He sounded surprised and said no, he hadn't.

"But you gave Alec a key to our apartment?" she demanded.

"I lent it to him once, ages ago, and he never returned it," Harold said. "Do you want me to ask him for it?"

Jane bit her lip. She didn't want Harold having any more stress at the moment. "Leave it to me," she said. "I'll deal with it."

Jane waited a few moments, gathering her thoughts. A line had been crossed today and action must be taken. Enough was enough.

She walked upstairs and tapped on Alec's door. When he answered he didn't invite her inside, but stood blocking the way.

"Alec, I'm giving you notice that we want your rooms back," she said. "Harold and I need more space. We'll give you time to look for somewhere else, of course."

Alec's eyes narrowed. "Does Harold know about this?"

"Of course he does," she lied. "We talked about it not five minutes ago. Remember we said from the start that it was a temporary arrangement? This is our home and we want it for ourselves." She spoke in a pleasant tone, and even smiled, although her heart was pounding.

"I don't believe Harold wants me to leave. Why don't you go instead, Jane? How long before you admit that your marriage is a sham?" His face was twisted with spite. "Harold is fed up with you interfering in the magazine and forcing your agenda down everyone else's throats. You'd be doing us all a big favor if *you* moved out."

"Yes, you'd love that, wouldn't you?" Jane snapped. "Then you could bully Harold even more than you bully him already. His health is suffering and you are in large part to blame. I'm serving notice that you should quit the premises, and if you force me to, I will get a legal eviction notice served on you."

Alec leaned against the wall, as if to signify that he had no intention of leaving, and cocked his head to one side. "It always amazed me that Harold married someone quite so plain. Plain Jane. With those looks and your shrill personality, it's a miracle you got a husband at all, never mind such a brilliant man."

Jane had been patient long enough; now she was riled for a fight. "You're not really impotent, are you, Alec?" she said. "Some folk think you're a homosexual, but my opinion is that you use that old mumps story as an excuse because you are too *fat* and too *nasty* to get the kind of girls you would want to be seen with. Did you seriously think you had a chance with Neysa? Or me, for that matter? Try working on your personality as well as your waistline if you don't want to be single your entire life."

"You think I was ever interested in you? That's laughable. I despise you, Jane. Always have."

She knew it was a lie. They had been friends, way back when—just not since she married Harold. "Why do you alienate everyone who cares about you, Alec? Me, Dottie, Harold . . . You're going to be a very lonely old man if you carry on at this rate. Sometimes I wonder if the person you dislike most is yourself."

He slammed the door in her face, so hard that a mirror rattled against the wall. Shaking with anger, she marched back down to their apartment. She would have to tell Harold what she had done, and force him to support her, but she had no regrets. It was unbearable living under the same roof as someone who was antagonistic to them; Harold needed a peaceful home to return to, not another battleground.

She telephoned the office, but Harold was in a meeting. She had to rush back to the *New York Times* to write her story for the morning paper. She would talk to Harold later, and just hope that

Alec didn't harangue him in the meantime with his own distorted version of their seismic falling-out.

It WAS LATE when Harold got home, and he smelled of whiskey. He shouldn't be drinking because of his ulcers, but Jane refrained from criticism.

"Did you speak to Alec?" she asked, and he nodded.

"I would try to mediate but I guess there's no way back from this," he said, exhaustion etched all over his face. "Alec says he is looking for somewhere else to stay."

"Good," Jane said. "The atmosphere will be a lot more peaceful without him."

Harold went to the bathroom and she heard him opening the cabinet to get his pills and running the tap to fill a glass of water. Next he would brush his teeth. After five years of marriage, she knew his routines backward, just as he must know hers.

She knew the little groan he made when he bent to remove his socks; she knew he would fling them toward the laundry basket and miss; she knew he would fall asleep within minutes of getting into bed, so soundly that a hurricane blowing through the bedroom wouldn't wake him.

She liked watching his sleeping face with its daytime furrows relaxed, his cheek sliding into the pillow, his breathing so slight it was scarcely discernible. The love she felt for him in those moments was pure and uncomplicated: it wasn't about their shared past, it wasn't about the future she hoped for. It was in the moment and it filled her from top to toe with happiness.

THE NEW YORKER staggered on through the summer without having to cease publication and, just as they were about to run out of money, Raoul Fleischmann conjured up a loan from his mother that would keep them in business with cash to spare. The magazine's fortunes turned around in the fall when an article entitled "Why We Go to Cabarets" was syndicated worldwide, bringing them thousands of new readers. It seemed there was an appetite for insider knowledge about the city's nightlife, so Harold commissioned Lois Long to write a new column called "Table for Two," in which she gave lively descriptions of her own racy comings and goings in clubs and speakeasies across town.

Jane and Alec carefully avoided each other at 412. If she heard him in the communal dining room, she stayed inside their apartment. If he was in the hall, she waited till he had left before going out herself. He had said he was looking for an apartment, but progress seemed slow, and there was no sign of him packing up.

Harold's ulcers flared up after Christmas, and eventually, under doctor's orders, he checked into a sanatorium for a two-week rest cure. Jane encouraged him to go—it was exactly what he needed. Her life was easier to manage when she just had her own job during the day, and her own friends to see in the evening. Not having to shop and cook for a houseful of men was a relief. She spent time with Dottie, Winifred, and Peggy, on their own and together. She and Dottie went dancing at a club in Harlem called the Savoy Ballroom. They liked it because it was one of the few nightspots where blacks and whites could mix. She avoided the Gonk entirely, and scarcely ever set foot in *The New Yorker* offices.

On the day Harold was due to leave the sanatorium, she called and asked if she should get the train to meet him and accompany him back to Manhattan. She wasn't sure how weak he might be. Maybe he could use help on the journey.

"No need," he told her. "But I do want some peace to convalesce, so I've booked a room at the Webster Hotel, just for the time being. The doc told me to avoid all sources of tension."

"I'm your wife!" she protested. "I hope I'm not a source of tension."

"No, but the situation at home is . . . difficult for me," he said.

Damn Alec that he hadn't moved out yet, Jane thought.

"Shall I come and meet you for dinner later?" she asked.

"Tomorrow. I'll need to rest tonight after the journey."

She wondered if he was angry with her about the fight with Alec. The two of them had been best friends before this. She could see it put him in a tricky spot, but she was his wife and he should take her side.

"I understand," she said. "It's just that I miss you, sweetheart. I can't wait to see you."

"Miss you too, mushkins."

Jane hung up the telephone feeling disappointed. She'd been counting the days till their reunion, but she supposed it would have to wait. His health came first. Poor Harold.

# Chapter 42
# DOTTIE

After Peggy stopped seeing Alvan, Dottie didn't return to analysis. It would have been awkward. Besides, she didn't feel they were making progress. She understood more about *why* she reacted the way she did to certain triggers—in particular, why she was so sensitive to "the emotional upheavals of romantic relationships," as Alvan put it—but she didn't feel she'd been given any tools to help her change. Maybe she would always be that way and had to learn to live with it.

When she had come out of the hospital after her overdose, Winifred had offered to treat her to an afternoon at her favorite beauty salon. She said she went there once a week.

"It's not that I'm vain," she insisted, shamefaced. "It's important for my job that I'm well turned out."

Her regular salon wasn't an expensive Upper East Side one, but a place in Chinatown run by Egyptian immigrants. It was clean, with low lighting, plump floor cushions, and gentle Egyptian music playing in the background. Dottie was looked after by an older woman in a veil, who cupped her face gently, examining her from one side, then the other, before pronouncing that she would benefit from a hot oil massage of her head and shoulders, then a facial.

Dottie lay on cushions as the woman dotted fragrant oil across her skin and began to smooth it in, slowly and sensuously. Before long, she sank into a kind of torpor, feeling protected, nurtured, and entirely at peace with the world. When the woman started kneading her scalp, every muscle in her body relaxed, and she felt almost tearful. It was wonderful to be so well cared for. Alvan would probably have told her that the beautician was a mother substitute—but it didn't matter. She was talented at her job, and Dottie never wanted the treatment to end.

"If you were a man, I'd ask you to marry me," she said afterward.

"And if I were a man, I'd say yes," the woman beamed.

Dottie turned to Winifred. "I swear, the last hour has done me more good than a year of psychoanalysis. Someone should tell Alvan he's picked the wrong profession."

Thereafter, they met at the salon every Friday afternoon for a beauty treatment or two, then went for a soda. Dottie liked Winifred's gentleness and tact. Peggy and Jane were forever quizzing her about whether she was eating properly, how hard she was working, and especially how much booze she was drinking, but Winifred waited for her to volunteer information and was never pushy.

They generally talked about feminine matters, such as fashion trends and beauty tips and magazine articles they'd read, but one day Dottie blurted out something she'd heard that morning that upset her badly.

"Did you know Charlie MacArthur has gotten married to Helen Hayes?" she asked, then paused for a moment to control herself. "Bob called to break the news."

Winifred pursed her lips in sympathy. "I did hear."

"Why her and not me?" Dottie asked. It felt as if she'd been stabbed in the back, although she supposed she had no right to be upset. "You know her, Winifred. What's she got that I haven't?"

Winifred shook her head, as if baffled. "She hasn't got your wit or intelligence, but I suppose she's pleasant enough."

Dottie laughed. "I hope you never call me 'pleasant enough.' You make it sound like the direst insult."

"Maybe Charlie wanted a peaceful life, with a compliant wife. You'd never have been that."

Dottie snorted. "Alec told me he was unfaithful before the last of the wedding cake was eaten. Good luck to her. I need to steer clear of the Charlies of this world. I'm not resilient enough for the type of men who make your heart beat faster."

"So what's the alternative?" Winifred asked. "Date someone you like, but who doesn't give you that thrill? I think sex without lust must be like a cocktail without the booze."

Dottie agreed. "Or you can sleep with married men for sex, safe in the knowledge it's never going to work out anyway. I've been trying that recently."

"That doesn't sound very nurturing," Winifred said. "I'm sure it's possible to have it all—love, sex, and friendship too—if you choose carefully." She smiled to herself, a faraway look in her eyes.

Dottie noticed her expression and asked, "Is there something you're not telling me?"

Winifred shook her head quickly. "I was wondering about that man I saw you with at the Gonk last week. Young-looking. Brown hair in a side parting. So devoted to you he was positively lapping up your every word."

Dottie thought back. "You must mean Seward. Seward Collins. He's a literary journalist who's trying to start a new magazine about books and wants to commission me."

"He looks like he wants to do more than 'commission' you—unless that's a euphemism." Winifred gave a cheeky wink.

It was true. Seward doted on her, which she found amusing. He wasn't her type: mousy-looking and only medium height, not nearly as handsome as Eddie or Charlie, and six years younger than she was, which was far too young. All he had going for him

325

was that he was intelligent and wealthy, heir to a chain of tobacco shops.

"My typewriter is older than him," she told Winifred, "and a good deal more use to me. I suppose the attention is flattering."

"Why not give him a chance? Take the friendship a little further," Winifred said, her eyes suggestive. "He might surprise you."

Dottie wrinkled her nose. "I've never gone to bed with anyone without being swept off my feet with passion—or too drunk to care. Making rational decisions is not my modus operandi when it comes to love."

"How's that been working for you?" Winifred asked, with the kind of complex look—part teasing, part serious—that only an actress could pull off.

After their conversation, Dottie gave it some thought. She was fed up with the sneaking around you had to do with married men: the way you couldn't call them at home, or make plans in advance, and you always came second best in their priorities. It was a poor substitute for a relationship, and there was still the risk of falling in love and getting hurt. Seward already adored her, and he was single. . . .

She remembered Winifred saying that he might surprise her and decided to test him. If he was good in bed, she might consider an affair; if he was a flop, she'd move on.

Seward seemed nervous when she invited him to her suite one evening, sat him down, and began kissing him. He'd been pursuing her for months, yet when the opportunity came, he held back.

"Are you *sure* you want to?" he asked, incredulous.

She practically had to undress him before he realized that she intended to make love with him, and then he became an enthusiastic participant. Not as talented as Charlie, but he'd probably not practiced with such a wide range of women—and that was no bad thing.

The evening after their first night of passion together, Seward presented her with a Cartier gold watch studded with diamonds. It was delicate and expensive, with an Art Deco face set in a scallop-shell bracelet.

"You'd have gotten a cheaper deal at Polly Adler's," she told him, fastening it around her wrist and admiring the effect. "The girls there only cost ten dollars, or so I hear."

He flushed. "I didn't mean it as payment for last night. It's a gift! I like you a lot, Dottie. I want you to know that my intentions are serious."

"You sound like a Realtor pursuing a property deal," she said, but she was touched by his eagerness. It was nice having someone keen on her. And a wealthy man who was keen on her seemed like a bonus. Who knew? Maybe she could try falling in love with him after all.

IN APRIL, NEYSA called to invite Dottie to visit her and Jack at a house they had built on Sands Point in Manhasset Bay.

"It's not as grand as Herbert Swope's place," she said, "but it has stunning views. We want to introduce you to little Joan. Now that she's crawling and chattering in baby language, she needs to meet her aunt Dottie."

"Can I bring a fella?" Dottie asked. "He has a car so he can drive us there."

It was nice having a beau she could invite to things, and she wanted to show Seward off to Neysa. She'd been so patronizing about Charlie that Dottie wanted to prove once and for all she was completely over him.

She and Seward arrived on Friday evening, both ravenous after the drive, but for some reason Baby Joan wouldn't go to sleep, so dinner was delayed. By the time food was served, they had all drunk far too much whiskey—Dottie had long given up any pretense at abstinence—and she argued with Jack about South American politics, a subject about which she knew precisely nothing. Seward looked embarrassed but kept his head down and didn't intervene.

Dottie woke next morning with a bad headache, but when she ventured downstairs to ask for an aspirin powder, Neysa thrust the infant into her arms.

"She's eaten all her breakfast like a good girl," she cooed in a grating baby voice. "Now she's going to stay with her aunt Dottie while Mama finds an aspirin for Auntie's sore head."

Dottie had never held a baby before but she'd seen mothers bouncing them, so she bounced Joan up and down in her arms. Joan gave a gratifying chortle so Dottie bounced her more vigorously, whereupon the baby opened her mouth, made a slight choking sound, and vomited yellowy-orange goo down Dottie's silk dressing gown.

"Joan!" Dottie exclaimed, holding the baby at arm's length as she surveyed the damage, then pretending to scold her: "I have a rule that I ditch friends who are sick on me. You're on your final warning."

The baby's face crumpled and she started to cry. Neysa sprinted across the kitchen to snatch her away. "Dottie, for goodness sake, she doesn't understand adult humor."

"Neither do you, it seems," Dottie muttered.

From that unfortunate start, the day only got worse, as Dottie discovered that their entire schedule had to be arranged around little Joan: meals, outings—nothing could take place unless she was settled and happy. Seward complied like a polite houseguest but Dottie found it difficult. She couldn't help thinking about her baby, Jacob, who would have been almost four now. He would have been running around laughing and chatting away, and she was sure he would have been far more interesting than Neysa's bland little bundle, who did nothing much except cry and poop.

Neysa had changed. Dottie had been looking forward to resuming the gossipy adult friendship they used to have when they lived across the landing. She didn't recognize this person who spoke in a baby voice and wasn't interested in any subject except her miracle child. She missed her old friend, and wished she could at least catch a glimpse of her.

After lunch, she sent Seward to sneak her a gin from a decanter in the living room, to make her feel more mellow and less snarky. Drink in hand, she wandered out to join her hosts in the garden, but somehow failed to notice that Joan was crawling on the grass. When she spotted the baby underfoot it was too late to stop, but Dottie had the presence of mind—and agility—to throw herself clear so at least she didn't step on her. In the process, she banged her shoulder and twisted her lower back, but she was sure she hadn't touched the child, who nevertheless began to squawk at the top of her formidable lung capacity.

Neysa jumped up and grabbed the precious bundle, and began searching every inch of her skin for evidence of an injury. "How *could* you!" she repeated several times. "She's a *baby*."

Both Jack and Seward hastened to assure Neysa it had been an accident and fortunately no one was hurt, whereupon Dottie exclaimed, "No one hurt? Don't I count, just because I'm out of diapers?" She rubbed her shoulder, which felt bruised and painful.

Neysa and Jack retreated inside the house to put Joan down for her afternoon nap. Dottie's drink had spilled so she sent Seward to fetch another.

"Well, that was awkward," he said, handing her the glass. "But I must say your fall was spectacularly elegant. Or elegantly spectacular."

"I'm doing my best," she told him, "but I don't think I'm cut out for this baby-adoration game. I'm sure Joan will grow up to be an exceptional young woman but right now she's boring as hell."

"What did you expect?" Seward asked. "She's a bit young for tap dancing and flute recitals."

"I expect all babies are boring," Dottie said. "In the wild, lots of animals eat their young and, looking at dear little Joan, you can see why."

"You utter bitch!"

Dottie turned to see Neysa standing in the doorway. She had heard every word.

"Oh shit," Dottie muttered under her breath.

"How dare you!" Neysa spat. "You've done nothing but complain since you arrived. I've never known such an ungracious guest. I don't know why you bothered to come if we're so tedious."

"Nostalgia, I guess," Dottie said. "I knew you back in the days when you used to have a personality."

Seward stood abruptly.

"Dottie," he said. "I think it's time for us to go. Why don't you pack your bag and I'll drive us back to the city?"

"What a good idea," Neysa agreed, visibly quivering.

Dottie shrugged and went upstairs to pack, taking her drink with her.

"Was I out of order?" she asked Seward on the ride home, still clutching her gin. "Or did Neysa overreact? I mean, honestly, wasn't that one of the dullest babies you've ever come across?"

"Yes, yes, and yes," he said.

"Bang goes our invitation to spend the summer with them. Such a shame to miss any new skills little Joan may have mastered. They'll just have to find some other guest to bore into an early grave."

Privately, she was saddened by the end of the friendship. Maybe

330

it could be resumed one day in the distant future when Neysa checked out of the cult of motherhood and became fun again—but somehow she doubted it.

DOTTIE AND SEWARD spent most of the summer together, going for trips to the beach in his car. He bought her a Scottish terrier called Daisy, a cute little thing who turned out to have unerring taste when it came to human beings, always growling at Alec but leaping up to greet Winifred with tongue hanging out.

Seward was a passable conversationalist, and had many useful suggestions for selling Dottie's writing, but gradually his adoration began to grate on her nerves. He was always willing to find her a soda or a sunshade, granted, but that eagerness made him less manly in her eyes. The appeal of sleeping with him began to pall. As summer turned to fall, she clung to the relationship, because it was preferable to being single, but she found herself getting increasingly tetchy with poor Seward.

One evening at the Gonk, she called to him, "Sewie, can you go upstairs and fetch my cigarette case? It's on the bureau." Instantly, he leapt to his feet.

"You didn't even say please," Peggy remarked once he was out of earshot. "You treat him like a doormat. It can't be much fun for you, and you're breaking that poor boy's heart."

Dottie felt guilty and made a point of thanking him when he returned.

Another evening, Bob asked her: "Where's the houseboy tonight? Is he upstairs polishing your shoes and darning your stockings? I hope you're paying him a decent wage."

Dottie was chastened. The more her ardor cooled, the more Seward pursued her. Was this how Charlie had felt when she kept chasing after him toward the end of their relationship? Was it cruel of her to give Seward hope? Would she be his Great Egret one day?

331

She tried forcing herself to be nice to him, but it was clear the end was approaching.

Would she ever manage to fall in love with a man who loved her in return? Or was she destined only to fall for the ones who didn't love her back? On the evidence, she wasn't hopeful. But at least she had managed an affair of several months' duration in which her heart hadn't gotten broken and she hadn't felt like killing herself afterward. For those small mercies, she would be eternally grateful.

# Chapter 43
# WINIFRED

Winifred invited Eva to the launch party for Dottie's first poetry collection, *Enough Rope*, which Elinor Wylie was hosting in her apartment. The room was mobbed by the time they arrived, and it was standing room only, with such a crush around the table where drinks were being served that it was impossible to get close. Jane waved them over. She had cleverly nabbed an entire tray of drinks and was able to hand one each to Winifred and Eva.

"I don't know why the party had to be here, instead of at the publisher's office," she complained. "I think Elinor wants to steal the limelight."

"You have to admit she's a good sport to allow the hordes to trample her Persian carpet and spill liquor on her antique chairs," Eva said, looking around.

"Good sport or coattail hanger? Look!" Jane showed them a copy of the book, with a smart gray-and-yellow dustjacket. "Dottie's dedicated it to Elinor. She clearly favors new friendships over old."

Winifred was surprised to hear Jane sounding jealous. "She told me Elinor was a big help in editing and arranging the poems," she soothed. "I expect that's why she gets a mention."

Jane was not mollified. She scowled at a portly literary editor who bumped her elbow as he squeezed past.

"I see Dottie didn't invite Seward," Winifred said, gazing across the room at her. She looked pretty in a crimson dress Winifred had advised her to buy; with her dark hair and eyes, she looked stunning in crimson.

"He's had his marching orders," Jane said: "We all saw it coming."

"Shame, though," Winifred said. She had thought Seward brought Dottie stability, but that clearly wasn't a quality she looked for in a man. "Where's Harold? Is he coming later?"

Jane hesitated before answering. "It's not his kind of thing," she said. "He's never been a fan of parties. Besides, he has a deadline for the next issue."

She didn't look at them as she spoke and Winifred got a feeling she was hiding something. She wondered what it might be.

"Talking of which . . . ," Jane continued, although it wasn't clear what she was referring to, ". . . I wonder if you two can shed any light on this?"

She pulled out a copy of "The Actresses' Guide to Directors," the poem that Winifred and Eva had co-written, and handed it to them.

"How on earth did you get hold of that?" Winifred asked, trying to keep a straight face. "We only gave copies to a few people."

"I can't divulge my source," Jane said. "But I think it's fun, while making a serious point. Harold's keen to publish it in *The New Yorker*, if he can get the permission of the author—or authors." She glanced from one to the other.

Winifred was suddenly wary. "He wouldn't mention any names, would he?"

"I could ask him to make it anonymous."

Winifred gave Eva a look that said: *Why not?*

"I think I can speak for the authors in giving you permission," Eva replied. "So long as their names aren't connected with it."

"Excellent!" Jane said. "I'll let you know—"

She was interrupted by Elinor calling for silence so she could make an announcement. Bill helped her to climb onto a footstool, so she could be seen over the heads of the crowd. She began by raving about Dottie's unique genius, in a speech peppered with glowing superlatives and much dropping of names.

Dottie was visibly cringing, and interrupted her a few minutes in by tugging her sleeve, nearly causing her to fall from the stool.

"Forget the hyperbole, Elinor," she drawled. "Just tell them to buy the goddamn book!"

AFTER THE LAUNCH Winifred and Eva went for dinner and speculated on what the reaction might be if Harold printed their poem in *The New Yorker*.

"The directors we named will hear about it," Winifred worried.

"So let them," Eva said. "What can they do, except change their behavior to try and disprove the allegations? I only wish we had named. . . ." She mentioned the man who had raped Winifred.

"God no! I would hate for him to think I was involved." She shivered at the thought.

"He can't hurt you anymore," Eva soothed. "And if it makes him think twice about hurting someone else, then we've done a good thing."

"What do you think the Theatre Guild will say?" Winifred asked. The board had recently invited her to become the first-ever director of an actors' training course they were starting, and she had been honored and overjoyed to accept. She would hate for anything to jeopardize her new role.

"They have no way of finding out," Eva told her. "Don't give it another thought."

After eating they wandered back to Winifred's place. Eva lived in New Jersey, where she shared an apartment with three other women, so they always stayed at Winifred's, despite the crush. She had thought she would feel invaded when Eva started leaving clothes and toiletries behind, but in fact she loved it. On evenings when Eva wasn't there, she found herself stroking her pearly pink silk robe and sniffing its jasmine scent, still marveling at her astonishing good luck.

Falling in love with a woman was a revelation, entirely different from her previous relationships with men. They were equals, for a start. Neither dominated the decision-making, but they discussed and agreed on everything, and she never felt intimidated or overpowered. They shared the cooking and cleaning; they talked about their work and supported each other's plans. It was like having a best friend and a lover rolled into one. Winifred reveled in the intimacy, as well as the exquisite lovemaking.

The only thing she struggled with was thinking of herself as a lesbian. What would her devout Catholic mother say if she found out? How would it affect her career? What about her friends? Would they disown her?

"There's no need for anyone else to know, is there?" Eva said. "Our friends assume we spend time together because of Arnold Rothstein. Your mother thinks I'm a new pal. Colleagues think we're working together. Easy!"

But what happens next? Winifred wondered. If Eva were male, they would consider getting married one day, but they couldn't ever do that. She began to wonder if they might look for an apartment together. They could find one with two bedrooms, so visitors wouldn't suspect they were anything more than roommates. Was it enough?

"You worry too much," Eva said. "Just enjoy yourself." She stroked the hair back from Winifred's neck and let her lips linger on the sensitive skin just below her ear.

THE POEM IN *The New Yorker* attracted much comment, virtually all of it supportive. From the named directors, there was silence.

The word was out, and Winifred thought it was worthwhile if it made young actresses a little safer.

When the telephone rang one morning and she heard Jane's voice on the line, she assumed she was calling about the poem, but instead Jane said: "Just a heads-up that Walter Winchell wrote about you and Eva in his 'Mainly About Mainstreeters' column in the *Evening Graphic* last night."

Winifred's heart began to pound. "He did? Why? What does it say?"

"He refers to you as a 'well-known lesbian couple,' and quotes so-called friends telling him that you are inseparable."

Winifred was shocked. "Who could he have spoken to? What friends would say that?"

Jane hastened to reassure her. "It might not have been a friend; that's just something columnists say. There were lots of reporters at Dottie's book launch and maybe one of them saw you together and jumped to conclusions. . . ." She paused. "He also says you vacationed together over the summer. Is that true?"

Winifred was distraught. "How could he have known? It's intrusive and . . . scary."

Jane sounded surprised at her reaction. "Isn't this what we wanted? Arnold Rothstein is bound to be convinced now."

Winifred could see she was being contrary. "I didn't mind a few people knowing to stop him pursuing me, but this is different. Readers will assume it's true because it's in the papers."

"Who reads Walter Winchell anyway?" Jane said. "Don't give it a second thought."

But it seemed lots of people did read his "Mainstreeters" column. Next time Winifred popped into the Gonk, Alec Woollcott raised his glass to her.

"Here comes our new friend of Sappho. You'd better cut those long nails, honey."

"Shut up, Alec!" she snapped, walking around the table to sit near Dottie.

"When a man and a woman get married, they need a marriage license," Alec continued. "But when two lesbians get together, they need a lick-her license."

A couple of folks snickered, but Dottie intervened. "Cut it out, Alec. You're not clever, you're not funny, and you're only drawing attention to the fact that your sole sexual experiences involve hoisting your own petard."

There were bawdy roars of laughter around the table but Winifred couldn't bear to stay. She turned on her heel and strode out.

Eva urged her not to let it get to her, but Winifred felt defiled, as if strangers were spying through her bedroom window. What's more, she was worried the Theatre Guild would change its mind about her new job when they read Walter Winchell. It was acceptable for an actress to be homosexual, but what about a teacher who worked with young women? Perhaps they would fire her for being an immoral influence.

When she went for her first board meeting to discuss the actors' training course, she looked around at the establishment figures in the room, waiting for someone to mention it, but the subject didn't come up so she assumed they hadn't heard—yet.

A few days later, she had lunch with Max, and of course the story had reached his ears.

"I think it's terrific." He grinned. "Your reputation has been far too serious, not sexy enough, but since the column appeared, I've had lots of offers for you to play femmes fatales."

Winifred shook her head. "I'm not interested. I'm stepping back from acting." She told him about the actors' training course she would be running.

Max lit a cigar slowly and regarded her through a puff of smoke.

"The offers will soon dry up if you don't keep acting, and—I'm sorry to be frank, my dear—you're not getting any younger."

She smiled. "I know I'm not. *Saint Joan* was my swan song. It was a great role but it taught me that I don't want to live my life in the limelight. I love theater but my future is behind the scenes. So I'm afraid that means I won't be needing your services any longer."

She could tell Max was annoyed. His eye twitched, and he took a long gulp of his drink. "You are an odd one," he said at last. "I must say I was relieved to hear you have Sapphic tastes. There was me thinking all that time you were frigid."

Winifred had to laugh. "Why? Because I never opened my legs for you? What an arrogant shit you are."

"You're not as great as you think," he said. "Pretty girls like you are ten to the dollar. Here today, gone tomorrow."

Winifred stood up and slid her arms into her jacket sleeves. "I'm glad you won't have any trouble replacing me then. Goodbye, Max." She had wanted to part on businesslike terms, but that didn't mean she should take abuse from him.

As she picked up her handbag, he muttered "Bitch!" under his breath.

She hadn't touched the martini she'd ordered. She considered throwing it in his face, but changed her mind at the last minute and aimed it at his crotch, where it stained the pale gray flannel as if he'd wet himself.

"That's for the ripped stockings," she said before she left.

She'd promised Eva that she would stop hitting men, but surely that didn't count?

# Chapter 44
# PEGGY

Peggy rang Jane to suggest that she might host a bridge club meeting at 412, the first in ages. Now that *The New Yorker* sales were climbing, she hoped the pressure on her had eased.

"Alec still hasn't moved out," Jane told her, "and the atmosphere's toxic. If he knew you lot were coming, he'd crash the party and be vile."

Peggy said in that case she would host instead, and they set a date.

Winifred was the first to arrive. She was twenty minutes early, so Peggy set her to work making tuna-fish canapés. They hadn't seen each other since the Walter Winchell story appeared and Peggy couldn't resist asking about it. She was surprised when Winifred's eyes filled with tears.

"I don't mind telling magazine readers what shade of lipstick I wear, but it's no one's business who shares my bed." She dabbed her eyes with a handkerchief, careful not to smudge her makeup, then focused on heaping tuna onto crackers and balancing a sliver of cucumber on top.

"So it's true?"

Winifred's lip trembled. "Yes, I have been"—she chose the word with care—"*involved* with Eva."

Peggy was astonished at first, and then, when she thought about it, it made perfect sense. Winifred and Eva were well matched: their intelligence, their love of theater, their stylish wardrobes—and they both had warm, easygoing personalities. She felt gratified that she had acted as matchmaker, albeit inadvertently.

"You seem upset. Is it serious between you two?"

"I love her," Winifred whispered, "but I don't see how we can continue." She sliced some cucumber, crying out when the knife slipped and slit the tip of her finger.

Peggy retrieved her first aid kit from a kitchen drawer. Out of the corner of her eye she saw Winifred dabbing away more tears, and decided to speak her mind.

"Why not? Because some muckraking journalist mentioned you in his column?" She took Winifred's hand and dabbed the cut finger with a piece of lint soaked in antiseptic.

"Have you considered how few times in our lives we fall in love?" she continued, warming to her theme. "My parents—just once. Jane and Harold—once. I haven't managed it yet, and perhaps I never will. Dottie struggles with love."

She wound on a bandage, trimming it and tucking the end under neatly. It was one of the skills she had learned in France after the war.

"Yet it is said to be the single most important, life-affirming experience we humans ever have. So if you've found happiness with Eva, then it would be criminal to give it up." She felt quite fierce about it. "And to give it up because of something that appeared in the papers over a week ago, that most people have forgotten already, would be lunacy."

Winifred gave a weak laugh. "It's not because of what he wrote."

"Why then? And don't tell me it's your Catholic guilt, because you know what I think of that."

Winifred turned to gaze out the window. "I'm living a lie,

341

because I'm not a lesbian. I've always been attracted to men. It's not fair to Eva."

"I don't care if you're a mermaid or a . . . a unicorn. What if this is the only time in your life you fall in love? Are you prepared to cut it short because of a narrow-minded definition of who we are supposed to love?"

Peggy was surprised at her own reaction. She'd been thinking a lot about love as she wrote *Tin Wedding*. The main character was an aging beauty, an Elinor Wylie type who feigns a sweet childishness to the outside world but inside is struggling to cope with the fading of her looks. She imagined her in a rather distant marriage, and examined the unique mixture of frustrations, sorrow, and rare happy moments as she and her husband grew apart over the years. What makes a good marriage was much on her mind as a result.

She knew she had done the right thing in breaking up with Alvan. The further she got from the relationship, the more she realized it had been convenient for both of them but had never come close to being love. The fact that he hadn't tried to change her mind reinforced it.

Would she ever find someone to love, or was she too analytical? Maybe love disintegrated when you broke it down into component parts and tried to catalogue it, as if in a laboratory experiment.

Winifred seemed surprised by her vehemence. "I wondered if you might be shocked," she said. "I certainly didn't expect you to command me to stay in the relationship."

"What does Eva think?" Peggy asked.

Winifred shook her head. "She doesn't see there's a problem— but it's different for her. She's had other women lovers, men too, and she's comfortable with that. Am I being a prude?"

"Perhaps." Peggy pursed her lips. "Give it time. Don't make a rash decision you might live to regret."

Dottie and Jane arrived together. Dottie was triumphant that *Enough Rope* was reprinting for the third time as Boni & Live-right struggled to keep up with demand. *The Bookman* review had called her "a giantess of American letters," Edmund Wilson said she was "a distinguished and interesting poet," and the *New York Herald Tribune* referred to her work as "whiskey straight."

"Congratulations," Peggy said, swallowing her tiny niggle of envy. Dottie already had a reputation as New York's funniest woman before her book came out, and that's why it had become an instant bestseller. There was no comparison to be made between them.

Tommy Smith had told her that *The Back of the Book* sold reasonably well for a first novel, and he was sure sales would build with the second. She wished she could earn enough to give up her advertising job, which became more tiresome by the day, but in truth she was grateful to be published at all.

Jane was subdued as they took their seats at the card table, and Peggy thought she looked tired.

"How's Harold?" she asked, wondering if his recent illness might be taking its toll.

"I hardly see him. He's married to *The New Yorker*. At least my rival is not another woman." She gave a wry smile.

Peggy handed out gimlets—a cocktail made with gin and lime cordial—in some fancy crystal glasses her mother had given her as a gift on publication of her first novel.

Dottie tried it and smacked her lips appreciatively. "One of these will improve my bridge; two and I'll be dancing on the table; three and I'll be trying to seduce Winifred."

They all laughed, even Winifred.

Peggy began to shuffle the cards.

"By the way, did any of you notice if I said or did something to upset Elinor at my book launch?" Dottie asked. "I'd had a couple

343

of drinks, but I can't remember urinating on the furniture or kissing Bill in the kitchen. . . . Yet she won't take my telephone calls anymore."

"You cut off her speech," Jane said. "She's quick to take offense, isn't she? I remember the first time we met she was upset because Winifred was named as one of the most beautiful women in the world and not her."

Peggy racked her brains but couldn't remember Dottie misbehaving. "Have you asked Bill?"

"Yes. He says she's not seeing anyone right now, but I don't know if it's true. It's rather eccentric behavior, don't you think?"

Jane chortled. "You're talking about a woman who claims to have regular conversations with an ancestor who was a sixteenth-century witch, yet *this* is your evidence of eccentricity?"

Dottie had to laugh. Peggy dealt the cards and they played a few rubbers, with the usual good-natured ribbing.

"Dottie, why didn't you lead with a heart?" Peggy asked in frustration. "It may not be a successful strategy in the rest of your life but it would have won us this rubber."

"A girl can never have too many diamonds," Winifred told Jane, waggling her ring finger, in a heavy-handed hint about what to play next.

They were still dismally poor bridge players, Peggy thought, but they'd at least reached the stage where they could appreciate the skill of the game. And they were having fun and forgetting their worries for a couple of hours.

At two a.m. when they left, giggling and unsteady on their feet, Peggy gave Winifred a quick squeeze.

"Don't forget what I said," she whispered. "We only get one life."

That phrase echoed in Peggy's head as she nursed her hangover the following morning. It had been seven months since she stopped seeing Alvan and she hadn't had so much as a sniff of interest from another man. She went to talks at the library, to the theater, to art gallery openings, but she always seemed to get stuck in the corner with a crusty old gent.

She had started popping in to the Gonk more often to see if there were any interesting men there, but apart from Alec they were all married womanizers. Bob Benchley was always in love with some girl or another, while his long-suffering wife stayed home raising their offspring; and Charlie MacArthur was incorrigible as ever, despite his recent marriage. Dottie hung out with Bob and Charlie a lot. No wonder she was cynical about love!

The birth of Peggy's sister's baby—a little girl they called Adelie—was a time of pure joy. She rushed home to Newburgh and spent the entire weekend holding the warm little bundle with her sweet scent and kitten cries. She may not be able to have a child of her own, but she resolved to be a loving aunt to this one, and perhaps to help shape her personality and tastes.

When she got the train back on Sunday night, she counted her blessings: she was a published author; she earned enough to support herself in Manhattan; she had a stimulating group of friends; and she had her health. It was more than most.

TIN WEDDING WAS published in May and press reviews praised the novel's depth of psychological insight. The comment pleased Peggy. Her goal had been to delve deep inside a marriage and uncover the tiny secrets spouses keep from each other, and she hoped she had succeeded. Tommy Smith seemed pleased, and asked her what she was writing next, so she was hopeful he would publish the third novel that was taking shape in her head.

One morning Tommy rang to say that *New York World* wanted

to run a feature on her. She was amazed and a little shy. Why would anyone want to read about *her*? She was a thirty-three-year-old spinster who lived alone, had a dead-end job in advertising sales, and came home most nights to sit at her typewriter. It would be the most boring article ever.

Heywood Broun was chosen to conduct the interview, and he suggested they meet at the Gonk, telling her *New York World* would pay for lunch.

"I requested the Plaza," he said, "but they wanted me to observe you in your natural habitat."

Peggy laughed. She had known Heywood for years, and that made her more relaxed than she would have been with a stranger. "I hope you won't tell your readers that I'm one of the so-called Vicious Circle." The term had been coined by Frank Case's daughter, who wrote a memoir about the Round Table habitués in which she rather glorified the truth. "I'm afraid I agreed with Dottie when she said they are just a bunch of lightweights laughing at each other's feeble jokes instead of doing an honest day's work."

Heywood scribbled down her words.

"Don't print that," she said with alarm.

"Don't worry," he said. "I'm writing a puff piece."

She hadn't come across the term, but it sounded fine.

"You're a good friend of Dottie's, aren't you? How often do you see each other?"

Peggy glanced around. Dottie hadn't appeared downstairs yet but it was only twelve, which was too early for her. "We often have lunch together—my office isn't far from the Gonk. And we're in a bridge club together." She told him they had started it in response to the men launching their Thanatopsis poker club, which had since disbanded.

"Does your club have a similarly pretentious name?" he asked, with a complicit smile.

Peggy grinned. "No, nothing like that. We don't even play much bridge. It's more about catching up on gossip and drinking cocktails."

"Ah, so you're supporting the bootleggers, are you? Very charitable."

"Yes, I suppose we're like a Bootleggers' Benevolent Society. Can't have the poor fellows starving in the streets!"

He scribbled that down. "When do you see the other two? Just at bridge club?"

"I always take Winifred shopping with me," Peggy said. "She has a great eye for style. Jane knows everyone who's anyone in New York City, so that's useful. And she's a wonderful dancer, as is Dottie. When I go dancing with those two, I sit and watch, feeling like the country cousin."

"I suppose they must provide entertaining material for your novels?" he asked, pencil scribbling away.

Peggy considered that. "The hide-and-seek party in *Tin Wedding* has some similarities to parties I've been to with the bridge girls, but that's as far as I'll go."

When the article appeared a week later under the headline "Manhattan Girls," Peggy was astounded that Heywood had made her sound like a carefree girl about town, swanning from one party to the next with Dottie, Winifred, and Jane. She rather liked his version of Peggy Leech; she was much more intriguing than the real one.

"Brilliant!" Tommy telephoned her to say. "If that doesn't boost sales, I'll eat my homburg."

A FEW DAYS after the article came out, Peggy received a letter from the owner of the *New York World*, Ralph Pulitzer, saying that he was a fan of her writing and wondered if he might invite her to lunch. He asked her to telephone his secretary to set a date.

Peggy rang and a lunch was booked more than three weeks hence, because Mr. Pulitzer was out of town until then.

Peggy was curious about the invitation. She telephoned Jane and asked if she had met him.

"I've bumped into him at a few functions. He's quite reserved and stuffy. Did you know he's the heir to Joseph Pulitzer, the newspaper magnate who founded the Pulitzer Prize? I wonder what he wants?"

"It sounds as though he's a book lover and wants to talk literature," Peggy said. "What age is he? And is he married?"

"He's married to a Vanderbilt but I can't remember which one." Jane paused. "And he's older than us, probably mid to late forties."

So it wasn't a romantic invitation. Peggy felt even more puzzled. Perhaps he had a writing proposition for her. Maybe he wanted to poach her to work in advertising sales for the *New York World*. She'd have to wait and see.

The day before the lunch, his secretary rang to say she had booked Voisin on Park Avenue, at twelve-thirty. It was a classic French restaurant, the kind with a menu that didn't show prices.

"You'll be elbow to elbow with the muckety-mucks," Dottie commented. "No belching or slurping of soup."

Peggy wore the dove-gray suit Winifred had helped her to choose, with a pale pink blouse and a string of pearls. She hoped she looked chic and literary at the same time.

Ralph was already seated at their table when Peggy was shown through the cavernous interior lit by chandeliers. He rose to shake her hand, and she saw that he was tall, with a high forehead, graying hair, and round spectacles.

"I'm delighted to meet you, Miss Leech," he said. "I was already a fan after reading *The Back of the Book*, but Tommy Smith recently slipped me a copy of *Tin Wedding* and I must say you have surpassed yourself."

"Thank you." Peggy smiled. "That's what every writer longs to hear. If we don't get better with each book, why keep writing?"

"The portrait you paint of a distant marriage is remarkably astute. You've got the shrewdness of Edith Wharton—or George Eliot."

"Those are two of my favorite authors," she admitted, glowing with the praise. "So that's a promising start to our acquaintance."

A waiter brought menus and poured glasses of water.

"If you like lobster, I can recommend the thermidor," Ralph said. "But please choose whatever you want."

Peggy scanned the lengthy menu. She was glad he hadn't insisted on choosing for her, the way Alvan used to. The implication that she might not be familiar enough with the names of dishes to choose for herself had felt patronizing.

After they had ordered, he asked about her job at Condé Nast and she described her daily routine. In an effort to be entertaining, she confided in him about her irritating boss, who wandered around buoyed up by his own self-importance and seldom did any real work.

"When I write reports for him, it amuses me to include words that I know he won't understand," she said. "Just this morning I slipped the word 'prescient' into a memorandum."

Ralph chuckled. "I bet he will use it to try and appear intelligent but he'll pronounce it 'pre-sigh-ent.' What's this man's name?" he asked, and when Peggy told him he exclaimed, "Ah, I beg your pardon, but I know him. He's a fine fellow."

Peggy realized she had been horribly indiscreet and tried to backtrack, whereupon Ralph started laughing. "I'm teasing you!" he confessed. "I've never met him and hope I never do."

From that point, they slipped into an easy companionship. They talked of literature and he wanted to know what she thought of *The Great Gatsby* (she liked it but found it flawed), her honest opinion of Edna Ferber (mixed), and whether she was a fan of Melville (very much so).

Two hours passed easily, but when he called for the check Peggy was still none the wiser about the reason for the invitation.

"I very much enjoyed meeting you," he said, "and I wonder if you might consider having dinner with me sometime?"

"Dinner?" she repeated, idiotically. "In the evening?"

"Yes." He laughed. "That's normally when I have it."

He didn't seem like the faithless womanizing type but in Peggy's experience they came in many guises. Much as she had enjoyed Ralph's conversation, she had no desire to become his latest mistress.

"Perhaps your wife would like to join us?" she asked, watching for his reaction.

"My wife and I divorced last year," he told her. "I hope you don't find that shocking."

Peggy shook her head quickly. "Of course not."

He spoke seriously. "I was tied up with work, and not paying enough attention to the marriage—somewhat like the husband you describe in Tin Wedding. The upshot was that my wife fell in love with our sons' tutor, to whom she is now married. We have two boys," he added. "Ralph Junior, who is twenty, and Seward, who is fifteen, both living with me. A long answer to your very fair question." He smiled. "Knowing all that, might you consent to have dinner with me?"

"I would love to," Peggy said, without hesitation. "Yes, please!"

# Chapter 45

# JANE

arold had been told by his doctor to eat small but regular meals and he started frequenting a tiny restaurant near the office, run by a motherly woman named Katarina, who described herself as part Slovak, part Croat, and part Serbian. Every day she served a set menu of flavorsome stews with meat and vegetables, and she prepared dishes especially for Harold that wouldn't make his ulcers flare up.

Jane always dined with him in the evening if she didn't have another engagement. It was the one time of day when she got him to herself, because, much to her dismay, he was still staying in the Webster Hotel. He claimed he slept better there, and it was handier for the office, and if he woke in the night he could get up and work without disturbing her. It was simply practical, he insisted, but she worried there was something else going on. She was yearning to make love with him and sleep in his arms in their own bed. Why didn't he feel the same way?

Alec still hadn't moved out of 412 and Jane was sure his hostile presence was the core of the problem. She got furious thinking about it. They'd had such high hopes for their communal living experiment, and it had worked well for a while until Alec drove a wedge down the middle and ruined everything. After their fight he had stopped paying rent, which made Jane wild with rage. If she heard his key in the door, she hovered inside their apartment until he had gone past because she knew if she came face-to-face with him, it would be impossible to stop herself from slapping him.

Every day she brought Harold clean clothes from home, along with any books he'd requested, and she picked up his laundry from the hotel. After they had eaten together he invariably returned to *The New Yorker* to do more work. He had asked her to stop coming into the office after she fell out with Alec, because he didn't want to risk open warfare breaking out yet again between his wife and one of his best friends. He was too exhausted for their conflict.

"You're going to have to be the one to make Alec get the hell out of 412," she told him over dinner one night. "Put your foot down."

"He promised he's looking for somewhere," he assured her. "I expect it won't be long."

"I hope it won't," she said. "I can't remember the last time we made love." She slipped her foot out of her shoe and rubbed it on his inside leg, the long check tablecloth hiding her movements from other diners.

He grinned. "It's been too long, I agree. It's my fault. Overwork and fatigue combined with a bad gut have turned me into a eunuch."

"Couldn't you ease up on work?" Jane asked. "Raoul told me the circulation has topped ten thousand and is increasing steadily. Surely other people could take some of the load?"

"Hmm," Harold said, chewing a mouthful of food. "I still need to supervise the content. There's no one else I trust to strike the right balance between droll and serious. And we're nowhere near the circulation of *Smart Set*; they have four hundred thousand readers and it's my mission to tempt them all to jump ship."

"How about preparing a couple of issues in advance, then taking two weeks off to vacation with your wife?" Jane asked. "I'll help. I could chase the writers, sub copy, deal with the printers—you name it, I'll do it."

"It's an appealing idea," he said. "Leave it with me."

She knew him well enough to realize that was a brush-off. Even if she did manage to drag him away on vacation, he would spend the entire time on the telephone to the office or reading submissions.

Back at 412, Jane stretched diagonally across their double bed, missing him with an ache deep in her heart. She wanted her husband back. She had always accepted they would have to make sacrifices to start a new magazine, but sleeping apart was a step too far.

*This too shall pass*, she thought, in the words of King Solomon. Once the magazine was firmly established and Alec had gone, she would make sure they got their marriage back on track.

ALEC MOVED OUT of 412 in late spring, with much crashing and banging of suitcases and boxes of books. Jane didn't ask where he was going. She didn't care if he had to sleep on the street, although she doubted that would be the case. His wealthy family gave him an allowance to supplement his earnings from writing.

She went upstairs to check his rooms and saw he had left them in a squalid state. The rug was stained, the bedding was torn, and it seemed nothing had been cleaned for many moons. But he was gone. Jane breathed deeply. She would hire the Chinese ladies to clean up. She couldn't bear to touch his mess herself.

Back downstairs, she called Harold at the office. "He's finally left!" she said. "Church bells should be ringing and ships in the harbor sounding their horns, like they did at the end of the war. I can't tell you how relieved I am."

"That's good," he said, and from his guarded tone she could tell there was someone in the room with him.

"I was planning to broil a chicken for dinner tonight. Would you like to join me, dearest husband of mine?" Chicken was his favorite.

"I can't tonight," he said. "I'll be here till late."

Jane frowned. It wasn't the night when he sent the next issue to press. "What's the emergency?"

"Oh, just the usual. I'm up to my ears. Can I call you back?"

"I was planning to collect you later, and help you pack your stuff at the hotel, so you can move home again. Do you want me to do it myself?"

"About that . . ." he said, and she could sense he was uncomfortable. "I've taken the room for another month. It's just convenient staying there. I have to go now, Jane. I'll call when I have a moment."

She hung up the telephone and sat down at the table, the raw chicken in front of her, wondering what the hell was happening. She had thought Alec was the main reason Harold didn't come home; now he claimed it was work. But lots of men managed to hold down a job and a marriage at the same time. She and Harold had always given each other plenty of freedom—perhaps too much. An alarming thought sprang into her mind: was he having an affair?

The minute it occurred to her, Jane began to fret. Almost all the married men of their acquaintance had affairs. Why had she assumed Harold was different? Had she been blind to the warning signs?

*He's not like that*, a voice in her head told her. His eyes never followed cute waitresses; he didn't know how to flirt.

And yet, before they were married, he had pursued her with funny love letters and thoughtful gifts. He'd been quite determined to win her. If he had met another woman he wanted to seduce, he'd be perfectly capable of it.

Jane had two choices: she could sit at home and worry about it or she could investigate. She stuffed the chicken in the refrigerator, pulled on a long trench coat and gray cloche, and hurried across Midtown to West Forty-Fifth Street.

First of all, she peered through the window of Katarina's restaurant but Harold wasn't there. She found a spot in a shadowy alley with a view of the entrance to *The New Yorker* offices and waited, smoking cigarettes to pass the time. *Could he be having an affair? What would she do if he was?*

She watched as other members of the magazine staff left for the evening, waving and calling goodbyes, some of them heading around to the Gonk, but Harold wasn't among them. It was after seven when he emerged, alone, and walked down to Katarina's. He was slightly stooped, and looked much older than his thirty-four years. Jane yearned to rush over and throw her arms around him, but stopped herself. She had to find out the truth.

He ate alone in Katarina's, staying there no more than half an hour before he walked back to the offices. Jane's stomach was growling but she couldn't risk leaving her post in case she missed something. She jumped at a rustling sound behind her and turned to see a foot-long brown rat rummaging through a discarded grocery sack. She threw a stone to scare it off.

Two hours later, she was shivering and her feet were numb when Harold emerged from *The New Yorker*, and walked slowly along the road to the Webster, then disappeared inside. Jane watched as the light went on in his room on the third floor. She ached to rush over and surprise him, but after waiting so long, it would be a waste to abandon her spying mission now. Maybe a secret mistress was on her way.

He didn't close the drapes at first, and she could see him pacing around with black garters holding up his shirtsleeves. He ran his fingers through his hair while reading a sheet of paper, in a gesture she knew so well. Past eleven o'clock, he was still working. No wonder he had ulcers.

Just before midnight he closed the drapes, and the light went off not long after. No other woman had joined him. His excuse that he couldn't come home because he was working appeared to be true. But he was going to make himself ill again if he didn't have a day of rest occasionally. If only she could spirit him home and take care of him properly.

Jane lit another cigarette, the last in her pack, and walked back to 412, feeling bereft. It was agony to know he was there and not be able to join him. It seemed he didn't miss her the same way she missed him, because she couldn't bear to sleep alone knowing that he was just a few blocks away.

She didn't doubt that he loved her—he had married her, after all—but perhaps he didn't love her as much as he used to. She had never felt so lonely in her entire adult life.

TWO WEEKS AFTER Alec's departure, when Harold still hadn't returned to 412, Jane decided the time had come to talk. She waited till the day after he got the week's issue to press, then joined him for dinner at Katarina's.

She was so full of dread, it felt as if a rock was lodged in her chest. They chatted about news first, and Jane described some stories she was working on for the *New York Times*, trying to keep her tone light. She waited till they had finished eating before raising the subject that was foremost in her mind.

"It's beginning to feel as if we're becoming best friends rather than husband and wife," she said with a wan smile. "Don't you agree?"

He looked her right in the eye. "That's not such a bad thing, is it?"

Jane wondered if he would ever understand how much that sentence destroyed her. She'd devoted her life to this man. She adored the bones of him, and wanted to be his lover, not his friend. She struggled to control herself.

"What about our marriage vows, to love and cherish till death do us part?" she asked, her hand shaking as she lit a cigarette.

"I'll always love you," he said right away, putting his hand over hers. "For the rest of our lives. That part is true."

"But you don't seem to want to live with me anymore," she whispered.

He was silent for a long time before he replied with words that broke her heart in pieces.

"No," he said. "I'm afraid I don't."

# Chapter 46
# DOTTIE

D ottie was stunned when she heard that Jane and Harold were separating. It was a friendly separation, Jane assured her: she still did his laundry and they ate dinner together most evenings, but they had agreed to live apart.

"How can that be?" Dottie demanded, feeling a flutter of anxiety. "If the most compatible couple in the world can't make their marriage work, what hope is there for the rest of us?" She'd been aware Harold had a room at the Webster Hotel but assumed it was only temporary.

"We let the passion slip away when we weren't looking," Jane explained. "It's my fault. I should have worked harder at that side of our marriage. We became too focused on the magazine at the expense of romance. And although we love each other dearly, it seems that's not enough."

Shock waves traveled through the Gonk crowd like the aftermath of a bomb blast. All their friends were convinced it was a phase they would work their way through. Jane and Harold breaking up was inconceivable. Dottie didn't tell Jane that Alec alone was triumphant, saying he had predicted it years earlier, because Jane insisted on wearing the pants in their relationship and no man should have to put up with that.

Winifred invited Jane to the beauty salon for their Friday afternoon session, in an attempt to cheer her up, but although Jane succumbed to a haircut, she didn't seem able to relax and enjoy the sensual pleasure of the treatments the way Dottie did.

"Let me be sad for a while," she said, a frog in her throat. "I need to grieve first. I hope I'll feel better over time."

Dottie remembered that when Eddie left and then Charlie, in quick succession, she hadn't been able to imagine ever being happy again. Jane had always been tougher than she was. Maybe it was easier when you were in your thirties and had more life experience. You realized that no matter how bad things got, there was usually something bright and shiny around the corner. For her it had been a bestselling book. For Jane? Who knew?

ELINOR WYLIE STILL refused to see Dottie, and her silence was increasingly hurtful. Dottie wrote letters but received no replies, and Bill gave her the brush-off when she telephoned. She rang the doorbell once when she was in the area but there was no reply, although she was sure she spotted a twitch of the living room drapes. She had clearly been dropped.

The more she thought about it, the more convinced Dottie became that she must have said something unguarded and caused offense, the way she had when she called Neysa's baby boring. What could it have been? It would be nice to know what she stood accused of and to have a chance to defend herself.

Work was busy: *McCall's* wanted a monthly column from her and she had taken over *The New Yorker*'s book reviews, which gave her regular income. Boni & Liveright was pressing her for a follow-up to *Enough Rope*, and she had a title—*Sunset Gun*, reflecting her themes of beauty and death—but she could have used Elinor's help in selecting poems. She was drowning in scraps of paper covered in random illegible scribbles that resisted any attempt at organization.

Jane and Harold's separation was much on her mind. Her own love life lurched on, through occasional tumbles with married men and a few unrequited passions, but without any regular bed-fellows. Sometimes she wondered if she should have stuck with Seward: he was a good man, but he simply didn't light her fire. At least they had stayed friends. She wouldn't have called herself happy, but she wasn't unhappy either.

One morning, when she was wandering around in a peignoir, sipping a cup of coffee and contemplating the chaos in her rooms, there was an urgent knocking at the door. She opened it to find Jane outside.

"Oh, hello," Dottie said, surprised. "Come in! I'm afraid it's standing room only. The poems got the best seats."

"I'm sorry to say I'm the bearer of bad news," Jane said, stepping carefully over piles of paper on the floor. "I just heard that Elinor Wylie has died."

Dottie felt cold creep over her skin as if she'd been plunged into an ice bath. "Dead?" she whispered. "But how? Was it suicide?" They had talked about it so often. Had Elinor finally done it?

"I don't know the details," Jane said. "The *Times* is preparing an obituary to go in tomorrow's paper. You could telephone Bill."

Dottie shook her head. "I don't want to hear about it on the telephone. I'm going there. Are you sure your people couldn't have got it wrong?"

Jane shook her head. "I doubt it." She hesitated. "I wasn't Elinor's greatest fan, but I'll come with you if you want company."

"Would you?" Dottie clutched her arm. "I'll get dressed. There's coffee . . ." She waved toward her tiny kitchen area.

As she got ready, Dottie was aware of the beating of her heart. How could it be that Elinor was gone? Her heart was no longer beating and her brain was no longer thinking. How had she done it? An overdose seemed most likely, but why didn't Bill find her

360

in time? She felt awful that Elinor had died without them being reconciled. And now she was dead—*dead!*—and it was too late.

Dottie thought of all the people she knew who had died: her mother and stepmother, her father and uncle, all of them older than Elinor. She should have had so many more years.

For once, Jane didn't complain about taking a taxi. The occasion seemed to warrant it. They arrived at 1 University Place to find the drapes closed and the house in silence.

Dottie rang the bell and waited till a white-faced Bill opened the door and ushered them inside.

"I knew you would come," he said, his voice cracking. "I've been waiting for you."

"Is she still here?" Dottie asked, wondering if Elinor might be lying peacefully on the bed with her hands folded over her chest. She would have liked to see her one last time, to kiss her goodbye.

"No," he said. "She died yesterday evening. The undertaker took her away last night." He suppressed a sob.

They stood with him in the kitchen while he prepared a pot of tea and the words flooded out as he explained what had happened.

"She wouldn't let me tell you, Dottie, but she had a stroke in England last summer that made her fall downstairs and injure her back. I brought her home in a wheelchair and she started getting treatment, but it didn't work. She was never able to walk again."

Dottie sat down, covering her face with her hands. Poor, poor Elinor. She would have hated that. Jane put a hand on her shoulder as Bill carried on.

"Then in November she had another stroke that made her speech slurred and her face lopsided. She refused to see anyone— even you—and she wouldn't let me tell anyone either. She didn't want company when she was looking less than her best." He choked on the words.

"I wish she'd told me," Dottie whispered. "I thought I'd upset her."

"Not at all. She couldn't bear being disabled. Couldn't abide it. It was a mercy that she was taken when she was or I'm convinced she would have killed herself. I was careful never to leave pills within reach, just in case. But instead, last night, I left the room for a few minutes and when I came back she had slumped in her wheelchair and she was gone. No breath, no heartbeat. She just slipped away."

"She was so young!" Dottie exclaimed, horrified. "Far too young to have a stroke."

"I agree, she was only forty-seven," Bill said.

Dottie blinked. "She told me she was in her mid-thirties. I remember being puzzled that she had fit in three husbands and eight babies but just assumed she was a fast worker. I guess it's a woman's prerogative to lie about her age."

"She looked incredible for forty-seven," Jane said. "She was a beautiful woman."

They took their tea into the living room and Bill told them about the funeral Elinor had planned for herself, with poetry readings, in a room full of scented lilies and candles. "She wants you to read," he told Dottie.

"Of course I will."

It was strange sitting in Elinor's living room without her presiding from her pink Louis Quinze armchair. Dottie wondered if her spirit might be hovering nearby, listening to their conversation, but all she could feel was absence. The finality of it hit her; the realization that she would never see Elinor again. There may or may not be an afterlife, but even if they met there one day, it wouldn't be the same. Elinor wouldn't be able to help her edit her poems, or to entertain her with colorful, eccentric anecdotes. She would never hear her voice, with its strange transatlantic accent.

"Bill?" she asked. "Don't you think Elinor captured this exact feeling in her poems? The vacuum left by death."

He nodded. "I was thinking the same thing earlier."

He took out a handkerchief and pressed it to his eyes for a few seconds before he spoke again. "I always knew she would die first of the two of us. I just didn't realize quite how hard it would be."

AFTER THEY LEFT the house, Jane and Dottie went to a speakeasy in a basement around the corner. It felt as if the occasion called for a stiff drink. Jane knew the doorman and Dottie murmured: "Useful to have connections in *low* places."

It wasn't lunchtime yet and the bar was empty, apart from a thin barman who served them generous sloshes of whiskey.

They toasted Elinor, then Jane asked, "I'm curious: what made you think she might have committed suicide?"

"We talked about it a lot," Dottie said. "So many people around her had killed themselves, and her work often deals with suicide. We agreed it's contagious, like measles. Once you know someone who's done it, the possibility takes root at the back of your mind."

Jane shivered. "Did you know anyone who had committed suicide before you tried it?"

"No, but . . ." She hesitated, wondering whether to tell Jane. "Don't be cross, but it was an interview with Elinor in the press that started me thinking about it. She made it seem like a way out of intolerable circumstances, just at a time when I was looking for an escape route."

"That was irresponsible of her. I wonder how many other people she inspired to try it, and whether any of them were successful?"

Dottie noticed that Jane had a furrow between her eyebrows that hadn't been there before. Looking closely there were a few gray hairs at her temples. "Writers can't be held responsible for the way readers react to what they've written. If you think that, how many failed love affairs would be my fault? Jeez, the rising divorce rate could be blamed entirely on my writing."

She spoke without thinking, then noticed a look of pain flash across Jane's face. "Oh shit, I'm sorry. Me and my out-of-control tongue."

"It's OK."

"You and Harold aren't getting divorced, are you?"

Jane sipped her drink. "It hasn't been discussed."

Dottie watched her, privately sure they would be reconciled before much longer. They had to be.

"Do you think you would ever try it again?" Jane asked. "Suicide, I mean."

Dottie had discussed this at length with Alvan in their sessions. "I can't guarantee I wouldn't. For the rest of my life, I will have to be on guard in case I slip down into that dark place where there seems no other way out. If I catch the signs early enough, I hope I can distract myself." She took a deep breath, then continued: "As I get older, I feel more anchored. Financial security helps. Friendships help. But I have to be aware that when I fall in love, I turn into the village idiot every time."

"I've always wanted to ask if there's anything I could have done. Tell me how I can be a better friend."

Dottie was touched that she should ask. "Stay in contact. If you haven't heard from me for a while and I'm not returning calls, arrive on the doorstep bearing whiskey." She gave a little smile. "Do you know that since my overdose, Peggy brings me lunch several days a week, and never a day passes but she telephones?"

Jane didn't seem surprised. "Peggy has a gift for friendship. I'm glad she is looking after you."

"I can't imagine what I did to deserve it. I've sometimes been mean about her behind her back, but I never meant it. I don't know why I say these things. The words slip out, like pickles from a salt beef sandwich."

"You're just Dottie, being Dottie. Would you like *me* to call you every day?"

"No, but we should go dancing more often. We could make it a regular date."

"I'd love that," Jane said. "I don't like being home alone at the moment. I need to keep busy."

"Is that how to deal with heartbreak?" Dottie asked. "Keep busy?"

"It's my way," Jane said. "I'm gritting my teeth and carrying on."

Dottie made a mental note of that. She was wary of falling in love again, in case it shook her newfound stability. If a decent, single man came her way, she gave him a wide berth because love terrified her now. Maybe it wouldn't always be that way. Maybe someday she could channel some of Jane's strength and let herself try loving again.

All of those thoughts came to her in an instant, sitting across the table from Jane in a basement speakeasy near Washington Square, the day after Elinor died. It was one of those rare moments when the world felt full of possibility and—unusual for her—she was at peace.

# Chapter 47
# WINIFRED

E va invited Winifred to come to Paris with her that summer, saying she was excited to show her all her favorite haunts. She wanted them to sit in sidewalk cafés drinking red wine and eating *crêpes suzette*; she wanted to see Josephine Baker's famous show at the Théâtre des Champs-Elysées; she wanted them to stroll around the Tuileries, where Edouard Manet painted his iconic pictures. It all sounded divine, but Winifred didn't want to commit herself. She knew Eva was hurt by her indecision. She had to give an answer soon.

There was no question she loved Eva. It made her smile when her lover walked into a room, because she was such a bundle of jaunty energy. There was no one whose opinion she respected more, or whose conversation she found more inspiring. She couldn't bear to think she might hurt Eva, and that's why it was important that she was totally honest with her.

When she weighed them up rationally, the difficulties in their relationship seemed insurmountable. She didn't want to announce herself publicly as a lesbian, and she also didn't want to lead a double life, so how could that be resolved? She lived in fear of someone at the Theatre Guild finding out her secret and firing her. Her mother had met Eva and liked her, but she would react differently if she ever discovered the truth. Her father would disown her.

Winifred wondered if she had only fallen for a woman because she had been treated so badly by men over the years. Being considered a "great beauty" had been a handicap. Men didn't talk to her the way they did to, say, Jane or Peggy. While she spoke she could tell they were watching her mouth move rather than listening to her words. They couldn't resist touching her, as if she were public property. They wanted to possess her, without stopping to find out who she was.

Perhaps most of all her mistrust of the opposite sex dated back to that audition when she was at college and a director at the very height of his fame had raped her. Was that why she was with Eva now? Because of him? She thought she had gotten over his attack but maybe she hadn't; maybe she never would.

WINIFRED WAS HORRIFIED when she heard that the Theatre Guild had invited the famous director to their annual dinner. She had successfully avoided him in the years since the attack, and the thought of being in the same room made her nauseous. She had been asked to speak at the dinner but she couldn't go, she wouldn't go. She'd have to cry off.

"You're the director of their brand-new actors' training program and deserve your place at that table," Eva told her. "If you stay away, you're letting him win."

It wasn't about "winning," though. Winifred knew she couldn't shake his hand and smile and welcome him to the Guild, as if nothing had happened between them. Every cell in her body protested at the thought. She would have to find a way to avoid that handshake. Even then, she felt sick when she pictured being near him—and scared, too, as if he still had the power to harm her.

As the dinner got closer she began to dream about the attack, dreams so vivid she could recall the scent of his hair oil and feel his hand pressing her head down onto the desk, so roughly she was scared her neck would break. She remembered the bruises on her hips, and her terror as she counted the days afterward until her monthly arrived. Most of all, she remembered the shame. He'd treated her as a girl of no consequence, and made her feel worthless. Perhaps he wouldn't recall that he once raped Winifred Lenihan before she was famous, but she would never forget.

She fantasized about walking up to him and slapping him, hard. But that would cost her her job. There had to be another way. And then it came to her. . . .

WINIFRED DRESSED FOR the evening in a midnight-blue satin dress that left her back entirely naked, and she applied matching eyeliner that accentuated her eyes. She had to be at her confident best if she were going to pull this off.

The Guild had hired two large rooms at the Biltmore Hotel, one for predinner drinks and the other for dining. Winifred arrived early and walked around inspecting the name cards that had been left by each place setting, moving a couple of them to suit her plan. When the guests began arriving, she cornered one of the other board members, an elderly gent, and kept him engaged in conversation with one eye firmly glued to the door.

The director arrived alone, suave in a tuxedo, white teeth matching his white shirt. She felt her face grow hot and her palms sweaty. He stood tall, smiling as he greeted her fellow board members, all cock of the walk and brimming with entitlement. When he headed in their direction, Winifred dodged behind a pillar so he couldn't see her, not yet.

They were called in to eat, and guests wandered around the table till they found their name cards. Winifred sat at the opposite end of the table from the director, in a seat that had a good view of his. She saw him pick up the printed menu in front of him, then notice the copy of "The Actresses' Guide to Directors" she had left underneath, just as it had been printed in *The New Yorker*.

He quickly folded it in half without reading it, and Winifred guessed he had seen it before. Clearly rattled, he glanced around the table to see if anyone else had the poem. Winifred hadn't distributed them, but she held up her own copy ostentatiously and pretended to read. He noticed, his eyes flicked to her face, and there was a moment's recognition followed by a look of horror. He *did* remember her. She was glad of that.

The meal was served, and she chatted to her neighbors on either side. She could feel the director's gaze on her but refused to meet his eye.

After the plates were cleared, three of the Guild's directors, including Winifred, were to make short speeches about their work. She had memorized hers till she knew it backward and didn't require notes.

"I am honored and excited," she began, "to be the first director of the Guild's actor training course. We are teaching forty students this year, and the aim is to increase that number to about a hundred next year."

There was polite applause, and Winifred waited for it to die down before talking about the techniques they were teaching, everything from elocution to fencing, and stagecraft to Shakespearian verse.

She continued: "Many of our students are still in their teens and have left home for the first time to live in the city. I myself was only seventeen when I started my training and I remember clearly how young and vulnerable I was." At this she looked directly at the director, addressing her words to him. "We all know there are some unscrupulous members of our profession, and young actresses can be at risk when they go for auditions. Of course, they are desperate to get their first job, and unsure how to protect themselves from abuse by those in positions of power."

A few members of the audience noticed her focus on the director and seemed puzzled by it. He kept his head down, not meeting anyone's gaze.

"So that's why I propose the Theatre Guild hire someone responsible for student welfare, a trusted person they can turn to if they encounter any problems in the pursuit of their career. It's our Christian duty to look out for them. We'll need to raise funds for this position, and I would like to ask if anyone here tonight would care to contribute." She sharpened her tone. "How about you, Mr. —?"

She hadn't directly accused him, but her message couldn't have been clearer.

He coughed. "Of course."

"How much can I put you down for?" Winifred asked.

"How much do you suggest?" His voice was hoarse.

"Perhaps you could start by donating a thousand dollars . . ."

A gasp traveled around the table. Winifred had been planning to ask for a hundred, until she looked at him and the upwelling of repressed anger nearly choked her.

He agreed. He had no choice. Winifred concluded her speech and sat down, blowing out slowly through her lips to control her racing heartbeat.

As soon as the other speeches were finished, she slipped away. She had done what she set out to do, but she wouldn't shake hands with him afterward and give him any sense that he was forgiven. Her forgiveness was not for sale.

AFTER THE GUILD dinner, Winifred hoped to feel a sense of release. She had confronted her attacker and put him in his place. But Eva was still waiting for an answer to her invitation to Paris.

It wasn't fair to string her along. Winifred had to make a decision about their relationship, one way or another.

Once a month, she went home to Brooklyn for Sunday lunch with the family. She never knew who would be there. Her brothers and sisters used their mother as an unpaid babysitter so there was always a handful of children rushing around. Her father would join them if he wasn't in bed with a hangover. An aunt she was fond of often came, and together she and her mother made a meal that could stretch to feed an army if necessary.

"Chuck a few more potatoes in the pot," her mother would call when newcomers walked in twenty minutes before they were due to sit down at the table.

After they'd eaten, the young ones were roped into doing the washing up, and Winifred asked her mother if she fancied a walk down to the bay. She looked surprised, but agreed, slipping off her apron and fluffing her hair. It was a warm spring afternoon, so there was no need for coats.

Winifred hadn't planned the conversation. She simply wanted time alone with her mother, but as they reached the waterside a question popped into her head.

"When Pa asked you to marry him, did you say yes right away or did you take a while to make up your mind?"

Her mother smiled at that, gazing fondly over the glittering water. "He was so nervous, poor man, I had to put him out of his misery."

"You didn't have any doubts?" From Winifred's point of view, it had been a disastrous marriage. Although her father had earned a decent living on the docks, his weakness for drink had darkened their lives.

"We've had our ups and our downs, for sure, but I knew he was the one God intended for me."

Winifred shivered at the mention of God. He surely wouldn't

intend Winifred to be with a woman. "*How* did you know?" she persisted.

"Well now, you do ask some difficult questions. Some things you just know." She picked up a flat stone and skimmed it over the water. "I didn't dream of turning him down because I couldn't bear the thought of losing him. That's the closest I can get to the truth."

Winifred thought about losing Eva: never again being able to lie in her arms and make love with her. She didn't think they'd be able to stay friends, like Jane and Harold. There was too much passion for it to work as a friendship. She faced a stark choice: all or nothing.

"How's your friend Eva?" her mother asked, making Winifred jump. "I wondered if you might bring her today."

"No, Ma. I wanted to spend time with you." She slipped an arm around her mother's waist. "Eva's fine. Actually, she's invited me to Paris in the summer. She's got family there."

"That sounds exciting," her mother said. "Will you go?"

Winifred shrugged. "It depends."

"Seems like an opportunity not to be missed," her mother said. "She's a lovely girl. I warmed to her right away."

"Good. I'm glad you like her."

Winifred switched the conversation to family matters: a cousin's forthcoming wedding, her elder sister's fifth pregnancy, her brother's new house.

They walked home and had a cup of tea, then it was time for Winifred to head for the subway back to Manhattan. Her mother came to the station with her and hugged her hard at the entrance. Winifred inhaled her familiar scent of home baking mixed with a hint of lilac talcum powder.

"All that matters to me is that you're happy," her mother said. "I hope you know that."

"Thanks, Ma." Winifred hugged her back.

"So I think you should go to Paris with that lovely girl Eva. You only live once, after all."

Winifred froze. What was her mother saying? Did she suspect about them? Might she have heard about the Walter Winchell column?

"Your father doesn't have to be told everything, now." Her mum kissed her cheek. "There's your train. Off you go. Send me a post-card of the Eiffel Tower."

Winifred sat on the train, stunned. Of course, she hadn't needed her mother's permission to love Eva, but it felt as if it had been given, and that helped her to make up her mind.

She couldn't wait to get back to Manhattan to call Eva and say yes, I'll come to Paris with you. As for the rest, they would figure it out along the way.

# Chapter 48

# PEGGY

Peggy woke early on the morning of her wedding day and stretched out in the soft fine sheets of her bed at the Hotel Astor, feeling happiness flow from her fingertips down to her toes. Sun was slanting between the brocade drapes. The buttermilk silk dress Winifred had helped her to choose was hanging in front of the armoire, and the air was full of the subtle scent of a bouquet of rare orchids Ralph had sent the previous evening.

His courtship had been traditional, although briefer than most. They didn't leap into bed, but after that first lunch they began dining regularly and talking on the telephone every day. He introduced her to his sons, who were polite, well-brought-up boys with their father's gentle sense of humor. After three months, Ralph had surprised her one evening by announcing his intentions.

"At the risk of scaring you away, I want you to know that I've fallen in love with you," he said. "You probably think it's far too soon for me to propose, and I'm willing to wait as long as it takes, but I wish you would give me a hint if I am barking up the wrong tree."

It made her smile to think of it now.

"I believe you've got the right tree, so please carry on barking," she had replied.

Before accepting the huge diamond engagement ring he offered, she told him she had a couple of conditions. "Would you consider having a child with me, if I am able? I've always wanted children." She was thirty-four to his forty-eight so it might be too late, but she couldn't give up her long-held dream.

He beamed. "I can't imagine anything I would like more."

"Also, I will give up my Condé Nast job with great pleasure, but I won't give up writing, so you would have to accept a wife who works."

"I wouldn't have it any other way," he replied. "You have far too much talent not to write."

There was no dancing in the moonlight, no serenades or love poems: it was a carefully considered decision, but everything about it felt right.

Dottie's reaction on hearing the news was priceless. "So, Peggy Leech, explain to me why you are marrying a millionaire with a vast Fifth Avenue mansion and a seaside palace at Sands Point because I, for one, am at a loss to understand."

Funnily enough, for Peggy, the money hadn't come into it. "Because we have fun together and he lets me be myself," she answered—and that was the truth.

THEY EXCHANGED VOWS in City Hall, then were driven in Ralph's Rolls-Royce back to the Hotel Astor, where three hundred guests were waiting in the stunning rooftop garden. Flowers climbed the pergolas and lined shady arcades, and waiters hovered with drinks and canapés. Dinner was in the glass-roofed restaurant, with trailing ferns and vines creating a gently undulating wall of greenery, then there was dancing on an open-air dance floor to the music of Duke Ellington's band, whom Ralph had hired for the evening after Peggy raved about them. Below, New York was a twinkling carpet, with the silvery Hudson River turning pink in the sunset.

Peggy had often heard other brides say that the day passed in such a whirl they scarcely had time to enjoy themselves, and she was determined that shouldn't happen to her. Instead, she made herself notice every detail. Ralph wiping away a tear as the vows were read. The boys—her stepsons—looking impossibly grown up in their tuxedos. The elderly aunts who were accidentally given the alcoholic punch rather than the fruit one, and became very garrulous and gay.

Winifred and Eva took to the dance floor for a foxtrot, both so tall and striking that there was a lull in conversation as the guests turned to watch. They were wearing frocks in complimentary shades of mulberry and blueberry and looked like elegant long-stemmed flowers in a summer garden.

Peggy looked around for the other bridge club girls and spotted Jane sitting at a corner table with Harold, their heads close as they talked intently. Peggy had asked Jane's wishes before adding Harold to the guest list and right away she had said to invite him, but not Alec. Please not Alec. She had lost weight recently, Peggy noticed. The day must be bringing back difficult memories of her own wedding eight years earlier—but, being Jane, she was putting a brave face on it.

Dottie had disappeared from the dance floor and Peggy couldn't see her anywhere. She seemed more stable these days but Peggy knew she would never stop worrying about her. Ralph joked that he had two children under his care and Peggy had one—but hers was far less obedient.

She noticed her stepsons seemed unsteady on their feet and guessed they'd been sneaking drinks from the bar. She went over and told them that they would be welcome to go to their hotel room if they wanted. They'd done their duty for the day.

"Thank you . . . Mom," Seward said, sounding uncertain what to call her.

Peggy held up her hand. They already had a mom. "Please, call me Peggy."

"Thanks, Peggy," Ralph Junior said. "Can we take sodas to the room with us?" He caught eyes with his brother.

"Of course you can have *sodas*," she said, smiling that they thought she hadn't guessed their secret. "Get some cake too."

As she watched the crowd, Ralph appeared at her elbow and slipped his arm through hers.

"Are you taking notes for your next novel?" he asked.

"I think I may be," she replied, turning to hug him. "By the way, have you seen Dottie anywhere?"

"I have, as a matter of fact," he said. "She's kissing Charlie Mac-Arthur in an alcove. Do you think we should intervene?"

"She's *what*?" Peggy shrieked. It was a disaster. How could Dottie even consider it, after all she'd been through? And Charlie—well, she would have some choice words for him. His wife had stayed home because she was in the late stages of pregnancy. "Which way?"

Ralph pointed and she hurried off in that direction, stopping to pick up Jane and Winifred in case she needed reinforcements.

Dottie was sitting on Charlie's knee in a darkened corner, eyes closed and mouth locked to his. Her arms were looped around his neck and his hand was stroking her thigh beneath her silver lamé frock. The three women surrounded them and Peggy tapped her on the shoulder.

"What the hell, Dottie?" Jane demanded, hands on hips.

Dottie looked up, all smudged raspberry lipstick and feigned innocence. "Sorry! I was busy learning from one of my mistakes. Did you need me?"

Peggy tugged her arm, forcing her to stand. "I want a moment alone with my bridge club girls. Come with me, all of you."

Keeping a tight grip on Dottie's arm, she led them to a railing where they could gaze out across the skyline. There was a finger-nail of new moon glinting against a black sky, and buildings were sooty silhouettes dotted with blinking yellow lights stretching into the distance.

"I wanted to thank you three for helping me get where I am today," Peggy said, turning to face them. "Remember when we talked about our ambitions at the first bridge club meeting? Not only am I a published author now, but I'm also a married woman." She held out her left hand to admire the wedding band on her finger. "I couldn't have done either without you egging me on."

"'Course you could," Winifred said, putting an arm around her. "But I know what you mean. Becoming friends with you girls gave me the confidence to find a more fulfilling career in theater, not just standing onstage spouting someone else's words."

"Harold and I got *The New Yorker* off the ground, at least," Jane said. "And that means a lot." She turned to Dottie. "What was your ambition? It should have been to steer clear of the Charlies of this world."

Dottie screwed up her forehead, trying to remember. "I think it was to become a genius. And I seem to remember the *Western Kansas World* review of *Enough Rope* called me one."

Jane gave her an indulgent look, head cocked on one side. "Necking with Charlie tonight—was that a work of genius? Or stupidity?"

Dottie pulled a comic face worthy of a five-year-old. "I've always thought the difference between genius and stupidity is that genius has its limits."

The opening bars of Duke Ellington's popular song "Creole Love Call" drifted out from the dance floor. Dottie flicked up the hem of her frock, Jane shimmied her shoulders, and the four women began to dance, each in her own individual style.

# Acknowledgments

I'm indebted to Lucia Macro, my editor at William Morrow, for encouraging me to write about Dorothy Parker. I've long been fascinated by Dottie, but did I have the nerve to invent dialogue for the wittiest woman in the world? Lucia thought I could, and she also suggested that I write about a group of women friends, so the resulting novel is very much her brainchild.

A small team of friends helped. Anna Sullivan gave invaluable advice on Winifred from an actress's point of view, and also helped me to understand the separate worlds of theater, vaudeville, and motion pictures in the 1920s. Dave Yorath helped with humor as well as advice on the intricacies of bridge. Peggy Vance was a stand-out contributor; she was a beta reader of the whole manuscript and added some excellent one-liners. Her mum, Claire Nielson, also gave valuable feedback. Other beta readers were the ever-brilliant Karen Sullivan and Lor Bingham, who gave me pages of detailed notes and helped to make this novel infinitely better than it would otherwise have been.

A huge shout-out for the William Morrow crack team of Liate Stehlik, Asanté Simons, Amelia Wood, Danielle Bartlett, Sophie Normil, Jennifer Hart, and Michelle Meredith, as well as Lucia Macro. I couldn't wish for a better publisher. Special mention goes to my copyeditor Kim Lewis, who is the best I've ever worked with—and this is my eleventh novel.

In the UK, big love for the energetic and creative Avon team of Molly Walker-Sharp, Becci Mansell, Eli Slater, Ellie Pilcher, Oli Malcolm, and Helen Huthwaite. Every time, they pull rabbits out of hats.

Gratitude to my agents at Sheil Land Associates—especially Vivien Green, to whom this book is dedicated. It was one of the best decisions of my life when, back in 1999, I went for a meeting in her attic office a couple of doors along from Dickens's old London home and accepted her offer to represent me. Thanks also to the amazing Gaia Banks, Alba Arnau, and Nishta Hurry, who get all the lovely foreign sales.

Publicizing novels in the COVID years has been made easier by the dedicated book-lovers producing online interviews and podcasts. They make it look easy, but I know a lot of time, skill, and effort goes into it, from devising insightful questions through to editing. Many thanks to everyone who invited me to chat about my last novel, *The Collector's Daughter*: Jeff Rutherford at *Reading and Writing*, Cindy Burnett at *Thoughts from a Page*, Carolyn Pouncy at New Books Network, Julia Kelly at Ask an Author, Diana and Michele at *Wine, Women and Words*, Erin Branscom at My Level 10 Life, Ashley and Tegan at *Bent Biblios*, Book Chat with Kim the Bookworm, and Charlie Place at *The Wormhole*. Hugs to author friends Dinah Jefferies, Hazel Gaynor, Jenny Ashcroft, and Tracy Rees, who are always game for a Facebook Live. Thanks also to the bloggers and readers who posted reviews. It makes such a difference, and I'm grateful for your time and effort.

Love and thanks to my sister, who gives copies of my books to all her friends, and my niece, who is teaching me how to use my phone. To Lor, who makes incredible videos and memes, and to Hope for her photos. To Hasan Demir for letting me have outdoor launch parties at his wonderful North London restaurant (zararestaurant.co.uk). To my swimming friends for chats and hypothermia advice. To Christina Jansen for my author portraits (cjansenphotography.com), and to Lee for fixing my computer. To Sue for her perennial wisdom, and to Karel for being such a unique and fun person to live with. Last but not least, to my brother, Gray, for his dry humor, even in the worst of times. I'm so lucky to have you all in my life.

# Historical Afterword

At some point in either 1921 or '22, Dorothy Parker, Jane Grant, Winifred Lenihan, and Peggy Leech started meeting once a week in each other's apartments to learn bridge. Marion Meade mentions the group in *What Fresh Hell Is This?*, her excellent biography of Dottie, and Jane Grant also recalls it in her memoir. The women had a meeting at Dottie's apartment soon after her first suicide attempt, and she greeted them with black bows tied around her wrists. The bridge group may not have been particularly long-lived, but I decided to use it as a device to link the stories of these four remarkable women during that momentous decade.

What appealed to me was that each of them was fascinating in her own right, and each achieved great things in her career during the 1920s, despite the fact that it was still very much a man's world—and despite the fact that they were all quaffing home-distilled alcohol, which was more or less pure ethanol.

Of the four women, Dottie is by far the best known. There is a wealth of information available about her, so the difficulty lay in deciding which bits to select then shaping them into a narrative arc. Her fans will ask why I didn't include Bob Sherwood, her sister Helen, her married lover Deems Taylor, or the trip to Europe with Seward, and they would probably like to have seen more about the work she published in those years. They will spot where I moved events to fit mytimeline and all the material I made up. The main facts of her life are true, but the dialogue and thoughts are invented (give or take a few original lines that I cheekily paraphrased), and every scene is fictionalized. I guessed at the roots of the anguish that led to her two suicide attempts in the 1920s, finding clues in her stories and poems, but of course no one knows for sure what was going through her mind.

Jane Grant wrote a memoir of the years when she and Harold were trying to get *The New Yorker* off the ground, but it reads in a very factual, unemotional way, even when she is talking about the breakup of her marriage, which must have devastated her. There is no bitterness toward Alec, although it's obvious he was a divisive force. She doesn't complain about the sexism of her journalist colleagues or about her arrest for alcohol violations, despite the fact that it was the men who drank most of the booze at 412; she even brushes off Harold's gambling losses, saying, "I knew it was no time for recriminations." The memoir was published in 1968, many years after the events, by which time we can suppose the emotional impact had faded. I get the impression that Jane was a tough, no-nonsense type who rolled up her sleeves and got on with things, so that's the way I portrayed her.

My knowledge of Peggy Leech's character comes mostly from the three novels she wrote, in which I can hear her sharp intelligence and keen insight into human nature. She analyzes the difficulty of relations between the sexes in an era when many women yearned to be more than "little wives in the suburbs," while the men wanted to keep them safely tucked away at home as they led independent lives. I know from others' memoirs that Peggy dated Alvan Barach for a while, but I am only guessing that they broke up because he was Jewish and unlikely to marry her. She could have met Ralph Pulitzer long before they became romantically involved, because he was a peripheral figure in the Round Table crowd, but I decided to have him appear near the end of my novel just when she was about to give up hope of ever meeting a decent man.

I know little about Winifred Lenihan beyond what is on her

Wikipedia page and in reviews of productions she appeared in. I'm guessing from the surname that her family was Irish. The question I wanted to answer was why, having achieved such great success in *Saint Joan*, she stepped away from acting and into teaching and directing. Perhaps she wanted more control over her career. It's true that she was voted one of the most beautiful women in the world by *McCall's* magazine readers, so I'm sure she was often pursued by predatory types like Rothstein and the unnamed theater director. I gave her a female lover because there were many lesbian actresses in the Gonk crowd, and it seemed to fit her storyline, but it's probably not true that she was gay since she married at the age of thirty-five (see page 9 of the P.S.).

I enjoy writing biographical fiction in which I give a voice to interesting women whom I feel have been misrepresented in the history books—or written out of them entirely. On balance, it's easier when less is known about a subject, because I have more wiggle room to massage their stories into the overall shape of the plot. In fact, *The Manhattan Girls* fell into place very easily once I formed my opinions on each of the four women's characters and felt I could predict what they would have done in the circumstances.

It's a novel, not four interlinked biographies, but I hope it is truthful to the challenges women faced when trying to have a fulfilling career and a mutually respectful relationship in the 1920s against a backdrop of the doomed Prohibition experiment. I loved writing it, and just wish I could hop back in time to join the women for a highball or three, while nibbling on Peggy's canapés and hearing the inside scoop on Dottie's latest doomed romantic adventures. ∾

# Reading Group Guide

1. The novel opens with Jane phoning in a story to the *New York Times*. Why do you think the author chose to start with her rather than one of the other three women?

2. Dottie is chaotic and frequently needs rescuing. Most of us know someone like that. Did you sympathize with her dramatics or want to give her a shake or both? How do you think she would have coped with social media had she lived a century later?

3. What happened to Winifred at the audition with the unnamed theater director is reminiscent of stories emerging through the #MeToo movement of the twenty-first century. What are the differences between then and now?

4. For the first half of the novel, Peggy is an observer, forming opinions on others, without much going on in her own life until she starts dating Alvan. Did you agree with her observations of the other women?

5. This is a novel about friendship, with some characters being better at it than others. What makes a good friend, in your opinion? Which of the four women would you most have wanted to be friends with?

6. What do you think of the men in the novel? Do you sympathize with any of them? Was their bad behavior a symptom of the times rather than their character flaws?

7. There's no doubt that Prohibition encouraged otherwise law-abiding folks to become criminals during the 1920s. Do you think it had a long-term effect on American attitudes toward the law? Or toward alcohol?

8. What is the purpose of Elinor Wylie in the novel? Did she care about Dottie?

9. Do you think all four characters changed or learned something about themselves during the course of the novel? Their story arcs are quite different. Did you identify more with one woman than the others?

10. Would you like to have lived in 1920s New York, dancing to jazz, wearing flapper dresses, and drinking hooch in speakeasies? What were the downsides?

# Further Reading
## (and Watching)

ON 1920S WOMEN:

Marion Meade, *Bobbed Hair and Bathtub Gin: Writers Running Wild in the Twenties*, 2004

ON DOTTIE:

Wyatt Cooper, "Whatever You Think Dorothy Parker Was Like, She Wasn't," article in *Esquire*, July 1, 1968

Kevin C. Fitzpatrick, *A Journey into Dorothy Parker's New York*, 2005

John Keats, *You Might as Well Live: The Life and Times of Dorothy Parker*, 1970

Marion Meade, *What Fresh Hell Is This?*, 1987 (in my opinion, the best biography)

Marion Meade, editor, *The Portable Dorothy Parker*, first published in 1944 (but I used the revised and expanded 2006 edition)

The Dorothy Parker Society has a lot of information online at dorothyparker .com and it also organizes walking tours in New York.

ON JANE:

Jane Grant, Ross, *The New Yorker and Me*, 1968

ON PEGGY:

Margaret Leech, *The Back of the Book*, 1925

Margaret Leech, *Tin Wedding*, 1926

Margaret Leech, *The Feathered Nest*, 1928

ON WINIFRED:

*Jigsaw*, the 1949 film noir in which she has a small role, is available on YouTube

ON NEYSA:

Brian Gallagher, *Anything Goes*, 1987

ON EDNA:

Julie Gilbert, *Ferber: Edna Ferber and Her Circle*, 1978

ON ELINOR:

Evelyn Helmick Hively, *A Private Madness: The Genius of Elinor Wylie*, 2003

ON PROHIBITION:

Michael A. Lerner, *Dry Manhattan*, 2007
Ken Burns and Lynn Novick, *Prohibition*, PBS documentary, 2011

ON THE ALGONQUIN ROUND TABLE:

James R. Gaines, *Wit's End: Days and Nights of the Algonquin Round Table*, 1977
Aviva Slesin (director), *The Ten-Year Lunch*, PBS documentary, 1987
Alan Rudolph (director), *Mrs. Parker and the Vicious Circle*, 1994 (I'm not a fan of this movie, starring Jennifer Jason Leigh as Dottie, but it's worth a look.)

ON BROADWAY IN THE 1920s:

Moss Hart, *Act One*, 1959
Gilbert Maxwell, *Helen Morgan, Her Life and Legend*, 1974 ∽